DEADLY SAVAGE

a Peter Savage novel

DAVE EDLUND

Deadly Savage (Peter Savage, #3)
Dave Edlund
www.petersavagenovels.com
dedlund@lightmessages.com

Published 2016, by Light Messages
www.lightmessages.com
Durham, NC 27713
Printed in the United States of America
Paperback ISBN: 978-1-61153-161-9
Ebook ISBN: 978-1-61153-160-2

This is a work of fiction. All characters, organizations, and events portrayed in this novel are either products of the author's imagination or are used fictitiously.

To the men and women who have served our country tirelessly and selflessly. We are forever in your debt.

ACKNOWLEDGEMENTS

FROM CONCEPT TO COMPLETION, there are many to acknowledge and thank for their contributions to this project.

First, I want to thank Sargent Seth Lombardi for analyzing the tactics imagined in Deadly Savage. Your feedback and suggestions are greatly appreciated. Also, I want to acknowledge that Sargent Lombardi has made a career serving in the United States Army, and is a veteran of two tours in Iraq and two tours in Afghanistan. Oh, by the way Sargent, next time you're invited to the President's Inaugural Ball, may I tag along?

I also want to acknowledge Siggy Buckley and her novel (based on factual events) There is No Going Back. This short story retells how Russian soldiers abused, raped, and murdered German civilians, driving them from their homes in Eastern Europe as the Red Army advanced on Nazi Germany. It is a sad tale of ethnic hatred and cleansing, a tale which shaped the way I created some of the characters in Deadly Savage.

Sometimes it takes only a suggestion and spark of imagination to lay the foundation for a novel. I want to thank my editor, Elizabeth, for that suggestion—two years ago, if memory serves me well. It was right after we completed and launched

Crossing Savage, and the Russian invasion of Crimea was news. I hope you enjoy what has grown from that conversation.

So, I go from concept to completion. Finishing a book involves editors—people with very special and indispensable talents. A huge thank you, Elizabeth, for your contributions to make this novel better.

I will quickly point out that the job of rooting out and correcting errors in the manuscript prior to publication is a daunting task. And although many have contributed magnificently to finding and correcting spelling, punctuation, and other grammatical errors, in the final analysis it must be said that I am the one who put them there in the first place.

Last, but hardly least, I want to offer my heart-felt thanks to you, the fans of Peter Savage, James Nicolaou, and the rest of the crew. And a special shout-out to my friends from Hiram Johnson High School who have been so generous in your support of this crazy dream I'm committed to pursuing. I write these novels for your enjoyment, and would love to hear your comments and questions on my web site PeterSavageNovels.com.

AUTHOR'S NOTE

IF YOU ATTENDED ELEMENTARY school in the United States prior to 1973, you were, in all likelihood, vaccinated against smallpox. The last naturally-occurring case of smallpox was diagnosed in 1977 and on May 8, 1980, the World Health Organization (WHO) declared smallpox eradicated globally.

Smallpox is a deadly viral disease for which there is no medical cure. There are several recognized, naturally occurring strains of smallpox, including hemorrhagic, flat type, variola minor, and variola major. The hemorrhagic and flat type have nearly 100% mortality rates, variola major has a mortality rate of about 30% to 50%, and for variola minor the mortality rate is <10%. Perhaps for these reasons smallpox is the only disease to have been completely eradicated worldwide.

A global vaccination program to rid humanity of smallpox was proposed by the Soviet Union in 1958, and the leadership pledged to provide 25 million doses of vaccine each year to the program. The program began in earnest in 1967 under the direction of the WHO. Historians have stated that without this large contribution of vaccine from the Soviet government, the program would not have succeeded. But this apparent act of generosity took new meaning when, in 1992, a high-level Soviet defector (Dr. Ken Alibek) revealed the depth of bioweapons research and development in his former country.

According to Dr. Alibek, the Kremlin ordered the development of a genetically modified smallpox virus, derived from the India-67 strain, as well as means to disperse the active virus from ballistic missiles and bombs. And Alibek was certainly in a position to know—from 1987 until he defected in 1992, Dr. Alibek was the Deputy Director of Biopreparat, a pharmaceutical company that fronted for the Soviet bioweapons program.

At the height of the Cold War, the main Russian bioweapons testing range was Vozrozhdeniye Island in the Aral Sea. In 1971, a civilian boat sailed too close to the island, the prevailing wind blowing from the test range to the ill-fated boat. At least one of the crew, and possibly more, were infected with smallpox. The crew went on to spread the disease to the port town of Aralsk. Three people died and the entire populate of 50,000 was vaccinated to stop the spread of the disease.

This is all a matter of public record, some sources are listed here:

- New Scientist, 17 June 2002, by Debora MacKenzie, www.newscientist.com/article/dn2415-soviet-smallpox-outbreak-confirmed.html
- Science, 18 June 2002, by Martin Enserink, news.sciencemag.org/2002/06/bioweapons-test-fingered-smallpox-outbreak
- GlobalSecurity.org, globalsecurity.org/wmd/intro/bio_smallpox.htm
- The American Prospect, 20 Nov 2001, by Wendy Orent prospect.org/article/return-smallpox

Why would the Soviet government apparently change their policy from providing enabling support for global vaccination against smallpox, to developing a genetically modified strain of the virus as a weapon? Perhaps the leaders in the Kremlin never were altruistic. Perhaps, they were carrying out a long-term plan to eradicate the disease, leading to a cessation in mass vaccinations and with that, vulnerability of future generations. The truth may never be known.

According to the U.S. Government and the WHO, there are only two repositories where samples of live smallpox are stored for experimentation; one is the Centers for Disease Control and Prevention in Atlanta, and the other is the Vector Research Center in Koltsovo, Siberia. However, a shocking discovery on July 1, 2014, refutes this official position. Six glass vials dated to 1954 containing smallpox were discovered in a cardboard box in an unsecured FDA laboratory Bethesda, Maryland campus of the National Institutes of Health. Even after 60 years, the virus in two of the vials was still viable and capable of causing infection.

How many other samples are out there, unaccounted for? And given that the Soviets were manufacturing 20 tons of weaponized virus annually in the mid-70s, how certain can anyone be that it was all destroyed?

Given that our youngest generations have never been vaccinated against smallpox, and those who did receive vaccine in the 60s and 70s have a compromised measure of protection, modern population centers have never been more vulnerable to this terrifying weapon.

So far, sane minds have managed to prevent smallpox virus from getting into the wrong hands—but for how long? And with nationalist fervor driving an expansionist Russian Federation, will old Soviet plans be revisited?

-DE

CHAPTER 1

Sary-Shagan, Kazakhstan

BUNDLED IN A WOOL SWEATER, scarf wrapped around his neck, and wearing fingerless knitted gloves, Ulan Bayzhanov prepared his workstation. The space was utilitarian with walls constructed of concrete blocks and painted a pale mint green. A few small square windows and one chart, listing the ampacity of copper and aluminum wire pasted to a wall, broke up the expanse of green. Scuffs and rub marks around the doorjambs hinted at the age of the facility. Natural light, forcing its way in through the small windows, was supplemented by overhead fluorescent fixtures that buzzed softly.

Ulan's workbench was cluttered with pliers and wire cutters, screwdrivers, electrical test equipment including several handheld multimeters and two oscilloscopes. Scraps of wire were scattered across the surface in no apparent order. Located in a stand above the workstation was a long, horizontal metal rod that held spools of electrical wire, the multicolored insulation offering welcome relief from the otherwise monotone environment.

Summer was still a month away, and without adequate

heating the research facility would remain cool until the outside temperature warmed. The thick block walls and small windows helped against the bitterly cold winter weather and the furnace-like summer temperatures. For now, Ulan layered his clothing to stay warm. The fingerless gloves were the only compromise he made, dexterity a necessity for his work.

Ulan Bayzhanov was born in a small house not far from Sary-Shagan. The son of sheep ranchers, he was raised an only child, two other younger brothers having died in their first year. The arid land and sparse vegetation made for a hard life, with a small relief found in the ground water that allowed his mother to grow some vegetables during the hot summer months.

Driven by ambition, Ulan had no interest in following in the footsteps of his father. As a child, his schoolteacher recognized the drive and instinctive intellect behind Ulan's sparkling brown eyes. He always had questions: how the machines worked; why the sun and stars moved as they did across the sky; why water existed as a solid, liquid, and a gas. But mostly, Ulan was fascinated by electricity.

One day, when Ulan was only seven years old, the schoolteacher brought a simple generator to share with the students. It was made using three large horseshoe magnets and a coil of copper wire that was turned within the magnetic field using a hand crank. A light bulb was connected to the generator, and then the children took turns cranking the handle to make the light bulb illuminate.

Ulan was immediately surprised by how hard it was to turn the crank to make the light bulb shine, but when the light bulb was disconnected from the generator, it was much easier to crank.

"I don't understand. Why does this happen?" Ulan asked.

The teacher, who had been educated in Moscow, explained that when the light bulb completed the electric circuit, cranking the generator handle caused electricity to flow through the circuit. Since electricity is energy, it requires energy to make it. "That is you, turning the handle. You supply the energy. It is hard, because it is work."

Ulan thought, allowing a few moments for understanding to take root. "Ah. So, if the light is not connected to the generator, there is no path for the electricity to flow. That's why it is easier to turn the handle." Ulan beamed with pride having learned this new lesson.

Whereas other classmates wished they could be doing almost anything other than school, Ulan looked forward to lessons every day. He read books borrowed from his teacher, and continued to excel in all his studies, but especially in science and mathematics.

The day Ulan completed school, his teacher met him with a rare opportunity. Facing no hope of further education, and desperate to pursue a path other than tending sheep, Ulan accepted an apprenticeship at the research facility in Sary-Shagan. He was only 14 years old.

That was the beginning of Ulan Bayzhanov's career as an electrical technician at the Russian research complex not far from the shore of Lake Balkhash. For the first three years, Ulan walked to and from work six days of every week. Fortunately, his family home was not too far away, and in good weather Ulan could make the walk in about an hour. When he turned 17, the director of the electrical and electronics lab gave Ulan a car. It wasn't much—with peeling paint, dented quarter panels, and torn and stained upholstery—but the engine ran, most of the time anyway. Still, it was the most beautiful gift Ulan had ever received.

Eight years later Ulan was still driving that same car. It required regular maintenance, but he learned to be a good mechanic and parts were always available, even if he did have to remove them from junked vehicles.

Today, Ulan was working alone to complete the quality assurance testing on two batteries, a test he'd started a week ago. Already he had completely discharged the batteries at the prescribed rate of five amps, and then fully charged the batteries to 13.2 volts. With the batteries fully charged, he carried out a series of tests to ensure they would provide more than the minimum rated power at three different discharge rates. Finally, the batteries had been left unattended for three days, and now he was about to measure the degree of self-discharge.

First, Ulan measured to voltage of the batteries and then he sampled the liquid acid electrolyte within the batteries and measured its density. Satisfied that the electrical and chemical characteristics of the batteries were correct, and passing all other minimum acceptance criteria, Ulan placed a self-adhesive seal on each battery housing with his initials and date.

Ulan slapped his hands together and rubbed them, the friction warming his fingers. He glanced out the window, and in the distance he saw a tan amorphous mass at what should have been the intersection of the ground and sky.

"Another dust storm," he muttered. At age 25, Ulan had never traveled more than 150 kilometers from his family home, the place of his birth. His world was dirt and sand and dust-- frigid winters and hot, dry summers. He'd never experienced a large, bustling city, although he had read about Moscow, Paris, New York, Berlin, and other popular metropolitan centers.

Someday he thought for the thousandth time.

With the two batteries tested, his next task was to complete the electrical assembly on the two black plastic cases. He moved to a second workstation on the opposite side of the small room. Here he had bright overhead lights and an illuminated magnifying lens mounted to an adjustable arm, especially handy for detailed soldering.

With one of the cases open, Ulan began to assemble the various electrical components. His job was to install the power supply and electrical system, plus an air blower and an electrically driven auger; a helical shaft that he thought served the purpose of moving a powder or granular material to the blower. For what purpose he had no idea; the work instruction did not identify the device by name or function, but this was not new to Ulan. Much of the work he performed was secretive.

Once the batteries were fixed within a mounting box, he installed the wiring harness and then inserted the three printed circuit boards—these were the brains of the device. Portions of the wire harness plugged into the circuit boards, as did several sensors that were already in place. Ulan firmly tugged the wires to ensure secure connection.

Finally, he referred to his work instructions on a sheet of white paper within a clear plastic cover. Along with the instruction was the quality assurance report for the three circuit boards, also manufactured at a neighboring location in the complex. It was the job of the design engineers to provide the assembly instructions Ulan was now reading.

With the various parts in place inside the black case, Ulan used special test equipment to ensure the electrical connections were correct. Then, using a signal generator and test leads that he pressed to small metal pads on the circuit boards, Ulan completed the final quality assurance tests.

Satisfied that all was correct, he signed off the work instruction sheet and inserted it along with the battery test report into the plastic sheet protector. Being a technician, Ulan did not have authority to pass the two cases on to the next department. In fact, the work instructions did not mention where the cases were to go next, presumably for final assembly. So, Ulan used the wall-mounted rotary phone to call his supervisor, Nartay Karimov.

"Doctor Karimov, I have completed my work on the two black cases, as you instructed."

"Excellent, I will be there right away," Karimov answered.

Two minutes later Karimov strode into the electrical lab. He was more than twice Ulan's age, with gray hair and deep creases furrowing his face. Ulan was leaning over one of the cases with his hands folded behind his back, conducting a thorough visual inspection. His expression was studious and intense, eyebrows squeezed together creating a series of parallel wrinkles in his forehead.

"Is something wrong?" Doctor Karimov asked, startling Ulan.

"Uh, no," he said, shaking his head as he stepped back. "I was just thinking. I installed a barometric pressure sensor, airflow sensor, and humidity meter. Plus, the air blower I installed there," he pointed with his index finger, "will draw ambient air inside the case. I think this is an automatic air-sampling device. But I don't understand what it does that common-place air sampling stations are not already doing?"

Nartay Karimov considered Ulan's questions. His thin face was severe with a sharp angular nose, chiseled chin, and obvious cheekbones. He squinted his eyes and stared directly at Ulan for an uncomfortable minute.

"You have always been someone I can count on, Ulan."

"Thank you sir."

"You do good work, and you get your tasks done on time. You have a future here, provided you continue to do as you have done."

"Yes sir." Ulan dipped his head, uncomfortably holding Karimov's gaze.

The mentor placed a hand on Ulan's shoulder and spoke gently. "Do not let your curiosity get the better of you. Some questions are best left unspoken."

Ulan nodded, and shifted his gaze to the floor.

"Now, I have a question for you. I have heard that you have affections for a certain young lady. Is this true?"

With a smile Ulan looked up, his eyes sparkling and his face slightly flushed. "Her name is Aida."

"Ah, to be young again." Karimov smiled. "You and Aida have so much to look forward to, and I wish you both a lifetime of happiness." He paused momentarily. "Now, shall we return to the task at hand?"

"Of course, sir." Ulan bowed his head slightly.

Doctor Karimov doubled checked the paperwork while Ulan watched in silence. He then used a digital multimeter to check a few voltages and resistance readings, and ensured a good ground had been established. This was normal, expected by Ulan, as Karimov had done this on a hundred other projects he had worked on.

After five minutes of double-checking and triple-checking Ulan's work, Doctor Karimov grunted approval.

"Take these down the hall to the biochem laboratory. I will phone and have someone meet you there."

Ulan followed the cart down the hallway. He had never been into the biochemistry lab and wondered why they needed these devices that were obviously meant to measure weather conditions. He stopped outside the door as instructed, and soon the door was opened by a middle-aged woman with platinum blond hair. It was cut short, making her look rather masculine. Beyond her frame, Ulan glimpsed an inner chamber and another glass partition. The inner chamber had several white suits hanging from hooks, and several hoods with large clear face shields. Ulan recognized these as full-body protective suits.

"Under the direction of Doctor Karimov, I'll take these," the woman said. Her voice was cold and detached. Ulan thought he knew everyone who worked at the facility, since the total number wasn't more than about 100, but he didn't recognize this woman. She wasn't a native Kazakh, and he thought her accent to be Russian.

Ulan watched as she wheeled the cart into the inner chamber. Just before the door closed, Ulan saw her take one of the white suits from the hook. This is very odd, Ulan thought, but he knew better than to ask any questions.

With the door closed, Doctor Maria Lukin donned a biohazard suit and then wheeled the cart through an airlock and into the laboratory. "Take this to the assembly lab," she instructed a technician. "You are to install a canister containing the new strain."

"The hemorrhagic variation?" the technician asked.

"Yes. The experiments with our primates confirmed the high infection and mortality rates. And last night the autopsies of three human subjects was completed. The results confirmed internal bleeding and organ failure resulting in death 85 to 100 hours after infection. So we can conclude the cell culture-method was successful."

The technician displayed a blank look, not comprehending the significance of the brief explanation. For a moment, Doctor Lukin considered explaining that growing the virus in a culture of human cells was a breakthrough in mass productivity over using chicken eggs as the growth medium. She quickly dismissed the thought—she was not here in this God-forsaken corner of the world to teach these ignorant fools.

"When you are done, make certain the case is thoroughly decontaminated. If you can't perform the task correctly, maybe you will find yourself a subject of future experiments."

CHAPTER 2

Bend, Oregon

WITH BON JOVI SINGING ABOUT LIFE ON TOUR, the classic rock radio station provided background music as Peter busied himself cooking breakfast. Bobbing his head to the guitar riff, he threw some diced ham into a hot skillet, already colored with red and green peppers as well as potatoes, when the phone rang.

"Hey buddy, how's your Saturday morning?" Gary asked. Gary Porter and Peter began their friendship in high school—they had since grown as close as two brothers ever could be. Hearing his friend's voice, Peter immediately conjured up his image; curly blond hair and infectious smile, cobalt blue eyes that were at home with his easy-going, gentle spirit. But Peter also knew Gary could be hard and unyielding if pushed too far.

"Not bad, Gary. Cooking up a breakfast skillet and then I'm going on a walk along the Deschutes River trail. What's up?"

"Have you heard about the military action in Latvia? I looked at the map; that's pretty close to Belarus."

They had been planning a trip to Minsk for about three weeks. Gary was doing some cyber security consulting for the

Belarusian State University, or BSU, and Peter wanted to visit his father who was presently collaborating with faculty in the chemistry department of BSU. He planned to bring along his children, Ethan and Joanna—Ethan wanted to apply as an exchange student and Joanna was interested in sightseeing and visiting her grandfather.

"No, I don't pay much attention to the broadcast news. Seems I hear soon enough from my government contacts when things go bad. What type of military action?" Peter was already changing the radio station and landed on Oregon Public Broadcasting where a panel of journalists and commentators were discussing current events.

"Based on what I read in the newspaper, a bunch of pro-Russian militiamen took control over a railway station in a small town near the Russian border, then they moved on to another city and there they were met by the Latvian army. There was a big fight and the militia lost."

"Who's in control now?"

"According to the Latvian government, they are."

"I'll research what the wire services have reported, and I'll also call Jim, but it sounds like the skirmish might be over."

Jim Nicolaou, Commander of the Strategic Global Intervention Team, had been a friend of Peter's ever since they were kids. Having followed separate careers, the paths of the two men crossed again a couple of years ago when Jim was working a case in which terrorists were systematically murdering petroleum scientists, a group that happened to include Peter's father. Since then, Peter had occasionally worked with Jim and SGIT in an unofficial capacity.

"You don't think Russia is planning to invade Eastern Europe, do you?" Gary asked.

Because of Peter's work designing and manufacturing silent magnetic-impulse pistols, which his company EJ Enterprises sold to the U.S. military, he had regular communication with various colonels stationed at the Pentagon. Based on those conversations and other off-the-record statements he had overheard, he was somewhat familiar with the unofficial take on Russian ambitions as they related to the former Soviet Bloc countries. Few officers in the U.S. military believed Russia would risk a full-scale war to retake territories lost when the Iron Curtain fell, despite the invasion and annexation of Crimea.

"No, I don't," Peter answered without hesitation. "But let me check my sources and see what I can learn. The fact that I haven't already heard about this is a good sign. But if I have any concerns the violence will spread to Belarus, you'll be the third person I tell--right after I inform Ethan and Jo that the trip is cancelled."

"Fair enough."

Peter placed his phone on the granite-surfaced cooking island just in time to stir the mix of potatoes, ham, and peppers before they burned. The moderator on the radio program introduced a story about a smallpox outbreak in Tbilisi, Georgia. Several dozen people had been stricken and were hospitalized; already 14 had died, including a two-year old child and her mother. The discussion from the panel's members was brief; one journalist pointed out that smallpox had been declared eliminated in the 1970s and that the source of the virus responsible for this outbreak was under investigation, but so far the World Health Organization had not organized an investigative team.

"That's what happens when you stop immunizing the population," Peter said, carrying on a monolog with the voices on the radio, all the while knowing how irrational his behavior was. He stirred the skillet one more time and then turned off the burner and placed a large scoop in a bowl.

As Peter sat at the counter separating the kitchen from a spacious great room, the moderator moved to the next topic of discussion. “Now I’d like to shift our attention to the Baltic States, and Latvia in particular. Last week we witnessed a remarkable series of events as the Latvian government put down, swiftly and decisively, what appeared to be another civil uprising involving pro-Russian militias.”

“That’s correct,” said the liberal commentator, a reporter with the Washington Post. “This seems to be a recurring event in Eastern Europe, only this time the outcome was much different from what happened in Georgia and Ukraine.”

“And why is that?” the moderator asked, spurring the discussion along.

The conservative panelist jumped in. “Well, the most significant difference is that Latvia, like Estonia, is a member of NATO, whereas Ukraine and Georgia are not. Plus, the Latvian government must certainly have planned for this possibility having seen the protracted and savage fighting in Ukraine and the annexation of the Crimean Peninsula by the Russian Federation.”

Peter was still thinking about the defeat of the pro-Russian militia in Latvia as the talking heads moved on to national events. Hearing what he sought, Peter tuned out the conversation and fired up his tablet between bites of potatoes and peppers. He focused only on the wire reports.

> May 17
> Sophia Janicek, The Associated Press
> ZILUPE, Latvia (AP) — Two days after the first gunshots were fired, pro-Russian militia have reportedly secured their occupation of the train station in this small town of a few hundred inhabitants close to the border with Russia.
>
> Considered strategically important because of the

major rail and road routes passing through Zilupe into Russia, armed militiamen claiming allegiance to the Russian Federation launched an assault on the railway station two days ago. The pro-Russian militia encountered very little resistance. The militia commander claims to have captured two Latvian soldiers, however that report is denied by a spokesman for the Minister of Defense.

The railway station in Zilupe is strategically located on the Riga-Zilupe train route, which is one of the longest passenger rail routes in Latvia. The town is also near the A12 road, which becomes the M9 highway after the border crossing into Russia.

Armed militiamen wearing black facemasks and carrying automatic rifles can be seen on the grounds surrounding the quaint timber-and-stone railway station. Sandbag bunkers have been erected as makeshift guard stations at the road leading to the station.

Local residents report that trains are arriving from Russia carrying male passengers with green duffle bags. The trains do not travel further west into Latvia. It is believed these male passengers are Russian soldiers.

However, a spokesman for President Vladimir Pushkin vehemently denies that any Russian military service members are in Latvia fighting on behalf of the militia. “This militia is comprised of local citizens,” said a spokesman for President Pushkin. “We have seen this before in Eastern Ukraine, South Ossetia, and Abkhazia. The people who live there are weary of their corrupt and weak governments, and seek repatriation with the Russian Federation.”

Subconsciously, Peter had stopped eating, even though the fork still rested in his hand. He moved to the next two hits.

May 19
Sophia Janicek, The Associated Press
RIGA, Latvia (AP) — The Minister of Defense announced today that seven Russian soldiers were captured near Zilupe in an overnight skirmish between government soldiers and pro-Russian militia. No casualties are reported on either side.

This news comes less than one week before scheduled talks between President Vladimir Pushkin and European and NATO leaders in Berlin.

Quoting an anonymous source in the Russian Defense Ministry, the Russian news agency Interfax reports that "the soldiers were on patrol near the border and apparently got lost. It was night and the forest is dense, it would be easy for anyone to lose their way."

U.S. Secretary of State Paul Bryan has accused the Kremlin of stirring up violence in this peaceful Baltic nation. A former member of the Soviet Union, Latvia restated their independence on May 4, 1990, charging that the occupation by the former Soviet Union was illegal.

"Once again we see the Russian government initiating civil unrest and violence in an effort to gain influence and territory," Bryan said. "It is becoming increasingly clear that Mister Pushkin covets a greater Russia, even if it means violation of international law."

May 20
Karl Church, Global Times
RĒZEKNE, Latvia (GT) — In a daring night-time

assault, government forces recaptured key buildings in this city of 36,000 residents. Approximately two dozen militiamen are reported killed and more than 150 captured. Most of the pro-Russian militia fled under cover of darkness.

Russian President Vladimir Pushkin, stressing that he supported an end to the bloodshed, urged the Latvian military to cease using force against its civilian population and threatened to withdraw from bilateral trade talks unless the violence ends.

Situated 39 miles west of the Russian border, Rēzekne is a major transportation hub for both highway and rail. The Moscow-Riga railway and the Warsaw-St. Petersburg railway intersect and pass through Rēzekne.

A spokesman for the Minister of Defense said that the assault commenced at 1 a.m. local time. "The raid was executed with professionalism by members of the Special Tasks Unit," he said.

The Latvian Special Tasks Unit is the equivalent of Special Forces. The Ministry of Defense would not comment on the number of men participating in the nighttime raid. A member of NATO, Latvia has frequently participated in joint military exercises and is considered by military experts to have a skilled and professional force.

A Pentagon source, who asked not to be named, said that the Special Tasks Unit received support from the U.S. Army in the form of non-lethal material. When asked what type of non-lethal material, the source replied, "night vision goggles and advanced communication equipment, plus intelligence reports."

At dawn this morning the main railway stations in

> Rēzekne were under control of Latvian soldiers, and regularly scheduled train travel is expected to resume by noon local time. Soldiers wearing Latvian uniforms were visible on the streets and in government buildings through Rēzekne as the government made a dramatic show of force.

No longer hungry, Peter pushed his bowl aside, staring at the tablet. Based on the news reports, the Latvian government was firmly in control and the violence had seemingly ended. There was no evidence to support fears that a Russian annexation was imminent, or anticipated.

Still, Peter called Jim Nicolaou, who answered on the second ring.

They efficiently passed through introductions and pleasantries before Peter got down to business.

"I'm not asking for any classified information, just your general take on the region," Peter said.

"The Latvians slapped down the militia rather quickly, and that sends a message to other militia groups that might think they can actually win a civil war. These Baltic nations are very different from Ukraine, and we don't expect a repeat of what happened there."

"So you wouldn't advise me to cancel my trip to Minsk?"

"No, I wouldn't. Look, you know I can't guarantee your safety. Who knows what might happen tomorrow, or in a week, or month… or never. All I can say is that the intelligence community does not predict further acts of violence by militia groups against any of the Eastern European countries. And if that changes, I'll let you know.

"By the way, how is the Professor doing? Last time we spoke he was rather anxious to get his research back on track."

"Still is," Peter chuckled. "Dad was frustrated by his perceived lack of progress, and he felt it would be helpful to work with colleagues at the BSU campus. Sounds like he's made some good friends. We've had a few phone conversations, and he sounds excited again about his research."

"I'm glad to hear that. Tell Ian hello for me when you see him, okay?"

They ended the call, and then Peter phoned Gary to relay the news.

Shortly later, Peter was walking along the Deschutes River. The morning was comfortably warm and sunny, a beautiful spring day. The rhythm of the walk was like a moving meditation, and soon Peter was lost in his thoughts.

Although he had many friends plus colleagues from EJ Enterprises, Peter still felt alone. Ethan was attending the University of Oregon in Eugene, a two-and-a-half hour car trip to the west. Joanna, or Jo as she liked to be called, was building her own independent life even though she lived in the same city as her father.

It had been a difficult transition as the children left home, perhaps more so because he didn't have his wife Maggie for support. The years since her death in an automobile accident had not softened the pain. Left brain-dead from her injuries, the hardest thing Peter ever had to do was instruct the doctors to remove her from life support. That was Maggie's final wish, and it still haunted Peter. Mostly at night, when it was quiet and the solitude was overwhelming.

Yes, it will be good to be with Ethan and Jo, and to visit Dad, Peter thought as a smile crept across his face.

CHAPTER 3

Sacramento, California
June 12

COMMANDER JAMES NICOLAOU sat hunched over his desk studying the morning intelligence update. He paused when he reached the paragraphs describing the latest events in Eastern Europe and the DIA analyst's interpretations. As commanding officer of the Strategic Global Intervention Team—SGIT—he led an exceptional team of intelligence analysts and military operatives. Given that the bloodshed over the past months had been limited to a few cities in Latvia and Ukraine, and no Americans had been killed, SGIT had not been called into service, but that didn't mean that he wouldn't stay abreast of all that was occurring in the region.

Although the pro-Russian militia, equipped with heavy weapons that could have only come from Russia, still occupied the city of Baltinava on the Ukrainian border with Russia, as long as talks were underway with Pushkin's government Europe and the U.S. were not willing to use force. As distasteful as it was to accept small enclaves ripped from sovereign nations, the idea of risking war in Europe was even more distasteful.

Everyone in the intelligence community knew that Russia was behind the military actions, including using Russian special ops soldiers dressed as so-called pro-Russian militia, supposedly civilians rising against their central governments. With the aggression largely unchecked, civil unrest was spreading throughout Eastern Europe; pro-Russian civilians versus pro-independence nationalists.

For now at least, the conflict in Latvia had been quelled, but in private conversations, military analysts admitted that Georgia was likely to be annexed by Russia unless the U.S. and Europe forcefully intervened—not a political possibility for President Taylor. Memories of the Iraq and Afghanistan wars were still potent in the public's mind.

For his part, President Vladimir Pushkin had played his hand brilliantly, correctly interpreting the vulnerability of Europe by virtue of dependence upon Russian energy supplies—which would serve to mitigate implementation of harsh economic sanctions—as well as U.S. reluctance to enter into yet another far-away conflict that would cost thousands of American lives and trillions of dollars.

As Commander Nicolaou read further, his ebony eyebrows pinched together. He pressed a button on his desk phone, and two seconds later the speaker came to life.

"Lacey," the voice said.

"Lieutenant, gather up everything you have on this possible plague outbreak in Georgia. I want a detailed briefing in one hour, conference room A."

"Yes, sir." Lieutenant Ellen Lacey was a veteran of SGIT, a loyal team player who led the group of analysts, all recruited from the DIA, NSA and Office of Naval Intelligence—all extremely bright and accomplished.

Lacey was of Irish decent with red hair and a well-proportioned figure. In the civilian world she had many want-to-be suitors, but she had yet to find any man who held her intellectual interest for more than a couple weeks. With few outside distractions, Lacey dedicated her talents—brilliant logical reasoning and savvy reading of human and political behavior—to her work at SGIT.

Jim hunched over the report, rubbing his index fingers against his temples. He knew as well as anyone that President Taylor was unlikely to commit to military intervention unless a NATO country was overtly attacked by Russia. The problem was that Pushkin had been stirring up trouble under the guise of civilian Russian sympathizers. These civilians were usually armed with sophisticated weaponry, including advanced long-range guided missiles, and they wore Russian military uniforms lacking unit designation or nationality patches. It was a thin disguise, but the frequent media reports referring to the aggressors as civilian militia served to reinforce a reluctance of the American people to get involved.

He turned to his computer and entered a search phrase. The firewalls between SGIT's super computer—named MOTHER—would ensure security even when using the most popular search engines.

Jim quickly scanned through the first five hits and followed the links. Scanning more than reading, he scrolled through the documents.

What he read worried him, and he absent-mindedly rubbed his chin in a gesture that had become his tell. Closing the file and moving back to the search hits, he clicked on a PDF document published by the Centers for Disease Control and Prevention in Atlanta. The document was ten years old, but the report was timeless. As he read the five pages and studied the color photos, he felt a wave of nausea. Pushing back from his desk, he rose and filled his mug from the carafe resting on the credenza at the side of his office. The hot coffee settled his stomach, if only a bit.

Jim Nicolaou, former SEAL and veteran of innumerable missions, nearly every one of them off the record, was no stranger to death and destruction. He was a warrior, an experienced killer.

Yet, the sight of children suffering from horrendous injuries and ailments—all the product of armed conflicts that were often rooted in power struggles or ideology, still bothered him deeply. It was one thing to take the life of another man doing his damnedest to end yours, but in Jim's code of honor there was no room for harming innocents, especially children.

Jim looked across his office at the computer monitor and the printed intelligence report, his hand-written notes in the margins.

If Pushkin is behind this, perhaps he has finally gone too far, he thought. With coffee mug in hand, he left his office for Lacey's briefing.

CHAPTER 4

Sacramento, California

LIEUTENANT ELLEN LACEY was already seated at the conference table when Jim walked through the door. She was flanked by two of her analysts, Mona Stephens and Beth Ross. Ross had provided pivotal insight into many SGIT assignments over the past five years, including the Venezuelan affair when civilian scientists were targeted by terrorists on U.S. soil.

Stephens was a relative newcomer, and Lacey appreciated her analytical reasoning skills fed by a voracious appetite for reading everything from major international newspapers to intelligence briefings. Her petite frame and blonde hair may have given the opposite sex the impression that she was all looks and no brains, but that could not have been further from the truth. She was intelligent, ambitious, and not about to sit by quietly if she wanted to make a point.

Jim nodded to Lacey. "Good morning."

"Stephens and Ross have been following the events in the former Soviet Bloc countries of Eastern Europe. I asked them to participate, if you don't mind, sir."

"Of course." Jim looked over the three faces. "What do you

have?"

"Well, sir," Lacey began, "in addition to the daily briefings you see, there have been three reports, all classified secret, from the DIA relating to disease victims in Georgia. I've uploaded the reports onto MOTHER. Over the past five days, hospitals in Tbilisi have been inundated—mostly civilians, but also Georgian military. Three hospitals ran out of rooms and have taken to parking patients on gurneys in the hallways. The first cases were reported twelve days ago, and the numbers have been steadily increasing. The reported symptoms include fever, headache, chills, nausea, vomiting, malaise and fatigue, and purple to red lesions over the patient's body."

"That's what it says in the briefings," Jim said, "and why I called this meeting. These symptoms are consistent with smallpox or Ebola."

"Yes sir, that's mostly correct. What was omitted from the general briefings, but captured in the classified reports, is that bleeding from the nose and mouth is also reported in later stages of the disease."

"Mortality rate?"

"About 80 percent to 90 percent of the patients have died."

"That was also omitted from the general briefing."

"And so far the extraordinarily high death rate has not been reported by the major wire services either."

"Okay, so someone is keeping a lid on this. Cause?" Jim asked.

Stephens replied without hesitation. "The symptoms are consistent with hemorrhagic smallpox, a rare form of the virus."

"Are you sure?" Jim asked.

Stephens nodded. "The bleeding and high fatality rate differentiates hemorrhagic smallpox from the more common form known as variola major in the medical community. Cowpox is much less severe, typically with limited but painful rashes that fade after two to three weeks. Monkeypox causes swelling of the lymph nodes, so far that hasn't been a reported symptom. Monkeypox and cowpox are seldom fatal."

"How can you be confident it's not Ebola or Marburg virus?"

"Without laboratory confirmation of cultures, I can't be absolutely certain. However, we've been in contact with doctors at the CDC. They've explained that Ebola and Marburg result in rapid onset of severe flu-like symptoms, including diarrhea, which is absent in the outbreak victims. But more significant is that the victims suffer from bleeding under the skin that appears as a red or purplish rash beneath small lumps."

"According to the experts, these are text-book symptoms of hemorrhagic smallpox," Lacey added.

Stephens glanced at Lacey and Ross, before returning her attention to Jim. "It's the most logical conclusion, the only one that fits the symptoms. A majority of analysts at DIA also concur…" her voice trailed off, and Jim sensed that there was more to it. But before he could ask, Lacey jumped in.

"There is an inconsistency."

"Go on."

"Hemorrhagic smallpox was extremely rare prior to the eradication of the disease in the late 70s."

"How rare?" Jim said.

"Only about 2% of smallpox cases were of the hemorrhagic variety. And since 1977 there have been no reported natural infections of smallpox of any variety."

"It's extremely unlikely that a smallpox outbreak of the magnitude reported in Tbilisi would be due to a naturally occurring infection," Stephens offered.

"Probabilities can be misleading. Smallpox vaccination hasn't been carried out for decades. Why wouldn't we expect the disease to reappear?"

Ross nodded. "We've thought about that. There are other examples, such as measles and polio, diseases that are causing more infections annually as a result of lax immunization programs. But if that was the case here, regular smallpox—variola major and variola minor—should have been the strain to reappear."

Lacey continued. "Hemorrhagic smallpox is rare, so rare that little is reported about the symptoms and progress of the disease."

"Perhaps Ebola or Marburg has mutated, giving symptoms that are confused for this variety of smallpox?" Jim said.

"Without cultures and a full DNA sequencing, that remains a possibility." Lacey said.

"There is one other possibility, sir." Stephens spoke in a low, confident voice. Lacey glanced at her, and nodded subtly.

"I think I know what you are going to suggest, but go on." Jim's dark brown eyes were steady, his expression firm as he waited several seconds for Stephens' reply. She took her time, collecting her thoughts, perhaps judging the possible reaction to the hypothesis she was determined to share.

And then she answered. "Weaponized virus—from U.S. or Russian stores."

Jim eased back in his chair, his eyes shifting between Lacey, Stephens, and Ross. "A Russian release of the virus was my suspicion after reading the briefings, and you've independently confirmed that. But why do you suggest the source could be U.S. stores? Aren't all smallpox cultures secured at the CDC?"

"We're looking into that sir. So far, I'm not getting any useful information. The CDC simply repeats the standard policy that smallpox and other hazardous category A pathogens are stored safely and with limited access. They insist there has never been a breach in security." Lacey said.

Jim leaned forward placing his fists against the conference

table for support. He recalled the color photographs in the CDC report he read a short while earlier showing angry raised red lesions on arms and legs, patches of darkly colored skin, the surrounding tissue red and inflamed. The clinical description, virtually sterile and devoid of emotion, proclaimed how the infected persons suffered high fever, their bodies racked with pain and convulsions. And then he thought of the women and children causalities mentioned in the intelligence briefing, and the barbaric suffering they were subjected to. His stomach began to tighten again.

Pushing off the table, Jim straightened and focused on Lacey. "What is being done to contain the outbreak?"

"The Russian Ministry of Healthcare was quick to respond with vaccine and medical personnel to administer it. They've said they plan to vaccinate the entire population of Tbilisi. That, combined with a city-wide quarantine implemented by the Georgian government, is expected to contain the virus and stop the spread."

"It sounds as if the Ministry of Healthcare was well prepared."

"Like they knew it was coming," Ross said.

Jim considered the comment. "Assuming for the moment that you are correct, what is the motive? What would Pushkin gain by releasing such a dangerous virus?"

"Demoralize the civilian population, kill Georgian soldiers, destabilize the government," Ross replied without hesitation.

"Maybe, but we have to be certain. Could this be a natural outbreak? Contaminated water or something?"

Lieutenant Lacey pursed her lips. "Unlikely. Smallpox was eradicated globally by 1977. Vaccination has not been carried out in the U.S. since 1972."

"The outbreak is localized and massive," Ross added. "These facts are not at all consistent with a natural outbreak, and suggest a targeted release of weaponized smallpox. This conclusion is supported by the rarity of the virus strain based on reported symptoms. However, without samples for DNA testing, we have no proof, only speculation."

Lacey drew in a breath and exhaled. "The World Health Organization has requested permission to enter Tbilisi and collect samples from patients, as well as environmental samples from around the capital. So far, the Georgian government has been very cooperative but President Pushkin's government is objecting, accusing the U.S. and NATO of a plot to plant evidence and blame Russia. The situation is complicated by the fact that the Georgian military cannot guarantee protection to a WHO field team. Consequently, the WHO is backing down and suggesting a delay until the situation in Georgia stabilizes and the quarantine is lifted. The UN Secretary General is supporting their recommendation."

"This all plays into Pushkin's agenda," Jim said. He frowned and began pacing back and forth, his frustration contributing to the tension in the conference room.

"Has President Taylor taken a position?" Jim said.

Lacey sighed. "No sir, not yet."

"So that most likely means that neither the U.S. nor Europe are willing to put troops on the ground to secure the WHO team while they collect evidence of a possible biological weapon attack." Jim continued his pacing.

Jim stopped, and turned to face his team. "If this is weaponized smallpox, how was it deployed?"

Lacey frowned. "The DIA isn't speculating. But, despite the cease-fire, five artillery shells are reported to have been fired on Tbilisi 15 days ago by the pro-Russian militia. One or more of those shells could have contained the virus."

"It's also possible that a few dozen infected persons entered Tbilisi about that same time," Ross observed. "Smallpox is highly contagious and is easily spread from person to person by inhalation, direct contact, or contact with clothing and linens that are contaminated."

As Jim listened to the timeline, he felt something was missing. "You're suggesting the initial infection occurred only a few days—three to be exact—before the first report of diseased victims. Isn't that a bit fast even for smallpox?"

Lacey and Stephens exchanged a glance before Lacey cleared her throat. "No sir, not this strain. However, we must acknowledge that if this is a weaponized virus, it may have been genetically altered."

Jim held Lacey's stare while he absorbed the implications. "If our theories are correct, and there is another outbreak somewhere else, what's to stop it?"

"Short of a mass vaccination program within the first three days of the virus being released, nothing. And if the disease spreads beyond a small geographical area…"

Jim finished her statement. "A global pandemic with a 90 percent fatality rate."

"It would take too long to manufacture and administer sufficient vaccine to curb the spread," Stephens said.

Jim considered the implications. Just one infected traveler on an international flight could spark a chain reaction. With the virus burning through an unprotected population at an exponential pace, how many would die before the disease extinguished itself? Hundreds of millions… maybe billions.

"Anything else to add?"

"No sir, that's the extent of our briefing," Lacey said.

"Have a summary report in my inbox by end of day. I'm going to forward it to Colonel Pierson. Maybe there's a role for SGIT to play in getting those samples."

CHAPTER 5

Minsk
June 15

THE BUILDINGS OF THE PRESTIGIOUS Belarussian State University surrounded a large park-like commons, with the science wing to the right of the main entrance. After climbing the stairs to the second floor of the chemistry building, Peter turned into the long hallway flooded with natural light from the row of windows on the left. He was closely followed by his two children, Ethan and Joanna, and good friend, Gary.

Peter strode to the nearest door opposite the wall of windows. It was stained dark brown, perhaps the color of years of accumulated patina. The nameplate on the door read 'Professor Ian Savage'. Peter knocked and then opened it cautiously, peeking around the edge of the door, not wanting to disturb the inhabitant. He had nothing to fear since the office was empty. Closing the door, he took a step back into the hall and examined the door again. It's the right name.

"No one home?" Gary said. Ethan and Joanna stood back while their father conducted his search.

Dressed casually in blue jeans and polo shirt, Ethan equaled his father in height, but was 15 pounds lighter. His light-brown hair was straight and slightly unkempt; obscuring any evidence of prior combing. Jo was a few years older than her brother, and she loved everything related to drawing regardless of the medium; pastel, pencil, crayon, but especially digital. Her straight brown hair, with a subtle tint of red, extended to the middle of her back. Like her brother, she had blue eyes that reminded Peter very much of their mother.

Peter looked to the next door and saw the name-plate at eye level: 'Professor Dmitri Kaspar'.

He knocked again, and didn't have to wait long before it opened.

"Peter!" Ian Savage greeted his son. "How are you?"

"I'm fine, Dad." Peter wrapped his father's slim frame in a hug, then stepped back, his entire face smiling as he greeted his father. Professor Savage showed a twinkle in his eyes at the sight of his only son. The moment passed too quickly, the unspoken emotion receding once again.

"We arrived last night, exhausted of course, so we slept in this morning."

"I understand. It's a long flight."

"Dad, you remember Gary Porter I think?" Peter gestured to his friend and Ian extended his hand.

"Of course I do! Good to see you again Gary."

Professor Savage squeezed between the two men, arms outstretched and a huge grin across his face at the sight of his grandchildren. Ethan and Jo each wrapped an arm around the elder Savage in a three-way hug.

"Hi Pops!" Jo greeted. Professor Savage preferred not to be called grandpa or granddad—he said it made him feel too old. The nickname Pops suited him better.

"It's good to see you," Ian said, his eyes sparkling as his gaze shifted from Jo to Ethan.

Standing in the office was another man, rather rotund in stature and with black hair, streaked with silver. His large round nose was covered in a web of tiny red lines, suggesting years of heavy drinking and eating. He was clean-shaven and his cheeks were ruddy. Although similar in age to Ian, they were polar opposites in appearance. With his white hair and beard, and lean physique, Professor Ian Savage had the stereotypical appearance for his profession.

Ian turned, drawing his family's attention to his colleague. "Here, I want to introduce you to my friend, Dmitri Kaspar. He is a professor in the Department of Chemistry." Ian Savage was on sabbatical from his tenured post in the Department of Chemical Engineering at Oregon State University; Ian and Dmitri were investigating new theories of abiogenic oil formation.

Dmitri stepped forward and shook Peter's hand. "Welcome, Peter!" he said with a booming, cheerful voice that seemed to naturally fit his appearance. "Please, come in." Dmitri led everyone into the spacious office. Besides the well-worn desk, furnishings included two narrow upholstered chairs and a low-back sofa. If it hadn't been covered with a thin blue slip cover, the stains and thread-worn cushions would have betrayed the furniture's true age. Along one wall was a large bookcase, the shelves overflowing with journals and texts, many in English.

Peter noticed a framed photo of a woman, a few years younger than Dmitri, on his desk next to the computer monitor. She had worn a pink blouse for the portrait, with a simple strand of pearls high around her neck. Her face was lean with pronounced cheekbones and sky-blue eyes. Time had faded her hair to gray. It was the only photo in the office.

"It's a pleasure to meet you, Dmitri," Peter said. "My father has mentioned you often. I understand you have been very generous in making Dad welcome here at the university."

Dmitri waved his hand dismissively. "It was nothing. Besides, what are friends for?"

Ian smiled at Dmitri's modesty. "Well, I'll say this. I arrived in Minsk a stranger, not knowing anyone, not really. Dmitri met me at the airport and took me into his home."

"I thought you and Dmitri have been colleagues for close to two years," Peter said.

"Yes, of course. That's why I wanted to take my sabbatical here, so we could work together. But our exchanges had been limited to professional conversations, a few phone calls, but mostly email. I didn't actually meet Dmitri until I arrived at the Minsk airport."

"My house has plenty of room," Dmitri explained. "Nowadays, it is mostly empty, so it made no sense that Ian should rent an apartment."

Ian turned to Dmitri and clasped his shoulder. "You have been a most gracious and generous host, my friend—a true ambassador of good will for your country."

"Ah, it is nothing. I know what it is like to be an outsider, a stranger, if you will. Besides, I am honored that you should choose to collaborate with me."

"You have traveled a lot?" Peter asked.

Dmitri shook his head. "No, not so much. Our funding is limited, and our government leaders would prefer that we do not visit Western countries."

Peter interpreted 'we' to mean the scientific staff at the university.

"Your travel was fine?" Dmitri asked to no one in particular.

Gary nodded. "Yes, uneventful and on schedule," Peter added. "We walked around Independence Square before coming here; had lunch outside at a nice restaurant."

"And the hotel? You are staying at the Crowne Plaza—it is okay?"

"Dmitri made the hotel reservations for all of you," Ian said.

"So it is you I have to thank. Yes, the hotel is wonderful and the staff are very friendly, thank you."

"It was nothing. The Crowne Plaza is usually where international guests of the university stay."

"I understand your campus tour is tomorrow?" Ian asked, looking at Ethan.

Ethan nodded. "I'm supposed to meet at the administration building at 9:00 am."

"Oh, that's very close," Dmitri said. "Are you planning to apply as an exchange student?"

"Yes sir. I'm studying chemistry at the University of Oregon."

Dmitri beamed with pride. "You know, this is the best university in Belarus, and it's in the top ten of all universities in Europe. And Minsk is a lovely city, with something for everyone."

"The architecture is beautiful," Jo said. "The city has preserved so many older buildings."

"You know, some of the oldest structures date to the invasion of Napoleon's Grand Army. We are fortunate that the Nazis didn't destroy everything during the War. Much of the rebuilding was done by the Soviets when they took their turn occupying my homeland." Dmitri's cheerful tone faded when he referenced the Nazis and Soviets.

"There aren't many students on campus now," Ian explained. "Summer break."

Ethan nodded.

"Your grandfather," Dmitri said, "speaks very highly of your academic achievements. I would be pleased to put in a good word for you with the department chairman. We have been colleagues for more than 20 years."

"Thank you," Ethan replied, feeling a tinge of embarrassment at being the focus of attention.

Sensing his discomfort, Peter shifted the conversation to Jo. “My daughter is interested in seeing some of the art treasures here in Minsk.”

“You won’t be disappointed, my dear. Please, allow me to serve as your guide at the National Art Museum. Tomorrow morning, after breakfast? It is forecast to rain lightly tomorrow, so carry an umbrella if you have one.” Dmitri’s charm was irresistible and Jo smiled.

“That would be wonderful,” she said.

“Are you also here on vacation, Gary?” Professor Savage asked.

“Not really. My company was recently hired by the university to review their IT security. When Peter mentioned he was coming here for a few days, it seemed like a good time to tag along and conduct a site audit. But I should be able to squeeze out a day of sightseeing.”

“Only one day? But there is so much to see,” Dmitri objected.

“I’m sure there is. I suspect I’ll be back to review recommendations to enhance security and reduce successful attacks on the servers,” Gary replied, not wanting to offend his new friend. “Hopefully then I’ll have more time to enjoy the city.”

The small talk wound down, and following a pregnant pause, Peter looked at his father. “How is the work going, Dad? You haven’t said much about it.”

Dmitri cast a sideways glance at Ian, unsure if there was something more to the question.

“We’ve made some progress, but lately the results have been… discouraging.” Ian looked at his son, an austere expression on his face.

“Come now, Ian. You make it sound as if we have nothing

worth reporting," Dmitri scoffed.

Ian faced his friend. "No, of course that's not the case. But you have to agree, the data over the past month has not been positive."

"Perhaps…" Dmitri shrugged. "However, negative results also provide valuable knowledge. I am reminded of a statement by a very famous American inventor, Thomas Edison. You know, he tested over a thousand different materials before he finally found a carbon thread that would serve as the filament of his electric lightbulb. When a reporter asked about all his failures, he replied that those experiments were not failures, rather he had succeeded in identifying a thousand materials that were not suitable for his invention."

Ian frowned. "Yes, I suppose you're right. Sometimes I'm too impatient, I know that. Not necessarily a good trait for a scientist." He forced a smile, and Dmitri returned a huge grin.

"Forgive me," said Dmitri, "I am being a poor host. Allow me to show you our laboratories. Our facilities are first rate, including an advanced electron microscopy lab. After the tour we will enjoy some wine at the faculty club. Of course, you will be my guests for dinner. I know a delightful restaurant that serves wonderful Belarusian cuisine."

"That sounds marvelous, Dmitri. Thank you. I hope your wife will join us also," Peter said. He assumed the woman in the photo was Dmitri's wife.

For a second, the gleam left Dmitri's eyes, and his smile—which had been almost constant since they met—faded. "No, she will not."

Peter immediately sensed the awkwardness of the moment, and regretted the question. "Dad tells me your labs are very well equipped," he said, deliberately selecting a safe subject for conversation.

"Yes, we are rightfully proud of our facilities," Dmitri said, cheerful once again. "Shall we start?"

With pride and purpose to his step, Dmitri turned right into the hallway with his guests one step behind. After passing a half dozen offices, he spoke over his shoulder. "The laboratories are in the basement so if there is any spill of water or reagents it cannot leak into the offices or conference rooms. Just ahead, we will take the stairs."

Suddenly a voice boomed down the hallway from behind the group. "Ostanovis!" Dmitri planted his feet and turned, expecting to see a colleague or administrator who had issued the command to stop. Instead, he saw three men dressed in military uniforms. The lead man had thick salt and pepper hair and a bulky, muscular build. Although he appeared to be around 50 years of age, his physique was fit, lacking the belly bulge so often plaguing middle-aged Americans and Europeans. He had a rifle slung over his shoulder but the two following him were holding their rifles with both hands, still casually pointing downward.

Ethan and Jo hadn't noticed Dmitri's concerned expression and, failing to understand Russian, did not interpret the order to stop. They continued walking toward the stairs, speaking softly to each other. In contrast, Gary, Peter, and Ian had turned when Dmitri did and immediately recognized that something was wrong.

The trio of soldiers approached quickly, and seeing that the young man and woman had not halted, the leader issued his order again. "Stop where you are!"

This time Jo and Ethan noticed and turned to face the commotion. They were only two steps from the double doors at the entrance to the stairwell.

The leader was now standing within arm's reach of Dmitri and his American friends. Peter's head spun toward Ethan and Jo. "Go! Run!"

Ethan bounded for the doors, yanking one open. His sister right behind, they dashed through and sprinted down the stairs two at a time.

Crack!! The gunshot echoed in the hard confines of the hallway, obscuring the sound of the bullet shattering the glass door as it automatically swung back toward the closed position. Peter launched himself into the soldier still recovering from the recoil after firing his AK-74. He ducked his head, planting his shoulder in the man's belly, slamming him into the wall. Still holding the rifle with both hands, the soldier slammed it down across Peter's back, but Peter refused to release his grip around the man's midsection.

Gary was poised to spring forward, frozen only a few feet from the muzzle of the second AK-74. The leader appraised Dmitri and Ian with discerning eyes, unconcerned with the scuffle. Without averting his gaze, he pulled a pistol from the holster at his side, point the gun to the ceiling, and fired.

Reluctantly, Peter released his grip, his back deeply bruised from the beating. He knew he could not win, but was satisfied Ethan and Jo were not being pursued. Peter stood upright, easily three inches taller than his adversary who still clutched his rifle, the barrel pointed at his chest. Before Peter stepped away the soldier swung the rifle butt connecting with Peter at the belt line, doubling him over.

"Nyet!" Dmitri shouted and Ian rushed to his son's aid.

Cocking his head to the side, the leader announced, "You are my prisoners. Raise your hands and do not move, or you will be shot."

CHAPTER 6

Minsk

WITH ONE HAND ON his holstered pistol, still standing in the hallway, the leader spoke to Dmitri in Russian, receiving short replies to his questions. Perspiration began to appear as glistening beads on the face and neck of the Belarusian scholar. He addressed his friends. "This is General Gorev. He is in charge of the pro-Russian militia—"

"You are Americans?" Gorev interrupted. "Yes?" He paused, scrutinizing Ian and Peter while waiting for their reply.

"Yes, American," Ian said. He raised his head and looked Gorev directly in the eyes as he replied. "I am working here with Professor Kaspar as a guest of Belarus. I'm on sabbatical."

As he listened, the corners of Gorev's mouth twitch and his eyes narrowed. He held out his hand. "Passports."

Reluctantly Ian removed his passport from his pocket and handed it over to General Gorev. Gary followed suit. Peter stared at the officer, not uttering a word, hands still raised.

Gorev opened the passport and glanced quickly at the photo of Ian Savage, reading his name and city the passport was issued from. He then placed the document in his breast pocket.

He repeated the process with the second passport.

"Mister Porter," Gorev said.

"Yeah, that's me. You have no right holding us at gunpoint—"

"Silence!"

Gary's eyes burned into Gorev, but the general absorbed every bit of the anger and outrage without a flinch. Shifting his gaze to Peter, he repeated his demand.

Peter shook his head slowly. "I don't have it. I left it at the hotel."

Gorev issued a short order and the two soldiers quickly frisked Peter. All they found was some local currency and a street map.

"Which hotel?" Gorev asked.

"The Holiday Inn." Peter's lips were drawn tight, his eyes hard and fixed on the general.

Gorev took a moment to measure the three Americans, looking them over from head to toe. The older one certainly fit his image of a professor, wearing khaki slacks and a light-blue long-sleeve shirt, the sleeves rolled up to the elbow. His hair was whiter than snow, thinning on the top, and his goatee beard matched the pure white hair color perfectly.

The other two Americans were troublesome. The one named Gary Porter definitely had an attitude, but had so far been easy to intimidate and control. The other man, though, he was different. His defiance was obvious, having already attacked one of the militiamen, and there was a recklessness in the way he responded to questioning, as if he was looking for a fight. He stood slightly taller than the older man—a little more than the general's own height of 1.8 meters. His thick brown hair was cut short, but not a military haircut. His frame was slender but fit; there did not appear to be an ounce of fat. General Gorev scrutinized his face again, focusing on the steel blue eyes, reading defiance and determination.

"Are you also a visiting scholar?" Gorev said.

"I'm just passing through. Was lost and asked these nice men for directions."

Gorev's mouth pulled back in a smile that was not reflected by the remainder of his features. "You are a funny man. How do you say it… a comedian, yes?"

"Yeah, I'm a comedian." Peter paused for a moment before adding, "I'll be going now." He lowered his hands and was immediately jabbed in the back by a rifle barrel. He raised his hands over his head again.

"What is your name, funny man?" Gorev said.

"Peter."

Gorev frowned. "Peter? That is all, just Peter?"

"Peter Savage."

"Ahh," Gorev said, his eyebrows raised. "You are related to Professor Ian Savage. His son, maybe?"

"That's right."

"I see." Gorev paused, looking over the three men. Dmitri was sweating profusely now, and his eyes were wide in fear. In contrast, the Americans appeared to be in better control over their emotions.

The doors to the stairwell opened and five more militiamen emerged from behind Peter, Gary, and Ian. General Gorev, speaking in Russian, asked if they captured the young man and woman who fled down the stairs minutes earlier.

Two of the militiamen exchange a confused glanced. Peter did not understand what was said, but suspected it was related to Ethan and Jo. He leaned toward Dmitri. "What are they saying?" he asked in a whisper.

"Your children, they escaped."

Inwardly Peter smiled. Thank God, they made it.

General Gorev shifted his stare to Peter. "No matter. My

men will find them before they leave the campus and hold them with the other students and staff." Then in Russian, he issued a command to the militiamen, and they moved swiftly down the hallway searching every office. If the door was locked, they kicked it in. Four of Dmitri's colleagues were found hiding in their offices and were herded down the stairs with Dmitri and the three Americans.

CHAPTER 7

Minsk

A TOTAL OF 36 FACULTY PLUS Peter, Ian, Gary, and Dmitri were corralled on the ground floor in the large main conference room just off the spacious lobby and principle entrance. Two sets of double doors connected the lobby to the conference room. A large oval table was centered in the room surrounded by standard black office chairs, sufficient in number for the hostages, while additional padded chairs lined two of the walls. Overhead fluorescent tubes provided illumination, emitting a constant, soft buzz. Blackout draperies were pulled closed, preventing any view of the campus through the large picture windows. Off in a corner, General Gorev sat at a small, utilitarian metal desk, conversing with two militiamen.

Every person had been searched, and their keys, wallets, cell phones, and money were all taken and placed in a rucksack stashed underneath the desk where Gorev sat. Soon all the hostages had found a seat, forming small clusters around the room. Conversation was sporadic; voices were hushed.

Peter was carefully scrutinizing their guards. The number of guards was frequently changing as men would enter and leave. Peter thought he had counted seven unique faces, but he could not distinguish any unit patches or rank badges on the uniforms.

Abruptly Peter stood and walked toward General Gorev, only to be quickly intercepted by one of the guards. With an AK-74 poking Peter in the belly, the message was clear though no words were spoken. He returned and dropped into a chair next to his father.

Ian Savage leaned close to his son and spoke in a low voice. "Be careful. Don't antagonize these men."

Peter nodded almost imperceptibly, although his tense posture and stern expression told Ian that he did not fully accept his advice.

Gary scooted his chair so it was just to the right and behind Peter. He bent over pretending to adjust the laces on his shoes. "You're up to something; I know it. You didn't really leave your passport at the hotel, did you?"

"It's in my boot." Peter whispered and tapped one foot against the other.

Gary surreptitiously glanced at Peter's brown-leather motorcycle boots. "Anything else hidden in there?"

At first Peter didn't answer. He turned his head and body slowly, scanning around the room and taking in both the hostages and the militiamen. At the moment, no one was paying any particular attention to the Americans.

Eyes still flitting around the room, he said, "A composite Zytel-ceramic blade."

"Jim taught you well."

At the mention of his friend, Commander James Nicolaou, Peter felt a minute uplift to his spirits. Soon enough, Peter reasoned, the news of the pro-Russian militia taking over the BSU campus and, most likely, other government buildings, would leak out to the world press. But it would still be days before anyone in the U.S. government knew that Americans were among the hostages. And how long would it take for Special Forces to rescue them? Days? Perhaps weeks?

Dmitri was silent—his head down and hands folded on his lap. To Peter, he appeared resigned to their fate.

"Professor Kaspar," Peter said, modulating his voice to avoid attention.

He raised his head and looked at Peter.

"Some of your colleagues were in their offices when we were captured. They must have heard the gunshots. Did anyone call the police?"

"They said the phone lines were dead. But two managed to call using their cell phones."

Peter nodded, imagining the local police organizing a rescue, also knowing it would take time. Then his attention landed on Gorev.

"What are they talking about?" Peter said, referring to the conversation between General Gorev and two other militiamen. They made no attempt to subdue their voices, and in the quiet room the sound carried easily.

"See that the tall one with blonde hair? His name is Major Leonov. General Gorev ordered him to make certain the machine is ready, and to set up a radio in the office of the Department President."

Major Leonov was decidedly taller and younger than General Gorev, also more muscular. To Peter's eye, Leonov looked like an elite, professional soldier.

"What machine? What are they talking about?"

Dmitri shrugged. "I don't know."

Although puzzled by the reference, Peter let it go for now. "Most likely the radio is so they can coordinate their actions with other groups. Have they said anything about government buildings also being taken? Anything about the police?"

"I think so. One of the men said that a police station was captured. Also the KGB Headquarters."

"KGB?" Gary said.

"Yes, the State Secret Police still use that name, a carryover from the Cold War when Belarus was still part of the former Soviet Bloc."

"What else are they saying?" Peter said.

"It sounds like they plan to question us."

Peter tilted his head to the side and raised his eyebrows. "That's curious. Why? What are they looking for?"

Dmitri shrugged his shoulders. "I don't know. Perhaps they are interested in our research?"

"There have been several successful breaches of the university servers. That's why I was contracted," Gary said. "The hacks have been mostly aimed at data from the science departments."

"We save our data, as well as drafts of publications, to the department server—we share it with the physics department—it makes it easier to collaborate with our colleagues."

"There's more to this than scientific espionage. What else are they discussing?" Peter said.

"Major Leonov and one other man were sent to the roof. General Gorev told them to find the..." Dmitri hesitated. He closed his eyes tight and rubbed his forehead. "I don't know the word, but I think it is air draw. That's what the General told them to find."

Peter turned away, thinking. Air draw. Air draw.

Suddenly he looked again at Dmitri. "Air intake, is that it?"

A quick nod. "Yes, air intake."

"Do you think that's important?" Ian asked, keeping his voice low, almost a whisper, like the others.

Peter leaned back in his chair, wincing when his bruised back pushed into the backrest. He slowly swiveled to face Gary, who sat with his arms folded across his chest.

"You thinking what I'm thinking?" Gary asked.

"Makeup air." For a few moments Peter just sat there, running scenarios through in his mind. He kept returning to one possibility.

"Dmitri. Are there exhaust ventilation hoods in the laboratories?"

"Yes, of course."

"I thought so. And since those hoods draw a large amount of air out of the building there would be air intakes on the roof to bring a supply of fresh air back inside, makeup air."

"Yes, it is necessary to balance the air pressure in the building so the ventilation hoods draw properly."

"Why is that important?" Ian asked. "They can't poison us, not when the militia is still guarding us. They're breathing the same air we are."

"I don't know," Peter replied. "Dmitri, anything else?"

Professor Kaspar shifted in his seat. "Well, the conversation is a bit odd. The General doesn't show much respect for the guards, and he talks as if he is from a different unit. His accent is wrong. I think he is not from here."

"Why is that strange? I'd imagine many of these militiamen are from other cities in Belarus."

"No, that's not what I mean. I think General Gorev is Russian military. Major Leonov, too."

"Maybe the Russian army has advisors helping the militia?" Ian said.

Peter watched as Gorev interacted with several guards. "Not advisor, but active participant. We need some proof of Russian military involvement."

Gorev sent two guards out with the rucksack, and then engaged in animated conversation with another militiaman. Judging from the gesticulations, Peter assumed Gorev was not pleased with the direction the discussion was going. Abruptly the two men walked out, followed by the remaining two guards. With the room momentarily empty of militiamen, Peter decided to check out Gorev's desk.

"Gary, plant yourself by the door and cause a commotion when the guards come back in."

Many of the other civilians watched Peter and Gary with a mix of curiosity and amusement. Peter swiftly walked up to the desk and grabbed the top sheet of paper. The writing was in the Cyrillic alphabet. Stuffing the paper inside his jacket, he returned to Dmitri just as the guards entered again. Seeing Gary standing close to the doors, one guard shoved him away, causing Gary to stumble in the process, knocking a chair aside with exaggerated movements.

Peter innocently placed the document in Dmitri's hands, then turned toward the doorway in time to see Gary picking himself up. He stared back at the two guards. "What was that for?" The guards ignored the question and moved off to the side.

Dmitri quickly read the paper while Peter stood with his back to the guards, preventing them from observing Dmitri. "This appears to be a directive from the Russian military command. It references Spetsnaz troops here under command of General Gorev. The Spetsnaz troops are to ensure safety of the ethnic Russian civilians."

"What else?"

Dmitri handed the paper back to Peter, who folded it and stuffed it inside the waistband of his pants. "That's all. I think it continues on another page."

"Got a visitor coming," Gary mumbled, and then he nodded his head to the side indicating an approaching militia guard. Everyone quieted and looked at the floor.

The guard spoke to Dmitri, his rifle casually pointed at him.

"He says we are to go with him."

"What does he want?" Peter said.

"No. Not you. Only Ian and myself."

Peter rose and the guard planted one foot back and snapped the AK-74 to his shoulder, sighting down the barrel at Peter's head. Gary grabbed Peter by the shoulders. "No Peter. Not here."

Ian held a hand out toward his son. "I'll be fine. They probably just want to ask a few questions. Probably about the research Dmitri and I are doing." Ian forced a smile, but it didn't fool Peter.

The guard escorted the two professors out of the room, Peter still restrained by his friend.

"I'm done with waiting. It's time for some answers," Peter said, seeing that Gorev had returned.

"What's the plan?" Gary was ready to go along with whatever Peter had in mind.

"A short chat with the General."

Peter started walking toward the desk where General Gorev was conversing with various militiamen—he had not yet noticed the missing document. No one stopped Peter this time. He stood at the desk, Gary at his left, and looked down at the General. A militiaman moved in behind Peter.

"General Gorev. What do you want with my father and Dmitri?" Peter asked, interrupting the conversation.

Gorev ignored him, further infuriating Peter. He snapped his hand out and latched onto Gorev's arm. "I'm talking to you!"

As soon as contact was made the guard swung the rifle butt into Peter's side, connecting just below his ribs. Peter gasped, loosening his grip and twisting to the side.

Gorev stood, glaring at Peter and Gary, while the guard had his rifle aimed at the Americans. "It would be much easier just to shoot you now; unfortunately that would be counterproductive.

Lock them in the store room."

With rifle barrels pressing into their backs, Peter and Gary were escorted out of the conference room and into a long corridor. Shortly, they stopped in front of a room. One of the guards unlocked and opened the door, then turned on the light. It was a small, windowless room, with cleaning and other supplies stacked on shelves along the walls. Opposite the door was a utility sink, and next to the sink stood an industrial air compressor, bolted to the concrete floor.

Peter and Gary were shoved in and the door slammed shut behind them, followed by a click indicating the lock had been engaged. Gary immediately tried the handle, but it wouldn't turn. He examined the latch and surrounding cover plate, failing to find machine screws holding it in place.

"The latch must be fastened to the door from the outside."

"The hinge pins?" Peter asked.

"Tamper resistant. We'd need a special tool to remove them and I'm guessing we don't have it."

Still favoring his right side, Peter slowly took in the contents on the shelves—a collection of cleaning supplies plus electrical components and plumbing parts. For a couple minutes he said nothing, focused on his new surroundings.

"You got a plan coming together?" Gary said.

Peter nodded slightly. "Ever watch MacGyver on TV?"

CHAPTER 8

MINSK

"DON'T TELL ME YOU WANT to play TV trivia," Gary said.

"Nope. But our host just made a big mistake by locking us in this room." Peter replied.

Gary looked around at the walls and shelves. "The walls are concrete block, no way we're digging out anytime soon. What do you see that I don't?"

There was a large battered metal box underneath the sink. Peter opened the top to reveal a tray containing various tools. He spotted a rusty hacksaw, pliers, hammer, and assortment of other hand tools.

Next Peter examined the air compressor. The machine was dusty and the electric motor and finned metal cylinders were connected by a pair of pulleys and a worn belt. The pressure gauge read just shy of 1.2 MPa.

"If this gauge is correct, we have about 175 psi of air in the tank," Peter said as he continued his inspection. A large valve was fitted close to the receiving tank, and iron pipe extended from the valve to an elbow and then to the wall. From there the pipe travelled vertically up through the ceiling.

Peter tested the valve. He grabbed the lever handle and pushed to the side until the handle was perpendicular to the pipe. He stepped back, studying the run of iron pipe.

"See if there are a couple of wrenches in that tool box," he said.

Gary kneeled beside the sink and rummaged through the tools, working his way down to the bottom of the box. He stood and handed two worn pipe wrenches to Peter.

He clamped one of the rusty tools onto a three-foot section of pipe that extended horizontally to the wall. He pulled on the wrench, but the pipe didn't budge. Again he tried, this time with both hands on the wrench, but the serrated jaws slipped on the iron, losing grip.

"Want me to try?" Gary asked.

"No, the threaded joints are rusted tight. If I pull too hard I could break the pipe."

"Isn't that the point?"

"No, I'm not looking for a club, rather something with more punch."

Peter retrieved the hacksaw from the toolbox. "I'll cut the pipe here by the wall. That will give us some leverage and together we should be able to turn the section of pipe 180 degrees so it's pointing toward the door."

Immediately Gary understood. "A compressed-air spud gun."

"That's the idea, but we aren't shooting potatoes out of the pipe. This shut off valve at the receiver tank will be the trigger."

"And what do you have in mind for the projectile?"

Peter was about a quarter of the way through the iron pipe where it was threaded into another elbow at the wall. Without looking away from his work, he nodded his head to the side. "That mop handle—if it fits inside the pipe."

Gary hefted the mop. "Primitive, but effective."

Peter completed severing the pipe and then handed the hacksaw to Gary. "Cut off the mop head and then saw a slot down the middle of the handle, about four inches long."

While Gary was busy Peter found some steel wire in the toolbox and grabbed the pliers. Then he pulled the composite knife from his boot. The knife was molded without a hand guard, although there were two holes through the grip, forward and rear, to help with lashing the blade to a pole.

Returning to the toolbox, Peter searched for a drill and bits—nothing. So he picked up a Philips screwdriver; it would have to do.

It took Gary another minute to finish. Peter fit the grip of the composite blade into the slot sawn into the handle. It was snug, but good. He marked the location of both holes on the grip and then used the Philips screwdriver to auger two ragged holes through the wood. Next, he used the wire to secure the composite blade, passing the wire through both holes in the knife handle and twisting securely with the pliers until the wire bit into the wood. Then he wrapped the wire tightly around the wood over and over, cinching the split handle tight against the knife grip, finally twisting the wire ends together.

Pointing to the iron elbow that connected the valve to the section of pipe Peter had just cut through, he said, "Put the wrench on this elbow and turn while I push up on the pipe." With a groan of rusted metal the pipe budged just a tiny amount at first. But as the years of rust broke free the pipe swung around until it was aimed directly at the door.

Gary tested the fit of the wood spear inside the pipe. "It's a bit loose." Peter noticed as well.

"We need a tight fit to build up pressure." Peter hurried to the shelves beside the door. A pile of rags, mostly stained and oily, yielded what he sought. Selecting what had once been a T-shirt, Peter ripped off strips a few inches wide. While Gary held the spear, Peter wrapped one of the strips around the blunt end.

"See if you can work it into the pipe, it may be too tight."

Gary twisted and pushed. Once he got it started the wood rod slid inside the pipe, although it took some effort. Together they rammed the shaft home, and then Peter took a final sighting along the length of the iron pipe, satisfied with the aim.

"That's only good for one shot," Gary said.

Peter nodded. He knew they needed more weaponry. "See what else you can find."

"There's a hammer in the toolbox, and those wrenches can be used as clubs."

"Not likely. You'll be shot before you get within arm's reach."

"Yeah, you're probably right. Are there any chemicals you can mix to make a bomb?"

Peter shook his head. "Not here. Maybe in the chemical store room, where ever that is."

"Well, I don't see anything to make a bow." Gary was methodically scanning the room. "And I don't see any arrows either." He paused. "Wait, is that a sprayer?" He pointed to the floor behind Peter and rushed to pick up the metal canister.

Like everything else, it was coated with grime and oil stains. Gary worked the pump and it felt like it was building pressure. The sprayer had a brass wand about two feet in length attached to a length of rubber hose. The hose was not very pliable anymore and the rubber was beginning to crack. He pointed the nozzle in a safe direction and squeezed the handle. A focused jet of foul smelling liquid squirted about six feet.

"It works! Maybe we can fill it with paint thinner or something and make a flamethrower."

"Not paint thinner, something more volatile." As Peter was talking he was moving cans of cleaning fluids. "This might work," he said and set a metal can on the floor, followed by a second one, identical in appearance. He removed the screw cap and carefully sniffed the vapors.

"What is it?" Gary asked.

"I don't know. The label's not in English. But it has the skull and crossbones, so it's poisonous, and it smells like solvent or hydrocarbons."

Peter poured a small amount of the clear fluid on the floor, then retrieved a book of matches he found next to some candles. He struck a match and extended the flame toward the liquid. As the flame approached the spreading puddle the liquid caught fire and burned with a blue-yellow flame.

"Excellent," Peter said. "Whatever this is, it's pretty volatile."

Gary dumped the previous contents of the sprayer down the sink and flushed the pungent smelling liquid with lots of cold water. Peter filled the canister with both cans of solvent.

"We need some means to light it," Gary said.

"I'll wire a piece of oily cloth around the nozzle. There's a can of machine oil next to the compressor."

It only took a few minutes for Peter to complete the ignition mechanism of their makeshift flamethrower.

"Under different circumstances, we'd test this contraption before betting our lives on it," Peter said.

"Come on, that'd take all the excitement out of it. Of course it's gonna work." Gary forced a grin, but it was fleeting.

"Now we wait."

"And when the guards come back?" Gary asked.

"We have to constantly man that air valve. When the door opens, we have to pop open that valve before the guard realizes he's looking at a home-made harpoon cannon. We'll only have a fraction of a second."

"Wish we had a real cannon and grapeshot."

"Me too. But this spear will do the job. Better get some rest buddy. I'll take the first watch."

CHAPTER 9

Sacramento, California

MONA STEPHENS GLANCED at the nameplate on the door; 'Lt. Ellen Lacey'. She knocked and was promptly answered.

"Come in."

Omitting the usual pleasantries and small talk, Stephens got right to business, advancing smartly to stop in front of Lacey's desk. She handed a folder to her boss. "This came in overnight from NSA. They're reporting multiple simultaneous attacks in Minsk by pro-Russian militia. The entire operation happened extraordinarily fast, obviously well planned and executed. A large number of civilian hostages are being held at several public buildings now under the control of the militia. They call themselves the Nationalist Proletarian Army, or NPA."

Lacey opened the folder and began to scan the contents. "Great. Before they were just kooks. Now they're organized kooks. What are the Russians saying?"

"The usual. President Pushkin is urging the Belarusian government to exhibit restraint, adding that Russia reserves the right to defend ethnic Russians should they be threatened or harmed."

“And NATO? How are the Europeans responding? And President Taylor?” Lacey stopped reading and shifted her gaze to Stephens.

“No official response from NATO yet, but the Joint Chiefs are conferring with Brussels in the event Belarus requests military assistance and President Taylor honors the request. The NSA and CIA are scrambling; seems they were caught totally by surprise. So far, the conflict is localized to a few government buildings and the main campus of the Belarusian State University. However, the situation is very fluid and, based on recent patterns in Ukraine and Latvia, it’s likely to escalate to the principle transportation hubs—airport, train stations. I’d imagine the leaders of France, Germany, and the U.K. will request a meeting with President Taylor to align their positions before anyone issues a public statement.”

“Reach out to Mossad and MI6. See what they are willing to share.”

“Yes, ma’am,” Stephens replied. “Should I also check with the German and French foreign intelligence?”

Lacey thought for a moment before answering. “Not yet, maybe later. The Germans are still bent out of shape that we spied on them, and the French seldom have anything of value they are willing to share.”

“Yes, ma’am. There is something else.”

“Go on.”

“It’s in the folder, a report from the U.S. Embassy in Minsk. Ethan and Joanna Savage, two American citizens, escaped from the university when the NPA stormed the campus. Their father is Peter Savage.”

Lacey’s eyes widened. “Has the Embassy contacted Peter?”

“That’s impossible. He’s among the hostages, along with his father Professor Ian Savage and a friend, Gary Porter. They were last seen by Ethan and Joanna on the second floor of the chemistry building, captured by armed militia."

"Does Commander Nicolaou know?"

Stephens shook her head. "I don't believe so. I just learned myself. The embassy report is time stamped 30 minutes ago."

Lacey flipped to the second page and read the scant details from the embassy. "It's likely President Taylor has already been notified that Americans are among the hostages. What do we know about the NPA? Do they have a history of taking foreign hostages?"

"Very little is known about the group. They seem to have sprouted from the pro-Russian militias that were part of the campaign in Latvia. The NSA is working to identify a command structure. It looks like this is the first time they've used the NPA name. But, the dominant militia in Latvia—led by Colonel Simenof, second in command was Alexei Gorev, he was a major at the time—is implicated in two massacres involving civilians. The city of Baltinava, near the Russian border, was quickly captured by the pro-Russian militia. Simenof is reputed to have gone door-to-door, his soldiers demanding passports. Any civilian with a Russian passport—very common in most Eastern European countries—was left alone. Those who could not produce a Russian passport were rounded up, taken to a soccer field, and shot. It all happened very fast, during the first day of occupation."

"How many were killed?" Lacey asked.

"Estimates range from several hundred to as many as 4,000. The local officials aren't very cooperative. The second massacre took place about a week later near the end of the conflict. Nine foreign journalists—including one American and one Brit—were captured and executed by gunmen wearing the camouflage uniform and black ski mask favored by the militias."

"Evidence?"

"Since the city is still under control of the militia, very little.

It was recorded and posted on YouTube. But the identity of the gunmen is unknown and Simenof is on record denying any involvement. And he may be telling the truth. Major Gorev and Colonel Simenof had a falling out when the Russians turned the tables and started providing heavy armor and weapons to shore up the pro-Russian militias in and around Baltinava. Simenof was satisfied with a limited victory, a small territory effectively under control of the Russian Federation, but Gorev wanted a bloodbath."

"So Gorev ordered the execution of the journalists? Why?"

"All speculation ma'am. But maybe he wanted to punish the West. Maybe he wanted to drag Europe into the conflict knowing they did not have the stomach to win a regional war against President Pushkin and the Russian military."

"So, we have to view the hostages as at-risk prisoners of a terrorist group."

"Yes ma'am. That's my conclusion as well."

"We need to brief Commander Nicolaou and get in front of the curve before Colonel Pierson asks for recommendations and a plan.

"Yes ma'am. I'll pull together everything we have from NSA, DIA, CIA, and foreign assets. It'll take an hour, maybe longer."

"You have 30 minutes. And see if there are any sat photos of the BSU campus. Pull in Williams and Ross."

"I'm on it," Stephens said over her shoulder, already at the door.

Lacey picked up her phone. "Sir, we have a situation developing in Minsk, and you're gonna want this mission."

CHAPTER 10

Sacramento, California

COMMANDER JAMES NICOLAOU sat at the head of the conference table considering the ramifications of the briefing. He was surrounded by his team of senior analysts—Ellen Lacey, Mona Stephens, Mark Williams, and Beth Ross—as well as his field operatives from Alpha Team—Bull, Ghost, Magnum, Homer, and the newest member of the team, Iceberg—so-named for his mop of snow-white curly hair. Tall and lanky, Iceberg, whose given name was Jerry Balvanz, played basketball in college for two seasons before joining the Army. He quickly worked his way into Special Forces and was a member of Delta when he was tapped to join SGIT.

In less than 24 hours, Minsk had turned from a city at peace to the epicenter of a full-blown crisis, possibly the initial wave of an invasion by pro-Russian militia and, potentially, Russian regular army and air forces. There was no denying that the map of Eastern Europe was being unilaterally redrawn by Vladimir Pushkin, and it was looking more and more like the former Soviet Union.

Stephens was just concluding her briefing. "Although only

three Americans are confirmed to be held by the NPA, it's likely the total will rise as we get more information. Real-time intelligence is beginning to trickle in; I've received three updates in the past hour. In addition to the BSU campus and buildings, the NPA holds the main train station, called Minsk Pass—short for Passazhirsky—and the Government House, which is the seat of local and national government. The parliament is located there but was not in session when the building was taken. The international airport is also under control of the militia; all flights have been cancelled. And they occupy the KGB Headquarters, plus a few less important government buildings. That's what we know as of this moment. But I caution everyone, the intelligence is sketchy, incomplete."

All eyes were scrutinizing a detailed satellite image of Minsk projected on a 100-inch flat screen monitor. Key landmarks were labeled in red font. The BSU campus and main railway station adjoined Independence Square, the location of the Government House. The KGB Headquarters was two blocks northwest of the square.

"Are there any reports of an actual attack on the KGB Headquarters?" Bull asked.

Sergeant Mark Williams was quick to reply. "No sir, nothing through our channels and no mention on Twitter or Facebook."

"Significance?" Jim said

Lieutenant Lacey took the lead again. "Too early to say, sir. However, the State Security Agency—like that of South Ossetia and Transnistria—has significant ties to Russia. It's possible they are allied with the NPA. With the KGB providing support in the form of intelligence and manpower, it could explain how the militia was so successful in executing this action."

Jim absorbed this information for a moment, his eyes sequentially moving amongst the faces of his intelligence analysts and field agents. It only took a few seconds for him to recognize the pattern. "South Ossetia, with significant Russian military assistance, won independence from Georgia in 2008. The conflict lasted only about a week. Once the conflict ended, Russia signed a defense agreement with South Ossetia.

"Likewise, Transnistria, a small strip of land between Moldova and Ukraine, declared its independence from Moldova. A civil war ensued. The pro-Russian separatists would have been soundly defeated if the Russian Federation had not intervened, committing the Soviet 14th Guard Army to the conflict. Without external help, Moldova couldn't win. A negotiated settlement called the Primakov Memorandum was signed in 1997, I believe. Following Russia's annexation of the Crimean Peninsula from Ukraine, Transnistria has officially sought admission to the Russian Federation."

For the first time since the meeting began, Sergeant Beth Ross spoke up. "President Vladimir Pushkin is a nationalist fanatic. Since he came into power he's exerted continuous pressure on the former Soviet Bloc countries of Eastern Europe, and slowly but surely he's pulling them back into the Russian sphere of influence. Seems that no one is willing to stand up to his aggression."

"Stay on topic, sergeant," Lacey commanded while Jim raised an eyebrow at the ad-lib commentary. It was well known, ever since the terrorist action on Chernabura Island in the Aleutian chain, an action that many of the men sitting around the table participated in, that Beth Ross distrusted President Pushkin and his government.

"Yes ma'am. Sorry ma'am."

Jim pulled the briefing back to the subject matter. "Alright, for the moment we'll assume the Belarusian State Security Agency is, at the least, sympathetic to the NPA. What is the U.S. Embassy doing?"

"Everything they can, sir," Stephens said. "A couple years

ago the Belarusian government ordered a reduction in staff and the ambassador was recalled. They only have a half dozen staff, and they're trying to locate the Americans residing in, or visiting, the city."

"It's going to take some time", Lacey added. "And not all Americans have registered with the embassy."

"What is the Belarusian government saying?" Jim asked.

Ross was ready for this question. "Not much that we know of. President Alexander Yatchenko has officially notified NATO Command in Brussels. Most of what we know is coming from citizens who were in the area of Independence Square and the BSU campus. There are a lot of photos and videos uploaded onto social media, including from travelers at Minsk Pass and the airport. Plus the Belarusian military is deploying some special forces—spotters and snipers—on rooftops of buildings that have not been taken yet by the NPA. Those special forces are providing periodic reports to NATO."

Jim knew that it would take time for intel to filter through NATO and make its way to Lacey's team. "Get ahold of Colonel Pierson and explain that we need to cut through the bureaucracy and get those NATO intel updates without the usual delay."

Ross made a notation on her tablet. "Yes, sir."

"Lacey, what's the hostage situation? There must have been hundreds, maybe thousands of civilians at the train station and airport."

"According to eyewitness reports, no hostages were taken at either location."

Jim scrunched his face. "Why? We have an unknown number of hostages, presumably being held at the chemistry building of the BSU campus, but none were taken at other locations?"

"We're assuming they are still held at the chemistry

building," Lacey corrected. "But that information is rather stale."

Jim nodded, leaving his question unanswered, and then turned his gaze to his senior analyst. "Okay. Given the intel we have, what's the objective? And do we expect the hostages to be released?"

Lacey cleared her throat, but before she could answer, the speaker in the middle of the conference table buzzed. The voice was easily recognized as that of Sergeant Wells, the receptionist—and gatekeeper—of SGIT. "Colonel Pierson is on the line sir. I told him you were in a meeting but he insisted it couldn't wait."

"That's fine. Put him through."

A crisp voice emanated from the speakerphone. "Commander, who's in the room with you?" Colonel Pierson never wasted time with greetings.

"Most of my team sir. I have Lacey and three junior analysts, plus Bull, Magnum, Homer, Ghost, and Iceberg. We're in secure conference room A."

"Good. It's best that everyone hear what I have to say. This mess in Minsk has President Taylor's full attention. He's demanding answers from the intelligence community. He wants to know exactly where the Americans are being held. He said, and I quote, 'no more American hostages are going to be murdered on my watch!' There should be no doubt about his position."

"We've been following the intelligence reports on this, sir."

"I assumed you would. President Taylor has already authorized Operation Bright Star to forcibly win the release of the hostages. To expedite the timetable, assets already in Europe will be used. Intelligence is coming in, but we must know the exact location of the American hostages. Make this your number one priority."

"Already on it, sir," Jim said.

"Good. You have one hour." Before anyone could reply, a buzz indicating an open line emanated from the speaker. The Colonel had ended the call.

CHAPTER 11

Sacramento, California

IT HAD BEEN MORE THAN four hours since the NPA had taken over the BSU campus, plenty of time for social media sites around the world to receive postings of photos and videos. This was a rich source of real-time intelligence, and the focus of much of the effort of the SGIT analysts.

"The picture is pretty clear," Stephens said. She was updating Lieutenant Lacey with support from Ross and Williams.

Ross elaborated. "The Minsk police and Belarusian Army have spotters and snipers posted on all the tall buildings within 1,000 yards of the BSU campus. Their reports are confirmed by postings across all major social media sites. The hostages have not been moved. They must still be in the chemistry building."

"Mark, please pull up the building layout," Stephens said. The analysts were meeting in one of SGIT's secure conference rooms, all equipped with access to MOTHER, state-of-the-art encrypted teleconferencing, and flat-screen monitor.

"We estimate that between 20 and 45 hostages are being held, including Peter Savage, Ian Savage, and Gary Porter. Most likely closer to the high end of the estimate," Stephens said. "We have no reports, at this time, of other Americans being held captive."

"Confidence in that total?" Lacey asked. She knew this to be critical to the rescue planning.

Mark Williams answered. "Good. We factored in the number of full-time research assistants, subtracting faculty on vacation. Since it is the summer break, nearly all the support staff and students are away."

Lacey nodded. "Continue."

Stephens cleared her throat. They had covered the facts—as best they were known—and now she was venturing into speculation. "The building is constructed of concrete block and steel. It primarily houses offices and laboratories, as you can see in the layout." She used a laser pointer to identify the rooms on the plan projected on the large monitor.

"We believe it's most likely all the hostages are grouped together, in one room. It would be much easier to guard them and require fewer men. Although the laboratories are large rooms, we do not think they would be held there."

"Why not?" Lacey asked.

"The laboratories are in the basement. During an assault, the NPA guards would be trapped, the only exit being up to the ground floor."

"There is also the danger of chemicals being released during an engagement," added Ross. "That could result in a fire, or poisoning. It's just too risky from a defensive point of view."

"I agree," Lacey replied. She was studying the building plan carefully. "So, you think they are being held on the ground floor in the main conference room?" Lacey was pointing at the flat-panel monitor.

Stephens paused before answering. Ross and Williams were staring at her, waiting for the response. Stephens quickly reconsidered the facts and logical reasoning—it was sound.

"Yes, ma'am. That's where they're being held. The main conference room."

Stephens had just finished when the door opened and Commander Nicolaou entered, followed closely by Bull and Ghost. Jim stood at the front of the room, arms folded, while Bull, his second in command, and Ghost took seats with the analysts.

Bull, known publicly as First Sergeant Mark Beaumont, was a Marine Corp (Force Recon) veteran, following the family tradition laid down by his father and uncle. Having grown up on the streets of Oakland, on the east side of San Francisco Bay, Bull found wrestling as an escape from gang life that seemed to lure so many other young men from his neighborhood into a life of crime. An expert at hand-to-hand combat, Bull followed a daily regimen to maintain his immense strength.

Although not a small man, Ghost—Staff Sergeant Ryan Moore—appeared thin next to Bull's bulk. Just topping six feet in height and weighing every bit of 200 pounds, Ghost moved with fluid grace, a skill he honed to perfection after years of hunting the remote evergreen forests of northeastern Oregon and Western Idaho.

Jim addressed his assembled team. "Status?"

Lacey took the question. "We were just reviewing the most current updates from Minsk. Based on civilian and official reports, we are confident the hostages are still held in the chemistry building on the BSU campus."

"Do you have a specific location?" Jim asked.

"We believe they are held in the main conference room on the ground floor." Lacey aimed the laser pointer at the floor plan still displayed on the monitor and indicated the location of the conference room. It was a spacious room, just to the left of the foyer at the front entrance to the building.

"You believe?" Jim said. "I assume you attempted to reach

Peter on his cell phone? I know it's a long shot."

Stephens replied before Lacey could get her first word out. "Yes sir, no answer. Presumably, his cell phone was confiscated. Our analysis is solid, and we stand by it."

Jim's dark brown eyes met Stephens as he measured her confidence. He knew that lives were at stake, not only the hostages but the rescue team as well. Yet he also knew that intelligence work was a mix of fact, logical speculation, and sound reasoning. Everyone on his team was better than good, and he trusted them. Slowly he nodded, and then turned to Bull.

"Get Colonel Pierson on the line," Jim said.

Bull reached out to the speakerphone and punched in a series of numbers. Following one audible ring, a hard voice answered. "Pierson."

"Colonel, Commander Nicolaou here. I'm with my team; communication is secure. I have you on the speaker."

"Continue," Pierson said.

"Lieutenant Lacey's team has been sifting through and analyzing the intelligence coming in from Minsk. They believe they have the location where the BSU hostages are being held by the NPA."

Jim and Lacey reviewed their conclusions and reasoning. The few questions the Colonel had were right to the point. In the end, he agreed with Stephens' assessment.

"Commander, I want your report and supporting data right away; I'll make sure it gets to the right people."

Jim nodded to Stephens, who quietly left the conference call. She had the files organized so it would only take a few minutes to email them to Colonel Pierson.

"Operation Bright Star has commenced as of 1220 EST. Fortunately, C Squadron of the First Special Forces Operational Detachment was already positioned in Germany. They are presently airborne. However, in the event Bright Star is not successful, I want your team in position."

"Yes, sir, we're on it," but Pierson had already hung up.

"Bull, assemble Alpha Team, conference room B, fifteen minutes."

"Yes, sir," Bull replied, and he and Ghost rose and exited the meeting.

Jim addressed Lacey and the remaining members of her intelligence team. "Good work, but we're just getting started. Stay on this. If there's any hint that the hostages may have been moved I want to know ASAP. Also, get me everything you have on the NPA weaponry, especially air defenses. Lieutenant, I want you in the briefing with the strike team."

"Yes sir," Lacey said as Jim left the room.

Exactly on schedule, Jim pushed through the door to the conference room and sat at the head of the table. He was met by the faces of his five strike team members—Bull, Ghost, Homer, Magnum, and Iceberg—plus Lieutenant Lacey.

"Given the fluidity of the situation and the presence of captives, we're gonna follow the standard rapid response plan. Homer, get the C-130 ready for wheels up in two hours, not a minute later. Standard load of weapons and munitions. I want external fuel pods to avoid mid-air refueling and save time."

"Affirmative, sir," Homer said, lifting his eyes momentarily from his tablet where he was furiously scribbling notes with a stylus.

"We'll continue the briefing en route. Lacey's team will provide frequent intelligence updates."

Lieutenant Lacey nodded acknowledgement.

"Flight time will be about 12 hours. We'll update and refine the plan in the air."

"Sir, how are we going to insert?" Iceberg asked. If he was

nervous about his first mission since joining SGIT, it didn't show. Slouched in his chair, his expression conveyed nothing but confidence bordering on indifference.

"With the airport off line, I think HAHO is the best option. And the aircrew will likely appreciate maximum standoff distance." The high-altitude, high-opening jump was a practiced, but dangerous, means of parachuting into a hot location. Aided by GPS and using specially designed parachutes, they could glide more than 20 miles from the drop point, and land with precision. It was risky, for sure, but the payoff was significant.

"If there are no other questions, we have work to do."

As the assembled personnel gathered their tablets and exited, Commander Nicolaou called to Lacey. "Lieutenant, a word please."

Jim was still seated, and Lieutenant Lacey stood facing her boss. "Has the NPA established air defenses yet at the BSU campus?" Jim asked.

"They've placed mobile SAM launchers and AA guns at the airport, fortifying their position. But so far, we have no indication they've placed antiaircraft guns or missiles near the KGB Headquarters building, the Government House, the train station, or the BSU campus. All reports indicate the NPA forces that overran the campus are armed with light weapons only."

"They could still have shoulder-fired surface-to-air missiles and RPGs," Jim said.

"I would agree, sir."

"Given time, they'll have Russian SA-11 mobile launchers in there, too. Our C-130 will be an attractive target."

"MOTHER is processing the KH images, including searching for AA weapons systems," Lacey said. The KH—or Key Hole—spy satellites provided very high definition images in multiple spectral ranges including visible, infrared, and radar. "I'll also ask Colonel Pierson to request a Predator over flight. In addition to images, it will serve as a decoy to draw fire if there are any active anti-aircraft systems in place."

Jim nodded. "I like your thinking, Lieutenant."

CHAPTER 12

Minsk

IT WAS THE IMAGE THAT frequently haunted his dreams. Maggie was radiant, laughing and so full of life. Ethan and Joanna were young, giggling and running in the meadow that edged up to the cold, blue lake, the forested ridge rising from the opposite shore. Then the vision melted away, to be replaced by his wife lying unconscious on a hospital bed. A tube was inserted in her arm and oxygen was being forced into her lungs through a tight-fitting mask covering her mouth and nose.

Peter hated this part. He knew what was coming… knew this was a dream, and yet it still scraped against raw nerves. In his vision he saw himself telling the physician to turn off the life support.

"She will die," the doctor said, his voice bland.

"This is not life," Peter said. "She did'nt want this." The doctor turned and manipulated some switches and knobs out of sight.

Peter had been there, of course, at her bedside. And even in his subconscious memory he knew he would relive her death—as he had countless times before.

While Peter looked on for the last time, Maggie's eyes suddenly opened, although the rest of her body was still frozen in place. Inexplicably, the breathing mask was no longer over her face, and she spoke, all the while the doctor continuing his process to turn off the life support.

"I need to know, are they safe?"

"Yes, they got away, down the stairs." Somehow Peter instinctively understood Maggie was asking about the children's escape from the chemistry building. But how could that be?

She smiled, and appeared at peace. "I knew you would take care of them, like you always have…"

"And I always will."

Her smile faded. "No, Peter, you can't. Ethan and Joanna are grown now. They will live their lives and you cannot always be there to protect them. Just like…" She stopped, leaving the statement unfinished. Yet Peter knew exactly what she meant.

"Just like I couldn't protect you," he said.

"My love, there was nothing you could do. You must accept this. Please."

"What am I to do?"

In Maggie's countenance Peter saw understanding that went beyond anything rational or comprehensible. "Don't you see?" Her eyes were pleading. "You have done all that a father can do. You've shielded Ethan and Joanna from harm, not just today, but many times."

"How could you…" Peter's mind was spinning in confusion.

"Know?" she finished his question.

"No, this doesn't make any sense. How can I be here again? This isn't real."

"And yet, here we are."

The doctor was still busily working, oblivious to the conversation transpiring behind his back. Suddenly it dawned on Peter, Maggie was alive, not like all the previous dreams where she lay unmoving, unconscious. "I have to stop the doctor!"

"No, Peter. No. You cannot change what has happened."

Peter grasped her hand. It was cold and limp. "What can I do?"

"You have already done what is important. Our children are safe. There is nothing more. You must let go."

"I miss you so much. All I wanted was to live my life with you, to grow old by your side as we raised our family."

Maggie's smile returned. "When it is time. You cannot change the past, but there is still the future, and another time to be together."

Peter held Maggie's gaze, longing to embrace her, to feel her warmth again. He wanted to lean over and kiss her lips, but his body refused to comply.

"You are a special man, Peter Savage." For the briefest of moments, the sparkle was there in her eyes.

"Stop! Stop what you're doing! She's awake!" The doctor didn't seem to hear Peter, and he remained busy, his back still turned to Peter and Maggie.

"No," she whispered in a voice so low only Peter could hear it. "We both know I cannot stay." She closed her eyes.

"No! Stop! She's okay!"

Finally the physician turned to Peter, confusion etched into his face. "The life support is off. There are no vital signs. I'm sorry."

"No!" Peter heard himself shout, and knew it was a dream… a nightmare. He stirred.

The voices were jovial, punctuated with laughter. Although not terribly loud, it was enough to roust Peter from a light, restless sleep, sitting on the floor with his back to the storeroom door. At first he thought it was only his imagination, some perverted part of the nightmare, but then he heard it again. He drove the images from his mind, but not before he recalled his promise—I will always protect Ethan and Jo, always.

Looking across the small room, he saw Gary positioned beneath the harpoon gun with his legs drawn up to his chest, forehead resting against his knees.

Psst. "Gary, wake up," Peter said, his voice a whisper.

Gary raised his head and blinked his eyes. Awake and ready, he stood, hand on the valve handle ready to discharge the makeshift weapon upon Peter's command.

Peter also rose and pressed an ear to the door. The sound of voices was clearer. He could make out two distinct voices, and assumed a pair of guards was close to the door, on a break maybe.

"Be ready," Peter whispered. The flamethrower was near his feet and he struck a match and lit the rag at the sprayer nozzle. He pumped the handle a couple times to make sure the flammable liquid was still pressurized. They were as ready as they could be.

Pounding a fist against the door, Peter called out. "Hey! Open the door! We need help!"

Several seconds passed, and Peter pounded the door again, raising his voice and calling to the guards. "Hey! Hey! In here! We need help! Hey!"

Peter pressed his ear to the door and thought he heard footsteps approaching. He backed away to the side and picked up the flamethrower. At the same time he nodded to Gary.

They heard the faint metallic clicks of a key engaging the tumblers in the door lock. The knob turned and the door opened. Standing there, framed by the doorway, were two guards, one standing slightly behind the other. With droopy eyes and tired expressions, they looked like they had been drinking.

"Now!" Peter shouted and Gary slammed open the valve

releasing the pressurized air and propelling the wood harpoon forward with a whoosh. In the blink of an eye the staff speared the lead guard in the center of his chest, the sharpened point protruding through his back. The guard fell forward, unable to utter a sound.

The second guard was stunned, never expecting to meet such a primitive and deadly weapon. He hesitated, and when he finally raised his eyes from his dead comrade, he was greeted with a plume of fire erupting from the end of the spray nozzle brandished by Peter.

In an instant the guard's torso and head were aflame. He cried in agony, dropping his rifle and then his body to the floor, writhing in an attempt to escape the inferno engulfing him. Several seconds later, with a deep breath that drew searing and toxic gases into his lungs, the second guard also died.

Peter set the flamethrower down and retrieved the rifle, but with the guard's uniform on fire, it was impossible for Peter to search for spare ammunition.

"Grab the rifle and search him for anything of value," Peter said, referring to the lead guard. Then he turned his attention to the hallway, fearful that the screams had alerted other guards.

Quickly Gary found two spare magazines and a cell phone in addition to the key ring still hanging from the doorknob. Although he did not carry any ID, in his wallet were Russian rubles and a photo of a young woman, perhaps a girlfriend. He stuffed the items into his pockets, passing along one of the ammunition magazines to Peter. "Ready," Gary said. "Now what?"

"We find Dad and Dmitri," Peter said.

"Sounds easy enough. Where do we look?"

Peter shrugged. Without knowing exactly where his father and friend were taken for questioning, all they could do was search room by room.

"And if the doors are locked?" Gary asked.

"Maybe that key the guards used to open the storeroom door is a master key."

Gary looked at the key ring again and counted only four keys, far fewer than the number of locked doors. "I hope you're right."

"Stay close to the wall and be quiet. If you hear anyone, freeze and take aim before they spot us." Peter doused the burning rag on the nozzle of the flamethrower and double-checked that he still had a book of matches in his pocket. Next he inserted his arms through the straps and hoisted the flamethrower onto his back. The metal pressure tank rubbed uncomfortably against his bruised muscles.

Peter looked to the right and then the left. He knew the large room where they and the other hostages were first gathered together was to the left. "Let's try this way," he said turning to the right.

Silently placing one foot in front of the other, Peter moved forward, hugging the wall. Gary was right behind him. It didn't take long to reach the first closed door, but they bypassed it upon noticing the placard on the door indicating it was the women's restroom.

Silently they inched up to the next door. Peter check the door handle, locked. Not wasting any time, Gary inserted the key that was used to unlock the storeroom. He gave it a quarter turn and was rewarded with a metallic click as the lock opened.

Gary quickly checked the room while Peter stood guard outside the door. "Nothing. Looks like a break room."

Suddenly they heard the echo of boots pounding the tile floor. The sound was quickly growing louder. Peter pushed Gary back into the break room and then kneeled, leaning his shoulder into the wall for support, aiming in the direction of the approaching guards.

Peter took a deep breath and exhaled, relaxing his muscles, focusing on the sight picture along the barrel of the rifle. Two soldiers jogged around the corner at the far end of the hallway. They must not have expected to meet an armed adversary, as they held their weapons casually while they conducted their hasty search.

BOOM! *BOOM*! Both soldiers crumpled to the floor, their bodies carried forward a couple feet by their momentum before coming to rest in an unnatural position.

"Come on!" Peter said. "They'll have heard the gunshots and be prepared next time."

The duo had no sooner started toward the next room when a guard emerged into the hallway 20 meters away, rifle raised and pointed in the general direction of Peter and Gary.

Peter instinctively dropped to a knee and pulled the trigger at the same time Gary let go a withering barrage of automatic fire, killing the guard instantly.

Peter stayed ready, gun aimed at the open door, expecting another NPA soldier to enter the corridor and return fire. Instead, he saw a metallic orb flung into the hallway. It ricocheted off the wall and rolled lazily toward him.

CHAPTER 13

Minsk

"GRENADE!" PETER YELLED and then shoved Gary to the open door to the break room. Peter dived in, landing on top of his buddy.

The explosion was far louder and deeper than the gunfire and Peter's ears were ringing, but he was alive, the blast and shrapnel being absorbed by the concrete-block walls. A long section of overhead lighting was destroyed, plunging the hall into darkness.

Sliding off Gary, Peter picked up his rifle and aimed it at the open doorway. With one hand, he leaned over and nudged Gary.

"You okay?"

Gary nodded and rose to his feet. "This isn't going so well."

"You're alive, aren't you," Peter replied. But he also knew Gary was right. It was only a matter of time before their luck ran out if they continued to fight the NPA soldiers head on.

"Watch the hall," Peter said. "Let me see what I can find."

Peter quickly assessed the room and the first thing he noticed was another door on the opposite wall. Maybe another way out, he thought. There was a sink, plus a refrigerator, microwave, and coffee machine. In three strides he was at the sink.

Automatic gunfire reverberated through the corridor, the hard walls channeling the sound. Gary ducked back inside the room as bullets burrowed in the open door.

Under the sink, Peter found what he was looking for. He set his rifle down and grabbed both pint-size bottles, then slipped off the flamethrower and stashed it in the empty space.

"Why are you leaving that?" Gary asked.

"I can move faster without it. Besides, we may want a weapon stashed for later." Peter removed the screw cap from one of the bottles and was immediately greeted by a pungent smell that caused his eyes to water.

"This will buy us some time," Peter said. "Fire a burst to slow them down. I'm gonna heave these into the hallway."

"What is it?"

"Concentrated ammonia, industrial cleaner."

Gary stuck the barrel of his rifle around the edge of the doorframe and fired a continuous burst until his magazine was empty. Peter threw first one bottle and then the other in the direction of the approaching guards. The glass shattered on the tile floor, spreading the noxious liquid in a wide swath. Immediately the ammonia vapors filled the space, causing the NPA soldiers to gag and their eyes to water profusely, stopping their advance.

"Quick, there's a door out the back. I only hope it's an exit," Peter said.

Gary was right behind Peter, who paused only to grab his rifle while Gary rammed home a fresh magazine.

Cautiously, Peter opened the door. It connected to another, smaller room, with a large corkboard covered with notices on one side, and a wall of small wood-framed cubes on the other side. Below each cube was a name card, and envelopes were resting diagonally in many of the open cubes.

Straight ahead there was another door, and Peter and Gary moved quickly for it. Peter opened the door just a bit and saw another hallway. He was about to open the door further when three soldiers ran past, fortunately not noticing the door ajar. This corridor must connect with other one.

"Maybe your dad and Dmitri are back with the other hostages," Gary suggested.

Peter thought for a moment. The truth was he had no clear idea where his father was.

"It's possible. And if he's not there, we'll capture Gorev and make him tell us."

Peter eased the door open and slipped into the hallway with Gary right behind him as before. No longer concerned with checking any of the rooms, they moved quickly along the wall toward the building foyer where the hostages were held.

Looking something like giant robotic bugs and painted flat black, the sleek MH-X stealth Blackhawk helicopters flew low over Minsk, barely clearing the rooftops, the chop of the rotor blades muffled so that it sounded like the helicopters were far away. If they could have been seen in the dark night sky, it might have appeared they were in a tight race, the lead airship furiously trying to out distance its pursuer.

As they approached the Belarusian State University campus in tandem, they passed low over three smoldering police cars that had attempted to respond to the crisis, only to be stopped dead in their tracks by a combination of machinegun fire and RPGs. The smoldering wrecks marked a boundary line, beyond which the police moved relatively unrestricted.

They slowed to a hover, one Blackhawk in front of the main entrance to the chemistry building and the other above the roof.

Thick ropes were dropped and men were quickly disgorged.

Within 30 seconds their cargoes were off loaded and the birds slipped back into anonymity, circling high above the drop zone, audible only to the careful listener.

Peter stopped and eased an eye around the corner, steeling a quick glance. It was sufficient to confirm that the passage did indeed connect to the foyer as he had assumed.

"To the right is the entrance where we came in. The meeting room will be ahead and to the left."

"Is the coast clear?" Gary asked.

Shhh. Peter concentrated. With the ringing in his ears fading, he thought he heard a helicopter. "Do you hear that?"

Gary swiveled his head, trying to locate the source of the sound. "Yeah, it sounds like it's coming from that way." He pointed toward the front entrance.

Peter glanced around the corner. He didn't see any guards. "Let's go."

With rapid, silent strides, Peter and Gary reached the next corner and stopped to listen. The helicopter sound was gone. Peter edged his head around the corner.

The foyer was a large open space with a reception kiosk near the middle of the room, facing toward the glass-walled main entrance. Outside, beyond the steps leading up to the chemistry building, was the park-like commons area. Lighting illuminated the concrete steps and eight-foot tall post lamps dotted the commons, casting deep shadows from the scattered trees.

Two soldiers were pressed tight against the far wall of the foyer near the front entrance, their attention focused on something that seemed to be transpiring outside.

Peter returned his attention to the kiosk. It was configured with a semi-circular counter open to the rear. The wood-paneled counter was fortified with sandbags stacked two deep, packed tight against the back side of the kiosk. A NPA soldier was manning a machine gun, aimed at the glass entrance.

On the opposite side of the foyer from Peter's position was the room where he and Gary were taken with the other hostages. While he was watching, a door opened and Gorev and three guards exited. Gorev was shouting orders and speaking into a hand-held radio.

Peter pulled back from the corner. In a very low whisper he reported what he saw to Gary.

"I say we rush them, kill the guards, and shoot Gorev in the shoulder and make him tell us where he's holding your dad," Gary said.

"And if we miss?" Peter replied. The sound of breaking glass broke his concentration. He hazarded a glance around the corner again and saw the two guards on the floor, blood pooling around their bodies, one of the front windows shattered. The machine gunner was drooped forward across the kiosk counter, motionless.

Then all hell broke loose..

CHAPTER 14

MINSK

A SERIES OF EXPLOSIONS occurred in rapid succession outside the building, shattering the glass wall and propelling sharp fragments into the foyer.

"Good thing we weren't out there," Gary observed.

Gorev and his guards had retreated out of the foyer prior to the blast, scrambling back into the room and avoiding harm.

Peter had just started to move forward when three men dashed through the shattered remnants of the front entrance. Dressed in civilian clothes with black load harnesses, and brandishing H&K 416 automatic rifles, the Delta Force operators looked more like private-sector bodyguards than elite soldiers.

"Freeze! Drop your weapon!" one of the men yelled at Peter.

Before Peter could comply, gunfire rang through the hallway and bullets zipped through the foyer. The three men, Peter, and Gary simultaneously dove in front of the kiosk for protection.

"I'm American!" Peter said. "We're on your side!"

More gunfire and bullets slammed into the counter.

Fortunately, the sandbags offered ample protection. One of the Delta Force operators stole a quick glance to the hallway where the shooting was coming from.

"I count three shooters, Zeus," he said. One of the operators with a short red beard nodded his head, almost imperceptibly, in reply.

"Who are you?" Peter asked.

"We're here for the hostages," Zeus answered. "Do you know where they are?" His eyes blazed with an intensity Peter had seen before… in Jim Nicolaou's SGIT team.

"Yes, they're in there," Peter pointed to the conference room where he had last seen them hours ago.

"That's what our intel says as well."

More bullets gouged chunks of wood from the kiosk, followed by a grenade blast that shredded a portion of the counter. Still, the sandbag barricade stood.

"I need cover fire," Zeus said, "so I can turn around that machine gun. Ready?"

"You know how to use that AK?" one of the operators, a big man, asked Peter and Gary.

"Good enough," Peter answered.

Zeus decided they were as ready as possible. "Okay, now!" he ordered. All four men began firing short automatic bursts, taking little time to aim. Zeus stood up, pushed the dead body off the PKM light machine gun, and spun it and the ammunition box around so he could aim it down the hallway. He pulled back the charging bolt, ensuring a round was chamber, and then pulled the trigger.

Zeus fired short bursts to avoid overheating the barrel and conserve ammunition, aiming at the NPA soldiers when they emerged from doorways, forcing them back, at least for the moment.

"Bear, get a sitrep from Gunslinger. Tell 'em to get their

butts down here!"

"Roger," the big man said.

Without interrupting his aim, Zeus issued his next order. "Keep your AKs on the east hallway, where you came from. They'll try to pin us down from both directions." Immediately Gary and Peter shifted, rifles aimed and ready.

No sooner had Zeus finished speaking when a squad of five NPA soldiers arrived in the east hallway and opened up on the kiosk. Peter and Gary returned fire, pushing the squad back, leaving two dead on the floor.

Zeus was firing the machine gun again. For the moment, it looked like a standoff, neither side able to advance or eliminate the opposition. Another grenade careened off the wall, striking the kiosk, and then rolling a few meters away from the sandbags before exploding. Supported by the two other Delta operators plus Peter and Gary, Zeus kept firing, and then reached the end of the ammunition belt.

With the volume of fire dramatically reduced, an NPA soldier stepped into the hallway, raised an RPG, and fired. The shaped charge detonated on the sandbags.

Gunslinger was the second Delta team of seven operators that had deployed onto the roof of the chemistry building. The plan was for Gunslinger to approach the objective from inside the building, clearing all hostiles they encountered, while Outlaw blasted in through the main entrance and quickly took control of the conference room where the hostages were supposedly held.

The plan was simple enough. With Gunslinger providing fire support, Outlaw would usher the hostages out into the commons where they would be loaded onto the two MH-X Blackhawks, presently orbiting overhead, unheard and unseen.

Although the insert went well, encountering no resistance,

the plan quickly began to unravel. Outlaw team was decimated by antipersonnel mines strategically placed around the main entrance and remotely detonated. Zeus lost four of his team to shrapnel before they even entered the building. And once inside, they were pinned down by a crossfire from the east and west hallways, only ten meters from the objective.

"Move, move, move!" The team leader of Gunslinger admonished his men to rapidly descend the stairwell. He had memorized the essential details of the building plan on the flight from Ramstein Air Base in Germany and knew the stairwell would connect to the west hall on the ground floor, about a hundred meters from the objective.

The Delta operators moved down the stairs, single file with rifles pulled snug to their shoulders, both eyes open and simultaneously looking at the holographic red dot while taking in everything in their field of vision. Their bodies were brushing the gray concrete walls, ever pushing forward. Initially, they didn't encounter any NPA soldiers. When the lead operator approached the second floor landing, the door to the stairwell opened and two hostile soldiers rushed in, not expecting to meet American Special Forces.

The lead operator fired twice in rapid succession, killing the NPA guards. Gunslinger team continued following the stairs down, urgently moving to provide backup to the remnants of Outlaw. They were nearly at the ground floor.

General Gorev smiled inwardly. So far he had correctly anticipated the rescue attempt and meticulously planned a superior defense. Holding a remote detonator in his hand, he turning the rotary switch to position four and then depressed the button. A fraction of a second later the muffled sound of explosions was felt more than heard.

He tossed the small box aside and then keyed the hand-held radio. "Activate the SA missile batteries and shoot down all airplanes over the city." His communication would be relayed by the radio operator in the department chairman's office to the appropriate forces at the international airport where the missile batteries had been placed.

A tinny voice answered. "But what if there are commercial flights?"

"Very unlikely at this hour. You heard my order, now do it!"

"Yes, sir!"

"And quickly move two teams onto the roof armed with Igla missiles. Tell them to check the operational status of the machine and radio their report to me immediately, but they are to hold their position. When the helicopters return, destroy them."

Inside the stairwell Gunslinger paid little attention to the emergency lights mounted high on the wall at each landing; one aimed up the stairs and the other pointing down the stairs. The non-descript battery boxes with dual incandescent lights were designed to automatically turn on in the event of a power outage, lighting the way for evacuation of the building.

The Delta team had no way of knowing that the batteries had been removed from each box and replaced with a MON-50 directional antipersonnel mine. When detonated, the RDX high explosive propelled hundreds of short steel rods forward in an arc. In the open, the lethal range was 50 meters—in the stairwell, the steel shrapnel bounced off the hard walls and stairs, turning the confined space into a giant blender.

In the span of a single heartbeat, the entire Delta team had been eliminated.

Dust filled the foyer while debris was scattered everywhere.

Zeus took stock—Bear was alive and scrambling back into position, but his other operator, who had been directly in line with the RPG, wasn't so lucky. The large ragged hole at his waist, the clothing and tissue scorched around the edges, was ample evidence. Peter and Gary appeared unhurt, still firing whenever a target appeared.

"We can't stay here," Zeus said. He depressed the button on his throat mic and spoke rapidly. "Gunslinger! Gunslinger!" All he heard was static. He tried again. "Gunslinger! Report, over."

Nothing. His mission had just gone from bad to worse.

"Listen up! We're gonna bust through those doors," Zeus pointed at the double doors connected to one end of the large conference room. At the other end of the room was a similar pair of doors.

"Bear, I'll go first. I want you right behind me to throw your weight into the doors. I'll shoot the hostiles and you herd out the hostages. Get them out as fast as you can while I provide cover."

Bear nodded.

Zeus turned to Peter and Gary. You two stay here and keep firing. As soon as the hostages exit you join up with them. We've got two Blackhawks circling, and I'm not leaving anyone behind. Got it?"

Zeus didn't wait for an answer. He was dashing to the room. Then Bear heaved his considerable bulk into the double doors and they flew open. Off balance, Bear crashed into a chair and onto the floor.

The NPA guards were standing, dispersed around the room and caught by surprise as the Delta operator burst in. Bear shot the closest guard from his prone position and then rose to his feet, shouting for everyone to keep their heads down and get out.

Zeus was standing at the doorway, moving his rifle from

target to target, firing single shots, then moving to the next guard. Simultaneously he was speaking into his mic. "Outlaw to Overlord. Objective secured. Need immediate extract. Under fire and taking casualties. LZ is hot!"

The Blackhawk pilots didn't need to be told the landing zone was under attack, the sound of gunfire was clearly audible over the radio.

"Roger Outlaw," answered the pilot of the lead Blackhawk. "Will advise Spooky. Overlord One is inbound." His co-pilot was already in communication with the C-130 Specter gunship circling above the battle. Bristling with armament and advanced targeting systems, including a 105mm canon, the Spooky gunship was a military marvel that always held the high ground. Using thermal imaging, any person or vehicle on the opposite side of the Blackhawks from the chemistry building would be assumed hostile and targeted with either the minigun or the howitzer.

Gorev was surrounded by his men at the far end of the conference room, still clutching the hand-held radio. One of the NPA guards turned toward Zeus and Bear and fired, missing the Delta men but shooting several hostages.

The civilians were making it out, but not fast enough. Bear and Zeus were doing their best, but with the hostages running for the door and the NPA guards shooting back, it was difficult to get a clear shot.

Seeing only two Special Forces commandos, Gorev recognized his opportunity and split his force. "Into the foyer!" he ordered the closest guards. They rushed the doors and threw them open, expecting to cutoff the escaping hostages and kill the two remaining Delta operators.

"I'm out," Gary shouted.

Peter slammed home a fresh magazine and handed his AK

to Gary. "Keep shooting!"

The RPG explosion had punched a hole through the sandbag fortification and destroyed the kiosk counter, but miraculously the PKM machine gun was laying nearby. Peter reached over the Delta corpse and through the hole left by the explosion; he grabbed an ammo can, popped open the lid, and loaded the end of the ammunition belt into the receiver. He cycled the charging bolt just as the doors flew open.

As the NPA guards rushed out Peter let loose with the machine gun and mowed them down. Gorev was stunned and dropped behind the steel desk for cover. He was shouting into the radio he still grasped. "Order the perimeter teams to close on the front of this building from the campus commons. The hostages are escaping outside. Cut them off!"

Peter thought he had glimpsed Gorev, but when he finished shooting, Gorev was nowhere in sight. "Gary, time to go! I'll cover you." Peter stood and swung around with the PKM at his hip, firing short bursts at any NPA soldiers who presented a target.

Gary fired and retreated to the front entrance. He stood to the side, providing protection as the hostages left the building and descended the steps to the grassy commons.

"People! Gather at the bottom of the steps. A helicopter is coming to take you all to safety. Everyone, listen!" Gary was shouting, and slowly getting the message across to the hysterical crowd.

There were still a dozen civilians screaming and pushing for the exit where Zeus was trying to get clear shots at the guards when a bullet found its mark, striking Bear in the forehead.

Another guard fired his rifle in the general direction of the doorway, attempting to shoot through the hostages to kill the lone operator. He succeeded in hitting the last five civilians. Zeus took a grazing bullet in his arm.

With the last of the hostages out the door, and his entire team dead, Zeus had no choice but to fall back and lead the hostages onboard the helicopters as fast as possible.

Peter was outside, searching the ragged group for his father's face. "Dad!" he kept calling. Finally he saw him standing next to Dmitri, looking around like most everyone else, confused as to what they were supposed to do now.

"Dad!" Peter yelled again as he ran toward him. This time Ian heard and threw an awkward embrace around his son, carefully avoiding the machine gun hanging at Peter's side by a web strap, the remains of the ammunition belt draped over his shoulder.

CHAPTER 15

Minsk

OVERLORD ONE WAS THIRTY feet above the lawn and descending while Overlord Two hovered two hundred meters away, the door gunner searching the grounds for any nearby threat.

"Everyone, stay together!" Zeus shouted to be heard above the engine and rotor blades of the Blackhawk. Although the aircraft was designed as the second generation of stealth helicopter, it was still quite loud at this close distance.

Gary closed ranks with Peter, relieved they were reunited with Ian and Dmitri. As Gary joined them, Dmitri was agitated, talking about a machine.

"Who said this?" Peter asked.

"It was General Gorev. I overheard him talking to another officer; a captain, I didn't hear his name. Gorev said Major Leonov reported that the machine was set and ready to activate on schedule."

Suddenly, a brilliant white light, like a gigantic strobe, illuminated the entire commons area for a fraction of a second. It was accompanied by an ear-splitting, sharp boom. It looked and sounded like a lightning bolt had rent the sky above them.

The rhythmic sound of the Blackhawk engine was replaced by metal-on-metal grinding. The tail of the aircraft dipped and struck the ground, followed by the cabin, and the machine rolled onto its side, the rotor blades gouging out turf as it burst into flames.

"Get back inside!" Zeus shouted. "Everyone back inside!" Although Zeus didn't see it, a streak of white light lanced across the night sky above his head, the Igla-S shoulder-fired anti-aircraft missile homing in on the hot engine cowling of the second Blackhawk. The missile detonated on impact, rupturing fuel and hydraulic lines, and engulfing the helicopter in a massive fireball.

A random cacophony of screams came from the civilians as they turned direction and started to run back to the destroyed front entrance of the chemistry building. A few faculty and administrators chose to flee in the opposite direction, past the burning wreckage of the American helicopter, only to be gunned down by fresh NPA troops sweeping across the grassy expanse.

Attracted by the gunshots, Zeus turned in time to see a red line streaking downward, from a moving but invisible point high in the sky, to the lawn on the other side of the flaming wreckage. He knew these were tracers fired from the Spooky gunship, but due to the flames he could not see the NPA soldiers being targeted. A moment later two white points raced to the orbiting aircraft, exploding in a brilliant pyrotechnic display. The tracer fire ended and the aircraft, broken into four major pieces and on fire, arced toward the ground.

Peter caught up with Zeus, grabbing him by the arm and spinning him around. "We have to get these people out of here!"

"We just lost our air support. My entire team is dead. Our only option is to find cover inside. Out here we don't stand a chance!"

"Gorev will have his men search room by room. They'll find everyone. We have to get away."

"Do what you want," said Zeus. "My job is to protect these people."

The gunfire was getting closer, herding the civilians back inside, and Peter realized that Zeus was probably right. Outside, they would have to run a gauntlet of rifle fire to escape.

"Come on," Peter said. He ran up the steps with Gary, Ian, and Dmitri in close pursuit. Once inside the foyer, Peter stayed to the right and angled for the east hallway, planning to retrace the route he and Gary had followed earlier. As they slipped around the corner, out of sight of the foyer, the gunfire ceased. Peter could only hope that the hostages would survive long enough for a second rescue attempt.

"All right, gentlemen. Listen up." Commander James Nicolaou addressed his team within the cavernous cargo bay of the specially modified HC-130J Combat King IIB aircraft. He had just completed a lengthy satellite radio communication with Colonel Pierson. "We've been ordered to proceed with the mission. We are approximately five hours to the drop point. To get maximum glide distance, we jump at 35,000 feet and deploy chutes at 34,000 feet. GPS landing coordinates are already programmed into your jump computer."

Every team member wore a small computer strapped to his wrist. The screen was about the size of a credit card, as thick as a cell phone, and ruggedized to mil-spec. The device provided essential information for a HAHO—high-altitude, high-opening—jump, including altitude based on GPS readings, air temperature, plus direction and distance to the landing point. With favorable weather conditions, a skilled operator could glide more than 20 miles from 34,000 feet and land within a 20-

foot by 20-foot target.

"Simultaneous to our insertion, Marine ground troops from the Black Sea Rotational Force, backed up by B1s, F22s, and support aircraft flying from Ramstein and Spangdahlem air bases in Germany, will commence an all-out assault on the Minsk International Airport. Their objective is to seize control of the runways and flight facilities and eliminate all SAM and AA batteries by 1000 hours local time. With the airport secured, reinforcements and munitions can be ferried in by air."

Jim reviewed the faces of his team. What he saw was confidence and commitment. "Lacey will provide intel updates right up to the point of insertion. However, our landing point and objective is ten miles from the airport. It looks like we are going in blind and alone."

"Just the way I like it," Magnum said in a low voice.

"Can it," Jim said, his tone leaving no doubt about his mood.

Magnum squared his soldiers and raised his chin just a bit. "Yes, sir," he said.

"As you all know, SGIT was the backup—second string. Now we are first string. The primary mission was, and remains, rescuing the civilian hostages. You also know from the intelligence briefing that some of the hostages are American."

Jim paused, moving from face to face, trying to sense their emotions. "Here's what the briefing didn't say. Peter Savage and his father Professor Ian Savage are among those being held against their will."

At the mention of Peter Savage, a concerned glance rippled through the team. The veteran members of Alpha Team knew Peter personally from prior missions. Homer recalled fighting side-by-side with Peter in a remote patch of desert in western Sudan, and he would never forget the debt he owed.

"What I am about to share with you is of utmost secrecy,"

Jim said. "However, I think you gentlemen deserve to know." Jim paused again to make certain he had everyone's attention. "Approximately one hour and 20 minutes ago, two Delta teams—Gunslinger and Outlaw—inserted and made contact with the objective. Initial resistance was light, but both Blackhawks were shot down just before the civilians boarded. A Spooky providing air support was also shot down at the same time. It is believed all 14 Delta operators were lost."

The drone of the engines was the only sound while this information was absorbed and digested. Every man under Jim's command had the highest level of respect for the different Special Forces commands, and Delta was widely considered among the best of the best. To lose two teams following a successful insertion could only mean this was going to be a demanding mission against a well-trained and prepared adversary.

"You each need to focus on the mission and have confidence, as I do, in your capabilities and training. Remember that each of you was hand-picked from the most elite units, including Delta." Jim paused again, searching the face of each team member for any hint of doubt or fear. He didn't find any.

"Any questions before I go on?" Jim said.

Bull spoke up. "What's the status of the hostages?"

"Unknown. However, the crew of the Spooky reported a large cluster of persons, presumed hostages, grouped near the lead Blackhawk. When the helicopter was destroyed, other persons advanced on the group from across the campus commons, at which time the hostages re-entered the chemistry building. That's all we got before they were shot down."

"Do we still believe they are held in the main conference room to the left of the front entrance?" This question came from Iceberg.

"That is correct, but subject to change based on most current intel."

"Weaponry and defenses?" Ghost asked.

"The NPA has locked down the airspace over Minsk. That's why we are inserting from maximum standoff distance. Fortunately, the special mods to our one-of-a-kind luxury aircraft…" That earned chuckles from his team. "…allow the pilots to stretch the flight ceiling to 35,000 feet. If we are targeted, the EWO can actively jam radar guided SAMs. We'll insert from 20 miles out, too far for heat seekers."

The B version of the Lockheed Martin Combat King II was a prototype, and only SGIT had one. In addition to more powerful engines and increased on-board fuel tanks, the aircraft was packed with the latest radar systems for navigational and targeting purposes. The Electronic Weapons Officer (EWO) could jam targeting radar, including radar emanating from surface-to-air missiles, as well as radio communications. The EWO could also deploy ten AIM-7X Sparrow missiles for defense from enemy fighters or air-to-ground attack. The X designation was applied because these missiles were still classified experimental, although it had passed all development testing and was now in active trials. The specially modified munition was designed to home in on radar emissions or travel to a fixed GPS coordinate.

Finally Homer asked what he thought was on everyone's mind. "What about Peter?"

"His children, Ethan and Joanna, escaped and are under Marine guard at the U.S. Embassy. The President has ordered its evacuation, but until the SAMs are neutralized, it's too risky by air and local police cannot guarantee their safe passage by car."

"He's tough, sir," Homer said, referring to Peter's resiliency and ingenuity.

Jim's lips were drawn tight in a thin line, his jaw locked. He nodded but didn't voice his thought—he's tough, but he's not bullet proof.

CHAPTER 16

Washington, DC

PRESIDENT TAYLOR WAS SITTING at the Resolute desk, a gift from Queen Victoria to President Rutherford Hayes in 1879. He was joined in the Oval Office by General Hendrickson, Chairman of the Joint Chiefs, Secretary of State Paul Bryan, Secretary of Defense Howard Hale, and the Director of the National Security Agency, Colleen Walker.

"This is unbelievable," President Taylor said. "First you're telling me the Delta teams are likely dead—and now this? How can this be true?"

Colleen Walker had just completed briefing the President and his closest advisors on the smallpox outbreak in Tbilisi. The number of suspected victims was growing exponentially, overwhelming the medical facilities in Georgia. And now reports were coming in of people getting ill with smallpox symptoms in Odessa, Ukraine, and Vilnius, Lithuania.

"Blood samples have already been received by the CDC," she explained. "Secretary Bryan has been most helpful in securing samples without delay."

"Both the Lithuanian and Ukrainian governments were

eager to jump on this quickly," Paul Bryan explained.

"How soon before we have any information from the CDC?"

"Twenty-four hours, sir," Colleen replied.

Casting his gaze at his Secretary of State, President Taylor said, "If this is the beginning of a broad smallpox outbreak, an epidemic, we need to mobilize resources and provide all the assistance we can. I assume you are also discussing this potentiality with the World Health Organization and the EU?"

"Yes, Mister President. My staff is reaching out to their counterparts in the EU as well as directors at the WHO. The Russians have already started a vaccination program, and we have been asked to supply vaccine from our stores."

"Do we have any smallpox vaccine?" Taylor asked, looking across the faces of his advisors.

At first, no one answered. The Secretary of State cleared his throat. "I can't speak for the military, but my office has reached out to the CDC and the FDA. We're looking into that." Paul Bryan cast a sideways glance at the intelligence director, mentally encouraging her to get to the main topic.

Colleen cleared her throat. "Sir, there is a more pressing matter, and the reason I requested the presence of General Hendrickson and Mister Hale. It concerns a report from the Kremlin released about twelve hours ago. It's been broadcast through the Russian media, that's how we came across it."

"Go on," the President said.

"President Pushkin claims they have evidence that the smallpox infection in Tbilisi is an American biological weapon."

President Taylor blinked his eyes, then leaned forward. "Did I hear you correctly? The Russians are publically accusing us of dispersing smallpox upon the population of Tbilisi?"

Howard Hale leaned forward and stared at Colleen Walker. He knew her to be a very logical and intelligent person; one who checked and doubled checked facts before recommending a course of action. It was inconceivable that she would share such an inflammatory accusation with the President unless there was ample supporting evidence.

"That is correct sir," said Paul Bryan. "Ms. Walker shared the reports with me only a few hours ago. I made some phone calls, including to Viktorovich Denisov who confirms—"

"Well, of course," the President interrupted. "The Minister of Foreign Affairs wasn't going to contradict a statement from President Pushkin."

"My point," Paul Bryan continued, "is that he shared technical details—off the record, of course—but knowing we would follow through and check his data."

"And?"

"Samples of the virus were tested at the European Molecular Biology Laboratory in Heidelberg. They sequenced the genome of the virus, confirming it to be smallpox and confirming a match to a U.S. smallpox sample from Fort Detrick."

"How can that be?" the President asked for the second time since the meeting began.

"Impossible," Hale said. "There is no ongoing research at Fort Detrick involving smallpox."

"No one said there was." Colleen remained calm, her voice steady and non-threatening. "Fluid samples from deceased victims were delivered by scientists from VECTOR, the only lab other than the CDC in Atlanta that is allowed to store smallpox samples."

"VECTOR is, first and foremost, a Russian bioweapons lab," said Hale. "It's located away from major population centers in Novosibirsk, in Siberia, for a good reason. How can we be sure they didn't spike the samples with smallpox from their depository?"

Colleen turned to the Secretary of Defense. "Because we have a 99%-confidence match of the genome with U.S. smallpox.

The genetic sequence is unlike naturally occurring smallpox or the strains Russia developed. Think of it as a fingerprint, only more detailed, more precise. The lab was able to rule out other strains since the World Health Organization has a database of naturally occurring and weaponized viruses and bacteria. The database was constructed using genome sequencing supplied voluntarily by both the U.S. and Russia.

"The match could be to a strain developed by the Army as far back as the 70s during the height of the Cold War. We won't know until we get a full report from the lab."

Secretary Hale leaned back in his chair and folded his arms across his chest. "And you trust the data?"

"Yes, I do. The EMBL is well respected. Why would they play along with a con from the Russians? Besides, scientists from the WHO also witnessed the testing and verified the data. Regardless, the CDC is conducting their own analysis, but I am confident they will verify the European conclusion."

President Taylor rubbed his temples. "It doesn't matter if the data is authentic or not. What does matter is that the entire world will see this as an unbiased investigation and conclude that America used biological weapons in an effort to implicate the Kremlin." He sighed and turned in his chair, looking out the window to the gardens, rich with vibrant colors, the beauty in stark contrast to the ugly topic of his meeting.

When he turned his attention back to his advisors, his mood was somber. "This plays right into Pushkin's hand. He's been saying all along that we're stirring up conflict and staging attacks by groups that we label as pro-Russian rebels in order to discredit Moscow and gain influence over the former Soviet satellite nations. When this news spreads, we'll be lucky to have any allies in Europe, or anywhere else."

"I'll start damage control right away," offered the Secretary of State.

Taylor nodded. “Reach out to Germany first, since they conducted the analysis.”

The President narrowed his eyes and locked onto Howard Hale and General Hendrickson. “Tell me this is not a missing bioweapon from one of our stockpiles.”

“No sir,” replied the General.

Howard Hale jumped in. “All stockpiles of biological weapons were destroyed during the previous administration.”

“You’re certain of that? Because if there is any doubt, any doubt at all, I better hear about it now.”

General Hendrickson met the President’s glare. “That is 100 percent affirmative sir.”

President Taylor held the General’s gaze for a moment. “Very good. Now that we’ve established the smallpox virus is not of U.S. military origin, can someone please tell me where in hell it came from?”

“We’re working that problem”, Colleen Walker said. “The prevailing theory is that someone, Russian or Russian-sympathizer, or maybe someone just looking for a big payday, got a hold of weaponized smallpox… either from a weapon prior to destruction of our arsenal, or from samples at Fort Detrick when they still had samples, or from the CDC. The DIA and CIA are assisting.”

“General, direct your staff to oversee an immediate review of all U.S. biological weapons containing smallpox. And verify the inventory. If even one weapon is unaccounted for I want to know without delay. Howard, you make certain General Hendrickson has every resource he needs.”

“Yes, sir. But I doubt any weapons are unaccounted for. That inventory was checked and doubled checked when they were destroyed.”

“Then check it again! There is no room for error. And get

the DIA over to Fort Detrick. I want a complete accounting of all samples of smallpox virus they ever touched, or even thought of handling."

"Sir," Secretary Bryan began, "assuming Howard and General Hendrickson are correct, and I have no reason to doubt their veracity, then a sample of smallpox must have been acquired from other sources. About a year ago, I recall the Washington Post reported six vials of smallpox were discovered in an unsecured lab at the CDC. Apparently, the samples were misplaced and undiscovered for decades. What if other samples were misplaced?"

"You mean as in handed over to the Russians?" said President Taylor.

"More likely," Collen said, "an individual willing to make a small fortune by selling the samples. We'll need to conduct a complete audit of smallpox samples at the CDC, beginning with the lot that was lost and rediscovered last year."

"Get on it. You have my authorization to use any government resources needed. Howard, make sure the Director of the CDC understands the importance and urgency of this investigation. Tell him I expect nothing less than complete transparency. This is not about blame; we need to know where the misplaced virus came from and whether or not it's all accounted for. Later we can sort out how it happened."

"Thank you sir," Colleen said. "I think it worthwhile to have FBI agents question Aldrich Ames and Robert Hanssen. Maybe they have some relevant knowledge, something that was said by their Russian handlers."

Taylor nodded. "Do it." He stood, his signal that the meeting was over. As the Secretary of State and NSA Director exited, President Taylor addressed his military advisors. "Does this information have any impact on Bright Star?"

General Hendrickson answered without hesitation. "No

sir. The operation is underway. A combined Marine Corps and Air Force assault on the international airport in Minsk will commence at 5:30 am local time. At the same time, Alpha strike force from the Strategic Global Intervention Team will insert at the chemistry building on the BSU campus and secure the safety of the civilian hostages."

"President Taylor lowered his gaze. "It's a terrible loss, what happened to the Delta teams."

General Hendrickson nodded. "The SGIT operatives will be inserting by parachute from very high altitude, a stealth insertion. We have every confidence in their success."

"I know they'll do their best," said President Taylor. But the conviction was lacking in his voice.

CHAPTER 17

Minsk
June 16

PETER LED HIS FATHER AND friends back through the mailroom and into the break room where he'd stashed the makeshift flamethrower. Hefting the close-range weapon onto his shoulder, he addressed Gary. "I think the safest place for the moment is in the storeroom where we were locked up."

"Good idea. We can top-up the sprayer with more flammable liquid, too."

Peter grabbed the last bottle of ammonia from under the sink. It was only three quarters full, but it could be handy. Then the group entered the hallway and raced the short distance to the storage room. It was easy to spot from the blood stained floor, although the two NPA bodies were no longer there.

The door was ajar, and Peter pushed it open cautiously. Unoccupied, the small room was just as they had left it.

"Quickly," he encouraged them in and closed the door. "Do you still have the key?" he asked Gary.

With the door locked, Peter felt a small amount of comfort.

He decided the first order of business was to take stock of their weapons. Peter clung onto the light machine gun, and he estimated about 30 rounds of ammunition left in the belt. Gary had the AK-74 with a full magazine. And then there was the sprayer converted into a flamethrower, plus the bottle of concentrated ammonia.

"Not much to take on a modern army," Ian Savage said.

"Dad, take a look around and see if you find anything useful, anything we might have missed." Peter slipped the flamethrower off his back and set it against the wall.

Ian nodded and started a systematic search. If nothing else, the distraction would help to take his mind off thoughts of impending doom, if only for a few minutes.

"If we just had access to the chemistry stock room," Dmitri said. He and Ian both looked tired. They had been awake for close to 24 hours, but there was more to it, Peter knew. Fear was taking a toll.

"Dmitri," Peter said. "Tell me about this machine you overheard General Gorev talking about."

He gathered his thoughts before answering. "Well, he sent some of his guards to the roof to make sure it was ready, that it would still function."

"On the roof. Of this building?"

"Yes, that is my understanding."

"And what does this machine do?"

Dmitri shrugged. "I don't know. They didn't say—only that it is ready. It must be important."

Peter considered what Dmitri shared, trying to piece the puzzle together. "Dmitri, you said before that the air intakes are also on the roof, yes?"

Dmitri nodded. "Does that mean something to you?"

"It means something. Just not sure I know what." Suddenly Peter remembered the cell phone he took from the guard killed by the harpoon gun. He dug it out of his pocket and examined the display. Relieved that he had a cell signal and plenty of battery power, he dialed a number he knew would bring help.

The phone rang five times, and Peter was beginning to think it would go to voice mail. Instead he heard a feminine voice. "Who are you calling, please?"

"Uh, Commander James Nicolaou. Did I dial the wrong number?"

The voice paused for a moment. "Commander Nicolaou cannot take your call now. May I relay a message?"

"This is Peter Savage and it's urgent that I speak with him. Do you have an alternate number where I can reach him?"

Lieutenant Lacey drew in a deep breath. While on a mission, Jim's personal and office phones were programmed to ring through to a number she monitored.

"Dr. Savage. It's Lieutenant Ellen Lacey. We met following the incident in the Aleutian Islands. Do you recall?"

"Yes Lieutenant. Look, I need to speak to Jim, it's urgent."

"That's not possible."

Peter paused, trying to understand. "Why not?"

"Dr. Savage, this is an unsecured line."

Suddenly it made sense. So, Jim is on a mission.

"I need to ask you a few questions. But please phrase your answers carefully. We have to assume this conversation is being monitored."

"Okay, but I don't have much time."

"Understood. Are the civilian hostages safe?"

The question angered Peter at first, until he realized that Lacey could not possibly know all the details of what had transpired with the failed rescue attempt. "Uncertain. I lost contact following the destruction of the helicopters."

Lacey had hoped for a more positive answer. "Are they still held at the same location?"

"As far as I know. Look, I'm being hunted so I can't give you those details—"

She interrupted, "Do not state your location."

Peter slowed down and collected his thoughts, organizing what he felt he could and couldn't say. "There's no way out. This building is locked down and unless you have a spare battalion of Marines in the neighborhood, I don't see us fighting out."

"Something better, have some faith," she said. "Have heavy weapons—armor, mobile missile launchers—been moved in?"

"I don't know." Peter's tone hinted at his growing frustration. "I can't see the roads."

"Can you move to a location where you have visibility?"

"Yeah. Headed that direction anyway. Something I want to check out."

Lieutenant Lacey let the comment pass, focusing on the immediate priority. "Good. How soon can you call back?"

"I don't know, maybe 30 minutes."

"As soon as you can, it's important. I'll be monitoring this number. Out."

"Wait a minute." Peter caught her before she disconnected. "I need to know. Did Ethan and Joanna make it safely to the embassy?"

Lacey felt like an idiot for not telling Peter sooner. "Yes, they are safe and under protection of the Marine guard."

Peter closed his eyes and felt a burden lifting. He slid his back down the wall, oblivious to the deep ache, until he was sitting on the floor. Then Lacey was speaking again. "You need to focus Dr. Savage. This is important; we need your help. Don't worry about your children; they are safe and out of harm's way. Do you understand?"

"Yes." Peter's voice was heavy with fatigue and emotion. "I'll call when I have something to tell you."

"Make it soon, please."

CHAPTER 18

Minsk

PETER POCKETED THE PHONE and relayed the essence of the phone conversation with Lacey.

"You think Jim is sending help?" Professor Savage asked.

Peter nodded. "That's why she asked me to see what's out there in the commons or the street, anywhere I can get a look. Dmitri, can you lead me to the roof?"

"Yes. We must take the stairs. But the door to the roof is normally locked and I don't have a key."

"I suspect this is a master key," Peter said, removing the key from the door handle. "Gary, I need you to stay here with Dad. No telling if we may run into more guards; you'll be safer here." Then Peter handed the machine gun and ammunition belt to Gary. "If you get discovered, use this, but conserve your ammo. Let me have the AK, it'll be easier to carry."

"Good luck son. Be careful," Ian said. Then he faced his good friend. "Take care of him Dmitri--he has a knack for finding trouble."

"You have my word, Ian."

"Don't worry, we'll be back. It may take a while, so just stay here and wait. Since we only have the one key, maybe it's best to leave the door unlocked so you aren't trapped in here. But don't get any crazy ideas about coming to look for us."

In the hallway Dmitri spoke in a whisper. "Follow me." It didn't take long to reach the stairwell, the same one Ethan and Joanna had descended earlier. Fortunately, they didn't run into any NPA soldiers along the way.

Dmitri reached for the door, intending to open it when Peter grasped his shoulder. "Let me go first," Peter said.

He opened the door slowly, leading with the rifle. The coast was clear, and Dmitri quickly followed Peter. They climbed the stairs, Peter cautiously in the lead, sighting ahead with the rifle at every bend just in case the enemy was also there.

After a nerve-wracking ten-minutes, they had climbed five flights and reached the roof door. Grasping the rifle in his right hand, finger on the trigger, Peter tested the doorknob with his left hand. Locked, as Dmitri had warned.

"Dmitri, try this key, but squat low and to the side in case there are guards on the other side ready to shoot."

Peter stood to the side, the concrete block walls providing some measure of protection to both men, while Dmitri followed the instructions. With a soft click, the door latched turned. Dmitri shoved it open, expecting bullets to whiz through the doorway. Instead, there was only silence.

As before, Peter led the way with the rifle. He emerged onto the roof, Dmitri right behind him. "Stay here. I'm going to look around," Peter said.

The flat roof was bordered with a waist-high wall that served to enhance the esthetics of the structure from the ground level, the wall mostly obscuring the dozen or more ventilation stacks and air-intakes that penetrated the roof. The ventilation stacks were a foot in diameter and were located in a line running down the center of the roof, each stack extending to a height of 10 feet and capped to keep rain and snow out. The air intakes were built from two-foot-square ducting, also capped. They were much shorter than the ventilation shafts so as not to draw in any noxious fumes emanating from the stacks.

Squatting low, Peter scrambled to the edge and looked out over the commons. Although many of the lamps were dark, no doubt damaged from the battle that transpired in front of the chemistry building, the still-burning Blackhawk wreckage plus the remaining functional lights provided adequate illumination. Peering over the edge, he systematically scanned the expansive space.

A mechanical sound, still distant, caught his attention. It seemed to be coming from the opposite side of the building. He dashed across the roof and gazed down at the four-lane thoroughfare. The streetlights cast a yellowish glow and beyond the street was Independence Square. The mechanical rumbling was getting louder, coming from the northeast.

Peter recognized the sound. He'd heard it before, at construction sites—the sound of steel tracks clanking against drive sprockets, overlaid on the roar of heavy diesel engines.

He squinted, trying to make out details in the distance, wishing he had a spotting scope or good pair of binoculars. Still straining to make out detail, he glimpsed the first tank passed under a streetlight. He continued to watch until the last vehicle rolled into Independence Square.

A soldier—Peter thought him to be an officer because he seemed to take charge of the gathering of tanks, armored personnel carriers, and missile carriers—descended from his steel shelter and conversed with another soldier. The vehicles then revved up their engines and deployed around the BSU campus.

Peter retrieved the cell phone and dialed the number he knew Lacey would answer.

"Lacey," she said.

"I'm on the roof. The commons is clear, except for about 20 soldiers. Small arms. They could still have RPGs or shoulder-fired missiles, I can't be certain."

"Good, that's what we expected."

"No, it's not good. I just watched six tanks, six armored personnel carriers, and one missile launcher drive into Independence Square. Two men got out, had a short conversation, and then the vehicles moved to locations around the campus. I can see two tanks and the missile carrier still parked in the Square."

"Can you describe the vehicles, especially the missile carrier. That's the biggest threat."

"I'll tell you what I can, but I don't know how to identify these vehicles." Peter edged up and peeked over the short wall. "The tank has a really long barrel, and it looks squashed and modern, not like the World War II Russian tanks; I don't know how else to describe it. The personnel carrier looks like a compressed box on tracks. No guns are visible. And the missile launcher has four big missiles aimed upward. I think I can also see a dish antenna, and the missile launcher rotates."

"That's good. I'll make sure this information gets to the right people. Is there anything else that might be important?"

"Like what?"

"I don't know. Do you see anything that would indicate they have set booby-traps, or maybe an ambush?"

"No, nothing I can identify."

"Okay. Any names?"

"Yes, two. Major Leonov and General Gorev. He's in charge. Does that mean anything?"

"Yes. Gorev's known to us. That's helpful."

"I snatched what I think is an order from Gorev's desk. It's in Russian, but a friend translated the document and said it refers to Spetsnaz troops here under Gorev's command. Something about ensuring the safety of ethnic Russians. And we found Russian rubles and a photo on a dead guard."

"I get the currency, but the photo?"

"It has a stamping on the back. My friend says it's a popular chain of film developing stores in Moscow."

"Anything else?"

"Maybe, I don't know if it's significant or not. Gorev mentioned a machine. He was discussing it with Major Leonov and some other soldiers. I don't know what it's supposed to do, but Leonov was in charge of placing it on the roof near the building air intakes."

Lacey paused as she thought about this information, recalling the recent horrors of Tbilisi. "Can you describe the machine to me?" she said, a renewed sense of urgency straining at her voice.

"No," Peter answered. "I haven't looked for it yet."

"Understood. Try to find it and report back ASAP. But don't touch it; we don't know yet what we're dealing with. Out."

Peter returned to Dmitri, who was huddled next to the roof-access door, right where Peter had left him.

"We have a new assignment."

Dmitri responded with inquisitive eyes.

"Let's find that machine you heard Gorev and Leonov talking about."

CHAPTER 19

Air space over Central Europe

THE SGIT COMBAT KING AIRCRAFT was still speeding for their target, a point in empty space from which Alpha Team would descend into blackness. Commander Nicolaou was working the plan over and over in his mind; anticipating deviations and contingencies. He was keenly aware of the fact that plans seldom went as expected—there were simply far too many variables to anticipate, too much that was beyond his ability to control.

Bull approached. "Sir, Lieutenant Lacey requests a word."

Jim entered the communication suite and closed the door for privacy. "Nicolaou," he said.

"Commander. I've been in communication with Peter Savage. He's with his father, Gary Porter, and Professor Dmitri Kaspar."

"Good news. Are they safe?"

"Yes, for the moment, but they did not escape. We were speaking on an unsecured line—he dialed your number. I told him not to mention his location, but he slipped up and said he was on the roof."

"Of the chemistry building?"

"Affirmative. He's our only set of eyes that we can communicate with directly. He reported armor settled in around the campus about twenty minutes ago; tanks and APCs, plus one mobile SAM launcher. No doubt a defensive perimeter; they are likely preparing for another assault. I've already requested current satellite images. With the thermal images we'll have vehicle locations pinpointed shortly. The GPS coordinates will uplink automatically to the EWO's targeting computer."

"Roger. Any details on the SAMs?"

"The launcher set up in Independence Square. From Peter's description, likely SA-11 or SA-17."

"Medium range missiles. We will be deploying at the maximum engagement range, but it's still a credible threat. Looks like the flight crew will be busy. I'll inform the pilots and weapons officer."

"Sir, General Gorev is commanding the militia and, we suspect, Spetsnaz soldiers as well."

"Not surprising that Russian regular units are directly involved," Jim said.

"There's something more. We have a possible link to the smallpox virus."

"What?"

"Professor Dmitri Kaspar—Ian Savage is collaborating with him—overheard Gorev talking to some other officers." Lacey relayed the information Peter had shared.

"If that machine is designed to disperse weaponized smallpox as an aerosol," Jim said, "it'll be drawn into the air intakes and infect everyone in the building. That's why they haven't moved the hostages. Gorev doesn't plan to kill them, he plans to infect them and have them spread the disease."

"Yes sir, that's our conclusion as well."

"But why not just disperse the smallpox in the room where the hostage are held? This plan seems too complicated, too risky."

"We've considered that. Once the hostages are released following infection they'll report that the militia didn't deploy any weapon—they won't know about the release on the roof. Plus, Ross and Williams ran a rudimentary computer model to predict the size of the fallout zone. From the rooftop, with a favorable wind, the aerosol will spread over at least two square miles, exposing up to 100,000 people. Shortly after sunrise, as the air is beginning to heat, a gentle breeze will pick up—ideal for spreading the virus across the most densely populated part of Minsk. That's why Gorev hasn't already released the aerosol."

"And President Pushkin will blame the U.S. Gorev's plan was to let the Delta team insert, so he had evidence of American forces on the site, ground zero for the release."

"Sir, I've worked through several scenarios with my team. We believe Pushkin will claim that the U.S. is attempting to use biological weapons to kill ethnic Russians. At the very least, it will provide an excuse for a direct invasion by Russian forces. Assuming this smallpox virus matches the genetic fingerprint of former U.S. stockpiles, Pushkin is guaranteed to win popular support around the world. America will be perceived as the aggressor, and in violation of treaties banning the use of biological weapons."

"We had this all wrong. Gorev never was planning to kill the hostages—not directly."

"No sir," said Lacey.

"I'll brief the team. Our mission priority has changed. We're going to disable that machine before it releases the aerosol. Inform Colonel Pierson, and suggest he communicates this information directly to the Joint Chiefs and President Taylor ASAP."

After Jim terminated the call to Ellen Lacey and briefed his team, he updated the aircrew with the new intel and possible threats.

The navigator conferred with a digital map of Minsk and the surrounding area, overlaid with the flight plan. "Closest approach to the airport is about 30 miles. At 35,000 feet we'll be outside the effective envelope of any medium range SAMs. But with that launcher at Independence Square, we'll be cutting it close. Could take us down with a lucky shot."

The pilot turned to Jim. "Can your team insert from a greater standoff distance, say 24 miles?"

"Negative," Jim replied. "I'd need another 4,000 feet of altitude to get that much glide."

The pilot shook his head. "This bird won't go that high, we're already squeezing everything we can out of her."

This wasn't news to Jim. He knew as much about the capabilities of their one-of-a-kind aircraft as the flight crew. "Captain," Jim address the pilot, "those AIM-7X missiles strapped to our wings will home in on radar emissions. I'd like to suggest that the weapons officer power up two of those missiles as we approach the drop point. As soon as you get painted with a targeting radar, fire on it and destroy the launcher preemptively."

"I like your suggestion," the pilot said.

Looking over the shoulder of the weapons officer at the city map, Jim asked if the satellite images had uploaded. The EWO punched a couple buttons and a new image was overlaid on the map. He zoomed in on the BSU campus and surrounding blocks.

"These bright spots are heat signatures," the EWO explained. He rolled a tracker ball and zoomed in tighter. In remarkable detail, the bright spots became ghostly images of tanks, APCs, and the missile launcher. Four tanks were stationed within line-of-sight of the chemistry building.

"Captain, those tanks could represent a serious problem to my team," Jim explained. "We'll land on the roof, and if we can't enter the building quickly, they could easily shell our position. Can you also target those four tanks? They're stationary, so the AIMs should track to the GPS coordinates."

"That's an air-to-air weapon system, it wasn't designed to bust tanks," the EWO protested.

"True, but the missile will attack from above. Tank armor is thinnest on top. The 40-pound high-explosive warhead and tungsten penetrators will slice through the top armor, no problem."

The EWO, pilot, and co-pilot considered Jim's argument but could find no flaw in his reasoning. "Very well," the pilot said. "But the remaining AIMs stay in reserve in case we get jumped by fighters."

CHAPTER 20

Minsk

PETER LOOKED DOWN AT Dmitri. He was sitting with his back against the wall next to the access door. He looked tired, and the jovial, happy-go-lucky expression he had when Peter first met him was gone, replaced with… what? Remorse? Regret? Or maybe he was just resigned to his fate.

"How are you doing, my friend?" Peter tried to lift his spirits, even a little.

Dmitri shrugged. "This is not how I wanted to welcome you to Minsk."

Peter chuckled, thinking it a joke. But Dmitri wasn't smiling. Instead, he seemed to be contemplating deep thoughts.

"Well, you still owe me dinner. But first I'm buying the wine—the least I can do to thank you for your help. And for befriending my father."

He looked up at Peter. "How can you be so different?" His question sounded genuine.

Peter shook his head. "I don't understand."

"You and your father. You treat me with respect and courtesy. You call me your friend."

"Sure, that's what we do. You opened your home and your arms to welcome Dad. Why would I want to treat you any other way?" Peter didn't expect an answer.

"Because of my name." Dmitri answered in a low voice, ashamed, his head facing his feet.

Peter's forehead wrinkled as he tried to decipher the cryptic response. Then it dawned on him. "Kaspar. That's German, right?"

Dmitri nodded. "The Russians have a long memory."

"You're referring to World War Two? That was a long time ago."

"Not long enough." Dmitri raised his eyes, locking Peter in his gaze. "Near the end of the war all persons of German decent were forcibly driven from their homes in Eastern Europe by the advancing Russian Army. Women, children, young, old—there were no more men of fighting age. Many of the women were raped by the soldiers as they walked hundreds of miles west to Germany. It was a brutal winter, and they were walking a gauntlet of sorts. Their possessions of any value were stolen. They were beaten like rabid dogs, even murdered for sport."

"I didn't know," Peter said.

"No reason you should have. It was not important to the Allies, and has been all but forgotten by historians."

Peter felt a wave of guilt for his ignorance. "I'm sorry. Your family—they settled in Germany?"

"Yes, before coming back to Minsk. Of course, their home was gone, taken by a Russian family. My grandparents worked hard to make a new start, and my parents did better. They afforded me an education." Dmitri forced a smile.

Peter reached down and offered his hand to Dmitri. "Don't worry about Gorev and the militia. If they want to get to you, first they'll have to get past me."

This time his smile was genuine, as was the solitary tear.

"You would risk your life for me?"

Peter nodded. "That's what friends do."

Dmitri considered Peter, trying to understand and wanting to believe that people could be different from what he had grown up to know. But never in his life had he been treated as an equal by anyone outside his circle of family and friends—certainly not by a stranger. Dmitri felt hope for the first time in years. Not only for himself, but for humankind.

"What now?" Dmitri said.

"Let's find this machine. Based on what you overheard, it should be near the air intakes. I don't imagine it will be too hard to find."

Dmitri shuffled behind Peter like a tired old man.

The air intake ducts were spaced between the exhaust stacks. They walked past the first six intakes without observing anything unusual, before Peter spotted the dark box. It was nestled snug against the next to last intake duct, and difficult to see in the darkness of night.

Wishing he had a flashlight, Peter resorted to using the cell phone as meager illumination. The machine was packaged in a hard case the size of a large suitcase. Four latches ran along the top edge, each secured with its own padlock. A chrome-plated key lock was embedded in the top of the case next to three buttons and what was probably an LCD display, although it was not illuminated. A long, narrow vent ran across the top, and another vent was evident on the side. Otherwise, there were no other distinguishing features on the case. Seeing no wires running from the case, Peter assumed that any power supply must be internal. He nearly picked up the case before recalling Lacey's warning.

Instead, he dialed the Lieutenant.. She picked up on the first ring.

"Did you find it?" she asked, no longer concerned about

possible eavesdroppers. At the moment, unambiguous communication was the top priority.

"I'm looking at it now." Peter described the case, presumably containing the machine, as Gorev referred to it.

"It certainly sounds like it could be an aerosol dispersion device," said Lacey.

"It wouldn't make sense that this machine dispenses a cloud of poison or infectious disease," Peter observed. "Gorev and his men will be killed, or at least sickened as well."

"True, if it was poison—nerve agent or the like. But I don't think that's the plan. Based on other evidence, I'm certain this device will activate shortly after sunrise and spread weaponized smallpox virus spores."

"But everyone will be infected, including the pro-Russian militiamen."

"Getting exposed doesn't mean getting sick."

Then it dawned on Peter. "Of course not; you're right. If Gorev and his men have already been vaccinated, they won't contract the disease."

Peter heard Lacey's sigh over the phone. "You said the case is just sitting there?"

"That's right," Peter answered. "I can't see anything tethering it in place. There's probably a dumpster nearby. If I can get to it, I can just throw this case inside and close the lid. That should contain the spores." Peter was reaching for the handle as he was speaking.

"No!" Lacey shouted the command, causing Peter to freeze.

"Why not? It's the safest way to contain the threat."

"Think about it. No, it's too risky. Gorev would never allow the plan to be so vulnerable. The case is probably set with motion sensors and a small charge. If you move that case, even the slightest amount, it's likely to explode and send the virus up in a cloud that will drift over the campus."

"Well, if that was the plan, then why are there vents along the top and side of the case?" Peter said.

"The charge is a failsafe; it's not intended to be the primary dispersion means. Even with low-power explosives, the pressure wave and heat will render much of the biological agent inactive. Slowly dispersing the agent as an aerosol is more effective. There will be an internal blower, battery operated, that will expel a plume of the smallpox agent over the course of an hour or so. The control mechanism is likely to be rather simple, although we've speculated the release could be triggered by favorable meteorological conditions."

"So if it's raining the device won't activate. What a perverted use of science."

"It's likely it could also be set with a simple timing mechanism."

"What do you want me to do?" Peter asked.

"Nothing. Boss Man will deal with it."

"But I'm here! There must be something I can do to render the device impotent. Maybe I can douse it with flammable liquids and burn it."

"Don't touch it. Don't even lightly brush against it. The motion detectors will be extremely sensitive. And if it gets too hot, that could trigger the explosive. Now that we know what we're dealing with, we'll come up with a plan to neutralize it. But for now, just leave it be."

"I hear you." Peter wanted to ask when help would arrive, but knew the answer would not be shared on an unsecured cell phone. "Call when you need my help." He ended to call and looked at Dmitri. The man definitely looked his age plus ten.

"Come on Dmitri. Let's get back inside and see what we can do to beef up our defensive capabilities."

"You have something in mind?" Dmitri said.

"I do. Can we get to the chemistry store room?"

"Sure. It's on the second floor. But what if it's guarded?"

"I'm betting they won't post men there."

Peter led the way back downstairs, rifle pointing the way and Dmitri close behind. Their luck held and no one was encountered in the stairwell. On the second floor, Peter cautiously pushed the door open and peeked in the hallway. Two guards were patrolling, walking away for the stairwell. He motioned to Dmitri with his index finger at his lips and mouthed "Shhh. Which way?"

Silently Dmitri pointed to the right. Good, away from the guards.

Peter looked again just as the guards rounded the corner. The hallway was clear. "Come on."

Silently but swiftly they left the stairwell and moved down the corridor. Then Dmitri tapped Peter and pointed to a solid wood door. Without a sound Dmitri used the master key to unlock the door. Once inside with the door closed and locked, Dmitri felt for the light switch and turned it on.

In a near panic, Peter quickly grabbed a lab coat hanging on a hook and stuffed it against the crack between the door and floor. "Sorry," Dmitri whispered.

Peter looked at his surroundings. The room was of moderate size with a row of shelving running down the center of the floor and additional shelving lining all four walls. There was a door at the opposite end of the storeroom in addition to the one they entered through.

"These chemicals are mostly for the undergraduate labs, but some of the graduate research programs also purchase solvents and reagents through the store. In the adjoining room are the glassware, hot plates, and other laboratory supplies, including customized apparatus. We're fortunate to have a professional glassblower on staff."

Peter hadn't really been listening, but this last comment

caught his attention. "Glassblower. Let's take a look."

Dmitri led Peter through the far door and into the adjacent room. This time he stuffed a lab coat at the threshold of the outer door before turning on the lights. This room was even larger than the chemical supply room, and in the center was a long, charcoal-gray counter. Peter tapped it with his fist. "Soap stone."

An array of gas torches with rubber hoses connected to the gas valves were spread across the counter. There were also short lengths of glass tubing in different diameters, evidence of past projects. Peter turned slowly, mentally taking inventory. Shelving along the wall hosted a range of materials from batteries and coils of copper wire to large power supplies.

"Dmitri, how are your glassblowing skills? Can you make some glass balls from that tubing?" Peter was pointing to a rack well stocked with tubes ranging from small to large diameter.

"Just spheres? It's been some time since I did any serious glass work, but yes, I can do that."

"Good. If you will get started, I'll find the chemicals we need. Make the balls about the size of an apple. And leave a section of tubing a few centimeters long. I'll use that to fill the balls and then you can seal them."

Dmitri smiled. "I think I know what you are planning. I'll get to work."

What Peter really wanted was explosives. Given enough time, he was confident he could make black powder and flash powder from chemicals he'd likely find on the shelves, but time was in short supply. He went to the solvents first. The large four-liter glass bottles were placed in two yellow-steel cabinets, standard precaution for flammable liquids.

Peter passed over the nitromethane—although explosive it was difficult to detonate. Instead, he grabbed a jug labeled hexane. Closing the metal doors, he continued his search. The chemicals were organized alphabetically, and Peter found what he wanted in the B section. He put the bottle in his pocket and continued his search—not in the C section. Of course not, that's the English name. He thought for a minute, trying to recall a specific chemical structure and the corresponding technical name for the compound. "Pentamethylene diamine," he whispered. "Ah, there it is."

With the glass bottle in one hand and jug of hexane in the other, Peter returned to check on Dmitri's progress. He already crafted three glass spheres and was busily creating a fourth. Peter set the chemicals several feet away from the gas torch. Dmitri lifted his cobalt glasses—heavily shaded blue lenses that filtered out the yellow light from the molten glass—and examined Peter's find. "I thought you were going to make an explosive, maybe RDX or TNT?"

"No time. Plus I'd need detonators."

"Mercury fulminate? I know there is picric acid on the self."

Peter shook his head. "No, too dangerous. I have a better idea—less bang but still ample to persuade our guests to leave us the hell alone. Where can I find a mortar and pestle?"

"Over there, next to the beakers."

"Can you make six more balls?" Peter asked.

"Sure." He lowered the dark glasses and went back to work.

Peter removed one of the ceramic mortar and pestles and returned to the chemical storeroom where he quickly found potassium nitrate and powdered sulfur. Grinding first a quantity of potassium nitrate, he then cleaned the mortar and dumped in some sulfur for grinding. The yellow sulfur flour was combined with the potassium nitrate powder and carefully mixed before Peter poured a small amount of the concoction onto a paper towel. He spread the pale yellow powder into a long narrow line and then rolled the paper around it, like a long, thin cigarette. But no one would want to smoke this. He finished his handiwork with a twist and then a strip of clear tape to keep it from opening.

With three of these long fuses made, Peter returned in time to see Dmitri blowing air into the glass tube, the far end a glob of orange molten glass surrounded by a yellow fireball. Dmitri's cheeks puffed out as he forced air through the tube, expanding the fluid glass into a near-perfect sphere. Once removed from the torch flame the glass ball rapidly cooled and Dmitri cut the tube stub with a file and an experienced snap.

"I surmise you fabricated fuses," Dmitri said, pointing to the twisted lengths of paper towel Peter laid on the counter. "But, you said we don't have explosives. So what are we making—incendiaries?"

Peter smiled. "Incendiary chemical weapons. We're about to violate the Geneva Convention."

CHAPTER 21

Washington, DC

PRESIDENT TAYLER HAD JUST been briefed by Colonel Pierson. Present were Howard Hale, Paul Bryan, and General Hendrickson. At the suggestion of Secretary of Defense Hale, also participating in the meeting were Air Force General Collins and Marine Corp General Hopkins.

"How confident is your assessment, Colonel?" President Taylor asked.

"High degree, Mister President. Based on the description by Dr. Savage—"

"He's one of the American hostages who escaped the group held captive, is that right?" Howard Hale asked.

"That's right. He's been our eyes on the ground."

"Are you sure the information he's feeding you is genuine, not misinformation provided intentionally by the Russians?"

"As confident as we can be, Mister Secretary," Pierson said. "Voice print confirms it's Peter Savage, and the information he's provided regarding armor and missile batteries around the BSU campus is confirmed by satellite imagery."

"Please continue Colonel," the President interjected.

"Yes sir. I was saying that the description of the machine—the term used by General Gorev—suggests it is an aerosol generator, designed to disperse powdered materials into the air."

"Don't you have any photos of it?" Bryan asked.

"It's night time, on an open roof, surrounded by hostiles. Tell me, would you want to be taking photos?"

President Taylor stood and walked around the Resolute Desk, standing with his arms folded as he addressed the Secretary of State. "Never in my worst nightmares did I ever imagine President Pushkin would orchestrate such a heinous series of events."

"He's an ambitious man, sir," Paul Bryan said.

Just then Colleen Walker was led into the Situation Room. "I got here as fast as I could, sir."

"It's fine Colleen, have a seat." She settled into one of the black leather chairs arranged around the large mahogany table.

She didn't look up at the faces gazing at her, choosing instead to open the file she carried and began reading. "FBI agents grilled Hanssen and Ames, but got nothing of value. And I have General Hendrickson's assurances that no smallpox samples from Fort Detrick are unaccounted for. That leaves us with the CDC."

She turned a page, still not looking up. "Go on," the President said.

"This is where it gets interesting. In 1987 a sample of weaponized virus, a particularly nasty and lethal strain of hemorrhagic smallpox—lot number 87T-332, vial number two—was marked for destruction. It's standard practice to incinerate biological samples to eliminate the hazard of accidental release. However, we cross-checked the records, and vial number two was not reported as destroyed. In fact, there are no subsequent records of this sample. It's as if it just disappeared."

"So what happened to the sample?" Paul Bryan asked.

"I can't say definitively at this point in time," she said. "But here's the kicker. The genetic sequence was recorded, again standard procedure for purposes of tracking a possible release and infection. The genetic fingerprint of 87T-332 is a perfect match to virus samples from Georgia."

"Perfect?" General Hendrickson said.

"As in identical," she said.

"My God," President Taylor muttered and cast his eyes toward the ceiling.

"Well, now we know where the virus came from," Hale said. For a half minute the room was dead silent.

"Do we know how it got into the hands of the Russians?" President Taylor said.

"Not yet, sir. We're still working on that. It will take some time. It's possible we'll never know."

The President lowered himself into the leather chair and pulled himself up to the table. "Does this revelation have any bearing on Bright Star?"

General Collins glanced briefly at his boss. "Speak freely Bob," Hendrickson said, confident he knew what his colleague would say.

Bob Collins began flying in Viet Nam in 1972, F-4 Phantoms. He had been shot down once, but escaped capture by the Viet Cong. Later he commanded a B-1 Lancer—unofficially called the "Bone" by crew members, slang for B-One—in missions over Kosovo. He was well respected at the Pentagon and considered a brilliant strategist, extremely bright but also bringing combat experience in both fighter and bomber aircraft.

"Mister President," General Collins began, "this information strongly suggests that this is a state-sponsored action, not a simple case of a local terrorist group holding civilians hostage. If the Russians are deploying biological weapons, then they are certainly in league with the NPA militia."

"What are the implications for your mission?" The President asked.

"Our strike aircraft will be picked up on Russian radar long before they enter Belarusian airspace. There is a squadron of Su-27 fighters stationed in western Belarus. Those fighters are state-of-the-art. If I were the Russian commander, I'd dispatch those aircraft to intercept our B-1s and shoot them down."

"I thought our Raptor fighters would protect the bombers," Taylor said.

"The Raptors are flown by the best attack pilots in the world, and they can handle the Flankers—"

Hale interrupted. "Su-27 fighters."

"I'm following," President Taylor said. "Continue General."

"Our rules of engagement are to shoot back only if the enemy fires first. By the time those Flankers launch missiles, it'll be too late. The electronic and other defensive countermeasures on the B-1 are good, but against a barrage of missiles there is a reasonable chance at least one gets through."

Feeling a huge weight on his shoulders, President Taylor considered the obvious solution: change the rules of engagement to allow the Air Force to enter this mission on the offensive. But doing so would likely mark the U.S. as the aggressor, the party that fired the first shot in what could easily become a regional conflict, and possibly escalate to a European, if not global, war.

"General Hopkins, what is your assessment?"

First clearing his throat, the commander of the Marine Corp answered. "I agree with General Collins' assessment. I have over 200 Marines depending on those B-1s completing their mission and taking out the air defenses at the Minsk airport."

"The airport is heavily defended," explained Hendrickson. "The Marines will be ferried in onboard Osprey transports—an easy target for missile and gun emplacements. Sir, we have to ensure the B-1 crews are able to drop their ordnance before the Ospreys are within range of the airport defenses."

"And the SGIT team?" Taylor asked, addressing Colonel Pierson.

"Alpha Team will insert from high-altitude and glide to the BSU campus. They will land on the roof of the chemistry building. That is the hostage location. It's also where Peter Savage is. The insertion will occur simultaneously with the attack on the airport, drawing attention away from their lone aircraft and insertion. Once they secure the safety of the hostages, they will sit tight and wait for the Marines to arrive."

"Why not just send the Marines in right away to rescue the hostages?" the President said.

"The BSU campus is only ten miles from the airport," General Collins said. "The air defenses there easily extend that distance. We can't get aircraft in until those missile batteries and AA guns are removed."

"You just lost me. What makes you think Colonel Pierson's team can parachute in if the Russian missile defenses effectively extend over most of Minsk? Won't his team be at risk of being shot down?"

"No sir," Pierson replied. "Alpha Team is inserting by parachuting from high altitude. They can glide 20 miles using this technique and land on a pizza box. Their aircraft will never be in range of the air defenses at the airport."

President Taylor nodded understanding. "But the Flanker fighters do represent a credible threat." The President had caught up to the reasoning of his senior military advisors and was finding only one acceptable solution.

"Very well gentlemen. Thank you for your candor. I

understand your concerns, and agree that this new development strongly implies a deep involvement on the part of Russia. Given that, I cannot, in clear conscious, send our men and women into this conflict without allowing them every opportunity to prevail."

President Taylor brushed his hand across the mahogany tabletop as if he were brushing away imaginary specs of dirt, thinking through his decision one final time before voicing it. "I want each of you to understand that I am arriving at this decision reluctantly. However, I fail to see any acceptable alternative."

His eyes swept across those of his Secretary of Defense and Joint Chiefs. "As of this moment, I am altering the rules of engagement. All American military forces operating in Bright Star are authorized to shoot first if—in their judgment—imminent threat is encountered. That use of force will, however, be limited to Russian military and pro-Russian militia forces and assets."

"Yes sir, thank you, sir," Secretary Hale replied. He glanced at his watch. "The assault will commence in twenty minutes with aircraft stationed in Germany. The SGIT transport has been en route for several hours."

"Good. Keep me informed. Paul, do you think you can get Pushkin on the phone?"

"Given the circumstances, I think so."

"Good. See what you can do." Paul Bryan excused himself as he left the meeting.

"Colleen, if the Russians have cloned a sample of smallpox from our laboratory, is there any proof we can find of their involvement? Any way we can prove they are the ones who actually dispensed it, not us?"

"The best proof would be the contraption that Colonel Pierson's inside man found on the roof of the chemistry building. If we could analyze its construction, I'd expect to find many telltale indicators that its origin is Russian."

"Colonel, odds that your team can retrieve the device?" President Taylor said.

"If anyone can, they will."

President Taylor nodded.

"Can we glean any evidence of Russian involvement from the samples from Georgia?"

"Perhaps, Mister President. I didn't mention it before because the data is still preliminary. As you know the CDC is also conducting a detailed analysis of the samples. So far, they have nothing new to add to the report from the European Molecular Biology Laboratory. However, in two samples there are traces of foreign impurities, anticlumping agents. These chemicals are formulated specifically to preserve the smallpox virus as a finely dispersed powder, even after sitting for months, perhaps years, in an artillery shell. There are also microscopic residues of the bursting charge."

"Bursting charge?"

"Yes, sir," General Hendrickson replied. "It's a relatively low-power, low-heat explosive intended to shatter the shell casing and disperse the contents. In this case, the weaponized virus."

"And you're saying the analysis suggests this anticlumping agent and bursting charge are of Russian origin?"

"Yes, sir. That's exactly what I'm saying."

CHAPTER 22

WASHINGTON, DC

"THAT'S CORRECT MISTER PRESIDENT." Although Paul Bryan had an amicable relationship with the Russian Foreign Minister, Viktorovich Denisov, he had failed to persuade his counterpart to wake President Vladimir Pushkin for a conference with President Taylor. "Mister Denisov reminded me of the time in Moscow and said that I should call later at a more respectable hour."

"President Pushkin is going to get a rather rude awakening shortly.Perhaps then he'll agree to speak with me."

"There's still time, sir. I could phone Denisov and notify him that a joint NATO-U.S. training operation is about to commence over Belarus."

President Taylor shook his head and held out his hand to calm Howard Hale before he launched into a rebuttal. "Thank you Paul, but no. We've covered this and I won't risk harm to our aircrew by alerting the Russians. No, we're going to slug it out if that's what it takes, in which case the element of surprise will be to our advantage. Any news from the administration of President Yatchenko?"

"About five hours ago he spoke to the media from a heavily guarded police station. He and many of the elected representatives have vowed to resist what they have labeled as an invasion by Russian military troops. He also says he told Foreign Minister Denisov that Russia had 48 hours to withdraw all military personnel and machinery—most notably the half dozen Russian fighters stationed at Baranovichi Air Base. Since the Belarusian military has little power to enforce this edict, it's more symbolic, but clearly signals his government's displeasure with the Kremlin."

President Taylor turned to General Hendrickson and wondered how it could be that his uniform always looked immaculate, even after a long day.

"General, remind me again of the timetable."

General Hendrickson cleared his throat. "Very shortly two B-1 Lancers will enter Belarussian airspace, accompanied by three flights of Raptors. Russian medium-range radar will pick up the B-1s but they won't detect the F-22 escorts, six in total, due to their low radar cross section. Simultaneously, a dozen Typhoon fighters from the Royal Air Force are approaching from the north, over Lithuania, and four F-16s will launch from Lask Air Base in Poland just ahead of the B-1s. The mission of the F-16s is to draw out the air defenses at the Minsk International Airport and destroy them with anti-radar missiles."

"You said medium-range radar. Are you implying that long-range Russian radar will detect the aircraft sooner?"

"Yes, sir; I expect they are already tracking our aircraft," replied Hendrickson. "An experimental over-the-horizon radar and tracking system can detect the Lancers, probably also the conventional fighters, anywhere over Eastern Europe. This system is code-named 'Container'. But in order to achieve this range, the radio waves are bounced off the ionosphere, greatly reducing resolution."

"Very well, continue please."

"We have two tankers loitering over Poland to gas up aircraft as necessary to keep them on station for as long as needed. One Air Force E-3 surveillance and tracking aircraft has also been deployed over Poland. The tankers and the E-3 are protected by the Typhoon fighters. Data from the E-3 is being streamed through the Joint Air Operations Command and Control center at Spangdahlem Air Base in Germany."

"Any word yet on those Russian Flankers in Belarus?"

"No, sir, not at this time."

President Taylor nodded, but he felt is gut tightening. Men and women were flying into conflict, and the outcome was far from certain.

CHAPTER 23

Minsk

"OH, THAT SMELLS AWFUL!" Dmitri said, almost gagging as he helped fill the glass balls with a mixture of the chemicals.

"Butyric acid and cadaverine, or pentamethylene diamine. Mixed with some hexane for flammability," Peter replied.

"It's awful—smells like dog feces and rotten meat."

"That's the point. I selected these compounds based on a modern theory of non-lethal crowd control. Odors that cause a gag reflex. It's instinctive in humans to avoid these smells which signal toxicity, and they elicit a strong response that's hard to overcome."

"How do you know these things?" Dmitri asked.

Peter shrugged. "In my business, it comes with the territory."

Dmitri frowned, but decided not to probe further.

"Why the hexane? Why not just fill the glass balls with the butyric acid and cadaverine?"

"The hexane is my special modification. As the hexane burns it will heat the other chemicals and spread the putrid odor faster. Plus there's the natural fear of fire."

Peter was taping two-inch lengths of fuse to each glass ball after Dmitri sealed the glass stub with the torch. "Just light the fuse and throw. Pretty simple."

Two hundred miles to the west, two Lancers were about to enter Belarusian airspace, only two minutes behind four F-16 Falcon jets. The B-1s had been gaining on the Falcons for the last 200 miles, ever since they went supersonic. The bombers were under the command of Major Lorraine Doyle, a career Air Force officer, graduate of the academy in Colorado Springs, and with 23 years in the service of her country.

The U.S. offensive would be under the direction of Golden Eye, the E-3 Sentry airborne warning and control system aircraft (AWACS). Circling above Poland, its radar coverage extended all the way into western Russia.

Major Doyle's mission objectives were clear; destroy anti-air defenses at the International Airport and provide close air support to the Marines who would be deploying into what was assumed would be a very hot landing zone (LZ). Although the B-1 was initially imagined to be an intercontinental strategic bomber, its offensive role had evolved considerably, in part due to a change in U.S. doctrine concerning the deployment of nuclear weapons, and in part based on the aircraft's successes in Iraq and Afghanistan in the fight against the Taliban.

Flying at 500 feet over eastern Poland at a speed of Mach 1.2, Doyle had the two Bones—code named Hammer Flight and Anvil Flight—in very close formation, tight enough that the returned radar signature would appear to be a single aircraft. The Russian air controllers would naturally assume the return to be indicative of a B-1 due to the supersonic speed.

"Golden Eye reports the Falcons have engaged two SAM sites in western Belarus," Doyle reported to her crew as well as that of Anvil Flight. The F-16's mission was to attract search and guidance radar and then destroy the radar with HARM (high-velocity anti-radiation missiles) munitions. It was risky for the pilots flying the Falcons, but offered huge benefits to trailing aircraft. Without the guidance radars, surface-to-air missiles and radar-aimed antiaircraft guns were useless.

"Golden Eye is tracking four—no six—aircraft departing from the airfield at Baranavichi," Doyle reported as she was listening to the secure communication. "Departing in pairs so the assumption is Russian fighters. We know they have Flankers stationed there. Let me know when you have them on the scope, Nate."

Captain Nathan 'Nate' McKinley was the Defensive System Officer, or DSO. In order to reduce their electromagnetic signature, the Bones were flying without their radar on, instead relying on a data link with Golden Eye.

"Have it, Major," Nate said. "Six Flankers, airborne and picking up speed."

The Flankers were a formidable foe, and with advanced look-down, shoot-down radar, posed a serious threat to the Bones as well as the F-16s, code named Searchlight.

"They've got their targeting radar on, Major. They're looking for us. Climbing rapidly, probably plan to get above us, get a solid lock, and fire."

"See if you can jam them," Doyle said, but Nate was already working on it.

"Doubtful, still too far out, maybe in another minute. Four Flankers split off and are vectoring to the Falcons."

Golden Eye, of course, was tracking everything, all aircraft between ground level and 50,000 feet within a radius of 350 miles. Colonel Horn was the senior officer onboard, responsible for coordinating through the CAOC in Stuttgart and establishing the order of battle, which meant the priority of threat and assigning the best resource to neutralize the threat.

Colonel Horn was a career Air Force veteran, with several real combat missions such as this one under his belt, including Operation Checkmate, a classified intervention over Venezuela involving F-22 Raptors and B-2 stealth bombers.

"Sir, we have four Flankers vectoring toward Searchlight Flight," an airman reported to Colonel Horn.

Colonel Horn understood that the Falcons were lightly armed for air-to-air combat with only two heat seeking missiles each. He also understood they would not fare well in a dogfight with the Flankers.

"Get a couple Raptors over there to help out those pilots. They need to stay on task."

"Roger that, sir," the airman said.

"Guardian Flight, this is Golden Eye, copy?"

"Roger, Golden Eye. Guardian One."

"Guardian One, we are tracking four Flankers approximately 180 miles out from Searchlight. You are directed to split off two aircraft to engage and neutralize threat. You have the vector now."

Following a brief pause, the voice answered in the airman's headset. "Affirmative Golden Eye. Guardian Five and Guardian Six will engage Flankers."

From the monitors aligned in rows on the AWACS, blips representing the two F-22 Raptor fighters separated from a cluster of six, leaving four to defend the Bones. Flying at supersonic speed, Guardian Five and Guardian Six closed on the Flankers, but not before the Flankers were within range of Searchlight.

"Searchlight, you have four Flankers within maximum engagement range. Be advised, two Raptors approximately 30 seconds out," came the warning from Golden Eye.

In a dogfight, with aircraft flying at 700 miles per hour and missiles traveling at four times that speed, 30 seconds was an eternity.

In that instant, threat warning receivers began to sound in all four aircraft. Flying in a loose formation, they scattered like startled quail.

"Searchlight flight, this is Golden Eye. Punch afterburners and resume vector east, toward the airport. Missiles were fired from extreme range, best bet is to outrun them." Golden Eye was trying to buy seconds for the F-16s, to allow the two Raptors to engage.

With Searchlight back on flight plan and traveling in excess of the speed of sound, the pursuing missiles ran out of fuel and self-detonated.

The four Flankers continued their pursuit, the Falcons easily revealed on their radar screens. Knowing the American planes could not stay in afterburner for long due to the enormous fuel consumption rate, the Russian pilots chose to stay at full military power and hunt their prey. Soon they would close distance again, and this time they would not miss.

"Searchlight, you are clear of inbound threats, but those Flankers have not broken off. Stay sharp, Guardians will engage in seven seconds."

The Su-27 Flanker pilots had hoped to engage the Falcons in a dogfight. Some of the best trained pilots in the Russian Air Force, these men wanted combat experience. Plus they knew they had the upper hand given the American fighters were on a specific electronic warfare mission and would be lightly armed for air-to-air battle.

What the Flanker pilots didn't expect was a pair of stealthy Raptors approaching quickly, and invisibly.

"Guardian Five. Slaving targeting computer to data link." The pilot coordinated his targeting with Guardian Six to maximize the utility of their limited weaponry—six Aim-120D "Slammer" missiles each. The weapons were stored internally which, combined with the sleek lines and radar absorbing materials used in the aircraft skin, resulted in such a low radar cross-section as to render the Raptor invisible to radar at typical engagement distances.

"Roger. Guardian Six locking onto bogies three and four."

"Fire on my mark," Guardian Five said, already locking the guidance systems on two missiles to the blips designated bogy five and bogy six. "Mark."

"Fox three," came the reply from Guardian Six, indicating he had just fired two Slammers.

The four guided missiles, traveling at nearly Mach four, closed on the Su-27 aircraft at more than three times the speed of sound. Onboard the Flankers, life instantly changed as the hunter became the hunted. The aircraft split in opposite directions, diving, ejecting chaff bundles to confuse the radar guidance system of the missiles.

The lead Flanker pilot fired up the afterburners and jinked, trying to break the lock and evade the rapidly closing threat. The blaring alarm was increasing in frequency as the missile closed the distance. He pulled back on the stick, at the same time pushing to the right. He felt the blood draining from his head in the tight five-G turn.

Still, the alarm screamed. He ejected more chaff bundles and pulled up the aircraft's nose—in seconds gaining 2,000 feet in altitude, before pushing the stick forward and hard left. He squeezed his abdominal muscles to constrict the flow of blood into his lower body, trying to keep oxygen flowing to his brain. The turn was sharp, nine-Gs, and his vision dimmed, becoming black around the periphery. It was like he was looking through a black tunnel at the outside world.

The Flanker was now flying supersonic in its downward

descent. He pushed the stick harder, angling steeply toward the ground still 10,000 feet below—but approaching fast. Then he pulled back on the stick. The aircraft shot upward, its momentum plus the enormous thrust from the twin engines pushing it toward the black heavens. He knew the turn would have to be tight to have any chance of evading the missile. Squeezing his abdomen hard and grunting, still holding the stick back. His vision dimmed, and yet he refused to ease on the stick, grunting, gulping in air, he held fast. Then his vision went black.

The Flanker resumed a straight trajectory without any control input from the pilot. Two seconds later the Slammer's radar proximity fuse sensed it was at the target. The 30-pound explosive warhead detonated five feet above the aircraft, causing fuel lines and fuel tanks to rupture and ignite in a huge fireball that lit the night sky.

The other three Flankers met similar fates at nearly the same moment.

"I'm sorry to bother you sir, but I have Foreign Minister Denisov on the line, and he says it's urgent."

"Put him through Marge." Secretary of State Paul Bryan was expecting a call from the highest levels of the Russian government. He knew the approaching flight of aircraft would not pass without notice, or response.

"I have been instructed by President Pushkin to warn you that Russia will not tolerate American or NATO interference in events unfolding in Belarus. We have detected a large number of aircraft approaching Belarus from the west and the northwest. Their flight pattern suggests military aircraft."

"You say they are flying over European airspace, not Russian. Consequently, there has been no violation of Russian sovereignty. I cannot accept your objections."

"Then you acknowledge these are American warplanes?"

"I have not acknowledged anything other than the obvious," replied Bryan. Although the stakes were high, he still enjoyed these bouts of mental jousting.

"Understand me well, Mister Secretary. Russia has an obligation to protect its citizens, and we do have fighter aircraft stationed in Belarus. As you know, President Pushkin and President Yatchenko share a common interest."

"Perhaps they have less in common now. President Yatchenko does not appreciate Russian troops stirring up violence in Minsk. We expect he will request NATO and international support against Russian aggression within 24 hours."

There was a moment of silence, presumably for Foreign Secretary Denisov to digest this piece of information. "Russia has no troops in Belarus. However, we do reserve the right to defend ethnic Russians, including those in Minsk. If U.S. and NATO warplanes are intending to engage the pro-Russian militia in and around Minsk, they will be met with force. Heed my warning Mister Secretary. Russia does not seek a confrontation, but we will not look the other way while American aggression once again interferes with the internal affairs of Eastern European countries."

Paul Bryan was prepared for this insinuation. "You are referring to the alleged use of the smallpox virus as a biological weapon in Tbilisi?"

"Of course. The evidence has spoken clearly. And from a European agency nonetheless. The global stage of public opinion is already rising against this monstrous act by the United States."

"Very well, Mister Denisov. Thank you for getting to the point. Now, I shall return the favor. First, you and I both know very well that the United States has not dispersed biological weapons anywhere. Not in Georgia, not anywhere. Soon, we will present our evidence of Russian complicity behind the outbreak in Tbilisi. Second, and listen to me carefully, any real or perceived threat in the airspace over Belarus will be dealt with decisively."

The line was silent.

"Minister Denisov, do you understand what I am saying?" asked Paul Bryan, although he knew the answer.

"I understand your language better than you understand mine. You will soon regret this course of action."

CHAPTER 24

Minsk

"LET'S GO. I HAVE AN IDEA how we might disable that machine and prevent it from dispersing the virus," Peter said. Dmitri nodded and together, equipped with their improvised weapons, the pair slipped into the hallway.

They dashed toward the stairwell, intending to return as fast as possible to the storeroom where Ian and Gary were sequestered. They didn't have far to go and Peter was focused on the doorway ahead when a booming voice called from behind. "Stop!" The command was punctuated by a gunshot.

Peter slid to a stop and turned slowly. Dmitri did the same. The AK-74 rifle was slung over Peter's shoulder, tantalizingly close and yet impossible to retrieve and aim without being shot dead.

"Hello my comedic America friend. We meet again," General Gorev said. "Drop your rifle." Five guards rounded the corner of the hall and surrounded the General, all brandishing assault rifles aimed at Peter and Dmitri.

"We missed you," Gorev said with a mock frown. "You will come with me."

"And if I refuse?"

Gorev raised his rifle and shot Dmitri in the belly. He fell forward, clutching the wound, rolling on the floor in agony.

"No!" Peter yelled, rushing to his friend. Gently pulling away Dmitri's hands, Peter examined the red splotch, blood already seeping through his shirt.

"He needs medical help."

"He'll get nothing. His kind is not welcome here." Gorev spat the words out.

Dmitri spoke softly. "Don't try to understand Peter. I knew it would come to this." Dmitri grasped Peter's hand, but there was little strength in his grip.

"Please. A first aid kit, or bandage to stop the bleeding," Peter pleaded.

"Nyet," said Gorev. Then he aimed his AK and fired again. The bullet punch through Dmitri's chest.

Frothy, bright-red blood oozed from the chest wound, pooling on Dmitri's once-white shirt and mingling with the dark red-brown blood from his belly wound. Peter knew the bullet had penetrated his friend's lung, likely other vital organs and arteries as well. Dmitri was dying, and there wasn't anything Peter could do to save him. He placed his hand on the bloody spot, knowing that death would soon come from fluid filling his lungs.

"Hold on Dmitri," Peter begged.

Dmitri shook his head softly, his eyes nearly closed. He turned to face Peter, and squeezed his hand. "You are fortunate my young friend, to live in America." His voice was weak.

"No!" Peter shook his head. "I'll get help."

"It is time." Dmitri slowly blinked his eyes and then held them half open, looking beyond Peter, his breathing shallow and labored. "I go now; Helena waits for me."

Peter recalled the photo on Dmitri's desk. Helena was his

wife.

"Dmitri! Hang on! Please! I can stop the bleeding," he lied. Peter's mind was racing, a chaotic mix of thoughts—even if he had a first aid kit, there was no treatment that could be rendered to save Dmitri. Even if he were in a hospital at this very moment, his chances of survival we slim. Peter was completely powerless to prevent the inevitable, just as he had been when Maggie passed. The image of Maggie in her final minutes of life flashed in his mind, replacing his sadness with a raging anger.

Dmitri's eyelids closed. "It is good, I want to be with Helena again." As the words escaped his lips, the breath exited his bullet-riddled body for the last time.

The rage was building in Peter, and with it a clarity of purpose. He was no stranger to death. First his wife, and later, at his own hands on a cold rocky outcrop in the Aleutian Island chain, and again in a desolate desert in Sudan.

Yet, he still found the wanton taking of life deeply disturbing. "Why?" Peter stammered.

Gorev shrugged. "Why not?"

Peter stood. "I will see you in Hell."

Gorev chuckled and was joined by his guards. "Really? And you think you have that power? You are one unarmed man. My soldiers can shoot you anytime I please."

"Then do it—shoot me." Peter was no longer afraid. He was overwhelmed with a drive to do what was right, at any price. It was a familiar feeling, one that replaced fear and uncertainty with a demanding call to action.

"Perhaps… at a later time. It seems you have some information, some knowledge, about how to design and manufacture very quiet guns. I am told you call it a magnetic impulse gun, yes?"

Peter glared back in defiance.

"You have lost, Peter Savage."

"Let me ask you a question, Gorev. What is the most dangerous and deadly animal on Earth?"

Gorev forced out a short laugh. "A lion or tiger? Is that how I am to answer?"

"What you answer is up to you."

"You speak in riddles my comedian friend, but you are entertaining." Gorev waved his hands to both sides, silent reference to the five rifles pointed at Peter's heart. He raised his eyebrows, his lips twisted in a nauseating smirk, begging a reply to the rhetorical question.

"A man—who has lost everything. He is the most dangerous animal. You see, with nothing left to cherish, nothing left to live for, a man becomes the most deadly predator. Without fear of death, he will do anything to achieve his ultimate objective and destroy his adversary.

"I have met men like you before, Gorev. I have fought against them. And I have learned that, among other despicable traits, you all share a drive to lord over others through fear and intimidation. You're nothing but a bully."

General Gorev tilted his head slightly, conveying both curiosity and amusement, inviting Peter to continue.

"You threaten to kill to get your way. All those people you're holding against their will, that's only possible because you've terrified them."

"Yes, we agree, they are like sheep. So, what is your point?"

"It's very simple. Without their fear, you are powerless."

"Powerless? I don't think so." He extended his arm to the side again in a grandiose gesture.

"If your plan was to kill all of us, you'd have done so by now. No, that's not what you want. You want—need—our cooperation. And as long as you are allowed to intimidate and coerce those people, reluctant cooperation is what you'll get. But not from me. I'm not afraid of your threats."

"I can kill you now, just as I did that filthy pig Kaspar."

"Death is inevitable. It can be a means to an end—your end. A man who accepts his mortality and fears neither death nor destruction, that man has already defeated his enemies."

Gorev forced a laugh. "And you are this man?"

"Your first mistake was allowing my children to escape." Peter's face was firm, devoid of any expression.

Gorev's mind flashed back to their first encounter in the hallway when the young man and woman escaped into the stairwell.

"Your second mistake was allowing my father and my best friend to get away." Peter was gambling that they were still safe in the storeroom, and that Gorev knew nothing of their whereabouts.

"And your third mistake was murdering my friend."

Gorev's demeanor was stern, but he remained silent.

"I have you at a distinct disadvantage. You need me alive."

"True, I've been ordered to deliver you for interrogation." He paused to choose his words carefully before continuing. "But--do you know how many times I can shoot you and still leave you sufficiently alive for interrogation?"

"Something tells me I'm about to learn," Peter mumbled.

Gorev raised his rifle.

"Get down!" Peter immediately recognized the voice and threw himself to the floor. An instant later he was greeted by the roar of automatic fire as Gary leveled the machine gun and fired a long burst. Two guards to the left of Gorev were killed immediately. Gorev and the remaining guards dove around the corner, out of the line of fire.

Wasting no time, Peter held one of the chemical grenades in his hand and lit the fuse before throwing it where Gorev had stood only moments earlier. The glass sphere shattered, the burning fuse igniting the flammable liquid. He threw a second one at the same spot for good measure. Within seconds a sickening odor drifted to Peter. He forced back the urge to vomit.

Picking up the rifle, he stood and ran to Gary, who was holding the door open at the stairwell. “Let’s go!” Gary urged.

“Where’s Dad?” Peter said upon reaching his friend.

“Left him in the storeroom when I came looking for you. I heard two shots. Is Dmitri dead?”

Peter nodded. “Gorev murdered him.”

The door closed behind them as they descended two steps at a time. On the ground floor, they ran to the storeroom. Opening the door, Peter greeted his father. “Dad, we have to go.”

“Go where?” Ian asked.

“Back to the roof. I think that’s where we’ll be rescued.”

CHAPTER 25

Minsk

JIM WAS LISTENING TO THE PILOT'S update over the intercom. "Russian Flankers challenged our aircraft as they crossed into Belarussian airspace. We have to expect there will be more, and probably robust SAM and AA defenses in Minsk."

"Are you picking up any hostile radar?" Jim asked.

"Nothing at the moment. Assuming we're not shot out of the sky, we'll get you to the coordinates for your jump. Have your team plug into the nav computer and upload our GPS coordinates. With most of our fuel burned, I'll see if we can gain another 1,000 feet."

The SGIT team each wore a powerful navigational computer strapped to their wrist. By uploading their present position, the computer would have a precise starting point from which to calculate their descent to the landing point. A simple touch screen interface and four-color display made the navigational device easy to manipulate, even with gloved hands. The computer would plot a glide path ending at the roof of the chemistry building on the BSU campus, constantly updating for prevailing wind, glide speed, altitude, and other factors.

Each team member simply flew his parachute by pulling cords attached to each end of the canopy, adjusting the form of the air-foil-shaped parachute and, thus, the glide path.

Ten minutes later the interior lights of the cavernous Combat King were extinguished, replaced with a dim red glow. The pilot's voice sounded in Jim's headset. "Secure satellite com, says it's urgent."

"It better, be," Jim complained. "Put it through."

"Sir, it's Lacey."

"This better be important Lieutenant, I've got work to do."

"It is sir. The smallpox virus is definitely ours. Identical to a sample that went missing from the CDC and is presumed to have been sold to a Russian agent."

"Are you certain this is not some stupid scheme concocted by the CIA?"

"No, sir. I've checked my contacts in the Agency. They understand fully that bioweapons is a line not to be crossed."

"You better be right, Lieutenant."

"I'd stake my career on it, sir."

"Good, you already have. We'll get physical evidence, if there is any."

"Roger, sir. Good luck."

Commander Nicolaou led the men of Alpha Team to the open loading ramp at the tail of the aircraft. A cold wind whipped and swirled through the open cabin. With goggles over their eyes and weapons hanging from straps in front of their legs, the six warriors leapt into the black void nearly seven miles above and 20 miles west of the BSU campus.

While still in free fall, seconds before his chute opened, Jim saw four bright flashes streak across the ebony sky.

Sacrificing silence for speed, the trio ran to the stairwell clutching their odd assortment of homemade weapons and modern firearms. Peter let the door swing close behind them. They continued their rapid pace ascending the stairs to the roof.

Emerging into the cool pre-dawn air, Professor Savage sat beside the sturdy steel door with his back to the wall. He was breathing deeply, winded from the sprint.

Peter searched the flat roof for anything that could be used to barricade the door. All he found was a rusted length of one-inch pipe. He wedged one end against the door knob and the other into the hard surface of the roof. It was better than nothing, but he doubted it would keep a determined enemy at bay for long.

"Dmitri was a good man; he was my friend," Ian said.

"I know Dad. I'm sorry."

"He was married to his wife for 43 years. She died a few years ago, I think. Dmitri didn't speak of her much, but when he did I could hear in his voice how much he missed her."

Professor Savage leaned his head against the wall and closed his eyes. "It never ends, does it?" he asked, his voice low.

Gary was at the edge of the roof looking over the commons, machine gun resting on the short wall, ready for action. The only problem was he had just 15 rounds in the belt feeding the gun, enough for only two brief pulls of the trigger.

"What never ends?" Peter said, addressing his father's cryptic remark.

Ian opened his eyes and looked upon his son, wanting to drink in the innocence of youth. And yet innocence is not what he saw, and he knew that time had long passed. "The senseless killing of one another. It never ends. Governments the world over say it will. We all individually commit to it. And yet here we are. Killing, always killing."

Peter saw before him a withered shadow of the father he remembered. The spark of joy was extinguished from his eyes; hope for salvation absent in his heart. He was suddenly an old man, one who had completed his journey, his mission. And now, there was nothing more.

Peter shook his head. "I don't know. Maybe humans are just hardwired to destroy one another."

"We're a failed species," Ian said.

Peter had always looked up to his father. He was a strong figure and never tolerated poor behavior from Peter as a child. Yet Peter never questioned his father's love for him. As a teenager, Peter admired his accomplishments. Professor Ian Savage was well respected by his colleagues and had amounted an impressive record of scientific publications.

There was no mistaking the disappointment his father felt when Peter chose a career in business and product development rather than academic research—a disappointment that often gave rise to heated arguments. As so often happens, pride and stubbornness trumped logic and understanding. Since neither father nor son wanted to accept the validity of the other's path, preferring to think in terms of superior and inferior, a silent truce slowly developed, resulting in a wedge of indifference driven into their relationship.

It didn't help that Ian Savage was a professor of chemical engineering at Oregon State University and Peter opted to study chemistry at the University of Oregon. The two universities, the premier hard-science institutions in Oregon, were perpetual rivals.

With the passage of time, wisdom had eventually prevailed, and over the past several years Peter and Ian had regained the closeness that was absent ever since Peter had founded EJ Enterprises and embarked on a successful career developing magnetic impulse technology.

Seeing his father's shattered spirit, Peter decided he had one more reason to end Gorev's life.

A low woosh caught Peter's attention. It sounded like a

large bird of prey—perhaps an owl—had glided low and swiftly over the roof. As suddenly as the sound appeared, it was gone, leaving Peter to wonder if he had really heard the sound or just imagined it.

There was no reaction from Gary; he was motionless, vigilantly overlooking the commons, alert to new threats. Sensing something was wrong, Peter unlimbered the AK-74 rifle from his shoulder.

He turned slowly, straining his eyes while searching the deep shadows on the roof and beyond. He stopped when his eyes passed over the machine in the distance next to the far air intakes, and a chill ran down his neck and spine. He shivered, but not from the cool temperature.

Then Peter heard the woosh again, but it was louder than before. Abruptly, a dark figure dropped directly in front of him, followed a second later by another, and another. Soon, six wraiths were busily disconnecting their black parachutes and readying weapons. No words were spoken, each figure singularly focused on completing essential tasks with expediency. Although he couldn't make out the detailed movements, Peter had the clear impression they each knew exactly what to do.

Peter and Gary trained their weapons on the unrecognized figures who had literally dropped in. "Who are you?" Peter asked.

"Peter, it's Jim," a familiar voice came back.

Lowering his rifle, Peter exhaled silently and relaxed his muscles. "I'm glad you made it. We've been waiting for you guys to show up."

Jim strode up to his friend, only then did Peter discern the details. He was dressed in black fatigues and load harness, carrying black weapons, and donning night vision goggles. No doubt Jim and the rest of the team could see Peter, Gary, and Ian as clearly as if it were mid-day.

"Lieutenant Lacey briefed me on your conversations." As Jim spoke, the other five shadows dispersed with fluid grace to different strategic locations where they could see the park-like commons below as well as defend against enemy numbers who might attempt to storm their position on the roof.

"Show me this machine you described to Lacey."

"It's over there." Peter led the way, stooped over to reduce his profile in case anyone was looking. He stopped five feet away from the treacherous device, fearful of accidentally touching it.

"Magnum, what do you make of this?"

Sergeant Percival Dexter, call sign Magnum, was SGITs expert on booby traps and IEDs—improvised explosive devices. The suitcase device he was visually examining was totally foreign; he had never before encountered a suspected bioweapon.

Lacey's description was accurate: vent grill along the top edge and low on one side; lock, three buttons, and a small LCD display. Otherwise, the case looked very much like a hard-plastic packing case of the type used for tools, photographic equipment, scientific instruments, and other fragile goods.

Kneeling, Magnum leaned in close, almost touching the device. The latches were secured with padlocks, and there were no visible restraints to hold the case in place—just as Peter had reported to Lacey.

With few features to focus upon, Magnum was left with only the ventilation grills. He removed a small penlight from a sleeve pocket just below his shoulder before addressing Jim by his nom de guerre. "Boss Man, I need a look inside. Perhaps there's something I can see through the grills."

"Red lens?" Jim asked.

"Affirmative."

"Go ahead."

Clicking the light on, he first peered down through the ventilation grill on the top of the case. There was scant detail, only what appeared to be a plastic air duct, but he couldn't see beyond a bend in the white plastic. Next, he laid his head down and shined the red light inside the lower side vent, confirming his suspicions.

After a minute he raised up onto his knees and addressed Boss Man. "There's an air duct connected to the top vent. This one down on the side is the air intake. I was able to make out a large air blower and at least two complex circuit boards. My guess is that it's powered by an internal battery bank—"

Magnum's briefing was interrupted by the sharp staccato of bullets striking the metal air intake above their heads. It sounded like a woodpecker rapping its beak against metal flashing.

Everyone ducked as low as possible—everyone, that is, except Homer. More bullets ripped across the low wall at the edge of the roof, just below where Homer was sighting his Barrett rifle. A second later, he squeezed the trigger.

BOOM!

The M107 sniper rifle belched out its .50-caliber bullet. Less than a second later the machine gunner on a rooftop on the far side of the commons—about 1,200 feet away—lay dead, the large bullet having punched through the low cinderblock wall he was using as a protective shield, bullet and debris smashing a ragged hole through his chest.

The gunfire drew the attention of a half dozen NPA on the roof with the deceased machine gunner. They formed a skirmish line along the wall, firing back with automatic rifles and the machine gun. Bullets sizzled through the air over the roof of the chemistry building. Hunched over, Peter scampered back to his father, who remained sitting next to the roof access door. Professor Savage started to rise when he saw his son approaching.

"Stay down Dad!"

The elderly Savage eased back to his resting position,

overwhelmed by the firefight developing around him.

Homer was no stranger to being shot at. Ignoring the unseen bullets passing all around him, he spotted his targets and methodically aimed and fired. He was shooting through their cover, the cement-block wall barely slowing the .50 caliber bullets. Within a minute, all of the NPA soldiers were dead, but Homer knew better than to relax his vigilance.

"We're done here," Jim announced.

The team plus Gary, who had also remained on watch at the edge of the roof, quickly retreated back to the access door and formed up on their commander.

"Magnum, is there any way to disable that device before it's activated and spreads the virus?" Jim said.

"Assuming that's its function, which I can't confirm. I've never come across any device like this before."

"Can we open it for a better look?"

"Negative, sir. If it was that easy, the bad guys wouldn't have just set it there. They would have locked it down. The fact that they didn't strongly suggests that it's wired such that opening the case, or moving it, triggers an explosive charge. If Lieutenant Lacey is correct, and it is an aerosol dispersion machine, touching it will be very bad. The only way we're going to see inside is with a portable x-ray machine."

Jim knew there was no way they could get one in time. Maybe in a day or two, but by then it would, in all probability, be too late.

"There must be a way to disable or destroy it." Jim said.

"Negative. Any movement is likely to trigger the dispersion, and blowing it up will also disperse the virus spores." Magnum thought for a few seconds, then shook his head. "Even burning it is likely to trigger the internal explosive."

"There has to be something we can do?"

"I know how to disable it," Peter broke in.

CHAPTER 26

MINSK

"FRY ITS ELECTRONIC BRAIN." With all eyes on him, Peter announced his plan. It sounded simple enough, too simple.

"Easy enough if we have a powerful microwave beam," Gary added.

Jim rolled his eyes. "Can we get real? I need actionable options."

"Well, we can't move the case into a microwave oven," Gary explained. "So it has to be either a very high power non-directional microwave source, or a smaller and perhaps portable directional transmitter."

"We might be able to rig up something with the radio, but we'd need a highly focused antenna," Bull said.

"Maybe they have something in the physics department." Gary suggested, encouraged that Jim was considering his suggestion.

"No, we don't have time to conduct a search," Jim concluded. "Peter, is there another way?"

Peter rubbed his chin and glanced at his father, still sitting quietly with vacant eyes observing the conversation. "Maybe, but it's risky."

"Hell, doing nothing is risky," Jim said.

"Okay. Do you have any C4?"

"Never leave home without it," Magnum answered. "But as I already explained, we can't blow up the case."

"I didn't say anything about blowing it up."

"What then?" Jim's patience was wearing thin.

"An EMP bomb—high-energy electromagnetic pulse."

"Oh, that is totally awesome!" Gary exclaimed with a grin. "Yeah, that'll roast every microchip and transistor on those circuit boards in a microsecond."

Jim was skeptical. "What do you think, Bull?"

Bull was their communications and computer expert. "Two concerns: Does it work and what is the collateral damage. It could easily take out all our electronic gear, including radios."

"It would leave us cutoff," Jim said.

"Look, an EMP is nothing more than an intense electromagnetic pulse," Peter rejoined. In the darkness he couldn't see Jim's expression, but still he sensed the Commander's doubt.

Peter met Jim's stare. "Electromagnetics is what I do. It's the basis for my Mk-9 magnetic impulse gun. The fundamentals here are no different; we're just going to ramp up the power a few orders of magnitude."

Jim considered his options and arrived at no other possibilities. "What do you need?" he finally asked.

"A piece of pipe, some wire, C4, and a detonator. And a DC power supply. Oh, and a Leatherman or Gerber multitool—screwdriver, wire cutter, knife, and pliers."

"Is that all?" Magnum asked.

Peter brushed off the comment. "I know where to get the copper wire and a high-power rectifier. We can tap in to the AC electrical power supplying one of those exhaust blowers," Peter pointed to the line of ventilation stacks along the roof. They were the exhaust ducts that carried contaminated air from the laboratory fume hoods out of the building.

"What about the pipe?" Gary asked.

"There's some copper drain pipe in the storeroom, and a hacksaw."

"Tell me how much you need. I'll get it while you go after the power supply and wire."

Since Peter and Gary knew the location of the storeroom and the SGIT soldiers did not, Gary's suggestion made a certain amount of sense.

"Jim, can you send one of your men with Gary? I need about six to ten inches of pipe. The copper drainpipe is perfect. Gary knows the way."

"Iceberg, you're with Gary. You shield him with your life, like he was President Taylor himself. Understood?"

"Affirmative, sir."

"I'll take Dad with me," Peter said. "I know you need every man you have to free the hostages."

"I don't like your plan." Before Peter could answer he was issuing a new order. "Ghost, you will escort Peter and Professor Savage."

"No! I've seen what Gorev and his soldiers can do. They exterminated a Special Forces team and a half dozen civilians. You have to hit them hard and fast, or they'll kill everyone! You need every man in your team."

Professor Savage had been leaning forward while his son was speaking, and now he had risen to one knee. "He's right, Jim. You have to stop Gorev."

"Besides," Peter added, "while you're drawing their attention there won't be any NPA guards to get in our way."

Reluctantly, Jim agreed. Magnum presented Iceberg with a timer detonator and a one-pound block of C4. "When you're ready," Magnum instructed Peter, "Iceberg will help place the explosives and set the detonator. Give yourselves plenty of distance from the blast. A pound of C4, if you use all of it, will make a big bang. If it were me, I'd be inside the stairwell and down at least one floor."

Gary tapped Peter on the shoulder, and they stepped back away from the others. "I hope you know what you're doing, because I have no experience with EMP weapons."

"Well, that makes two of us," Peter admitted. "But I did read some instructions in a paper published by Los Alamos National Lab."

CHAPTER 27

Minsk

EXTREMELY CONFIDENT, THE TWO Russian pilots, Sergei and Alexander, vectored their Su-27 Flanker fighters toward the one radar blip thought to be an American B-1 bomber. Russian air defense systems along the western edge of the Russian Federation had been tracking the inbound American warplanes from the time they entered Polish airspace. Those powerful land-based radar tracking and computing systems had established data connections to the Flankers, and were presently directing the fighters to their prey.

Already anticipating the destruction of the strategic bomber, Alexander and Sergei, who had been inseparable since childhood and throughout their 10 years of service in the Russian air force, had developed what they believed to be a fail-proof plan of attack. They knew of the electronic jamming capability of the B-1 aircraft. Still, they would test the defensive systems of the American warplane with radar-guided and infrared-guided missiles. If that failed, they would use their 30mm guns to shoot down the defenseless bomber. They both knew it was destined to be a glorious day for The Russian Air

Force and the two pilots.

"Hammer Flight, Golden Eye. Be advised, two Flankers closing. Twelve o'clock, 15,000 feet. Fifty miles and closing fast."

"Roger," Major Doyle replied. "Nate, two bogies approaching dead ahead and at 15."

Nate adjusted his suite of defensive measures, looking for radiation from the attack aircraft. So far his scope was blank, no emissions originating from other aircraft.

"Nothing yet, Major."

"Keep looking. There out there. They'll have to turn on their radar to get a firing solution to upload to their missiles."

"They could attack with heat seekers," suggested co-pilot Captain Bill Harrison.

Doyle had already considered this possibility. "No, I don't think so. They'd have to come around and approach from our six to get good tone, and they know we can outrun them."

"Can't kill what you can't catch," Captain Harrison said in agreement. The fighters would have a poor shot approaching from the front. Training doctrine was to attack from the rear so the heat-seeking anti-aircraft missile could lock onto the super-heated engine exhaust emanating from the back of the target. With the B-1 already flying at supersonic speed, by the time the Flankers passed and turned to approach, they would never get within engagement range of Hammer and Anvil Flights.

"Bingo!" Nate announced. His scope suddenly showed emissions originating from in front of the Bones, growing exponentially in intensity as the aircraft approached each other at two times the speed of sound.

"We're being painted sir."

"Jam it."

Nate had already identified the frequency of incoming radiation and matched it with a high-intensity source from the Bone, essentially blinding the Russian radar.

"They're switching frequency Major."

"Stay on it; don't let them get a lock."

"Roger. Adjusting frequency, ejecting chaff."

Golden Eye was monitoring everything. With the Flankers within range, Colonel Horn responded without mercy. "Order Guardian to splash those Russian fighters."

The Raptors did not need to break formation since the Flankers were approaching directly. Guardian One and Guardian Two received the data link from Golden Eye. The flankers were now within 28 miles, well inside the kill zone for the radar-guided Slammer missiles carried by the Raptors.

"Guardian One, have tone on Bogy One."

"Guardian Two, lock on Bogy Two."

The Raptor pilots launched their weapons at the same time to minimize the reaction time available to the Russian pilots. Although the closing speed was close to Mach 5, the missiles would suffer from reduced maneuverability since they were attacking head-on.

Inside the Su-27 aircraft, the overly confident pilots were stunned to hear their threat-warning receivers go off with a screeching tone.

"What? That's impossible," Alexander said in confusion.

The pilots separated, Sergei pulling up while Alexander pushed the stick forward, forcing his plane into a steep dive. In the partial weightlessness, his body rose against the restraining strap and blood pulsed into his head.

They had 20 seconds to live.

As Alexander's fighter lost altitude, the missile retained its electronic lock and changed course, once again approaching the Russian aircraft. Alexander looked through his canopy and for a briefest of moments saw the white plume from the AIM-120 missile.

It was coming directly for him.

He pushed the stick to the left, and then to the right, but at only 2,000 feet he was essentially playing a two dimensional game. To point his aircraft upwards would cost him speed and shorten the distance to the missile.

Alexander ejected chaff bundles, and continued to violently rock his aircraft from side to side. As the threat-warning tone increased in pitch, he knew he was going to die.

When the missile warhead exploded, it was directly over the cockpit. Alexander's dreams of glory ended in a brilliant white flash that shredded his body as well as his aircraft.

Sergei fared no better. The incoming missile would not be fooled by the relatively motionless chaff bundles, and the powerful engines of the Sukhoi were no match for the nimble missile traveling at Mach 4.

The slammer detonated beneath the middle of the fighter, destroying the engines and causing both wings to break off. Sergei had no time to eject before the ensuing fireball and shower of metal debris ripped through the cockpit.

"Golden Eye to Hammer, do you copy?"

"Loud and clear Golden Eye. What's the update?" Replied Doyle.

"The Falcons have made two circles over the airport without drawing any radar or AA fire. Colonel Horn isn't buying it. Thinks the militia is holding back until your flight is within engagement range."

Doyle glanced at Bill Harrison, the message clear. "Understood, Golden Eye. What about the Raptors?"

"Guardian flight will stay on station providing a defensive cap. We're showing a couple dozen Russian aircraft, fighters, circling on their side of the border. Looks like they parked a gas station up there as well to keep the birds in the air for at least several hours. The Colonel thinks they may throw more pilots into the fight. If so, Guardian will engage them."

Major Doyle shook her head. "They don't have enough ordinance left to take on two dozen Sukhois or MIGs. Fuel is probably questionable, too."

The radio was silent for several seconds, suggesting to Doyle that another important conversation was taking place onboard Golden Eye. Then the airman came back. "Uh, roger that Major. Colonel Horn says you are to follow the plan. The Raptors can keep the enemy engaged long enough for you to finish the job and then get the hell out of Dodge. That's a direct quote from the Colonel."

Bill Harrison, who also had complete access to the communications with Golden Eye, smiled, imagining Colonel Horn instructing the airman to relay his blunt message.

"And the Wild Weasels?" Major Doyle asked.

"Negative. The Falcon's mission is to continue northwest." The crews of the two Bones had been briefed in detail on their job in this choreographed mission, but they did not know all the pieces in play. The Falcons were to clear a path from Minsk to the city of Vilnius in Lithuania. Just as the Bones would depart in this direction, the Marines would be flying in from a staging base in Vilnius.

"Five minutes to target, Major," Harrison said.

"Roger that. Jonesy, how we doing?" Captain Kent Jones—Jonesy as he was known by his flight crew—was the Offensive Systems Officer. His primary responsibility on this mission was to lay down their ordinance on selected targets at the Minsk International Airport. The DSO, Nate McKinley, was searching for ground-based targeting and attack radar in the vicinity of the airport.

"All systems are go. I've got green from left to right," answered Jonesy.

"Anvil, this is Hammer, copy?" Major Doyle broke radio silence knowing that she was revealing her flight was two aircraft, not the single bomber as it almost certainly appeared to the Russian radar operators hundreds of miles away.

"Copy Hammer," came the reply from Anvil Flight in a pronounced Southern drawl.

"We'll fly in low and fast on the first pass, just like we briefed. Once radar are located, I'll circle back at 10,000, weapons hot. You'll follow me but keep some distance in case we need to maneuver."

"Roger. Good huntin' Major."

Dominated by a futuristic terminal made of stainless steel panels and large, angled windows of tinted glass, the National Airport at Minsk was beautiful. The four-story terminal curved gracefully around the front street-level approach, the center of the terminal dominated by a tower capped with a bi-level octagonal structure, oddly reminiscent of a giant steel mushroom.

Screaming across the flat ground at close to 14 miles per minute, the two B-1 aircraft passed over Minsk Airport at 200 feet elevation. The double sonic booms shattered the windows in the gleaming terminal. NPA soldiers who had the misfortune to be outside clasped hands to their ears, but too late for many to avoid damage to their eardrums.

Scattered around the single long runway were six mobile anti-aircraft missile launchers. These systems had been hiding in the dense forest surrounding the runway, but with the bombers approaching, the militia commander, who understood the importance of holding the airport, ordered them into the open where they would have unobstructed clearance.

Major Doyle started her turn immediately after passing over the airport. At the same time, she bled off about two-thirds of the Bone's speed, climbing to 10,000 feet.

The DSO's console lit up with red and yellow lights as

warning buzzers sounded the alarm.

"Targeting radar all over down there, Major," Nate announced. "Transferring target coordinates to OSO."

"Clear to engage at will, Jonesy," Major Doyle said.

Jonesy flipped a switch that opened the bay door and selected weapons by using a stylus on the multi-color touch screen menu. Next, he used the stylus to press a box commanding the weapons system computer to accept all targets provided by the DSO. A red "fire" button illuminated, and Jonesy depressed it. From beneath the fuselage, a rotary missile launcher dropped a HARM missile, its engine igniting as soon the slender missile cleared the underside of the bomber, and it streaked toward the target. The launcher rotated and a second missile was fired. And so it went until eight missiles had been launched in less than ten seconds.

The first HARM missile was fired from a range of about five miles. It followed the radar beacon of the designated missile launcher and detonated on the target eight seconds after launch. Within seconds—less time than it took the militia commander to realize he was under attack—all of the tracking and attack radar systems were destroyed.

With the major threats eliminated, Hammer flight and Anvil flight proceeded to the second priority: neutralize all heavy weapons and fortified positions.

"Jonesy, how's the Sniper Pod working?"

The Sniper Advanced Targeting Pod was a recent add-on to the two Bones, having not yet been adopted across the fleet. Lockheed Martin, maker of the Sniper Pod, successfully lobbied the Air Force to trial the targeting and reconnaissance system to enhance the close air support function of the B-1 Lancer.

Captain Jones checked his panel, quickly running through the internal diagnostics. "HARM system offline. Sniper pod coming online now. FLIR functional. CCD-TV functional.

Laser functional. Bringing up visual imaging now."

"I want a wide angle scan for heat sources," Doyle ordered.

"Going to split screen." The infrared lens would pick up the heat given off by objects and people. Against a cooler background, engines and other machinery appeared white on the monitor. Jonesy panned the camera systematically, looking first near buildings—the passenger terminal and the airplane maintenance hangers—and then along the runway, taxi ways, and finally along the tree line.

"Picking up lots of heat signatures, Major. Confirming with visual. We've got tanks and armored personnel carriers. Also a mix of trucks. Can't determine if they are weapon platforms or transport. If the militia didn't get these heavy weapons from Russia, then they've got an amazing surplus military industry in this country."

"Are they stationary?" Doyle asked.

"Negative. The tanks and APCs are headed for the tree line, probably seeking cover—"

"Tracking radar, Major!" Nate said, his voice conveying urgency.

"They have a lock. Now second band. Missile is launching!"

Doyle pushed the stick hard right at the same time Harrison moved the throttles to full power. The four engines jumped to life, accelerating the Bone forward.

"Anvil, this is Hammer. Missile launch, evasive maneuvers. Get out of here!"

There was no reply from Anvil, and Major Doyle assumed the crew were necessarily very busy.

"Nate, jam that emission! Jonesy, take out that radar!"

Nate was working his panel, ejecting chaff and trying to swamp out the reflected signal from his aircraft. He wasn't having much luck, as the missile guidance system was randomly switching homing frequency.

The threat warning receiver was wailing. "Twenty seconds to impact!" Nate announced.

"Jonesy, this would be a good time to kill that radar," Doyle said.

"Working on it." Jonesy was frantically bringing the HARM system back on line.

"Got a start-up fault, initiating start sequence again."

"Fifteen seconds."

Doyle put the Bone into a tight downward turn, using gravity to aid the engines and accelerate her aircraft. The airframe shuttered as it approached the speed of sound. Suddenly, the shaking subsided as the craft became supersonic.

"Still gaining, ejecting more chaff. I can't hold a jam, the seeker is constantly changing frequency!"

"Weapons system online... locking source... HARM missile launched!"

"Major, level flight course bearing one-eight-one, maximum throttle," Nate said. He knew that they simply had to put as much distance as possible between their airplane and the incoming missile. It was a race, and if the HARM missile didn't destroy the radar guidance system on the launcher first, they were going to be hit.

Bill Harrison tried to push the throttles farther forward, but they were already against the stops, had been since the first warning of the missile launch. Major Doyle gripped the stick firmly, holding it steady, avoiding any small movement that would bleed energy and speed away from her aircraft.

"Ten seconds..."

Other than the roar of the engines, no other sound was present.

"Five seconds... ejecting chaff."

Two seconds passed. "Talk to me Nate," Doyle said.

Several seconds passed before he answered. "Lock

terminated. Missile fell away and detonated."

"That was too close," Bill Harrison said.

Major Doyle was on the radio. "Anvil, this is Hammer. Missile destroyed. Status?"

Her brows pinched together. Only static came back in her earphones.

"Anvil, this is Hammer. Report."

Again, only static. Then the radio blared.

"Hammer, this is Golden Eye, do you copy?"

"Roger Golden Eye. Hammer flight returning to station. That was tight."

A pause spoke volumes, before the voice of the airman returned. "Hammer. Anvil was hit. Four beacons active, but the Bone was lost."

Major Doyle could only hope that all four crewmembers of Anvil flight were safe. The fact that their beacons activated indicated they had all ejected.

"Understood Golden Eye. Hammer is returning to station to complete secondary priorities."

"Hammer, this is Colonel Horn. I want your aircraft at 30. No more chances with short-range air defenses."

"Roger sir. Hammer out."

Doyle turned to follow a direct course back to the Minsk National Airport, climbing to 30,000 feet. "Reduce throttles to half power."

Bill pulled back on the throttles, and as the Bone slowed his body pushing against the shoulder straps.

"Jonesy, Nate. We lost Anvil. Four good ejects."

The intercom was silent in response.

Sensing their concern, their fear, Doyle added, "Nothing to worry about. They'll be picked up and having cocktails before we finish the debrief."

"We're going back?" Jonesy asked, but he knew the answer

already, he felt the aircraft turning and climbing, and slowing.

"We'll complete the mission. Keep that HARM pod on line, just in case."

Major Doyle considered her plan and then a few seconds later she was issuing new orders. "Nate, you take over the HARM system. If you even think you detect a radar emission, you fire on it, understood?"

"You got it Major," Nate said. The DSO and OSO formally shared different functions, but their panels were interchangeable, one of the features designed into the B-1 to increase survivability in combat. And the DSO and OSO were extensively cross trained.

"Jonesy, get on the Sniper Pod. Locate those heat signatures, confirm with visual if you can. Regardless, I want a prioritized target list. Tanks and AA guns first, then APCs, lastly any trucks or vehicles with an engine.

"We'll circle above the airfield and use some of Uncle Sam's finest GBU-53s."

Jonesy and Nate both smiled at that. It was time for some payback, and a 250-pound, laser-guided bomb would bring a load of payback, more than enough to shatter even the heaviest battle tank.

CHAPTER 28

Minsk

"WE'RE SPLITING INTO TWO squads and will descend the stairwells simultaneously." Jim was pointing to Peter. "You, Gary, and the Professor will follow my team down." If there were any trip wires, he knew his men would see them.

"We've been up and down this staircase a couple times without any problems. If there were booby traps, wouldn't we have been blown up by now?"

"General Gorev knows we're here. If it were me, I'd put some grenades or mines at all the access points. He knows we have to come down to rescue the hostages."

"No arguments from me," Gary said.

Jim entered the stairwell, followed by Peter and Professor Savage. Iceberg was already glued to Gary, and Ghost took up the rear. Bull led Magnum and Homer across the roof to the west access door, where they disappeared from sight.

"Single file, hug the wall," Jim instructed.

They worked their way down, Jim shouldering his H&K 416 assault rifle, aiming wherever his eyes looked. They made it to the second floor without any delays. Peter, with his father right behind him, cracked open the door. The hallway was clear.

Peter hesitated and turned to Gary. "Do me a favor and get my sprayer. I left it in the storeroom."

"You got it buddy."

Peter looked at his father. "Ready?"

Ian Savage nodded. Silently, they dashed to the chemical storeroom and ducked inside.

Colonel Horn popped another antacid. He was vaguely aware that the airmen and women under his command had running side bets as to whether the Colonel chewed the fruit-flavored, chalky tablets because he liked the taste or to quell an overactive digestive system that did not respond well to stress. He leaned closer, taking in the detail on the color monitor, paying special attention to the distance marker.

"Notify Hammer and move Guardian flight into a blocking position in case those Russian fighters cross over the border." Then he turned to the adjacent airman. "Where's the nearest tanker?"

Referring to her monitor, which looked a lot like a civilian aviation control screen, she pointed to a triangle resting over a number. "We have a KC-46 here, sir, over eastern Poland."

"Position it over Vilnius; we're about to have a lot of aircraft in need of more gas."

Colonel Horn returned his attention to the area display. The airman was still conversing with Hammer flight.

"Roger that, Major. Guardian is moving to a blocking position."

Colonel Horn stood back and allowed his crew to do their jobs, preferring to watch and think through all options.

Jonesy programed a string of 41 tanks, AA guns, APCs, and

other vehicles into the targeting computer system, prioritizing as ordered by Major Doyle. "Ready when you are Major," Jonesy announced through the intercom.

"Nate, any hostile emissions?" Major Doyle wanted one last confirmation before committing her aircraft to a circling pattern above the airfield.

"Uh, negative, Major. Clear and quiet. Must have got all the radar systems."

"I wouldn't count on it. Bill, be ready with the engines. If we are targeted again we're gonna go to max power and get out of here."

"Roger that," Bill replied, edging his left hand toward the throttles.

"Okay Jonesy, this will be a text-book run. Since you have all the targets uploaded, this should go fast. Ready?"

"You're damn right I am, Major. Time for payback."

"Clear to release weapons. Let's bust some armor."

As Jonesy worked through his target list, releasing bomb after bomb, Major Doyle maintained constant flight speed and altitude. In a matter of minutes, all 41 of the guided bombs had been released.

Doyle continued circling above the airport, allowing time for Jonesy to complete a bomb damage assessment, or BDA, using both the infrared and visual spectra from the Sniper Pod. Even from 30,000 feet he could easily see direct hits as well as craters indicating a close hit. All of the tanks and mobile AA guns had received direct hits as they had no time to recover from the threat and attempt to move to a new location. The same was mostly true for the armored personnel carriers, although five were incapacitated by near hits. Whether the 250-pound bombs simply missed the mark or the APCs tried to escape, Jonesy would never know—and it didn't matter.

"BDA complete Major," Jonesy said. "All eight tanks destroyed. Three AA guns destroyed. Five APCs destroyed—

direct hits—another five are stationary, probable damage from close proximity detonation. Can't be certain of operational status. Twenty heavy and light trucks destroyed. Looks like three fueling tankers are on fire."

"Load up the coordinates for the five damaged APC, we'll hit 'em again."

"Roger," replied Jonesy, already at work.

"Are you picking up any stationary air defensives? AA guns?" Doyle asked curiously.

"Negative. Four sandbag bunkers—if you can call them that—on both sides of the runway. But no guns visible."

"They could have technicals with mounted dual or quad AAs inside the hangars," Bill Harrison commented.

Pickups with heavy machineguns mounted to the beds, so-called technical vehicles, seemed to be ubiquitous throughout the world's hot-spots. They were relatively cheap to make and anyone could drive them. Plus, they were fast and maneuverable.

Doyle nodded, understanding Bill's warning.

"Major, I have the five APCs," Jonesy said. "Coordinates uploaded..." He stopped, not finishing his sentence.

"Talk to me Jonesy," Doyle said.

"I'm showing a tug pulling a large aircraft out of one of the hangars. Only the aircraft nose is visible, can't offer positive ID yet."

At this point it didn't matter to Major Doyle. "Take it out while it's still attached to the tug and crawling. Push that aircraft to top priority. Designate two 53s."

"The 'ol double tap. Yes Ma'am."

It only required a handful of seconds for Jonesy to upload the coordinates where the nose of the aircraft was clearing the hangar roof. He figured he had at least 60 seconds to release the two-guided bombs before the unidentified aircraft was safely clear of the hangar entrance. Against an unarmored aluminum-skinned plane, even close would be good enough.

"Request permission to release ordinance."

"Granted. Let's finish this mission."

Just like he had done hundreds of times before in training exercises, and a handful of times in actual combat, Jonesy released the guided GBU-53 250-pound, iron-clad bombs sequentially. As the Bone continued to circle, he completed the BDA and reported to Major Doyle.

"Direct hit on all five APCs. The aircraft, whatever it was, is history. Looks like the pair of 53s hit the forward section of fuselage at the leading edge of the wing root. The fuel is on fire and will take out the hanger as well as everything inside."

"Good shooting Jonesy. Nate, any activity on your scope?"

"Negative, Major. If they have any functional radar down there, they're not turning them on."

"Understood. Bill, give me a heading for Vilnius. We'll top up the tanks on the way home."

Immediately upon entering the west stairwell, Bull's squad smelled the foul stench of corpses. The smell of guts—feces and urine—mixed with blood and warm meat assaulted their noses. It was unpleasant, but not yet sickening—that threshold would be passed within a few hours as the bacterial decay of the bodies accelerated.

The air was heavy with death. At the second floor landing they saw the dead Delta operators in the dim light from the exit sign. In Bull's mind, there was no reason to check for vital signs. There was no sound, no moaning, no call for help. And the bodies were all twisted and bent in unnatural positions, the result of the blast and hundreds of steel rods ripping through their limbs and torsos. There was also the blood and gore.

He held up his fist and the men stopped in their tracks, eyes alert and searching.

"There, in the corner," Bull said as he pointed to the olive drab rectangle at the base of the stairs, ten feet below. "Magnum…"

As their IED specialist moved forward to assess the danger, carefully stepping around the bodies, Bull activated his throat mic. "Boss Man. Be advised. We have a probable IED inside the stairwell at the ground floor. Also, this is where six Deltas bought it."

"We'll recover the bodies later."

"Affirmative."

"What are you dealing with?"

"Looks like a mine, AP. Magnum has the trip wire and is disarming it." Bull imagined that another antipersonnel mine, probably similar to the one they were now neutralizing, had killed the Delta operators.

"Roger. Advance on the lobby and hold until Ghost and I are in position."

Jim assumed he would also find an antipersonnel mine or grenades connected to a trip wire on the ground floor, and he was not disappointed. Just as Bull described, there was a military-green rectangular slab on the concrete floor in the corner. Jim's eyes moved from the AP mine across the stairs to a secure fastening point, in this case the railing post, and he saw the thin, high-strength-steel trip wire. It was only six inches or so above the steps, easily missed by someone not alert to the danger.

While Ghost kept a vigilant watch for any threat from the upper floors, Jim gently released the trip wire from the handrail post. Then he removed the detonator from the rectangular plastic-covered mine. He recognized it as a MON-50 antipersonnel mine, essentially a copy of the American

Claymore AP mine. Extremely lethal.

Jim shoved the detonator and trip wire into a cargo pocket. He slipped off his rucksack and placed the mine inside, saving it for later use.

Opening the ground floor door just a crack, Jim peered into the hallway. No soldiers were visible. He pulled the door closed. In barely a whisper, he said, "Coast is clear. Stay together and move sharp. Let's go."

The four men dashed into the hallway. Gary was still cradling the machine gun, the short ammunition belt hanging to the side of the weapon.

Jim and Ghost pushed ahead to the lobby. Iceberg motioned for Gary to lead the way to the storeroom. The pair split off and went in the opposite direction.

The blood-stained floor marked the spot, a grim reminder in case Gary had forgotten.

Gary opened the door and ducked inside. Iceberg took one quick look around to make certain no one was watching, then he, too, entered and closed the door without a sound.

"Tell me what to do," Iceberg said.

"Just watch the door and make sure no one tries to enter. Here," Gary offered the master key he was still carrying, "lock the door."

Gary took the rusty hacksaw from the tool chest and set to work cutting the copper drainpipe beneath the utility sink. Even though the blade was old and well-used, it was still reasonably sharp and made short work of the relatively soft copper pipe. With a ten-inch length of pipe in hand, Gary stood. "We're done here."

With Jim and Ghost at the junction of the east hallway and the lobby, and Bull, Magnum, and Homer at the west hallway adjoining the lobby, both squads saw the battle zone, imagining the struggle that had transpired hours earlier. The shattered kiosk was clearly the epicenter of combat.

Ahead, to the right of the expansive lobby and still out of sight, was the conference room where the hostages were believed to be. As soon as the two squads cleared the corner to enter the lobby, any guards stationed outside the conference room—and certainly there would be guards—would see them.

With weapons raised, each man aimed through the optical sight while keeping both eyes open to see everything transpiring in their field of vision. Jim ordered his squads forward. Hugging the wall, they advanced, steadily, silently.

Bull's squad saw them first. He fired one shot then quickly moved to the next guard, getting off a round before the guard knew what was happening. Homer was behind Bull, and he fired a second shot into each guard, ensuring they were out of the fight—permanently.

Even through closed doors, Major Leonov and his men recognized the sound of suppressed weapons being fired. "Inform the General we are under attack. Call in reinforcements," he ordered his radioman while a dozen NPA soldiers knelt behind sandbag barricades—hastily stacked following the first rescue attempt—weapons aimed at the two entry points, ready to let loose a wall of lead when the intruders burst through the doors.

Leonov mentally counted down the seconds. In his mind he saw the two outside guards killed, and the assault team cautiously approaching the doors. They would swiftly search for trip wires and, finding none, would prepare breaching charges to blast the doors open and stun the defenders. Yes, right about now…

He picked up the black box, pushed the toggle switch forward and then depressed the button. His efficient movements were rewarded with a deafening blast that rattled the walls and threated to breach the closed doors.

CHAPTER 29

MINSK

THE MINSK AIRPORT, ONCE A GLEAMING, modern hub of civilian air transportation, stank of burning diesel and rubber. Black smoke wafted over the terminal building, freely entering through dozens of shattered windows.

The NPA militiamen were stunned. Many were dead and even more were injured. Almost to a man, they conveyed defeat. But not so the professional Russian soldiers who were better trained and prepared. They recognized this attack for what it was, and the greater danger that was soon to follow.

Vadim Zolnerowich, a career veteran with the rank of Colonel, was in charge of the Russian Spetsnaz unit. He had been in the control tower during the attack. Fortuitous, since the Americans had no intention of destroying the essential assets of the airport, including the control tower. They needed this port to be functional to swiftly bring in men and supplies.

Zolnerowich was on the radio, addressing the NPA commander. "Prepare your men for an invasion. Get the technicals out of the hangers and position them along the tree line on either side of the runway."

"But Colonel, our armor is destroyed, along with our missile batteries. We cannot defend this position. We must withdraw!"

"Listen to me, you coward. You will do as I have ordered, or I will personally hang you by your heels and cut your throat. This battle is not over! Soon the Americans will attempt to bring in troops, and we are going to defend this runway. Is that clear?"

The radio was silent for a moment, as if the NPA commander was thinking over his options. "Yes, sir."

NPA militia and Spetsnaz poured out of concealment. The four technicals, each with a dual-barrel 23mm antiaircraft gun mounted to the bed of the pickup, sped out of two hangers, racing down the runway and then veering off the tarmac at about the midpoint. They stopped just inside the trees, the vehicles pointed toward the gray runway, engines idling and ready to pull forward to fire upon the anticipated American aircraft.

Unseen to the defenders, a dozen Marine Ospreys and two Air Force AC-130W Stinger II gunships were approaching from the northwest. The Ospreys, each loaded with 18 combat Marine troops, were approaching low, just above the treetops, while the Stinger gunships were flying in at 25,000 feet, ready to provide a protective cap over the battlefield.

In theory, it was a strong plan, just about guaranteed to succeed. That is, provided the air defenses had truly been eliminated as reported by the crew of Hammer flight.

About a mile away and still out of sight, the massive propellers and engines of the Ospreys could be heard—a deep throbbing that intensified to a rumble and, finally, as the odd-looking aircraft with huge propellers appear low on the horizon, an intense roar of engine and rushing air.

The transports came in three at a time, approaching the

runway more like helicopters than fixed-wing aircraft; the twin tilt-rotors turning progressively, steadily rotating to vertical, allowing the transports to slow and hover before descending the final ten feet to the tarmac. With the engines still roaring and the huge propellers whipping up violently swirling air currents, the rear hatch opened. Even before the ramp door hit the hard surface the Marines were running out, two-by-two, fanning out to both sides as fast as possible. In less than a minute, 54 combat-ready Marines were on the ground.

With the troops clear of the Ospreys, the pilot of each transport revved the engines and rotated the tilt-rotors forward to accelerate for a short takeoff—there were six more planes to land, 108 more troops to unload.

Shouting to be heard over the screaming aircraft, Captain Diaz ordered his men to move toward the terminal building. They would use the burning hulks littering the open grass shoulders for cover as much as possible, but eventually they would run out of cover as they neared the three-story structure.

With the advance troops safely on the ground, and not encountering any resistance, the path was clear for the remaining transports to come in quickly. No sooner had the roar of the first three Ospreys diminished when the next wave of three aircraft came in to land. This was the moment Zolnerowich anticipated, when the Ospreys, filled with American soldiers, were easy targets. Maintaining a safe distance between aircraft, the transports lowered toward the runway.

"Fire!" Colonel Zolnerowich ordered over the radio. "Destroy those aircraft!"

At once the four technicals gunned forward from their camouflaged positions within the tree line, the sound of the truck engines unable to compete with the thunderous rumble from the turboprops. Even while they were driving forward the 23mm antiaircraft guns opened up on the approaching aircraft. Explosive projectiles tore into the Ospreys where they detonated, shrapnel ripping into wire harnesses, hydraulic lines, and men.

Caught in a murderous crossfire, the pilots gunned the engines attempting to reverse downward momentum and gain distance from the AA guns. As bullets slashed through engine cowlings, two of the three aircraft lost power and slammed into the runway, bursting into flames. The third transport continued to claw at the air, the crew desperately willing the Osprey to accelerate away from the threat. They made it another 500 feet before fuel leaks inside the fuselage caught fire.

As the conflagration spread throughout the cabin, men screamed in pain and terror, electrical wires burned through, and hydraulic pressure was all but gone. As the engines were starved for fuel and with multiple electrical malfunctions, the metal beast cratered into the grass strip beside the runway, engulfed in a fireball that mushroomed upward in the pale blue sky.

Witnessing the carnage through the pilot's windscreen, the lead Osprey in the last group of six, aborted the landing, banking away from the runway to wait at a safe distance.

Immediately Diaz was on the radio to coordinate the close air support while his platoon was shooting at the technicals.

"Bravo squad, Charlie squad! Into the tree line ASAP!" he ordered over the radio. Moments later mortar shells rained down, landing short of the Marines but adding to the deafening racket.

"Stinger One!" Diaz shouted into the radio. "You've got to take out those mortars—we've got no cover here!"

"That's a roger. Do you have a visual?" The pilot's voice came back calm, measured.

"Negative!" Surrounded by his three squads firing rifles and grenades at the technicals, it was nearly impossible for Diaz to hear. "My men are within 300 meters of the burning aircraft! Between the wreckage and the terminal along the edge of the runway!"

The two gunships dropped to 11,000 feet searching the terminal building and nearby hangars using the targeting camera in infrared mode. Warm bodies stood out as white silhouettes against a grey background.

"Ghost Rider, this is Stinger One. We're picking up some activity on the central portion of the terminal roof, looks like a mortar team. Preparing to fire."

"You have to clear that roof!"

"Roger," came the disembodied reply from Stinger One.

The captain of the gunship opted to deploy the 30mm automatic cannon rather than laser-guided missiles. As the cannon opened up, the black and white video on the targeting display showed white splashes obliterate the images of the soldiers manning the two mortars. It took several seconds for the heat and smoke to dissipate. All that remained were white stationary blobs that had once been living men.

"Target neutralized," announced Stinger One.

"Stay on it!" Diaz shouted. "If anything moves kill it! I have to get a platoon of Marines on that roof!"

"Roger, Ghost Rider. Advise position."

It was a fierce firefight and Diaz and his squads were not letting up. One technical was totally destroyed, a charred hulk of twisted metal, the spilt gasoline and rubber tires still burning fiercely. The other three were on the move, picking up speed. Muzzle flashes from the tree line marked at least a dozen infantry. If they had mortars, or other heavy weapons, Diaz knew his men would be in a world of hurt. Already there were scores of dead and wounded, and his corpsmen could only reach a few.

A high-pitched screech rose above the sounds of battle as

three white streaks reached down from the heavens, terminating at each of the technicals in a horrifying explosion—Hellfire missiles launched from Stinger Two.

Although the remaining Ospreys were not visible, Diaz was certain they were holding position only a few miles away. He needed to open up a safe landing zone, and fast.

"Stinger One! We need you to clear the trees for 400 meters both in front of and behind my position! Estimate 30 to 40 infantry. They have us locked down!"

"Confirm your position Ghost Rider."

"I've got four squads between the tarmac and the tree line, popping smoke now." Diaz nodded to the radioman, and he threw two smoke grenades.

From 11,000 feet Stinger One and Stinger Two saw the purple smoke cloud a few hundred meters from the burning wreckage, just like Ghost Rider had said.

"We've got a visual on purple," Stinger One said.

"Affirmative, you are cleared to fire."

There was a short pause, and then the pilot came back over the radio. "Uh, negative Ghost Rider. That haircut's a bit too close."

Diaz felt his anger rising. "Stinger One, this is Ghost Rider! Clear that tree line, now, goddammit! Now!"

"I say negative, Ghost Rider. We're at 11k and I can't guarantee those shells won't hit your men. I'm not going to be party to a blue-on-blue investigation."

"Then descend to a lower altitude if you have to! Hell, you're welcome to get right down here on the ground and bleed with my men! I don't care how you do it, you just get those guns shooting and clear the damn trees! Those transports can't come in until this LZ is cleared! Do you understand me?"

A volley of rounds stitched along the ground only feet away from Diaz. Two of his men weren't as lucky, the bullets ripping through their bodies.

Diaz could have sworn he heard a sigh over the radio, and then the voice of the pilot came back. "On your authority, Ghost Rider. This conversation is recorded, and for the record my objections have been clearly communicated."

"Affirmative, my authority, whatever! Just light up the tree line, goddammit, while I still have men left to carry out this mission!"

A second later the trees were racked by 30mm cannons from the two gunships. It was a devastatingly violent barrage, each automatic gun firing 200 rounds a minute, the explosive shells ripping branches from trees and raining searing metal fragments into the NPA and Russian soldiers. Then came the deeper and louder explosions from Hellfire guided missiles blasting apart the protective vegetation. A large oak tree, hit squarely by a missile, split in half while Diaz watched.

The barrage lasted two entire minutes—an eternity to those on the receiving end—and it was so intense that none of the combatants on the ground exchanged fire. Everyone was keeping their head down and seeking any protection available. For the Marines in the open, that meant becoming one with the Earth. For the enemy within the trees, the light foliage and undergrowth offered no resistance to the shells and missiles.

Another minute passed, this time in relative silence. Inside the gunships the crews prepared additional cases of 30mm ammunition, ready for another battle. The Marines raised their heads and took in their surroundings. There was no resistance.

"On your feet!" Diaz ordered. "Washington, you hold Delta squad here, you're providing security for the birds. Once they've unloaded rendezvous with Charlie squad. Everyone else, spread out—we have a terminal to liberate!"

Already medics were rushing to treat the wounded. The first step was a quick triage—mostly a superficial examination of obvious wounds—if they weren't life-threatening, the medics moved on. They would come back later to deal with the less-serious injuries and to collect the dead.

In the distance, Diaz saw three Ospreys approach and then hover over the terminal. Sinuous black threads dropped from the open rear hatch of each aircraft. No sooner had the lines fallen when Marines rappelled down the ropes onto the roof, and then the Ospreys quickly departed.

The final trio of transports hovered just above the runway under the watchful eye of Delta squad, discharged their human cargo, and then departed to a safe staging area miles away. There they would wait, until the airport was under U.S. control.

The statisticians would mark this day for its heavy losses, and the battle was far from over.

Three squads of Marines slid down the thick lines in rapid succession, landing solidly on both feet and then immediately taking up defensive positions around the roof. Bodies of the NPA mortar teams were scattered about the two sandbag bunkers, also destroyed. The Marines didn't waste time to determine if the mortars were functional or not. Rather, as they passed, a Marine dropped a thermite grenade down the gapping maw of each weapon.

"Ghost Rider, Reaper here, over?"

"Ghost Rider reads you, Reaper," answered Diaz.

"Reaper has secured the roof—will enter the top floor through three access doors and work our way down."

"Roger. See you on the ground floor. Ghost Rider out."

Reaper was relieved his platoon had taken the roof without resistance. But he was certain that would change once they entered the building.

CHAPTER 30

Minsk

INSIDE THE CHEMISTRY STOREROOM, Peter walked past the shelves of chemicals, his father following in silence. It was in the next room, the one where Dmitri had fabricated the hollow glass spheres, that Peter would find what he sought. "This way, Dad."

On the shelf were spools of insulted copper electrical wire, no doubt used in a range of physics experiments. Peter grabbed a coil of large gauge wire and handed it his father. He side-stepped to a cluster of gray boxes. He had glimpsed these earlier and was fairly certain they were electrical power supplies. Now, he needed to examine them more closely to find exactly what was required—a power inverter that would convert the alternating line current to direct current.

Peter handed the AK-74 rifle to his father, freeing both hands for the search. After a couple minutes, and rummaging through a half dozen power supplies, he found what he needed. "Eureka."

The supply was heavy and Peter needed both hands to slide it off the wooden self. "Take that file, too; we can use it to strip the varnish insulation from the wire," Peter motioned with his chin in the direction of the glassblowing table and a triangle file laying there, a common tool for cutting glass tubing. Ian picked it up and dropped it in his back pocket.

"Are you ready Dad?"

Professor Savage nodded. With the rifle firmly gripped in his right hand and holding the copper wire in his other, he appeared alert and determined again. Once more, he had a purpose; and his will to avenge Dmitri Kaspar gave him strength.

"Hold," Jim ordered, halting Bull's progress. Something didn't feel right.

"It's too easy," Jim mumbled, just loud enough to be heard across the squad net.

"What's the order, sir?" Bull said.

Before Jim could answer, the space was shattered by a tremendous explosion that ripped through the lobby. The pressure wave blasted fragments of broken glass out the front entrance, itself deadly shrapnel, while hundreds of steel balls swept through the lobby at waist height. Propelled forward by the explosive, the projectiles slammed into the wall and the kiosk with great force, shredding sandbags and splintering the remains of the kiosk.

Safely behind the corners of the east and west hallways, the SGIT team was unscathed.

That was close, Jim thought. "Bull, they were expecting a breaching assault on the lobby doors. New plan. Take your team out the front entrance. Now! Move it!"

Bull and his squad didn't question, they ran for the shattered glass entrance. Hopping through the windowless frames and quickly picking their way around civilian bodies, the rest of the order came through the ear buds.

"On my mark you're going to breach the exterior glass wall while Ghost and I draw their attention to the lobby doors."

Bull, Magnum, and Homer stayed close to the wall, trampling flowers and pushing through shrubbery, stopping just at the edge of the large glass window. The heavy draperies were still drawn, shielding the occupants from prying eyes.

"Det cord, ten feet," Bull said.

Magnum grabbed a spool of yellow cord from his rucksack and peeled off a sufficient length. Slicing through the cord with his knife, he handed it along with a detonator to Bull. With practiced efficiency, Bull placed the explosive rope in place, securing it with duct tape.

The team stepped away from the window, still pressing their bodies tight against the wall. There they waited, counting the seconds, anticipating the signal. They didn't wait long.

"Bull, ready?"

"Affirmative."

Jim and Ghost each tossed a grenade in front of the nearest door. At the same time, they dove behind the destroyed kiosk and ruined pile of sandbags, sand still trickling out of innumerable perforations.

The simultaneous detonation of the grenades blew the lobby doors inward. At the sound of the explosions Bull detonated the explosive cord, easily blasting through the window. Bull was through first, quickly yanking down a curtain panel. His squad wasted no time jumping through the opening, weapons searching for targets—and there were plenty.

The dozen NPA soldiers were largely exposed. They were expecting a frontal assault through the two lobby doors and were hunkered down behind the sandbag barricades when the grenades blasted the doors inward. Only the assault didn't materialize.

Instead, Bull's squad rushed in from behind the soldiers,

who had turned at the concussion of the breaching charge. Bull, Homer, and Magnum opened up.

A few militiamen managed to swing their rifles around and point them in the general direction of the SGIT assault team, firing without taking time to aim. Time they didn't have.

Bullets flew wildly, shattering the remainder of the windowpanes behind the draperies, the sound of breaking glass mingling with gunfire.

Major Leonov was in a corner of the room, and in the confusion of battle he darted for the open doorway, planning to use the massacre as a diversion for his escape. He halted abruptly in the doorway, Jim's rifle pointed at his face. Ghost was a step behind and to the right of Boss Man, aiming his AA12 automatic shotgun at the Major, the huge 12 gauge barrel looking more like a canon.

"Stop right there," Jim commanded in an even voice. "Drop your weapon."

Leonov did as ordered and raised his hands.

As quickly as the attack started, it was over. Bull, Magnum, and Homer checked the NPA soldiers for signs of life and, concluding there was no further danger, turned their attentions to the hostages.

The men and women were clustered in a corner of the conference room. The terror-stricken civilians watched in silence until Bull approached, rifle down and hand held up, palm facing the petrified people.

Breaking the silence, a woman asked, "You have come to rescue us?" Her English was almost flawless, with only a mild accent.

Bull quickly realized they had recognized the American flag on the shoulder of his uniform. "Yes, we're going to get all of you out of here."

A man pointed his finger at the officer standing in the

doorway, hands raised at gunpoint. "That is Major Leonov. He is Russian Spetsnaz."

"Really?" Bull turned his head. "Did you hear that Boss Man?"

"Sure did." Jim was looking his prisoner in the eyes, appraising his mettle. "So, Major Leonov. You're a long way from home."

"And you are?" Leonov said.

"None of your concern. Ghost, bind his hands."

As Ghost zip-tied the prisoner's hands behind his back, Bull completed the head count. "Fifteen, sir."

"Several of our colleagues were killed during the first attempted rescue," the man who pointed out Leonov explained.

"What do we do now?" Ghost asked.

"We need to get these people out of here to a more secure location."

"Roger that, sir."

"Where to, Boss Man?" Bull asked.

Jim removed a folded paper from his breast pocket, a floor plan for the chemistry building. "Here." He stabbed his finger at a location on the map representing a large room on the ground floor at the opposite end of the building.

"Not many exterior windows, corner access, should be defensible," Bull observed.

"We have company coming!" Homer shouted. He was facing toward the campus commons. Wearing his night vision goggles, the approaching enemy soldiers stood out easily against the landscaping.

"Come on people—time to go!" Jim said. The civilians rose and exited the room as a tight group, following Bull and Ghost down the hall to the far end of the building.

"How many?" Jim asked.

"Looks like 20, maybe 25."

With Jim in the lead, Magnum and Homer each grabbed Leonov by an arm, and together they trotted down the hall, close behind the civilians.

CHAPTER 31

Minsk

LEAVING THE WIDE RUNAWAY BEHIND, Captain Diaz led his men toward the terminal. The control tower rose above the center portion of the curved structure, providing an unobstructed view of the tarmac and taxi lanes. A half dozen commercial aircraft were parked at the gates, stranded where they had the misfortune of being when the airport was taken over by the NPA. Several more cargo aircraft were sitting on a large concrete pad several hundred meters from the terminal, including one Antonov An-225, the world's largest cargo plane. Behind that behemoth was the flaming wreckage of another plane and hangar.

Aside from two shallow grass-covered depressions to collect runoff water from the expansive paved surfaces, there would be no cover until they approached very close to the terminal. Then they would have tugs, baggage carts, and the landing wheels and low-slung engines of the parked aircraft to use as shields.

As they crested the lip of the first depression, the Marines came under fire, bullets grazing the ground and tumbling out of control upward. Immediately they fell to the grass, seeking out targets.

Mortar shells were exploding behind them, and Diaz was unsure —his men or the second wave of Marines who were still coming off the runway. Glancing over his shoulder, he saw more explosions well down the paved strip, and he had his answer. He turned his gaze back to the terminal in time to see a cluster of 30mm shells rain down on the suspected mortar position behind a tug close to the An-225.

Machinegun fire was still raking his position, keeping his squads locked down. At least the mortars were silenced. Diaz glassed the various equipment close to the building, trying to spot the machinegun crews. Then he saw it, a brief muzzle flash and a second later a dozen bullets tore up grass to his left, close enough he could hear the ricochets making a zinging sound.

"Behind the main landing gear of the aircraft at the gate, third from the right," Diaz said to Nolty, the Marine next to him. "Pass it along, concentrate your fire on that machinegun when I open up."

The combined rifle and automatic fire was intense, a continuous ear-splitting roar. After three seconds Diaz ordered, "Cease fire!" shouting to be heard.

"Let's go!" Diaz was up and running first, immediately followed by the rest of the platoon. He was halfway across the taxi lane, a long strip of concrete that paralleled the runway but was only about half the width, when a machinegun opened up on his men again. The bullets split the air, some finding the running Marines, most just passing by in a mini sonic wave.

On the concrete there was nowhere to hide from the murderous automatic fire. Then another machinegun joined in. Diaz knew they had no choice but to run toward the weapons and dive into the grassy depression as fast as possible. But given the distance they had already covered and carrying 100 to 120 pounds of gear, the Marines were reduced to moving at the pace of a jog.

The gunfire continued unabated, and more Marines went down. Diaz heard screams of pain over the ringing in his ears.

"Medic!" The call rang out again and again. "Medic!"

At the lip of the depression, Diaz dove forward and tumbled down the gentle slope, followed by his radioman. He turned onto his side in time to see Nolty and then another dozen men scramble into position along the leading edge. It was still another 400 meters to the terminal, and nearly all that distance would be in the open. His platoon didn't stand a chance of making it to the building unless those machineguns were silenced.

Overhead the gunships were still orbiting, hunting any heavy weapons the enemy was trying to deploy. At the moment, he heard more 30mm canon shells exploding but couldn't see the impacts and assumed they were targeting weapons on the other side of the long terminal.

The machinegun fire slowed to sporadic volleys once the surviving Marines joined their commander in the shallow pocket of earth. Lying side by side on the cool, lush grass, they felt as much as heard a rhythmic and deep thumping, as if they were in a gigantic drum that was being rapidly beaten.

Four AH-1Z Viper attack helicopters flew fast and low over the Marines spread out across the open expanse of tarmac and grass, the pilots deftly flying their slender aircraft while the co-pilot sought targets. Diaz was going to help them. From their forward position, he could call in targets and spot for the gunners. Through his binoculars he spotted the second machine gun, revealed by the muzzle flash when it was fired.

He keyed the radio. "This is Ghost Rider. We are pinned down by two machine guns, request air support, over."

The reply came back almost immediately. "Ghost Rider, this is Shield. I have four Vipers locked and loaded and on station.

Tell me what needs killin', son."

"Machinegun underneath commercial aircraft at Gate 3, they're between the main landing gear. Second gun is on the second floor, about 10 meters to the left of the control tower. They're inside, shooting through a blown-out window."

"Roger that, Ghost Rider."

"Be advised; we have Marines clearing the building from the top down. Three squads, they're currently on the third floor."

Another volley of fire forced Diaz and several other Marines off the lip and further into the depression. Diaz didn't hear the reply of acknowledgement from the helo pilot. He inched back to the edge in time to see the four Vipers split into two teams and circle around the terminal from opposite directions. The attack birds were low, only 160 meters, and they made one pass to confirm the reported locations of machineguns. On the second pass the lead Viper of each pair locked onto his target and fired.

A pair of Hellfire missiles struck just before and after the wing root on the parked aircraft, shearing off the right wing and collapsing the landing gear. The two-man machinegun team was dead even before the 90,000-pound Airbus landed on them.

The other Viper hooked in ten meters above the tarmac. The pilot came to a stop and at the same time pivoted the nose of the helo so it was pointing at a row of blown out windows to the right of the control-tower base. At the sight of the attack aircraft, the Russian soldiers leveled their machinegun and fired.

Immediately the pilot pulled back on the cyclic stick, retreating the Viper directly away from the terminal. The co-pilot aimed the three-barrel Gatling gun and unleashed a continuous barrage of 20mm armor-piercing explosive rounds, walking the barrel back and forth for a full three seconds. Hundreds of bright flashes, like flashbulbs, marked the explosive rounds inside the building.

The pilot held his aircraft in a stationary hover, daring the defenders to attack, but their guns were silent.

Captain Diaz was in awe, having watched the devastating attack through his field glasses. Wasting no more time he ordered his men forward. They would regroup behind a smoldering armored personnel carrier about 120 meters from the terminal.

Facing only sporadic small arms fire, they made the dash suffering only two casualties, both minor grazing bullet wounds. The Vipers continued to circle overhead, firing missiles and 20mm rounds at targets of opportunity, while the gunships could be heard firing their canon at targets that were outside of visual range. The bulk of the Marine invasion force was coming up behind Diaz facing little resistance.

Diaz looked at the sweaty faces surrounding him. He did a quick head count and realized half of his men were absent—either dead or wounded. His back was pressed against one of the eight rubber tires as he saw Washington leading Delta squad. "Welcome back Sergeant," he said.

Every man in Delta squad was breathing deeply, trying to recover from the long run. "We couldn't catch up until the machineguns were put out of commission," Washington said. "Had us in that first depression by the runway. Man, that's a long sprint."

"Glad to have you back." Diaz gave everyone several minutes to rest while he considered their plan of attack. When he was ready, he addressed his men.

"Listen up!" All eyes were on their commander.

"Squad leaders, you will each enter the building through a

different doorway. We will clear the ground floor and meet up with Mike, November, and Romeo squads there. Any hostiles trying to escape will be caught between our forces. Beginning with Alpha squad, you will enter at Gate 2, Bravo Gate 3, Charlie, Gate 4, and Delta, Gate 5. Squad leaders, refer to your maps of the terminal." Diaz paused momentarily, paper rustling as the maps were unfolded.

"Our job is to secure and hold this floor while Mike, November, and Romeo clear from the top down. Alpha and Bravo, you will sweep right. Charlie and Delta, you will sweep left. Make sure you leave a rear guard. No one enters this floor unless they wear the U.S. Marine Corps uniform. Am I clear?"

Heads nodded accompanied by "Yes, Captain."

Diaz looked over the sweat-soaked faces of his men. Many were veterans who had seen combat, for others this was their first time. None showed fear.

"If you haven't already, drink some water. If anyone's low on ammo, get a couple mags from your buddies."

He stood and peered around the end of the APC, steeling a quick glance and then pulling back before he'd get his head shot off. He didn't see any enemy and hazarded a second glance. Still, no one was visible.

"Squad leaders, ready?" The men were all standing now in four tight groups. "Go!"

Diaz rushed around the APC with Charlie and Delta squads at the same time the other two squads ran around the opposite end of the destroyed steel beast. The Marines ran hard and fast, reaching their respective gate doors and lining up tight against the wall to the side of the doors. For security reasons the entrances were locked. The airport personnel would have used a personalized magnetic keycard to unlock the doors for baggage handling and catering.

Nolty, leader of Charlie squad, looked to Diaz and then

pulled a pistol-gripped shotgun from a scabbard alongside his pack. He pumped the action forcefully, chambering a breaching round, pressed the muzzled against the door latch, and pulled the trigger. The 12-gauge shotgun jumped back and Nolty kicked the door open, immediately darting inside. The rest of Charlie squad followed single file, filling a wide hallway. They moved forward, hugging the walls and shortly faced two doors, 90 degrees apart. Diaz checked his map, confirming that one door led to a service room with elevators to the second floor where the kitchens were located. The other door connected to the baggage claim and customs hall.

He looked at Washington and Nolty. "Nolty, your squad will clear the baggage area. Washington, you take the service room." Both men nodded affirmation.

"Look, once your space is cleared, wait for my signal. Both squads will enter the main arrival hall at the same time. I'm expecting heavy resistance, so timing is important."

The doors were locked, as expected, and on a silent count to three, the latches were simultaneously breached. The Marines rushed in.

Washington's men found little of interest in the large room. Several desks, some empty carts that may have been used by catering, three elevators along one wall. There was no way he could lock out the elevators—that would have to be done at a mechanical room or control panel. But he could do the next best thing. He had his Marines rig two trip wires and two Claymore mines, each located in front of the elevator doors and about ten feet apart such that the lethal arc of each AP mine covered all three elevators. The trip wires were arranged such that if one was activated it would not set off the other.

Delta squad was ready, there was nothing more to do than wait for the order from Captain Diaz. Washington gently tested the latch on the door leading to the arrival hallway. At least from the inside, it was not locked.

Charlie squad entered the large open room and spread out. Baggage carousels were spaced across the expanse. On the far side of the room was the customs declaration area, with five large steel desks where unlucky passengers were invited to open their suspect luggage to be searched. Beyond customs was the exit.

"Clear!" The shout was repeated by Marines as they swept their shouldered rifles across their respective fields of fire. No enemy were occupying the baggage claim area and the squad moved forward. Suddenly, Russian soldiers rushed through the exit doors stopping at the customs declaration counter. Both sides saw each other at the same time and opened up.

Rifles fired, grenades exploded. The Marines ducked behind the stainless steel luggage carousels and concrete pillars supporting the upper floors. The Russian Spetsnaz used the customs desks as protection. The confined space and hard surfaces amplified the horrendous noise, drowning out any attempt to verbally communicate.

One by one, the customs desks were shredded by explosions. The Spetsnaz, reduced to only two survivors, retreated back to the arrival hall.

Charlie advanced to the two sets of double exit doors. If they had been constructed of glass it would have been easier, but these doors were solid steel and locked. Unlike the service room cleared by Delta, the baggage and customs room was a secure space.

Diaz looked at two Marines. "Set up charges; I want those doors ready to disappear on my mark."

The Marines busied themselves placing detcord around the double doors and connected the explosive-filled cord to a single detonator held by Nolty. Completed with their task, they joined their fellow Leathernecks behind what was left of the desks.

Then Diaz activated the squad net. "Washington, you ready?"

"Affirmative Cap."

"On my mark were gonna blast these doors open and throw grenades out into the hallway. You do the same. As soon as the grenades explode get your men out the passageway as fast as possible." No need to elaborate on the reasoning; all the Marines knew the choke point was a killing zone.

Diaz locked eyes with Nolty and mentally reviewed all they had done since entering the terminal. He'd done it by the book, as they trained.

His Marines were ready.

The heat and pressure wave was simultaneous with the ear-splitting blast. No more than a second later Marine heads popped up and grenades were lobbed out the opening where the pair of double exit doors had stood resolutely only moments ago. Dust was still swirling in the turbulent air, but this wasn't a time to pause.

With Diaz, Washington, and Nolty in the lead, the rest stormed into the arrival hall, heads swiveling and each crack of gunfire announcing a possible target. The men of Charlie and Delta squads were not being stingy with their ammunition, knowing they had to press forward.

Ahead, in the middle of the hall was a bar and snack concession. To the right were several small stores selling liquor, upscale clothing, perfume, and tobacco products. On the opposite side was a restaurant. The stores were empty, and many of the higher value products had already been looted by the Russian and NPA soldiers.

Washington and Nolty ordered the Leathernecks to spread out as they advanced cautiously. Suddenly, a fusillade of bullets cut through the middle of the formation. Three Marines fell to the floor amid a cry of agony, truncated by the voluminous return fire from the combined squads.

Chips of wood flew violently from the bar as bullets punched through the ornate mahogany. Enemy soldiers rose from the depths of the restaurant and from behind shelves in the stores, firing their AK-74 rifles at the exposed Marines.

Nolty turned his aim from the bar to the restaurant. Through his peripheral vision he saw a young Marine die instantly, his head blossoming in a red mist. He dropped his carbine, allowing it to swing at his side by the sling, and brought a second weapon strapped to his back. It had a short barrel, yet was large in diameter, and with an oversized cylinder above the trigger—the cylinder holding six 40mm grenades.

Shooting the M32 from his hip, Nolty sent a fragmentation round into the restaurant, followed in rapid secession by a second grenade. Both exploded on the counter along the back wall, reducing the wood display case to splinters and silencing the rifle fire.

As his comrades focused their fire on the stores, Nolty shifted his aim. Each pull of the trigger was followed by a deep whump that sounded oddly out of place with the sharp crack from the rifles and machineguns.

A grenade obliterated a glass display case housing expensive perfumes, small shards of glass multiplying the lethality of the steel fragments. Two more 40mm rounds blasted apart shelving, sending clothes and leather handbags in all directions. The final grenade exploded amidst a dozen bottles of single malt scotch that had somehow been left untouched. The crack of the explosive was followed by a deep thump, the sound of vaporized alcohol exploding in a fireball.

Nolty opened the cylinder, ejecting the spent cases and slammed home six more—it was all he had. A third of his fellow Leathernecks were down, but they had to hold the ground floor until the Marines from the upper floors joined them.

Every rifle shot drew the combined fire of the Marines, and they continued to advance on the stores and restaurant. The enemy soldiers in the restaurant resorted to firing their AKs on full auto while trying to stay out of sight behind a litter of tables and chairs. A couple of lucky bullets dropped two more Marines, but they had approached to within 30 meters of the shops—close enough that they started to throw grenades.

Four of the deadly steel orbs bounced about amongst the table legs of the restaurant, only to detonate a second later sending chairs and shattered portions of tables into the air. When the chaos settled, silence descended on the restaurant. But defenders were still fighting from the shops on the opposite side of the hall. Now, the Marines turned their attention to the remaining resistance.

Clusters of AK fire erupted briefly from behind rows of shelves or display counters, only to draw concentrated return fire and hand grenades. The trained Russian Spetsnaz were shooting and moving, never staying in one place very long.

Three more Marines fell to Russian bullets.

Nolty aimed the M32 at a cigar counter, blasting it apart along with the soldiers seeking protection behind it.

Another volley of shots came from the clothing store. Nolty turned his aim, but could not see where the shots had come from.

"Washington!" Diaz shouted. "Sweep forward with Delta squad. I want the remainder of this floor cleared!"

"Yes sir! Delta, you heard the Captain! Let's go!"

As the Marines rose to follow Washington, a new burst of fire emerged from the clothing store, and this time Nolty got a bead on it—two soldiers shooting from the far side of a waist-high display island, about four feet wide and twice that in length. The sides were polished wood doors concealing stock held in reserve. A multicolor collection of sweaters was folded and neatly stacked on the top of the island.

Nolty fired two 40mm rounds into the island, blowing it apart and creating a rainbow of sweaters across the floor. The Spetsnaz soldiers staggered, suffering from the blast overpressure. Moving in slow motion, both men began to raise their rifles, and were instantly shot dead by the remains of Charlie squad.

A moment passed… and then a second moment.

"Clear!" the call was shouted out, and echoed down through the surviving Marines. A heartbeat later Marines from Romeo, Mike, and November squads rushed out of the stairwells.

Diaz got on the radio and reported their local victory. Nearly all the enemy combatants fought to the death; only a few had surrendered.

Outside, the sky was owned by the Marine Corps attack helicopters and Air Force gunships. Anything even remotely resembling a mortar or machinegun position was destroyed; any moving vehicle was ripped apart by Hellfire missiles.

With the elimination of all hostile forces throughout the terminal, the only real estate left to clear was the control tower. The tower was accessed by a stairway behind a locked door. Diaz summoned Washington and Nolty. "Any of your men speak Russian?" he asked.

"Pratchett completed three years at Monterey," Washington said, referring to the Defense Language Institute on the California coast south of the Bay Area.

"Good. Get him. We're gonna enter the control tower."

Diaz, Washington, and Pratchett hugged the concrete wall beside a metal door that they assumed opened onto the control center. Pratchett held a note he'd been instructed to write in Russian, ordering the occupants to surrender or Diaz would order the Vipers to light-up the control tower with 20mm canon and missiles.

Using hand signals only, Diaz instructed Pratchett to slide the folded paper under the door. Once done, he rapped the butt of his rifle against the door. The sound of muffled voices was heard through the door, and Diaz imagined someone was picking up the note.

The three Marines silently backed down the staircase, weapons ready just in case. They waited just one minute before a voice announced in Russian that they were surrendering. The voice was followed by four soldiers.

Pratchett questioned the men, who admitted to speaking only Russian. Whether it was true or not mattered little. Once their hands were bound and they were searched for weapons and papers, they were questioned further

"Who do we have?" Diaz said.

"They're not saying much. No ID, not surprising. But this one," Pratchett indicated a man of medium build with graying hair, giving him the appearance of being older than the other three prisoners, "had this photo." The picture was of a woman and a boy, both were smiling.

"Family?"

Pratchett posed the question in Russian, answered by a silent stare.

Diaz flipped over the picture—there was writing on the back. "What does this say?"

"Just their names; Sonya and Vadim Jr."

"So, wife and son. That would make our friend here Vadim Sr." At the mention of his name, his eyes moved to Diaz, who noticed. "Ah, you are Vadim?" Diaz placed the photo back in the prisoner's breast pocket.

"Vadim?" he repeated.

Finally, the man gave in. "Yes, he said in broken and heavily accented English. My name is Vadim Zolnerowich."

CHAPTER 32

Minsk

THE HALLWAY WAS LONG, more than a hundred meters. If Jim had been running, he could have covered the distance in 12 seconds. But with the out-of-shape, middle-aged former hostages, it was already close to a minute since they left the conference room.

With about ten meters to go, the first three soldiers rounded the corner and entered the hallway from the shattered lobby entrance. Instead of taking time to aim at the fleeing hostages, they fired quickly, too quickly. The bullets travelled harmlessly into the walls and ceiling.

They halted their forward movement to stand and aim, but Magnum had spun around quickly and opened up with the AA12. Spewing five rounds of buckshot a second, he didn't have to aim. The shot spread to a three-foot pattern by the time it reached the far end of the long hallway. After holding the trigger for two seconds, none of the NPA soldiers were left standing.

The brief firefight served as further encouragement for the former hostages to push through the open doorway, Ghost and Bull preceding them and rapidly sweeping the room for any hostiles. It was empty.

Magnum halted for a half second, but no other soldiers rounded the corner. He turned and started sprinting ahead, only a step behind Boss Man, Homer, and Leonov when shots rang out again. A ricochet slammed into his thigh like a hammer blow. Magnum lost his balance, falling forward into the trio. Boss Man and Homer were knocked to the ground, Magnum's weight pressing on their legs.

"I'm hit!" Magnum cried out, clasping his left hand on the wound to staunch the flow of blood.

Jim extracted his legs first and knelt, rifle already raised and squeezing off rounds. Homer pulled himself free and grabbed Magnum by his load harness, dragging him to the open door. Ghost rushed out to give him a hand, while Bull leaned against the wall and added supporting fire as Jim retreated backwards, constantly firing until he was next to Bull. The discipline of training took over, and neither man flinched even though bullets were thudding into the walls and ceiling around them. Finally, the last of the militiamen was dead or driven back, and silence set upon their microcosm once again.

Peter and his father heard the gunfire and explosions rumbling up from the ground floor. "Can the building take those explosions and not fall apart?" Ian asked.

An impossible question to answer, Peter shrugged. "It hasn't fallen down yet."

Quickly they climbed the steps, joining Iceberg and Gary at the top of the stairwell, just inside the roof access door. Iceberg didn't want to run the risk of being observed on the roof, especially since it was approaching sunrise and the sky was getting light. Before long the first rays of sunlight would fall across the roof, making it much more difficult to remain obscured.

"Did you get it?" Peter asked between deep breaths. He set the metal box down. The weight of the power supply and the hustle up the stairs brought beads of perspiration to his forehead.

"Right here." Gary indicated the flamethrower he had set behind himself in the corner.

"I meant the copper pipe."

"Oh, yeah." Gary proudly extended his fist holding the length of copper pipe. "Hope this will do. It's the longest section I could cut without digging into the wall."

The ends were still rough and ragged from the saw cut, but otherwise it was perfect for the job. Peter set the pipe down and took the copper wire from his father.

"Okay, here's the plan. We need a coil of this wire about a half inch larger in diameter than the pipe." He touched the pipe as he spoke.

"Iceberg, we need another piece of pipe, a little larger than this one to use as a form to wind the wire around."

"Can't you just turn a few coils, forming them by hand?" He asked.

"No, won't work. First, we need as many coils as we can get to make a strong magnetic field. Second, the wire coil cannot touch the copper pipe. If it does the device won't work."

"On the roof, there are some stand pipes—probably about the right diameter. I can bust one off."

Peter smiled. "That's what I was thinking, too. They're vent pipes for the plumbing lines, probably plastic. I'll get a piece of pipe, and I need you to stand guard. It's getting easier for NPA soldiers to see us on the roof."

"What can I do?" Ian asked.

"The power supply. For the EMP bomb to work we have to tap into the electrical supply for the ventilation blower closest to the aerosol dispersion device. That blower will be powered by alternating current, 220 volts. This power supply converts alternating current to direct current, but I think it has multiple outputs at different voltages. I didn't take much time to check it over closely."

"I'll cut the plug off the power cord," Gary said, "and strip back the insulation so the wires can be tied in at the blower."

"Good. Dad, find the output terminals. Pick the highest voltage direct-current option. That's where we'll connect the EMP bomb."

"Ready, sir?" Iceberg addressed Peter. "Daylight's coming on quick." He clutched the AA12 in one hand, the other resting on the door latch.

Peter rose. "Let's go."

Iceberg lead the way in a crouch, his head moving from side to side, eyes searching for anything out of place, any threat. He didn't expect to encounter NPA militiamen on the roof, but he was quite concerned about rifle fire from neighboring rooftops.

After moving to an open location on the roof, about 10 meters from the access door, Iceberg knelt and shouldered the AA12, still swiveling his head and torso in close to a 360-degree arc. Peter dashed to the closest roof vent. He wrapped a hand around the open end of the vent and pushed from side to side. It moved, flexing a little near the base. Good, it's ABS plastic. Should be able to break it off, Peter thought.

He held the length of copper pipe next to the black vent ABS for comparison. Satisfied with the pipe's diameter, Peter grasped the top of the vent with both hands and pushed, leaning his body into it. The ABS bent and then refused to move further. Peter tried again to no avail.

"I'm gonna need your help. I can't break it off."

Iceberg joined Peter and added his strength to persuade the pipe to shear off. At first, the result was no different. Then Iceberg shifted position. With his weapon slung over a shoulder, he placed his right hand on the top of the vent pipe and leaned back using his left hand to brace for the expected fall. Then he pulled the pipe toward his body while Peter pushed from the opposite side.

Their teamwork was reward with a crack and then a pop as the ABS fractured in a jagged break. Iceberg crashed onto the roof surface. Peter pivoted just enough to avoid piling onto Iceberg and the now-liberated piece of ABS vent pipe.

Peter scooped up the copper pipe and the black ABS pipe and hastily returned to the access door. Iceberg was right behind him, shotgun again in his grip.

Back inside, Peter set to wrapping the copper wire around the plastic cylindrical form while Ian held the section of pipe. He carefully laid the coils so that there was only a small gap, about the width of the wire itself, between successive wraps. When the coil was slightly longer than the length of the copper pipe, he stopped and slid the wire coil off the form.

"I need you to pack C4 inside of this pipe." Peter handed the copper section to Iceberg. "Place the detonator in one end just far enough to initiate the explosion. The idea is to generate a pressure wave that travels from one end of the pipe to the other."

"Got it."

"Also, we need to turn on the electric power to the coil at the exact same moment the C4 is detonated. I think I can modify the detonator to serve as our electric switch."

With a block of plastic explosive in one hand, Iceberg handed a timing device to Peter.

Peter slipped the back off the plastic box revealing the battery compartment. "Perfect," Peter said. "Let me have your multitool."

Iceberg handed over the folded stainless steel implement. Peter removed the fuse from the box and jumpered it with a short length of copper wire. A lot of current would be flowing through the circuit, and he didn't want the fuse to fail too quickly. In only a fraction of a second the timing device would burn out anyway from the high voltage and current, but a fraction of a second was a very long time for events that would occur at nearly the speed of light.

Peter clipped the positive wire lead from the battery and shaved off the insulation from the wire ends. He joined the timer to the copper coil by twisting together a wire from each; the remaining two wires, one from the timer box and the other from the coil would be connected to the output from the power supply.

"Is the power supply ready?" Peter asked.

Ian nodded.

"All we have to do," Gary explained, "is tap into the electrical supply to one of the ventilation blowers."

Peter paused, taking in their handy work. It was almost hard to believe the klujed contraption could possibly work. Peter traced with his eyes the pathway the electrons would follow, seeing a dozen ways it was certain to fail. And yet the electric circuit only had to hold for a millisecond, enough time to energize the coil and detonate the explosives.

It was a Rube Goldberg contrivance for certain, but it had to work.

"Time to move it in place," Peter said as he crossed his fingers behind his back.

CHAPTER 33

Minsk

THE SILENCE DIDN'T LAST LONG. "Where's Major Leonov?" Jim demanded.

"He got away when Magnum took you two down. Went around the corner," Ghost replied. "Probably out the nearest exit."

"Sorry sir," Homer added. "I was busy getting Magnum back to safety while Bull was providing cover fire."

Jim sighed. It was a bad break. He wanted to bring Leonov back for interrogation and, as a ranking Russian officer, possibly to stand trial for war crimes.

"How is Magnum?"

Bull was bandaging the leg wound as he replied. "He'll live. Took a round to the lower thigh, but the bullet barely penetrated the skin. Must'a been a ricochet. I popped it out and I applied antibiotic powder. When we have time, it would be a good idea to pull the skin together with three or four stiches."

"I'm good sir; ready to go."

Jim took in the room for the first time. The long tables with utilitarian chairs, rows of shelving supporting thousands of volumes, and three copy machines told him they were in the library.

The former hostages were clustered away from the windows. Watching the commotion unfold, praying it would end well. This time their prayers were answered.

Bull finished tying off the bandage. "Do you think they'll press the attack?" he asked.

"They will. Radio Mother Goose with a sitrep. I want to know how long until reinforcements arrive."

Mother Goose was the code name for the Joint Air Operations Center (JAOC). From their command center in Stuttgart, the JAOC was orchestrating the air and ground assault on the Minsk International Airport.

"Will do," Bull replied. While he was working the radio, Jim worked out a defensive plan. The hallway extended over a hundred meters to their right, and also straight away from the library double doors about 30 meters before joining up to the parallel corridor running along the opposite side of the chemistry building. Without positioning guards in the hallway, they somehow needed to defend against NPA soldiers from both directions.

Jim removed the MON-50 mine from his rucksack and addressed Homer. "This will take care of the approach from the right. I'll anchor it in the corner. Inside the top of those copy machines you'll find a plate mirror. See if you can extract one."

Homer understood. "We'll use the mirror to see if anyone is approaching from that direction…"

"And we don't have to expose anyone." Jim completed his sentence.

As Jim finished prepping the mine with a manual detonator, Homer returned with a rectangular mirror a little larger than a sheet of paper.

Using a couple bookends to support the slab of plastic,

explosive, and steel shrapnel that comprised the MON-50 antipersonnel mine, Jim ran the wires back inside the library. He would connect the wires to the detonator after everything was in place. Next, he stood the mirror in front of the mine and angled it so the reflection was of the far end of the corridor.

Satisfied, Jim's next order was to build a makeshift barricade, behind which his team would take up firing positions. "Listen up everyone! I need books. Lots of them. Stacked up right here." He tapped his foot in the middle of the floor directly in line with the double doors to the hallway.

Peter removed the screws from the junction box on the nearest blower and carefully cut into the power wires. If he made a mistake here and shorted the circuit, they'd have to go to another blower farther away, if they had enough wire to reach.

He had no idea what the effective radius of the electromagnetic pulse would be. It could be as little as a meter or as much as a hundred meters.

He spliced in the coil and the timer, and then Iceberg connected the timer to the detonator wires. Peter stood the copper pipe on one end and slipped the coil over the pipe. Finally, he made sure none of the wires were shorted. He nodded to Iceberg. "Okay. Set the timer for 60 seconds."

Iceberg punched in the time delay and then activated the device. Both men sprinted for the access door and, along with Gary and the Professor, descended one flight of stairs.

Iceberg was on the squad net. "Alpha Team. Timer activated. Turn off all radios and other electronics."

At Peter's urging, Jim agreed that the team would turn off all electronics as a final measure of protection. Although a powerful EMP was capable of burning out any electrical circuit, even if it was turned off, a weak EMP could still trigger voltage spikes in activated circuits, resulting in electrical damage.

Soon there was the muffled sound of the explosion. “Try your radio,” Peter said.

Iceberg turned it on and activated the throat mic. “Boss Man.” Static. “Boss Man, do you copy?” Still static. He shook his head.

“Try again.”

“Boss Man, do you copy, over?”

“Boss Man here. Read you loud and clear. Is the aerosol dispersion weapon deactivated?”

Peter was already bounding up the stairs.

“Give me a minute, sir, still in the stairwell.”

Iceberg was ascending three steps at a time and gaining on Peter. They emerged through the access door together.

The case was no longer there.

It took Peter a moment to find it. The force of the explosion blasted it twenty feet away, but from a distance it appeared intact. Good. Internal explosives—if there were any—didn’t detonate.

Just then the familiar sound of automatic rifle fire split the air, and Peter and Iceberg ducked. “I have to check it,” Peter exclaimed.

“Keep your head down!” Iceberg returned fire, but the enemy was beyond the effective range of his shotgun.

Peter scrambled to the case. One hinge was broken completely, and the lid was askew. On closer examination it was clear that all of the latches were also broken.

He spun the case and carefully lifted the lid. Inside, everything appeared intact. The circuit boards—all three of them—looked fine at first glance, although the tiny LEDs on the boards were not lit. Peter examined the inline fuse between the batteries and the circuit board. It was not blown indicating the current surge occurred only for a very short duration.

"We have to go!" Iceberg shouted.

Peter closed the lid, difficult with only one functional hinge, and wrapped his arms around the case. Hugging it to his side, he darted back to the access door. A volley of bullets gouged cement dust from the wall next to the access door.

Iceberg was there waiting for him, holding the door open. They passed through, the door clicking shut behind them.

"It worked!" Peter exclaimed.

"Never doubted you," Iceberg said dryly. "Let's go. We'll rendezvous with the rest of the team." Ever cautious of trip wires, Iceberg grabbed the sprayer by its straps and led the foursome down to the ground floor where they were greeted by Jim and Ghost.

"This way," Jim said. "We've taken up in the library. I'd like to get a look inside that case you're carrying."

CHAPTER 34

Minsk

THE LIBRARY, ONCE A BASTION OF ORDER, looked like it had been ransacked in preparation for a wholesale book burning. In the middle of the floor was a large stack of bound volumes—very large. Ten books deep and two feet tall, the barrier provided a measure of protection much as sandbags would have. Peter, accustomed to test-firing bullets into various media including dry, compressed paper, reckoned that the AK bullets would penetrate no more than five books—about 30 inches—before coming to a halt.

The three copiers were arranged end-to-end in an arc near a windowless corner. Layered with the copy machines were the library tables, turned on end and pressed close to each other, adding another two inches of solid oak to the defensive barrier.

Peter gently set the defunct bioweapon on the floor. He opened the case and removed the three circuit boards, one at a time, examining each carefully. What he found was satisfying—several capacitors and diodes on each board were scorched black, burned out. Most likely, the microprocessor chips were also ruined.

"It's dead," Peter concluded. "Electronic circuits overloaded and smoked."

"It's still potentially dangerous," Jim said. "Magnum, check it for an explosive charge. If you find one, disarm it. Colonel Pierson is gonna want to have this examined in detail."

Magnum hobbled over and tried to sit on the floor next to the case, only to grimace from the sudden sharp pain in his leg.

"Let's set it up on the stack of books, easier for Magnum to do his job," Peter suggested.

Peter set the circuit boards in the case lid and, with Jim's help, moved the open case. Magnum grabbed a chair and made himself as comfortable as possible, then started to methodically disassemble the internal components. It only required two minutes to find a small explosive charge by following the wires that ultimately led to the detonator. The charge was hidden behind a duct and metal container attached to an air blower. Peter, looking over Magnum's shoulder, suspected the blower was powerful—it would need to be to disperse the virus powder as an aerosol.

"Here it is, sir. I've clipped the wires and removed the detonator." Magnum placed the detonator next to the case. "Should I remove the charge as well?"

"No. Leave it for the techs back home. And put everything other than the detonator back in place. They'll want to document the construction."

"Do you think there are more of these aerosol machines?" Peter asked.

"Maybe, hard to be sure. I wish we still had Major Leonov—or General Gorev, or another officer to question." Jim gazed at the open case while Magnum carefully replaced the components. Recalling the photos of infected women and children covered in purple-red welts, some with blood dribbling from their nose and mouth, he felt his anger rising.

"Bull, any word on reinforcements?"

"Fighting at the airport is fierce, but the Marines landed okay and are taking control. A squad in three Humvees is on the way, ETA 20 minutes."

"Set up direct radio contact with the squad leader. And get word to Colonel Pierson; our primary objective has been achieved."

Peter joined his father and Gary, who were sitting next to two of the copiers. He sat down heavily on the carpeted floor, his back protesting. The pain was oddly welcome, a not-so-subtle reminder that he was still alive.

"Sounds like we'll be getting out of here soon, and with a Marine escort," Peter said, trying to lighten his father's spirits.

"Think they'll catch Gorev?" Gary asked.

"He should be put on trial and hanged," Ian said. "Just like we did with the Nazis."

"The bigger question is who's behind the virus aerosol machine. Gorev and the NPA must have had help with that," Peter said.

"That should be obvious. Over the years I've seen ruthless dictators come and go. But the likes of Vladimir Pushkin are rare."

"Professor," Gary said, "President Pushkin isn't stupid. He'd have to know that if he was ever connected to supplying biological weapons to pro-Russian militia, the consequences would be severe."

"I think Dad's right. Under Pushkin's leadership, Russia has sponsored invasions of Georgia, Moldova, and the Ukraine. The only repercussions were sanctions. That didn't stop him from annexing large swaths of land, including the strategically important Crimean Peninsula."

"You can add the civil conflict at the hands of pro-Russian militia in Latvia and now Belarus," Professor Savage said.

"Speculation," Gary objected. "Irrefutable proof is needed."

Peter nodded in agreement. "Well, that case," he pointed to the aerosol machine, "will be the first hard piece of evidence. If we can determine who made it using parts from what countries, then we'll be well on our way to determining who is behind this plan."

"Looks like we have company coming for breakfast," Ghost announced in a low and even voice upon seeing the reflection in the mirror. Homer, Magnum, and Bull snapped weapons to their shoulders. Jim conferred with Ghost who was kneeling behind the stack of books.

"Just a couple heads poking around the far corner of the hallway," Ghost reported.

"By the lobby?"

"Affirmative." Ghost kept his eyes focused on the mirror in front of the mine. It was their only means for seeing down the long corridor.

"There's another entrance at this end of the building. Bull, keep a sharp eye out. I'm betting they'll attack from both directions."

Homer made himself busy adding more books to the pile as quickly as he could.

"Peter, Gary, Professor," Jim called, "help Homer. We need to reinforce this barricade." The trio rushed to move armloads of books, both lengthening and deepening the literary bunker. Soon, the faculty and staff joined in, wanting to do anything and everything to help. In a matter of just a few minutes the pile doubled in size.

Peter slipped through the straps of the flamethrower. He figured it might come in handy if the attack arrived. In addition to extending to the right, the hall led 20 yards straight away from the library doors where it forked, the left branch connected to another entrance to the building. If an attack came down this corridor, the enemy would be close enough to engage with the flamethrower.

Gary took a prone position to the side, away from the bunker, positioning the machine gun atop a short stack of books and journals for a clear line of fire. The Professor took a spot next to Ghost and aimed the AK-74.

"You okay with that?" Ghost asked.

"Young man, I've done my share of shooting, if that's what you mean." Ghost almost smiled, and then he focused again on the mirror.

"More heads poking around the corner," he said. "Now three of 'em stepping into the hall—they're moving forward."

"Weapons?" Jim asked.

"AKs. Not seeing any RPGs."

"Let 'em come. Everyone stay sharp. When they come, they'll be real close."

"They're getting brave. Now I count eight, possibly twelve. Tight group," Ghost said.

"Let me know when they're about 40 meters out," Jim said.

Suddenly three NPA soldiers appeared directly ahead. Two dove to the floor, sliding to a stop. In unison they opened up with their rifles, firing into the library. Bullets plunged into the book barricade as well as the far wall.

Gary was ready, finger on the trigger, and he was the first to fire. The machine gun chewed through the short belt of ammo in two seconds, and when the echo of gunfire faded, the NPA soldiers were dead.

"I'm out," Gary announced.

"Here!" Jim handed his Para Ordinance Super Hawg .45 pistol to Gary.

"Still coming! About 60 meters."

"Shout out when they're at 40," Jim said.

Another wave rounded the corner and came head on at the

library. The SGIT team opened up, supported by Gary and Ian. Dozens of bullets buried deep in the stack of books.

"Forty!" Ghost shouted.

Jim stopped shooting and slammed his hand down on the remote detonator. For an instant, the world came to a standstill while the space immediately in front of the library doors was filled with an explosion that vaporized the mirror.

Instinctively the SGIT and NPA soldiers ducked, bringing a temporary halt to the firefight. With the mirror destroyed, Ghost was blind, unable to see down the long corridor to the formation of men ripped apart by the shrapnel from the MON-50 antipersonnel mine.

"Grenade!" Jim shouted as two metal spheres lobbed into the library. One stopped just inside the door, a lucky break for the defenders. The other made it further, resting against the pile of books.

Peter dove over a desk, holding the sprayer nozzle out so as not to roll over the flaming nozzle and extinguish it. Everyone else ducked down, as low as they possibly could.

Jim knew that as soon as the grenades detonated, the NPA soldiers would rush and overtake their position.

Time seemed to halt--then the grenades exploded.

CHAPTER 35

Minsk

THE GRENADE EXPLOSIONS were even louder than the mine. Peter was certain he couldn't hear anything other than the intense ringing in his ears. The stack of books had been demolished by the explosion. He looked over at his father—half buried under books—and then to Gary. Although both appeared unhurt, neither was moving.

"Dad!" Peter was sure he shouted, but it sounded so faint and distant to his ears. He saw Jim and Ghost trying to shake off the books. Jim was frantically looking at the doorway, struggling to bring his rifle to bear. They seemed to be moving very slowly, as if they had leaden limbs.

Peter swiveled his head to the opening just as the first militiaman reached the doorway, knowing none of the SGIT team could possibly get a bead on the attacking force. He pointed the flamethrower and depressed the trigger. Instantly an intense yellow tongue of fire shot forward, engulfing the enemy soldier.

Screams emanated from his writhing body. Weapon no longer in his hands, he dropped and rolled for a few long seconds, and then he laid motionless, dead.

Peter didn't stop to watch or grieve. He bellowed like a primal beast as his inner rage drove him onward, forward past the desk, to the doorway. Like a dragon of lore, the jury-rigged flamethrower was spitting an inferno that engulfed everyone in its reach. Peter advanced methodically, torching everything—and everyone. Soon, the corridor for 15 meters in front of the library entry was aflame. Fire clung to the concrete-block walls and tiled floor and bodies, and the smell of burning flesh was nauseating.

Finally, Peter released the trigger. There was nothing else to burn although his fury still smoldered.

By now Jim and Ghost were behind Peter, training their weapons down the long hallway that connected to the lobby, searching for targets. There were none. Only bodies of the NPA guards torn to pieces by the mine Jim had set.

Bull joined them. "Everyone's okay," he reported, thankful that none of the civilians appeared injured.

Peter dropped the sprayer from his shoulders, wincing as the metal canister slid against his battered and bruised back, setting it aside gingerly, like it might break if handled roughly. He turned and walked back to his father.

"Dad?"

Ian Savage moaned as he sat upright.

"Are you okay?" Peter asked again.

"You mean other than having a stack of books dropped on my head?" He rubbed the back of his scalp.

Relief washed over Peter at the sudden realization that his father was fine. Peter smiled. "Your head's too hard for a few books to cause any damage."

Ian looked up at his son. "You might think you're funny, but..."

He stopped at the sight of blood at Peter's side.

"You're hurt," he said.

Peter's expression conveyed his confusion.

"Your side—you're bleeding."

Bull was there, raising Peter's arm even before the sensation of pain fully registered in his mind. But as his arm was raised, the pain flared. "Oww!"

"Hold your arm up and let me have a look," Bull said. He expanded the tear in the shirt. The flesh was cut, but it didn't go deep.

"Looks like you were grazed by shrapnel. Lucky though, it didn't puncture your lung." Bull squeezed and poked a bit, confirming his diagnosis. "Boss Man, I need to put a few sutures in this laceration. Might as well stich up Magnum at the same time."

"Okay, but do it quick."

While Bull was busy treating his patients, the radio squawked. "Ferryman this is Ghost Rider, do you copy?"

Everyone heard the tinny voice; it was coming from somewhere within the rubbish pile of tomes and loose papers. "Ferryman, this is Ghost Rider. Do you copy? Over."

Jim pushed aside debris until he found the radio. "Ghost Rider, I read you. ETA?"

"Authenticate, Ferryman."

"Bravo bravo tango one zulu one. This is Boss Man; transmission is secure."

"Roger Ferryman. Authentication complete. Thank you sir. We are closing fast, no opposition so far. ETA three minutes."

Jim confirmed the GPS coordinates for their current location and briefed Ghost Rider on the recent battle. He closed with a caution that the NPA had control of the BSU campus buildings and Ghost Rider should expect resistance.

"Roger, we're coming in hot. Ghost Rider out."

Jim spent the next two minutes talking to the former hostages, preparing them for the departure. He didn't know exactly where they would be taken, or how they would get there. All in due time. But Jim was certain that the BSU campus and many of the neighboring buildings—the seat of Government and the KGB Headquarters—would be the scene of intense fighting over the next several hours as the Marines evicted the NPA.

Despite fatigue and fear, the chatter was upbeat until once again the sound of heavy gunfire entered the library. A moment later engines were heard revving to high rpms.

"Fifty cal," Homer said.

"And Humvees. I think the Marines are about to arrive."

BOOM! The deep, thunderous crack from an explosion sounded like it was just outside the library walls. But the experienced soldiers knew better. Attempting to ease the concern evident in so many faces, Jim explained. "Marines are coming for us— Force Recon troops from the Black Sea Rotational Force. Sounds like their driving multiple Humvees armed with heavy machine guns and TOW missiles. What you just heard was probably a missile busting through a wall or maybe an armored vehicle." Then he added, "Nothing to worry about—these guys are as good as they get."

"I can't wait to get a hot shower and sleep in a real bed," Gary said.

"Soon enough," Jim replied. "The next faces you see will be dressed in Marine uniforms."

Peter busied himself closing the aerosol machine and securing the lid in place with an electrical cord he cut from one of the copy machines. Then he sat next to his father.

"What are your plans?" Peter assumed his father would have a difficult transition with Dmitri Kaspar dead.

"I'm ready to come home."

"You're welcome to stay at my place in Bend, if you'd like. Ethan and Jo always enjoy spending time with you." Peter paused before continuing. "I do, too."

Professor Savage gazed into his son's eyes. What Peter saw was a portrait of sadness and grief. Before the Professor answered, Bull entered with a Marine officer. "Sir, this is Captain Diaz."

Boss Man kept the introductions short and then got down to business. "We have 18 civilians to evac. What's your plan?"

"Ran into some resistance, like you said. The approach to the campus and the commons is cleared, killed about 20 or so enemy soldiers out there. Took out a tank across the road at Independence Square. There are two other tank hulks burning and what looks to be the remains of a mobile SAM launcher. You guys do that?"

Rather than explaining the missiles were fired from SGIT's top-secret transport, Jim just nodded.

"Third and fourth platoons are clearing the other buildings. My team is completing a final assessment as we speak. If it's secure, we'll bring in an Osprey, land it right in the street. Weather is deteriorating slightly. Light rain, but wind is mild and ceiling is still above 3,000 feet— shouldn't impact bringing the bird in."

"What can my men do to help?" Jim asked.

"We picked up a few prisoners. No rank insignia, and they aren't talking. Found this on one of them." Diaz held a hard case, about the size of a cell phone. Jim opened it to reveal a syringe, extra needles, and an ampule of a clear serum. "If some of your men can guard them, it'll free up my team to finish clearing this building and provide security."

"Do you know what this is?" Jim asked.

"No, I assume it's some type of medicine. Maybe insulin or a pain killer." Diaz was a bit surprised by Jim's interest in the ampules.

"I think it's something else entirely." He called Peter over. "What do you make of this?" he asked, handing the case to Peter.

Peter replied almost immediately. "Vaccine." He looked at Jim. "They were selectively vaccinating their troops and anyone else they wanted to protect."

Diaz looked confused.

"Can you take me to them? Now?" Jim asked.

"Sure." Diaz turned to the open door and called. "Washington, Nolty." Two Marines hustled up to their commander. "Confirm the head count and get these people ready. Clothes on their backs only, nothing else."

"Yes, sir!"

Diaz addressed Boss Man. "Follow me." Jim followed the Marine captain with Bull and Ghost by his side, and Peter close behind.

CHAPTER 36

Minsk

"AH, MY OLD FRIEND MAJOR LEONOV," Jim said. The Spetsnaz soldier refused to look up.

"You know who he is?" Diaz asked.

"We've met. But I don't know the other three. We had Leonov, only to lose him in a firefight outside the library."

All four prisoners were sitting on the ground near one of the Humvees, hands bound behind their backs. The rain was intermittent, and not especially cold—certainly no risk of hypothermia although it was probably somewhat uncomfortable. Too bad, Jim thought.

"I'm glad you caught him," Jim continued. "I suspect he'll have a wealth of information to share with DIA and CIA analysts."

"We'll take them out with us in the Humvees after we get the civilians evacuated."

Jim knelt down in front of Leonov. "We disabled the machine--I thought you'd like to know."

Leonov barely reacted, only a brief glint of surprise, and then it was gone, his countenance neutral once again.

"You probably didn't think it was possible."

The Major remained silent.

"Who built the machine, Major?" Jim prodded, trying to goad him to open up. "We'll learn soon enough. The explosive charge has been disabled and the machine is intact. It won't take long to piece it together and figure out its origin."

Still Leonov refused to speak.

Peter lowered the open case holding the ampules. "Who was carrying this, Captain?"

Diaz pointed to Leonov. "Your blond buddy."

"This is vaccine—that's what it is, right?" Peter said. Leonov was staring at the case in silence.

"Well, this vaccine will be analyzed. The Army has a very good lab at Fort Detrick. The Centers for Disease Control will also conduct an investigation. The chemical composition of the vaccine will tell us clearly the country of origin." Peter was making this up, speaking his educated guesses with confidence.

He had Major Leonov's attention and pressed him harder. "The medium the virus was grown in, the method used to kill the cells--these are all part of the fingerprint. I've been told that no two labs use the exact same recipe."

"You think it matters?" Leonov scoffed. "You have nothing."

"We have the aerosol machine, plus this sample of vaccine. It has Russian labels and I'm betting the lab results will confirm it was made by a Russian pharmaceutical lab."

Leonov shrugged. "Believe what you wish; Russia is not the only country to use the Cyrillic alphabet. When the international media broadcasts video of women and children suffering and dying from smallpox, nothing your government says will be believed." Leonov raised his head and looked directly at Peter. "Time," he started to laugh, "it is not on your side."

"Come on Peter; we're wasting our time," Jim said.

Peter stood motionless, staring at the Major, processing what he'd said—and then it hit him. "Wait a minute!"

Peter faced Jim and Captain Diaz. "There's another device, another aerosol machine."

"What makes you certain?" Jim said.

"He knows we've already disabled the machine from the roof of this building. Yet Leonov is saying that people will be infected. So there has to be another one out there."

Jim reached down and grabbed Leonov by the collar, hauling him up to his feet. Then he slammed him back into the Humvee and leaned in close to his face, water droplets running down his nose and cheeks.

"Where is it?" he demanded.

Leonov's lips curled in a sickening smile.

Jim slid his hand around the man's throat, and squeezed. The veins on either side of his neck bulged as circulation and airflow were constricted. "Where is it!" Jim shouted.

"It's already too late," Leonov said with a laugh.

Diaz had his knife in hand. The blade was seven inches long and razor sharp. "Say the word Commander and I'll pop off his knee caps. We can start with the right leg, and see what he has to tell us."

The Major stared back at Jim, his eyes defiant and filled with vengeance. "Do it," Jim said.

Peter watched in silence. He knew he should object, try to talk Jim and Diaz down, but he also knew they needed information right now.

Diaz gave his weapon to Peter, who kept it trained on Leonov. Then Diaz reached down and cut a small slice in the camouflaged pant leg. Wielding the knife like a surgeon, he inserted the blade through the cloth, cold steel pressing against flesh, and enlarged the opening, fully exposing the kneecap.

Jim had the Spetsnaz soldier leaning backwards against the

Humvee, pinning him there with an iron grip on his throat. "Last chance. Once he cuts off your kneecap you'll never walk again."

His eyes widened and his breathing became rapid and shallow. Still, Leonov shook his head.

"Do it," ordered Jim.

"Wait!" Peter couldn't take it any longer. "You can't do this."

"Bull, I am ordering you to escort Dr. Savage back inside."

Bull grabbed Peter's arm. "Come on, let's go."

"This isn't right!" Peter said as he let Bull lead him away.

"The ends always justify the means," Diaz said.

Peter had his back turned, and the next sound he heard was a blood-curdling scream. He didn't have the stomach to turn and look.

At the moment, the Minsk International Airport was arguably one of the busiest airports anywhere. Marine and Army reinforcements were arriving onboard C-130 transports, while incoming equipment and cargo flights were landing at the rate of about one plane every 15 minutes. Nearly every square meter of tarmac was occupied with parked planes unloading men, equipment, and machines.

Then, once empty, the planes, operated by the USAF, NATO, the RAF, and the French Air Force, were rapidly refueled so they could take to the air again, returning to bases in Germany, Poland, Italy, Turkey, France, and Great Britain. Everything that would be necessary to wage war with Russia had to be flown in, and it was needed now.

In the span of hours, the airport had transformed into a huge port, dedicated solely to establishing a defensible foothold against an anticipated Russian counter attack. The Pentagon analysts expected that to appear first as an air assault, followed by a ground force, including armor, attacking within 24 hours.

The analysts were wrong.

"Bill, you have the stick," Major Doyle said at the sight of an incoming encrypted email message.

"Co-pilot has the stick," Bill Harrison said to acknowledge transfer of flight control.

"Looks like that hot shower will have to wait. We're not through yet," she said. It didn't take long to read the message.

"New target coordinates," she said to Bill.

With the destruction of air defenses at the airport and low on fuel, Hammer flight was on its way back to Germany, mission concluded. The plan was to fly northwest across Lithuania to avoid any remaining air defenses in western Belarus.

Doyle checked the fuel load, not good. She keyed the secure radio link. "Golden Eye, this is Hammer flight, acknowledge."

"Reading you, Hammer Flight. This is Golden Eye."

"Look, our tanks are pretty lean. Insufficient fuel to complete new sortie. Please advise, over."

Following a short silence, a new voice addressed Major Doyle. "Major, this is Colonel Horn. What is your fuel status?"

"Sir, we will go bingo fuel in five minutes at current speed."

Colonel Horn had built his career by making hard decisions, and this was no different. "Listen closely Major. That airport is essential. If we don't hold it—if we allow the Russians to retake it—we will not be able to reinforce and supply our troops." He paused to let that message settle in.

"Right now, there's a column of Russian armor approaching fast, and soon it will be within striking distance of the runway. Our aircraft and crew are fully exposed. You know as well as I the havoc those tanks can bring to bear on exposed aircraft. Best case, they shut down the runway and stall our advance. That's a win for Russia; time is on their side. We have to hold that runway and infrastructure—intact—at all costs."

"I understand, sir," Doyle said.

"Do you, Major?"

Without hesitation, Major Doyle answered. "Affirmative sir. This aircraft is expendable."

Colonel Horn sighed heavily. He hated this part of the job as much as he was proud to be associated with the the men and women who served under his command. "That's right Major. I wish it wasn't so, but I'd be lying to you to say otherwise. We don't have other strike aircraft in the vicinity with the capability to destroy that armor. What's left of the close air support is on the ground being refueled and rearmed. The militia and Russians didn't just walk away from the airport."

"We're on it sir."

"Godspeed, Major."

"If I can ask a favor, Colonel, move that tanker as close to our vector as possible. We'll be on fumes on the flight home."

Although Doyle couldn't see it, Colonel Horn smiled. "You've got it, Major. Golden Eye out."

"Turn us south Bill, you have the coordinates. Maintain 30,000 feet." No sooner had she completed the order and the aircraft began a tight banking turn.

"Jonesy, what ordinance are we still carrying?" Doyle asked the Offensive Systems Officer.

Captain Jones checked his stores before replying. "Uh, twelve GBU-49 and three GBU-50 if you really want to leave an impression. What's the objective?"

Doyle considered her options—mostly laser guided 500-pound bombs and a couple guided 2,000 pounders. Either was more than adequate.

"Suspected Russian armor. Golden Eye has detected a column heading toward Minsk on the M1 motorway. Location about 45 miles east of Minsk and closing fast. The column will reach the airport in about 60 minutes, maybe sooner. We are to confirm target ID using the Sniper Pod. If it's military assets, we'll take 'em out."

"Roger that."

They flew in silence for ten minutes. Bill had been running the numbers in his head, same as Major Doyle. "It's gonna be close," he said.

"That's right Captain. Even if we don't have to dodge or outrun any MIGS or missiles, we still may not have enough fuel to reach the tanker. We'll return at altitude, and if we flame out, we eject."

By the time the Bone was close enough to get a visual on the advancing column, it had closed to 25 miles from the airport, and still moving at top speed. Jonesy was studying the magnified images coming back from the Sniper pod. "We have tanks, Major," he said. "Probably T-90s. And a bunch of BTR 80s or 82s," referring to the eight-wheeled armored personnel carrier.

"How many?"

"Ten T-90s. A dozen… no, make that fifteen APCs."

"Prioritize the tanks. Without heavy armor the BTRs won't fair well against the Marine Viper attack helos."

"Roger that, Major." Jonesy designated all ten tanks. The Sniper pod would hold the laser designator on up to three separate targets. "We'll have to do five releases, Major, if you want to drop all our ordinance."

"No point in bringing it back home. Plus our fuel will go farther if we aren't carrying any excess weight."

"With ya one hundred percent," said Jonesy.

"Bill, bring us down to 20. That will reduce the drop time and we can get out of here sooner."

Captain Harrison nodded.

"I've got GBU-49s for each tank," Jonesy said. "That leaves two extra that I'll target on a couple APCs. Plus we have the

GBU-50s. I'll try to target those for a close group of two or three APCs—2,000 pounds of high explosive will go a long way on that light armor."

Doyle resumed control of the aircraft, placing it in a straight, level flight and pulling the throttles back to minimum airspeed. "You are go to release, Jonesy."

Three at a time, the 500-pound laser guided bombs fell free of the Bone, quickly pointing nose down. The bulbous contraption at the nose of the bomb followed the invisible laser beam reflecting back from the target. In seconds, the three bombs detonated simultaneously. Against the relatively thin armor on the top of the T-90s, the bombs were devastating.

Then the next three bombs were dropped. And several seconds later, three more—and then three more until all the laser-guided munitions were gone. Out of vision of the crew, all ten heavy battle tanks were blown apart—turrets completely separated from the chassis, tracks snapped, even the reactive defensive armor on the outer hull had detonated in a series of sympathetic explosions.

The BTR armored personnel carriers fared even worse. Of the fifteen vehicles, eight were destroyed by either direct or near hits from the 500-pound and 2,000-pound bombs.

As Major Doyle gently banked her aircraft and slowly climbed, she saw the telltale column of black smoke. "Were you able to get a BDA Jonesy?" she asked.

"Affirmative Major. All ten tanks are smashed, and at least half the APCs are history."

"Nice shooting, Jonesy, I'll share the good news with Golden Eye."

CHAPTER 37

MINSK

DIAZ SLAMMED THE POMMEL of his knife hard against Gorev's kneecap. Not hard enough to fracture the bone, but with enough force that it hurt like hell. Then, without pausing to give his prisoner a rest, he dug the tip of the knife into the soft flesh at the edge of the knee. Predictably, Leonov screamed in pain.

Diaz held back.

"Where?" Jim demanded, holding Leonov tight, bent backwards to the point that his back was also aching.

"Where! Tell me or so help me, I'll let him slice off your kneecap."

"I don't know!" He took a moment to control his breathing, slow it down, so he could speak. "It's not under my authority."

"Tell me!"

Jim tipped his head toward Diaz, who edged the steel deeper into Leonov's knee. He screamed again.

"I can't! I don't know where it is! I'm telling the truth."

"I think you do know and you're just holding out." Jim scrutinized Leonov's face—it was soaked, partly from the gentle rain and partly from perspiration despite the cool air. Jim slid his hand gripping Leonov's neck so he could feel his pulse—it was racing, maybe 150 beats per minute. And his breathing had returned to rapid and shallow. Leonov was terrified.

"Where is it?" Jim shouted only inches away from Leonov's face. Again Daiz dug deeper; again Leonov screamed in agony.

"I don't know!"

Jim relaxed his grip, allowing Major Leonov to fall to the ground.

"It's no good. I don't think he knows."

"He'll talk once his knee cap is on the ground," Diaz said.

"Yeah, he'll say whatever you want to hear. But that doesn't make it true."

"Okay then, now what?"

"When your medic has time, stitch him up," Jim said, and then he strode into the chemistry building. Peter and Bull were just inside the doorway. The sound of the tilt-rotor V-22 Osprey landing was very loud, even inside.

"Bull, time to get these people onboard that aircraft. Take them out the other way so they don't have to pass these charred bodies." The stench was still horrendous, but the fires had died out.

"You didn't have to do that," Peter said after Bull had left.

"I didn't do it," Jim replied.

"I heard the scream."

"Diaz smacked his kneecap, and then made a shallow slice in his flesh. The corpsman is probably suturing it now; doubt it requires more than five or six stitches."

"Okay, I guess you fooled me."

"That was the point, and you played the part marvelously. Once you were convinced Diaz was actually going to do grave harm, Leonov also believed it. The fear of torture is often worse than the actual act."

"I'll remember that. What did he tell you?"

"Nothing, unfortunately. I don't think he knows where the other machine is. Hell, for all we know there may not even be another machine."

"And what if there is? We have to find it!"

"Do you have any idea what you are suggesting? It could take weeks to conduct a thorough search of the city. Right now, we need to evacuate these people, get the aerosol machine into proper hands for analysis, and secure the area."

Although Peter didn't like it, he couldn't argue the point, not without at least a clue as to the whereabouts of the other device, or devices.

Jim placed his hand on Peter's shoulder. "I understand what you're feeling. After Major Leonov is properly interrogated, maybe we'll know more."

Peter nodded, "Okay."

Soft rain continued to fall off and on. The gloomy weather perfectly matched Peter's mood. He looked skyward, feeling the drops splat on his face, wishing the rain would wash away his despondence.

Captain Diaz approached followed by the SGIT soldiers of Alpha Team. "Time to go." He left four Marines to guard the prisoners.

Flanked by Marines and Jim's SGIT team, all of the civilians filed into the Osprey and were shuttled to the Renaissance Hotel in a more secure part of Minsk. The flight was very short, the Osprey never getting higher than 500 feet or transitioning fully to horizontal flight. Peter remained silent and brooding during the short hop.

The aircraft landed on the expansive front lawn of the hotel and lowered the rear ramp. Peter and Jim exited first, followed by the rest of the civilians, and finally by their Marine escorts and Alpha Team. Once clear of the downwash, they were met by a Marine Colonel.

The Colonel saluted Jim and then extended his hand to Peter. "I'm Colonel Garret. Follow me."

The lobby was surreal, devoid of patrons. The only people were hotel employees and staffers in Air Force and Marine uniforms.

"This way," Garret urged them on.

They passed through the lobby and entered a broad corridor with doors on both sides. Peter recognized these as conference rooms the hotel would book for conventions.

All of the doors were closed, and Garret led them to the last door on the right. It was at the end of the hallway. Marine guards dressed for combat were standing aside the double doors. Other guards were moving randomly through the hallway.

Inside the conference room were more armed soldiers. Peter looked to the front of the room and saw a stage with tiered seating.

"Ladies and gentlemen," Garrett addressed the group, pausing for his aide to translate into Russian. "Please take a seat; this won't be long." Garrett indicated the tier of chairs and people moved along the rows until the seats were mostly filled. Peter, Gary, Ian, and Jim were the last to be seated in the front row. Bright lights illuminated the many curious and confused faces.

"What's going on Gary?" Peter asked.

"You got me. Looks like they're setting up video cameras and other communication equipment."

Colonel Garret, who had removed himself to the side while everyone became seated, stepped up to Jim and Peter. "Please bear with us for a moment and we'll get on with this."

Peter was tired, and lacking patience for mysteries. "What, exactly, is going on here?"

"Some important people want to talk to you."

"How about later?" Peter said. "I'm exhausted and I hurt. Speaking for myself, I'd be quite happy just to have a good meal, hot shower, and some sleep in a real bed. I suspect my father and friend would agree. Then we can talk all you want."

"Ordinarily, I'd be inclined to agree with you. But circumstances are anything other than ordinary."

Peter started to object, but was pre-empted by one of the communications technicians. "Colonel, I have POTUS on the line."

CHAPTER 38

MINSK

"LADIES AND GENTLEMEN," President Taylor's image appeared on the monitor. Dressed in a dark suit and wearing a white shirt and royal blue tie, he was relaxed, sitting behind his desk in the Oval Office. It was an image cultivated and refined by the many other leaders who had gone before him. An image intended to convey confidence, security, knowledge.

"I want to welcome you to freedom. I know you have all suffered a harrowing ordeal." He paused to allow translation to Russian.

"Arrangements have been made for you to stay at the hotel, as guests of the U.S. government of course. Marine corpsmen will perform a short examination of each of you to make certain there are no physical injuries. We also have some questions we'd like to ask of each of you; call it a debriefing, if you will."

Although it looked like the President was looking directly at the gathered audience, in fact he was gazing at a video monitor. Off camera, and unknown to the gathered audience in Minsk, President Taylor was joined by the Joint Chiefs, his top intelligence advisors, and Secretaries Hale and Bryan. Taylor wanted the contents of the conversation to be heard directly by his trusted inner circle.

"I have requested your audience for two important reasons. First, I want to tell you about recent events that you have been, at least in part, witness to. A pro-Russian militia—the Nationalist Proletarian Army, or NPA—seized control of the BSU campus, the KGB Headquarters building, and the Government House. They also took control of the international airport." The President took his time reviewing the events so that the Belarusian citizens would understand what had happened, although he stopped short of mentioning the smallpox virus and the aerosol machine.

"Second, I want to ask for your help. Anything that you heard or saw may be of value. One of your colleagues, Professor Dmitri Kaspar, has already provided invaluable assistance."

President Taylor moved his head as if he could see through the camera, trying to spot Dmitri in the audience. "Is Professor Kaspar there?"

The faculty and staff of BSU stared back blankly. They did not know what happened to their friend and coworker, only that he was missing.

Peter answered, breaking an uncomfortable silence. "I'm sorry Mister President. Dmitri Kaspar was murdered by General Gorev."

President Taylor frowned, and took a deep breath before going on. "I'm very sorry. I gather he was a brave man."

"He was," answered Ian Savage, unable to hold back his emotions. A tear rolled down first one cheek and then the other. "And he was my friend."

"You are Professor Ian Savage, and I believe I was just speaking with your son, Peter?"

"Yes Mister President," Peter answered.

Gary nudged Peter, and he took the hint.

"This is Gary Porter, my best friend, and a brave man," Peter said.

"Mister Porter, it's a pleasure."

The video feed showed an aide approach the President and whisper in his ear. Then Taylor cleared his throat and resumed.

"During the time that you were held captive, did you see or hear anything to suggest Russian soldiers were present at the university alongside the rebels?"

"We heard them talking," a woman spoke up. "They spoke in Russian, but the accent was not of Minsk. More like Moscow."

President Taylor pinched his eyebrows and thought for a moment before continuing. "Commander, do you know if you encountered militia or Russian regulars?"

Jim answered without hesitating. "Both. We have documents of orders to Russian Spetsnaz and other physical evidence linking soldiers to Moscow. Some of the soldiers we fought were very well trained and equipped, more likely Spetsnaz than militia. Also, we have Major Leonov in custody. He is purportedly a member of Spetsnaz."

"I see. Well, I want to thank you all very much. I'm sure Colonel Garrett's men will have many more questions. You must all be exhausted. I will let you get some well-deserved rest."

There was a shuffle and people rose and began to move to the door, ushered quietly and respectfully by several Marines. "Uh, just a few more minutes, gentlemen," President Taylor said.

Peter noticed the monitor was still on. "Do you mean us?" he asked.

"Yes," the President replied and then he waited until the last of the university staff had left. Colonel Garrett gave a silent nod indicating the room was clear.

"There is an additional matter that I wish to discuss with

you. However, it is of the highest level of secrecy. Colonel Garrett, have you dismissed the technicians?"

"Yes, sir. The communications team has left the room along with all other civilians and military personnel. Only myself, Commander Nicolaou, Peter Savage, Gary Porter, and Professor Savage are present."

"Very well. Colonel Garrett, I must ask you to leave the room now."

Colonel Garrett turned and strode out. If he had any curiosity about the imminent conversation, he knew better than to ask.

As soon as the door shut, the President continued. "Will each of you please confirm that there are no other persons in the room other than yourselves?"

A chorus of 'yes' was heard in reply to the President's question.

"I understand that the four of you were intimately involved in deactivating the virus aerosol machine. Did you see any identifying markings on the machine?"

"Yes, and we've shared all this with Commander Nicolaou," Peter said. "The machine is in his custody."

"Please, tell me what you found inside the device."

"Well, circuit boards that looked to be made in Russia based on the Cyrillic markings. The same for the air blower and the plastic case itself. I can't say anything about the origin of the explosive—the military can make that call after a lab analysis is completed. Plus, Leonov had his men guarding the aerosol machine on the roof of the chemistry building on the BSU campus."

"Hold on just a minute. I have General Hendrickson here, also Secretary Hale." President Taylor motioned with his hand and his two advisors stepped into the image, standing slightly behind the President, who remained seated at his desk.

"It's very important," said Howard Hale, "that we know the origin of the machine. Based on what you have shared, it is likely it was manufactured in Russia. But we have to be certain."

"We can transport it directly to Ramstein Air Base in Germany," Jim suggested. "They should be able to complete a highly detailed analysis."

President Taylor waved his hand, dismissing the suggestion. "This is too sensitive. You four are part of the inner circle; we have to keep a lid on this. Everything related to smallpox or bioweapons or an aerosol dispersion device, everything, is on a need-to-know basis and carries the highest level of secrecy."

General Hendrickson chimed in. "Sending the case to Ramstein or any other air base is too risky; we simply cannot guarantee the information will not be leaked out. Commander Nicolaou, you have to conduct a thorough examination there, immediately."

"Yes sir." Jim was already trying to figure out how he could carry out the General's order.

President Taylor seemed to read the concern on Jim's face. "I have confidence in you Commander. You have two scientists on your team—"

Gary interrupted, raising his hand like a student trying to get the attention of his teacher. "Uh, three. Three scientists. I'm a software engineer." Gary turned to Peter and said, "That counts, doesn't it?"

General Hendrickson frowned. "Commander, you have operational control of this mission for as long as the case is in Minsk. Colonel Garrett has been advised, and he will support you fully. You will communicate sensitive information directly to Colonel Pierson. He's been fully briefed and is in frequent communication with the Pentagon as well as the White House. Any questions?"

"Sir, I will need to bring some of my SGIT analysts in on

this. Colonel Pierson will vouch for them."

The General nodded. "Anything else?"

Jim looked to Peter. "Yes," Peter replied. "We can remove the explosive charge—we've already removed the detonator. I'm recommending that we ship them immediately to a lab for analysis. Same for the virus. I presume it's in a powdered form enclosed within a metal box. The rest of the dispersion device can stay here."

President Taylor pressed a button to mute the speaker, and then he conferred with his two advisors. After two minutes, the speaker was activated again.

"Very well," said Hendrickson. "Have the explosive and detonator ferried immediately to Ramstein. We'll come up with a cover story before the samples arrive. The virus is more challenging. But the European Molecular Biology Laboratory in Heidelberg has been participating in genetic sequencing of samples from Tbilisi, Georgia."

Hendrickson paused for a moment, allowing Hale to break in. "We'll get it cleared, but they are the best resource at the moment. Later, we'll have the CDC check their results."

"One more thing," Peter said. "It's possible we have all been exposed to the virus simply by opening the case. You should think about getting a vaccination program started here right away."

President Taylor looked at Secretary Hale. "See to it Howard. Get 100,000 doses of vaccine on a flight ASAP; within the hour if possible. Draw whatever medical personnel you need from the Army and Air Force. Also coordinate with the CDC on a quarantine and vaccination plan. Move on this; I don't want any delays."

"I'm on it, sir." He stepped to the side to conduct a brief conversation with an aide.

There were no further requests from either Jim or Peter.

"Gentlemen," President Taylor said. "I need answers. The Russian Foreign Minister is scheduled to speak to the General Assembly at the United Nations in about twelve hours. He is expected to accuse the United States of using biological agents as weapons of terror against civilian populations. Right now, the evidence is in their favor, even though we know the accusation to be completely false. We must have this evidence; irrefutable proof that Russia manufactured this aerosol machine to spread smallpox in Minsk."

President Taylor shifted in his chair and his eyes narrowed. "If we fail, the court of world opinion will turn against the U.S. President Pushkin will be emboldened to use his proxy military to continue attacks on Eastern European nations, and NATO will have no choice but to go to war to prevent the map of Europe from being redrawn."

"I understand, sir," Peter said. "We'll wring as much information as we can from this machine, but it won't be easy."

"I need your results as soon as possible, hopefully not more than an hour, two at most."

Peter shared an uncomfortable look with Jim. He knew better than anyone that you don't promise research results on a schedule; often the science just doesn't cooperate. You learn what you can, as fast as you can, and whether it would take one hour or ten hours was anyone's guess. Fortunately, they would have assistance from the SGIT team of intelligence analysts, a group Peter had brief interactions with in the past and held in high regard.

President Taylor seemed to read his mind. "Do the best you can—that's all I ask."

"Mister President?" Peter said before he signed off. "What do you plan to do with this information? I mean, assuming we find confirming information that the device was assembled in Russia, then what?"

President Taylor stared into the camera, his eyes hard, uncompromising. "Leave that to me."

"Well, you heard it." President Taylor said. "Recommendations?"

Colleen Walker, Director of the NSA, answered. She had thought long about the options should proof that Russia was trying to frame the U.S. come into their hands. "We have to send a strong message. We should destroy whatever facility made that machine."

"And risk starting a war with Russia?" Paul Bryan retorted. "President Pushkin won't just sit on his hands if we bomb one of his nation's military labs."

"But you agree the machine was likely assembled at a military facility; you just said as much," Colleen answered.

Bryan rolled his eyes. "You're distorting what I said. Until we have proof, we really don't know who fabricated that device, or where."

President Taylor raised his hands, signaling an end to the verbal jousting.

Secretary Hale broke the tense silence that had settled across the Oval Office. "I agree with Colleen. Once we determine where the smallpox virus was made and the aerosol machine was assembled, we take it out."

Paul Bryan objected. "Are you assuming both were made at the same site, or are you recommending we attack and destroy two facilities, both possibly Russian?"

Hale wouldn't let himself be baited. "If we're lucky, we can use cruise missiles, launched from a safe distance."

"If we're lucky? Did I hear you right?" Bryan glared at his counterpart in Defense.

Taylor raised his voice. "Gentlemen. This is not the time."

Bryan and Hale both redirected to their boss.

"Paul, I want to speak with President Pushkin immediately. Please see to it."

"Yes, Mister President." As he left the Oval Office he hoped he would be more successful connecting the call this time.

"Cruise missiles… I don't know," Taylor muttered.

"They'll fly under their air defenses, no personnel at risk."

The President had taken up pacing behind his desk. "Won't we run the risk of spreading more smallpox if they have inventory on hand?"

General Hendrickson replied. "That would be true if we used conventional munitions." He paused, until he was confident he had everyone's attention. "There is another option."

"And that would be?" prompted the President.

All eyes now were on General Hendrickson.

"A tactical nuclear warhead."

CHAPTER 39

Washington, DC

PAUL BRYAN FOLLOWED THE CHIEF of Staff into the Oval Office. It had taken the Secretary of State less than ten minutes to complete a terse conversation with Foreign Minister Denisov who agreed that President Pushkin would receive a call from President Taylor within 30 minutes.

"Thank you Paul," President Taylor said. Then he paused, eyes seemingly looking through the Secretary of State. "Seems we've been here before."

Bryan nodded. "Too many times. I wish it wasn't so."

After a moment, President Taylor continued. "The Air Force destroyed a column of Russian armor headed for the Minsk airport. For the moment at least, the airport is firmly under our control, and we are not being challenged in the air."

"Congratulations sir."

"Not yet—this is far from over."

"If I may ask sir, suppose our hypothesis that the smallpox weapon was manufactured by Russia is confirmed. Do you intend to bomb the facility?"

Taylor look weary, the wrinkles on his face deep, his eyes

puffy and heavy with fatigue. “If we find such proof, and it is irrefutable, I have no choice but to vaporize the facilities responsible for manufacturing the virus and building the weapon.”

The sudden realization swept over Bryan, the revelation filling him with dread. His jaw dropped, and he was about to speak, but Taylor held his hand out, quashing any objection.

The nightmare scenarios raced through Bryan’s mind, painfully imagined and terrifying. What the President was contemplating was akin to standing in a vat of gasoline and lighting matches, then dropping them in the hope the flame would extinguish before igniting a deadly conflagration. Events could rapidly spiral out of control and lead to not only a large-scale war, but one involving the exchange of nuclear weapons, a horror the world had only witnessed once. And until his dying breath, Paul Bryan was determined to do everything in his power to prevent a repeat.

The voice of President Taylor pulled Secretary Bryan back to the present. The phone buzzed twice and he eased himself into a Chippendale chair. “President Pushkin. I wish we were not speaking under such grave circumstances.”

“You seem to take military conflict rather easily, Mister President. A pity. You would be wise to have higher regard for American lives.”

“Sir, neither of us has the time to play games. We both understand the gravity of the situation.”

“Indeed, perhaps you should have given it more thought before you interfered in the affairs of a sovereign nation. America has no right to use its military might to change the course of events in Belarus. Only the people of Belarus have that right.”

“I’m glad we agree on that point.” Taylor knew his sarcasm wouldn’t be lost on the Russian President.

"My country has an agreement with Belarus to provide protection in the event of an attack from outside forces. We have shown considerable restraint, but if America and NATO do not back down, I'm afraid we will have no choice but to honor our agreement."

"I have spoken with President Yatchenko, and he expressed his desire that Russian aircraft, troops, and vehicles leave his country immediately."

President Pushkin chuckled dramatically. "So, you order your military to invade Minsk and attack Russian aircraft, and I am to take your word that you were invited?"

"Believe what you will. The truth is self-evident."

"Indeed. Many of the citizens of Minsk hold Russian passports. Did you know that?"

Pushkin didn't wait for a response. "The Russian people are loyal to each other. I have a sworn duty to protect my people wherever they live. In Belarus, we have many citizens. Although we are separate nations on paper, that is a mere formality. Our people—my people—are very close.

"I sat down with President Yatchenko last year, and gave him my pledge of protection when we signed the formal agreement. Belarus is not a NATO country. You have no right to become involved militarily."

"The United States and our European allies are responding to our moral obligation to defend a peaceful country."

"International law in on my side," Pushkin said. "I must insist that you withdraw all American armed forces and military equipment within 24 hours."

President Taylor paused for a moment before answering. "Mister Pushkin, once Russian forces have fully withdrawn, along with Russian armor, antiaircraft batteries, and fighter aircraft, then, and only then, will U.S. and NATO forces leave Belarus."

"I see," Pushkin said. "So this is how you wish it to be."

"Spare me the indignation. We all know you are stirring up trouble in the former Soviet Bloc countries under the guise of independent citizen militias."

"You have no right to lecture me. My country is exercising its right to protect and support ethnic Russians wherever they may live. America is no stranger to sending armed soldiers into foreign lands to protect her citizens. Why should Russia be any different?

"In Europe, Asia, Latin American, the Middle East, it's always the same. You use bribes and threats to coerce governments to become pro-West, pro-U.S. If that doesn't work, you order your intelligence agencies to destabilize leaders and put your own puppet regime in power.

"You've united Western Europe under NATO and now you won't be satisfied until all of Eastern Europe is also economically and militarily allied against Russia!"

"Since 1945, it has been the policy of the United States to support democracy and freedom of the people to fairly elect their government. It's unfortunate you view that policy as a threat."

"So you say. In reality, my country's boundaries have receded in the west and the south as a result of persistent pressure from the United States. You have long stirred civil unrest and fomented rebellion in the border regions. These are lands that were united under one flag, the Russian flag, by Peter the Great and Catherine the Great long before the birth of America."

"I am familiar with Russian history. And you aim to reestablish those historical borders?"

President Pushkin remained silent.

"You've made mistakes this time."

Pushkin sighed, and President Taylor thought it a bit

theatrical. "You should know me better, Mister President. I do not make mistakes."

"Oh?"

"The world is already learning how America has used a biological weapon in Georgia to poison innocent people. Your weak attempt to blame my government is refuted by the evidence... evidence from none other than the European Molecular Biology Laboratory. It is time to face the truth; you have no credibility on the world stage.

"As I'm sure you know, my country has already briefed the Secretary General of the United Nations on these outrageous and provocative actions your administration has taken. How can you justify infecting thousands of civilians with disease and then blame it on Russia? How dare you! My Foreign Minister will soon address the entire Assembly, and lay out the irrefutable evidence of your guilt."

President Taylor had expected this, and listened calmly until Pushkin finished. "We have many captured Russian soldiers in Minsk."

"And what is your proof—that they speak Russian?" Pushkin laughed. "Your prisoners are militiamen—rebels—not Russian soldiers."

"We shall see."

"Mister President, heed my warning and withdraw your troops and airplanes before this skirmish escalates past the point of no return. Once the United Nations is aware of your crimes, America will stand alone."

"Did I tell you that we recovered an aerosol device from a rooftop in Minsk? It was designed to disperse weaponized smallpox virus. Clever contraption, really—it proved rather difficult to disarm." Now it was Taylor's turn to let out a short, mirthless chuckle. "But of course you know that. After all, the machine was made under your direction."

The line was silent for several heartbeats before Pushkin replied. "You say you recovered one machine for dispersing aerosols? Smallpox virus?"

"Yes, that's correct. Are you surprised?"

"Indeed. Did you deactivate the machine before it could dispense the virus?"

"Fortunately, yes. It is our understanding there has been no release in Minsk. The population is safe. But just to be certain we are initiating a small-pox vaccination program for the civilians who may have been exposed. We have good reason to believe the aerosol dispersion machine and the virus itself were manufactured by your government."

"Once again, a groundless allegation, Mister President. My government does not engage in biological terrorism. That, it would appear, is the sole domain of the United States."

"On the contrary, the device was assembled using Russian components, including Russian explosives and detonators. And the anti-clumping agent mixed with the virus powder is also of Russian origin." Taylor decided there was nothing to lose by overstating what he actually knew as fact. But Pushkin did not pursue the President's claims and remained silent.

"The virus itself is the interesting part. The analysis—genetic sequencing—is not completed yet, but we expect it will indicate the smallpox is identical to that used in research in the United States. A strain that was stolen and sold to a Russian agent."

"I am baffled. You admit the smallpox virus is identical to U.S. genetic strains, and yet you accuse Russia of building and deploying the weapon? Who will believe such nonsense?"

"There is no doubt it is of Russian manufacture." Hearing his words spoken aloud, President Taylor realized how ridiculous his accusation sounded. It would take a significant PR effort to spin this so that opinion did not swing against the

United States.

"Come now, we both know that your military has the resources to make this machine look like it was fabricated in Russia. Let me tell you, as a friend, if I were to make a bioweapon and deploy it in a secret attack, one aimed at civilians—"

"But, of course, you did just that," Taylor interrupted.

Unfazed, Pushkin continued. "I would instruct my scientists to purchase American parts and use captured American explosives. This would ensure that if the weapon was captured, it would not be traced back to my government.

"The virus itself, that is the tricky part of this thought exercise. Hmmm. I am told by my scientists that Russia no longer maintains live smallpox virus samples. We have a complete genetic code, which is sufficient should we ever have a need to manufacture the ghastly virus."

President Taylor was surprised at Pushkin's command of American slang, and then recalled Pushkin had attended both Harvard and Oxford in the U.K., each for two years, more than two decades earlier.

"Since the smallpox genetic sequence does not match Russian strains, but does match American strains, the logical conclusion is clear."

"We both know the truth."

"You speak of truth as if it were an absolute. There is no such thing. Truth is what others choose to believe."

President Taylor recognized the futility in further debating the issue.

"Mister Pushkin, we can either negotiate a peaceful settlement to this unfortunate situation, or the United States and its NATO allies will use all necessary force to bring an end to your government's aggression."

When Vladimir Pushkin replied, his words were clipped, his voice tight as if he was struggling to restrain a violent outburst. “President Taylor, I have indulged your insulting accusations long enough. You have seriously underestimated my resolve—the resolve of the Russian Federation and her people, and, ultimately, the resolve of the sovereign nations of the world. I warn you, tread carefully, for you are walking into a minefield.”

Before Taylor could reply, the line went dead.

“Okay,” Peter said. “Clearly time is of the essence.”

Jim opened the door and called for Colonel Garrett. He was involved in a conversation with a Marine sergeant, but Jim assumed his needs took priority over just about any other business.

“Colonel, I assume you know the essence of the conversation I just concluded.”

“I know that you are in charge of a secret mission and I am to provide whatever support and assistance you require.” Other officers may have felt denigrated by being sidestepped, cut out of the information loop, but not Garrett. He was confident in his abilities and the trajectory of his career and took no offense. Jim read that right away and decided to downplay his authority as much as possible.

“With your permission, sir, I’d like to get my team working on that case right here. We could use the video and secure com link to bring in my analysts at The Office.” The facilities that SGIT called home, located on a portion of the McClellan Business Park in Sacramento, was affectionately called The Office by the team.

“Whatever you need Commander.”

“Thank you sir,” Jim replied and then he called for Bull and the communication technicians who were hanging back in the shadows outside the room. Within a few minutes the case was resting on a long table. The technicians arranged bright lighting, and had already connected Lieutenant Lacey, whose image filled the flat screen.

Before he began, Jim dismissed everyone other than Peter, Gary, Ian, and Magnum, who would be needed to deal with the explosive charge. Colonel Garrett ensured the door was closed on his way out.

"Lacey," Jim began. "Everything we are about to discuss is 'need-to-know'; Sensitive Compartmented Information."

"Understood," Lacey replied.

"We are going to disassemble the aerosol machine. Magnum has rendered it safe by removing the detonator. The circuit boards are toast thanks to Peter's improvised EMP bomb—"

Uncharacteristically, Lacey cut off her boss. "Excuse me sir, did I hear you correctly?"

"Affirmative Lieutenant. Peter somehow managed to rig up a close-proximity electromagnetic pulse weapon that overloaded the electrical circuits of the machine. Very effective."

Lacey's mouth was agape and her eyes were wide as she listened from the SGIT conference room.

"Bring in Stephens and Ross, I want their eyes on this, too. And who's your best Russian translator?"

"That's Ross, sir," Lacey answered.

"Very good. Peter saw some writing on the circuit boards, maybe other parts as well. Ross can translate for us. We're looking for evidence as to the origin of this device. The explosive charge and smallpox virus—we're assuming that's what it is—will be transported to Germany for further analysis. Colonel Pierson has the details, but that is not our concern at this time. The device itself will be secured for any follow-up analysis at a later time."

Lacey placed the video conference call on hold while she summoned Mona Stephens and Beth Ross.

Jim grabbed a small hand-held camera, connected

wirelessly to the communication link so that his analysts, halfway around the world, would clearly see everything as Peter meticulously worked his way through the case.

"This is the device, removed from the roof of the chemistry building. It was placed adjacent to an air-intake vent," Jim explained as Stephens and Ross seated themselves in the conference room at The Office.

"I'll begin with the display and three buttons." Peter gingerly removed the circuit assembly and placed it on the table.

"Looks like a standard timing circuit," Gary said. "I'd imagine one of the buttons activated the manual timer, and the other two buttons are to increase or decrease the set time. This key lock is a simple switch to prevent accidental arming."

"Now, moving on to the circuit boards," Peter explained. There were a total of three, two large and one a little smaller, aligned in a row with about an inch of separation. Peter pulled the first board out of the slot with both hands. It was a snug fit. He placed the circuit board on the table under the light and Jim captured close-ups with the camera. They repeated the process with the next two boards.

Peter stopped, waiting for comment from any of the SGIT analysts. All three were framed on the large monitor, each sitting behind an opened laptop.

"This board," he held one in front of the camera for closer scrutiny, "appears to have sensors for measuring atmospheric pressure and wind speed. And this component here—" Peter pointed to a blue chip soldered to the board. "I think this is a humidity sensor. It looks very much like humidity sensors we have in portable meteorological instruments."

"I concur," Gary added. "These are most definitely sensors, not the typical transistors, capacitors, and resistors one finds on PCBAs."

"Mister Porter?" Ross interjected. "PCBA?"

"Printed circuit board assembly."

Beth Ross nodded as she continued typing on her laptop.

"I understand measuring humidity and atmospheric pressure, but I'd think wind speed would be even more important." This question came from Lacey.

"Oh, of course. Wind speed is inferred from a miniature pitot tube that connects to the air intake grill. It's right here," again Peter pointed out the component—it was longer and more slender than the other components soldered to the printed circuit board.

"A pitot tube measures air speed by a differential pressure," Gary elaborated. "They are commonly used on aircraft."

"Except in this case air speed is the wind blowing over the case," Lacey said.

"Correct." Peter maneuvered the board in front of the camera. "Can you see the writing clearly?"

Beth Ross answered. "Commander, can you zoom in on the center board?"

Jim did, enlarging the image two fold. It appeared as a smaller image on the lower left of the monitor, overlaid on the video of Lacey, Ross, and Stephens.

Ross studied the image. It was Cyrillic printing—several words that Peter assumed were a manufacturer name and board ID.

"Definitely Russian," Ross said. "Now, please focus on the left board, the writing along the edge, see it?"

"Got it." Jim zoomed in until the writing was large and clear.

"Hmm, that's odd," Ross said. Her lips moved in silence, like she was sounding out the words she was reading.

"What's odd about it?" Stephens asked.

"Well, the other two circuit boards have Russian markings indicating they were fabricated in Russia. But this board..." Ross shook her head. "No, this writing is not Russian."

"Are you certain?" Lacey asked. "It looks like Cyrillic characters to me."

"Oh, they are. But that doesn't mean it's Russian." Ross paused for a moment. "I think this is Kazakh."

Lacey and Stephens were focused on Beth Ross, hanging on her words. "Kazakh is the native language of Kazakhstan, and it's spoken by a majority throughout most of the country," Ross explained.

"And Russia operates several military and scientific research facilities in Kazakhstan, including missile and laser research. It makes sense," Lacey said.

Peter gently placed the air blower on the table, and Jim zoomed in on the label. Even though Peter didn't read or speak Russian or Kazakh, he could still interpret much of the printed information.

"It's a 12 volt blower, the specs are given here," Peter pointed with a screwdriver to the label. Again, the printing used the Cyrillic alphabet.

"The air blower is of Russian manufacture," Beth observed. "Let's see the batteries."

"First, I want to get the explosive charge out of the way," Peter said. It was packaged in a military-green plastic box. Even with the detonator removed, Peter felt his pulse quicken as he adroitly removed four mounting screws that held the explosive-filled box to a partition panel inside the case. Once free of its mountings, he turned it over and immediately concluded it was devoid of any markings. "Looks like a non-descript box—could be from anywhere."

Jim shared the images, turning the box so all six sides were photographed.

"Magnum, the detonator and charge are going to Ramstein. Package them up, detonator separate from main charge, and see to it that Colonel Garrett gets them on a flight ASAP. He understands the priority, but respectfully remind him anyway."

"Yes sir."

Peter moved on. "Now I'll remove the batteries."

The power supply was substantial—about the size of a motorcycle battery—and it was heavy enough that Peter held it with two hands as he set it down, although he tried to minimize his handling of it. "Probably sufficient energy stored here to keep the machine in standby, waiting to be activated, for at least a month."

Beth Ross studied the label, black printing on a white and green background. The battery casing itself was black plastic. But what was most interesting was a short message, hand-printed at the bottom of the label.

"Yes, the battery is also Russian made. However, see that handwriting on the label?"

"What does it say?" Peter asked as Jim zoomed-in the camera until the image dominated the frame.

"I'm pretty sure that's a QC certification, a name and date, but like before, that's not Russian. It's Kazakh."

Lacey looked into the camera, making virtual eye contact with Jim and Peter. "If Ross is correct, that means the device was most likely assembled in Kazakhstan, not Russia."

"There's no mistake in my translation," Ross said. "Remember, I grew up with a Russian grandmother, and was fluent in Russian by age seven. And I majored in linguistics in college. After graduation, I completed a 48-week course in Russian at the Defense Language Institute in Monterey. Kazakh is a Turkic language while Russian is Indo-European. They're completely different in grammar and vocabulary. To Westerners the written words look similar because the Cyrillic alphabet is favored now. But that wasn't always the case. Kazakh was first written in Arabic script. With Russian domination of Kazakhstan beginning in the early-20th century, use of Arabic script was banned. Anyone who is fluent in one language or the other can easily tell them apart."

"It does make sense," Peter said.

"Why do you say that?" Jim asked.

"Well, look at it this way. Someone has manufactured smallpox based on a U.S. strain of the virus in order to make it look like America used biological weapons. We're pretty sure it was Russia, and the Kremlin would have to know we would suspect them. So, they can't afford the risk of actually making this aerosol device on Russian soil. At the minimum, it gives them plausible deniability."

"Peter has a good point," Lacey said.

"Stephens, where are the significant Russian research facilities in Kazakhstan?" Jim asked.

"Give me a minute sir." She was already typing in the query. MOTHER, the SGIT super computer, would have a summary in seconds.

"Let's keep going, Peter. Maybe there are some marks on the sheet metal assemblies or other parts that'll give us more clues."

With the battery and control boards removed, it was a simple matter to unplug the wire harness and expose the ducting, and a box that presumably contained the weaponized virus.

"See if you can get a clear shot of the wires," Peter suggested. Jim focused on some letters on the insulation.

"The wire is of Russian manufacture," Ross said.

"Now you should be able to move the camera into the case. See this spot?" Peter pointed again with the screwdriver. "Looks to me like a stamp of some sort."

Ross studied the image. "Sir, can you zoom in a bit more?"

Jim moved the camera closer and played with the zoom and focus. "That's max magnification," he said.

It was indeed a stamped mark on the sheet metal ducting,

but not writing. Rather it was a symbol. Ross typed a search command and waited momentarily for the results. When it displayed on her laptop, she turned the PC around to the video camera.

The picture was a circle with a turquoise blue center and a yellow rim. Superimposed over the blue center was a yellow horse.

"This is the coat of arms for the Jambyl Province, or Oblast, of south central Kazakhstan," Ross explained.

"Bingo!" Stephens nearly jumped out of her chair. She began reading from her monitor. "Sary-Shagan. It's the major Russian missile test range in Kazakhstan. Also laser weapon development and testing and, back in the Soviet era, a nuclear test site. Mostly high-altitude air bursts to study EMP effects. The facility lies on the western shore of Lake Balkhash."

Jim said, "The site is very remote. Good location for weapons research and development."

"There's a strong cultural tie between Russia and Kazakhstan—" Lacey was saying when Ross interrupted her.

"That cultural tie, to the extent you can legitimately call it that, is recent. It only goes back a hundred years or so to when the communists seized control of Kazakhstan. The Kazakh people have more in common with Asians, having descended from the Mongols when Genghis Khan invaded and settled the land."

"Miss Ross," Lacey said, "I understand your dislike for the government under President Pushkin. But you will remain focused and professional."

"Yes ma'am," Ross answered.

"What I started to say, Commander, is that President Pushkin sees a cultural connection with Kazakhstan as evidenced by a similar alphabet and the fact that Russian is commonly spoken by the Kazakhs. The land has also been under

Russian control, gaining independence with the fall of the Iron Curtain. There are strong trade agreements between the two countries, including energy and other strategic resources, while at the same time Kazakhstan has turned its back on the West. It does not take a vivid imagination to picture Pushkin invading northern Kazakhstan following the same logic as the invasion of Eastern Ukraine."

Jim rubbed his chin, a habit when he was deep in thought. "So you're suggesting that the government of Kazakhstan is functioning as a Russian puppet?"

"In essence, yes. Some analysts within the DIA openly speculate that Kazakhstan will be the next Crimea, invaded and annexed by Russia."

Peter, who had been listening intently, felt he knew where the analysis was leading. "I'd certainly feel better if we had more evidence before concluding that this device was manufactured on the shore of Lake Balkhash."

"The package will be delivered to Ramstein Air Base tonight," said Lacey. "They have a well-equipped lab and can analyze the chemical composition of the explosive and detonator. But I'm betting they confirm both are Russian military. So, I don't see how that helps us. We already know the Russians are involved."

"I'm confident," Peter said, "this aerosol dispersion device was not assembled in a clean and sterile environment. There simply is no need for that given the nature of how the device operates."

"I'm not following you," Jim said. Lacey and the other analysts were listening carefully, trying to understand where Peter's comment would lead.

"Well, the device draws in air and then expels the fine virus as a dust or aerosol. Since ambient air is drawn through the device, why go to the trouble to assemble it in a clean environment? It's going to get exposed to dust and other air pollutants during operation anyway."

"Okay," Jim said. "But so what?"

"We need to look for a fingerprint that will confirm the location of assembly. That fingerprint is pollen and dust."

Lacey and Stephens were nodding as Peter spoke. "I agree, sir," Lacey said. "If the machine was assembled at Sary-Shagan, there will be traces of pollen from native plants."

"The risk," Peter said, "is that there may not be much native vegetation in that part of Kazakhstan. If I'm not mistaken, it's very arid."

Stephens read from her laptop. "The Ili River delta is close to Sary-Shagan, and it's lush—coastal cane, several varieties of reeds, and willows." She tilted her head and frowned. "Fairly common plant species—pollen analysis may not provide a definitive answer."

"That's why it's vitally important to also examine dust that is adhered to the plastic box housing the battery as well as other surfaces inside the case. Plastics are susceptible to acquiring a static charge, which attracts dust, so it's likely we'll find material on the box and elsewhere. We have to capture the dust particles and then analyze their chemical makeup using x-ray fluorescence spectroscopy inside the chamber of an electron microscope."

Jim objected. "But any samples—pollen or dust or whatever—that maybe found are already compromised since the device has been opened to Minsk city air. Not to mention the handling under our examination here."

"Your argument would be valid if we were trying to prove the machine was assembled in Belarus," Peter said. "But that's not the challenge. We want to know if, at any time, the device has been in the vicinity of Sary-Shagan. If the answer is yes, then the mostly likely reason is because it was assembled there."

Jim was convinced. "You sound like you know what to look for, Peter—where to find dust and pollen samples," Jim said.

"I've done this before, if that's what you mean. The magnetic impulse guns my company develops go through rigorous testing in the field before we release the design to production. Part of that testing is to disassemble a prototype gun and examine it for contamination by dust, dirt, and grit. Because the weapons generate strong magnetic fields, particulates that are predominately iron and nickel will accumulate around the solenoids, potentially causing a short circuit. We capture the contamination then analyze its composition using an electron microscope."

"Good. I want you to collect your samples now. Do you think there is an electron microscope at the BSU campus?"

Peter recalled Dmitri's comments when they met and he was planning to take them on a tour of the chemistry facilities. He had mentioned an electron microscopy lab. "Yes, it's my understanding they do."

"Can you operate the microscope?"

Peter nodded. "Yes, I should be able to get a simple elemental analysis of any particles we capture off the inner componentry."

"Good. What do you need?"

"Well, some cotton swabs and adhesive paper labels, and a piece of wax paper. Oh, and a pen and pad of paper… and several paper envelopes."

Jim sent Iceberg and Magnum in search of the items. "Start with the hotel manager. The office should have file folder labels. Maybe housekeeping has cotton swabs, and check the kitchen for the wax paper. And get some disposable latex gloves!"

Next, Jim addressed Lacey who was still on the video feed. "Lieutenant, find out where we're to send the virus package. I'll inform Garrett; he can commandeer a second aircraft once he knows the destination."

With a new objective, Peter returned to examining the components inside the case, as well as the plastic case itself. He squinted his eyes as he looked along the hinge and the metal reinforcing wrapping the edge of each half of the molded case, spotting areas to sample. Also, on the blower housing, which was plastic, he found a thin, grey-white coating of dust. He'd sample that with the adhesive label, same for the plastic battery box, and the fiberglass printed circuit boards.

Peter had mentally completed his course of action just as Iceberg and Magnum returned with the requested goods. He set to work documenting the sampling locations on a sheet of paper, in every case also drawing a simple sketch of the location from which the sample was acquired.

Carefully, Peter folded the adhesive labels between sheets of wax paper. Later, he would peel the labels off and, hopefully, the dust particles would still be retained by the sticky layer. Cotton swabs were wiped over edges and grooves to collect the particulates, and then each was placed in a separate labeled envelope.

It took about 15 minutes to complete the task. The last action was to remove the metal compartment that was suspected to contain the virus agent. Peter donned a pair of disposable gloves and held his breath while backing out a few screws that held it in place. Once free of its mountings, Peter slipped the metal box into a zip-lock bag. Finally, they closed the case, and Gary and Jim sealed it inside two plastic bags, taping the seams tight. Later, it would be ferried to Germany.

CHAPTER 40

Minsk

PETER PLACED HIS HAND ON Jim's arm. "You do know there's another machine out there. We have to find it."

"With no clue as to where it is? We've gone over this already."

"The situation has changed. I think I know where it's been deployed."

Jim studied his friend, looking into his steel-gray eyes, searching for any sign of uncertainty—and reading only confidence. "Right now our job is to get these samples analyzed. Whatever we find has to be communicated immediately to President Taylor."

"That's the wrong priority. So what if we know the machine was assembled in Kazakhstan. There's another one out there, and when it activates it'll expose thousands of innocent people; maybe tens of thousands."

"We have our orders." Jim let the message sink in before continuing. "Let's get the analysis done first. Then we will go hunting for the second aerosol device. Okay?"

Reluctantly Peter agreed.

"What makes you so certain you know where the second device is?" Jim asked.

"A process of elimination. First, the case would have to be placed at a location that is under control of the militia."

"Okay, that narrows down the field of search to the airport and a handful of buildings in downtown Minsk. It would take days to thoroughly search those locations."

"Not days, an hour at the most."

Jim didn't attempt to hide his skepticism.

"Look, the aerosol needs to be released into the atmosphere. That means the machine will be on a rooftop, like the one at the chemistry building. Furthermore, it will be most effective if it's on a very high roof to yield a greater dispersion area."

"That would be the control tower at the airport. That's got to be the tallest building."

Peter shook his head. "No, not the airport. Based on what the Marines were saying, that was an intense battle and now it's under military control until further notice. So there won't be commercial flights landing and taking off, which means few people to potentially be exposed to the virus. No, the location is Minsk. And the tallest building is the KGB Headquarters, which is also under control of the militia."

"Given the sensitive political situation, it'll be some time, maybe weeks, before anyone is allowed to search the KGB Headquarters."

"This rain is expected to break up soon, and when it does, when the weather clears, the machine will activate."

"How do you know this?"

"Because that's how the aerosol machine we captured is constructed. It's probably a simple logic sequence. With this weather moving out, the barometric pressure will rise and the relative humidity will decrease within hours. There may even be a gentle wind, all the better. As this information is recorded, the microprocessor will recognize the pattern and conclude that conditions are right. At that time it will activate the machine. The blower will be powered up, and the compartment holding the smallpox virus will open allowing a jet of air to entrain the tiny dust-like virus particles and spread it into the atmosphere."

"From the top of the KGB Headquarters it could expose all of downtown Minsk." Jim imagined the machine spewing out an almost invisible, deadly dust cloud.

"Yeah, and when it's done and the virus has been dispensed, some pro-Russian KGB officer will remove the case and destroy the evidence."

"It's the perfect plan… and we're gonna make sure it doesn't happen."

Peter's lips curled upward slightly, not quite a grin but close. "Knew you'd see it my way."

"First, let's get to the lab and analyze these samples."

Within a few minutes, Jim had his team rounded up along with Captain Diaz and Peter. With ammunition supplies replenished, they boarded the Osprey. The samples, 19 in total including three control samples, were placed inside an expandable file folder donated by the hotel business office.

Jim's plan was simple. The Osprey would shuttle the men back to the BSU campus, landing as close as possible to the chemistry building. He and Peter would find the electron microscopy lab. As Peter was analyzing his samples, Jim would communicate the results to Lacey.

With the massive tilt-rotors in a full horizontal position, the aircraft functioned like a gigantic helicopter. It hovered a foot above the pavement, the tail door open and ramp against the asphalt. The pilot deftly avoiding clipping any streetlights lining the wide avenue.

In five seconds everyone was out. The SGIT team, Peter, and

Diaz all jogged across the campus to the chemistry building.

A few Marines were scattered about the campus; Peter counted six by the time they entered the battle-scarred chemistry building. Diaz engaged in a conversation with another Marine while Peter followed the SGIT soldiers into the building. Already the bodies of the slain Delta operators had been slipped into black body bags and removed, soon to begin the long, solemn flight home.

Inside, the hall still reeked of fire and death, the walls scorched in front of the library. Bullet holes riddled the walls. Looking down the long hallway toward the main entrance, Peter saw large bloodstained swaths of tile flooring, but the bodies of the militiamen had all been removed.

"Which way?" Jim asked.

"I don't know," Peter said. "Our tour was interrupted by Gorev before it began. We'll have to search door to door. I think the upper floors are all offices, so let's start here and then go to the basement."

"Bull, organize the men and get the supplies Peter needs to build another EMP bomb. Iceberg helped before, so he should know what to get. You have the list?" During the short flight in the Osprey Peter drew up a list of the necessary items. The power supply was the big question as he wasn't confident the SGIT soldiers would know what to take from the storeroom, so he told them to grab anything that even remotely looked like a power supply.

Moving quickly, Peter and Jim started down the hall checking each door. Fortunately, none were locked. As they reached the end of the hallway, almost at the destroyed lobby, Peter opened a door and found what he was seeking. "This is it." He entered, turned on the light, and Jim followed.

The room was small, only about 150 square feet, and had no windows. Occupying the center of the floor was the large, gleaming white electron microscope. An office chair was resting in front of a console with many buttons and panel-mounted lights. To the left was a stainless steel vacuum chamber—a horizontal pipe with bolt-on flanges resting on a smaller section of vertical pipe. The vacuum pump was running, making a rhythmic thumping sound.

An old-fashioned cathode-ray-tube monochrome monitor was located to the right. At the moment it displayed a moving pattern, the logo of the company that made the delicate instrument.

Peter sat in the chair and studied the controls. "Let's hope that the explosions didn't damage the electronics."

"And if they did?" Jim asked.

"Then we're screwed." Peter answered somberly.

"What can I do to help?"

Peter set the expandable file folder on the console and gently removed the samples. He scooted to a side table with a Styrofoam holder lined with small metal buttons, each button connected to a metal post. Sharing the table was another machine with a clear squat cylindrical top about six inches in diameter.

Peter tapped it with his finger. "This is a sputterer. It deposits a thin coating of metal on the samples." Jim listened intently.

Lifting one of the metal buttons, Peter placed a small piece of double-sided tape on the button. Then he removed a cotton swab from one of the envelopes. The white cotton held darker specks of foreign material lifted from the case hinge. He rolled the cotton across the sticky tape, leaving the particles behind.

"Place the sample stage inside the sputtering chamber." Peter showed Jim how to do this. "Then turn on the vacuum pump and watch this vacuum gauge. When the needle is here," Peter pointed, "flip this switch and an electric discharge will cause metal from the target to coat the sample stage."

The entire process was over in about three minutes. Peter turned a valve releasing the vacuum inside the chamber, and then he removed the prepared sample. "Now, you get the next sample ready while I load this inside the vacuum chamber of the microscope."

"What's the purpose of the metal coating?" Jim asked as he was repeating the manipulations.

"Metals conduct electricity, right?"

"Sure, of course."

"Well, this instrument will shoot a stream of electrons—electricity—at the sample. The electrons will generate an image that can be magnified electronically. If the sample is not conductive then electrical charge builds up and blurs the image."

Peter loaded the sample while he was talking, and the chamber was pumped down.

"You know how to operate this microscope?" Jim asked.

"It's very similar to the one at my company. Same manufacturer, but an older model." He pressed some buttons on the console and then turned a dial to sharpen the image on the CRT. He turned three other dials to move the sample in the x axis and y axis, and to magnify the image.

"Right there, see that?"

Jim nodded, looking at the screen while the next sample was being sputtered.

"I'll magnify the particle and then aim the x-ray beam at it." Peter manipulated the controls until the speck of dust was a green image filling the CRT. A cross was superimposed on the image, the point of analysis. In a moment the magnified image was replaced by a white screen displaying a chart.

"There it is. That's the elemental analysis of that particle."

Peter printed the list of chemical elements and percentage in the sample. Then the process was repeated over and over until all 19 samples had been analyzed.

Finished, Peter looked at the printed elemental composition tables for each sample. "There's a pattern, all right. See this?" He pointed to a series of names and numbers on the paper. "Sodium, potassium, lead, copper, zinc... all in relatively high concentrations."

Peter set the paper aside and studied a second printout. "Excellent. This is a control sample obtained from the top of a door at the hotel in Minsk. See? No copper or zinc or lead, and very low levels of sodium and potassium."

Jim studied the data while Peter moved to another printout. "And this control sample is dirt from the grounds in front of the hotel. As before, no lead, copper, or zinc. Moderate sodium, almost no potassium. This pattern is repeated over and over. The samples from inside the case are very different from the control samples."

"I agree they're different in chemical makeup, but how does that prove the aerosol machine was assembled in Sary-Shagan?"

"At the moment, it doesn't prove anything. We need to fax or email these printouts to Lieutenant Lacey for comparison to dust and mineral records from the shore of Lake Balkhash."

"I know she's been working on it. I'll check again, maybe we have that information already." Jim reached into a cargo pocket and removed a handheld electronic device. It had a screen like a cell phone, but was twice as thick to accommodate the extra circuits for encrypting voice, text, and email communications. He tapped the screen to illuminate the list of recently received messages. The device had no chime or ring tone, a failsafe to ensure the sound could never occur at a compromising moment.

"Lacey sent a text 20 minutes ago." Jim pulled up the short message and read it. "Says she is still trying to get representative data on dust composition from the area north and west of the lake. But the region is known for dust storms. Since the lake is gradually shrinking with water from the feeding rivers being diverted for agriculture, the shoreline is saline. Also, copper, zinc and lead are mined in the region, and processing the ore has yielded contamination by these heavy metals over a broad area. Seems the Kazakhs are not overly concerned about environmental pollution."

"That pretty well explains the chemical makeup of our samples."

"Is that the message you want me to give Colonel Pierson and the President?"

Hundreds of times, Peter had performed exactly this type of routine analysis. But this time was far different. His conclusion could very well encourage President Taylor to authorize military action. Against who? Peter thought. An outdated Russian base at Sary-Shagan? Maybe against military or research facilities within the Russian Federation? And what if I'm wrong?

"Peter?" Jim prodded.

"We have the chemical fingerprint connecting dust contamination from the case to an area like Sary-Shagan. Plus, the quality control markings and other notations in Kazakh, and the symbol for the Jambyl Oblast. The only logical conclusion is that the machine was assembled, if not manufactured, in Kazakhstan."

Jim placed his hand on Peter's shoulder, understanding the burden that he felt. "You did a good job here, I know it's difficult."

Peter's expression was severe as he looked deep into Jim's eyes for some measure of reassurance and comfort.

"I just have one question," Peter said.

"Yeah, what's that?"

"What if I'm wrong?"

CHAPTER 41

MINSK

WITH THE UPDATE COMMUNICATED to Colonel Pierson and the President, Jim gave the sheath of data printouts to Bull, who transmitted them over an encrypted data link using a scanner in one of the Humvees. Once done, the stack of papers along with the samples were neatly placed into a pouch where they would remain safely inside Jim's rucksack.

The rain had stopped and Peter was glad to be outside, away from the retched, acrid smell and carnage. He was inspecting a small pile of wire, metal boxes, and pipe next to one of the Marine Corps Humvees. Two others were parked nearby.

"Do you have what you need?" Jim asked.

"This is the best power supply," he said. "We'll take this one. Looks like sufficient wire. Is there a bag or something we can put all this into?"

Ghost dropped a worn canvas bag taken from the back of the truck and then placed all the items inside while Peter held the bag open. The last item to go in was what looked like the same piece of plastic pipe Peter had used on the roof to wind the wire.

"What about the explosive?" Peter asked while Ghost gently laid the bag in the back of the truck.

"Magnum has C4 and detonators."

"I think we should pack the copper pipe now, and you can show me how to set and insert the detonator."

Jim raised an eyebrow at Peter, considering his request. "Look, we don't know what we're going to run into, but it is the KGB Headquarters building. My guess is they won't give us visitor's badges and an escort to the roof."

"You have a valid point. Magnum!"

It took Magnum less than two minutes to stuff a partial brick of C4 plastic explosive within the copper pipe while Peter watched. Care was taken to avoid air pockets, it was essential that the explosive detonate with uniform force along the length of pipe.

Finally, Magnum showed Peter how to insert the detonator—a short metal rod with two wires extending from the back end—and how to set the timer. It was a small digital device, powered by a 9-volt battery. "Remember to give yourself time to get well clear of the blast."

Peter stuffed the detonator and timer into a pocket, and placed the copper pipe into the duffle bag.

"Is that it?" Jim asked.

"Yes, that's everything."

"Diaz commandeered these three Humvees," Jim said. "We'll drive up Independence Avenue to the KGB Headquarters. It's not far—maybe a mile or so."

"Ready, sir?" Diaz asked. All of his men, except for Washington and Nolty, were ordered to secure the BSU campus.

Then another thought came to Peter. "Just a minute!" He turned and dashed back inside, leaving Jim with a questioning look. A minute later he returned with his flamethrower in hand. He heaved it in the back next to the duffle bag.

"That's it. I'm ready," Peter said.

The trio of Humvees was passing between Independence Square and the Belarusian State University on Independence Avenue. This main thoroughfare would lead directly to the KGB building, a massive stone and concrete structure with an imposing facade. Although the exterior was frequently photographed, sightseers were not welcome, and the only way to get a tour was to either work there, be a high-ranking member of government, or be arrested for crimes against the state. The later was definitely not a favored option.

Jim was riding shotgun in the lead vehicle, with Peter in the back, and Ghost on the .50 caliber machine gun. He had the weapon loaded and cocked, ready for action. "How far, sir?" asked Nolty from behind the wheel.

"About thirteen-hundred meters," replied Jim. "It'll be on the left. A large stone building with four huge stone columns at the main entrance. It's the tallest building around."

Staying close behind the lead, Washington was driving the middle Humvee with Diaz on the TOW launcher. The TOW missile was a wire-guided anti-armor weapon ideal for taking out tanks and armored personnel carriers. Taking up the rear position was the third truck armed with another heavy machine gun with Iceberg on the trigger. The lack of traffic on Independence Avenue gave the military vehicles wide clearance, and so far there was no opposition.

That changed as they drew within sight of the massive KGB building. Parked on the broad sidewalk to either side of the stairs leading up to the huge wood doors were two Russian tanks, sitting parallel to the building, engines idling. The tank commanders were standing with the upper portion of their bodies above the turret to take advantage of the fresh air. One commander appeared to be smoking a cigarette. Clearly, the tank crews were not expecting trouble.

Jim radioed the trailing Humvee at the same time Nolty pulled to the right. "Diaz! Two tanks ahead; take 'em out!"

Barely a second elapsed when the whoosh and white smoke trail passed on the left of Jim's vehicle. The guided missile struck the closest tank, low on the turret at the cusp where it rests on the chassis. The detonation set off sympathetic explosions inside the tank. White flame and heavy smoke rocketed upward thirty feet through the open hatch.

Without prompting, Bull shoved another TOW missile up to Diaz, who quickly reloaded the single-shot tube.

The Russian commander of the second tank dropped down inside the armor shell and locked down the hatch. As he called out the target, the turret began to traverse, the big 125-millimeter cannon tracing an arc through the air.

Diaz aimed, ignoring the impending danger. The shot had to be perfect; he and his crew would only get one chance. If the missile failed to kill the steel beast, their Humvee would be blown out of existence.

As before, he aimed at the junction of the turret and the chassis. This was a weak point in an otherwise heavily-armored construction. He held the cross-hairs…

Steady…

The canon barrel was just about lined up, and he was looking into its gaping maw.

"Fire!" Diaz shouted.

White smoke marked the path of the missile as it left the launch tube from the top of the Humvee at 300 meters per second.

Less than two seconds later the canon barrel stopped, having lined up on the Humvee.

A millisecond later the missile struck home and detonated in a blinding white flash that blasted the turret off the tank.

It flipped over, landing in the street upside down. Intense fire raged within the turret-less chassis as propellant and fuel combusted in a hellish conflagration.

The two explosions, separated by about 40 seconds, violently shook the Humvees, and Peter felt an instinctive fear rising within.

The tanks were ablaze, destroyed before either could get off a single shot. But the element of surprise, which Jim was counting on, had vanished. Guards wearing black uniforms poured out of the KGB building, several leaning against the large stone columns and firing AKs at the approaching Humvees. Many more ran down the stairs to take up firing positions from the sidewalk and street, using parked cars and the shattered tanks for cover.

The heavy machine guns opened up, firing short bursts that sounded like deep, booming drum rolls, only ten times louder. To Peter it was feeling almost surreal. He was a passenger, with no role to play in the gunfight, watching it unfold from the safety of his front-row, armored seat.

The enemy was falling fast, and although they were hitting their targets, attempting to shoot through the glass and body panels to kill the occupants, the trucks' heavy protection of Kevlar, ceramic and steel plates, and bullet-proof windows rendered the rifle bullets harmless. Peter watched as two guards attempted to shoot from behind a parked sedan as .50 caliber bullets ripped through the entire width of the car, seeking, and eventually finding, the guards. As the Humvee passed Peter saw their bodies, clad in black, lying motionless in expanding pools of blood on the white sidewalk.

"Drive up the stairs and bust into the lobby!" Jim ordered the driver. Nolty shifted into low gear and floored the accelerator, speeding up the stone steps, the truck bouncing wildly. Ahead, the columns seemed to move closer together, threatening to close the gap.

"I don't know if we're gonna make it, sir!"

"Yes we are—keep going!"

Everyone was thrown around violently inside the truck as it traversed the stairs. Ghost was tossed like a rag doll in the gun turret, but somehow he managed to hang on. The nose shot into the air and then slammed down at the top, but the forward momentum never ceased, and Nolty skillfully corrected the steering and shot between the middle two columns. Screeching metal signaled that the driver was right all along, the opening was too narrow. Luckily, the vehicle's unmitigated bulk and momentum carried it forward, gouging out chunks of stone from both columns.

The bumper of the Humvee slammed two guards into the ornate wood doors—each twelve feet tall—and then bashed the doors open, tearing them from their heavy iron hinges. The truck skidded to a stop 20 feet inside the lobby of the KGB headquarters.

Occupying one entire square block and constructed more like a fort than an office building, the structure had few windows; the limited light filtering in cast a dim glow supplemented by massive ornate chandeliers suspended from the 25-foot-high ceiling. Beautiful slabs of marble covered the floor, extending about a foot up the wall before transitioning to dark wood panels. Ahead was a bank of four elevators; wide staircases with marble handrails and posts were on either side of the elevators, a red carpet covered the marble steps. The newels also served as the base for sculpted bronze post lamps, each with five light globes.

The space had a feeling of immensity given its sheer size and tall ceiling. A large bronze statue of Lenin was off to the right, and a smaller bronze of Alexander Lukashenko, the former president of Belarus with strong ties to Moscow, was on the opposite side of the cavernous room.

Staffers and guards were running about in pure pandemonium. The guards were easily identified by their all-black uniforms and AK-74 rifles. Ghost was blasting away with the .50 caliber, devastating and demoralizing the enemy, taking care not to kill the unarmed staffers, who scrambled to leave what had become a killing field.

The second Humvee with Magnum, Homer, and Iceberg shot up the steps and came to a stop just inside the shattered front doorway. Iceberg manned the heavy machine gun, adding volume to Ghost's withering fire. Magnum and Homer bailed out of the truck, pausing just long enough for Homer to grab another drum magazine for his AA12 shotgun, and scampered to the lead vehicle. Jim had already exited, using the bulletproof door as a shield.

"Nolty, you stay with Ghost; make sure he doesn't run out of ammo!" Jim ordered. Just then Magnum and Homer joined up on their commander.

"Magnum, stay with Iceberg. The four of you are going to hold this lobby."

Homer was clutching his weapon. "You have frags for that?" Jim asked, referring to the explosive 12 gauge rounds.

"Frags and buckshot," Homer replied.

"Good, you're with me. We're taking Peter to the roof. Give me a hand with the gear."

Peter had already strapped the flamethrower on his back, the sudden stab of pain from his side and his back reminded him again of his wounds, despite the painkiller Bull had administered. He was struggling to lift the heavy duffle bag when Homer arrived at his side and grabbed a strap. With Peter lifting the other loop, they yanked it out of the cargo space.

Firing continued at a steady pace, and quickly the staffers cleared. Peter wasn't sure where they all went, but suddenly they were gone.

The third Humvee remained outside, taking up station at the base of the steps. Washington parked the vehicle with the front pointed across Independence Avenue, giving plenty of room to turn the truck to gain a better angle on Russian or NPA military vehicles and troops that might attempt to reinforce the KGB Headquarters. Two shoulder-fired Stinger missile launchers lay on the seat within easy reach. Commander Nicolaou had declared any aircraft not bearing U.S. or NATO-alliance insignias to be hostile, and ordered his team to shoot-first.

Inside, NPA guards in their camouflage uniforms were streaming down the stairs, firing their assault rifles as they ran. Bullets were zinging off the Humvees, while the SGIT team returned a devastating barrage.

Two groups of men split and took up positions on opposites sides of the lobby, attempting to flank the Humvees and trap the Americans in a deadly crossfire. They ran for the statues, Lenin and Lukashenko, diving behind the granite and bronze for protection.

"Ghost, Iceberg, get those fifties on them!" Jim shouted to be heard.

Ghost swiveled his gun to the right, Iceberg to the left. Each man fired a sustained burst. The legs of Lenin were cut in half by the large caliber bullets, and the thirteen-foot-tall statue toppled over sideways, smashing marble floor tiles where it landed. Ghost lowered the muzzle, forcing the bullets down, chasing the ducking heads. The stone base with Lenin's feet was chipped as if a crew with jackhammers were pounding on it. While the enemy ducked under the hail of bullets, Jim flung two grenades that rolled past the base of the statue. They detonated, silencing the NPA guards.

At the same time, Iceberg was shooting through the bronze

of Lukashenko. One NPA guard was leaning against the statue for protection. The bullets sliced through the soft bronze easily, killing him before he was able to hit Iceberg. Magnum tossed a grenade that bounced beyond the base and exploded, sending shrapnel into the two remaining guards who were ducked low behind the stone pedestal.

Shooting continued from the front, but it was noticeably weaker.

Jim keyed his throat mic. "Alpha Team. We're going up the right staircase. Ready… Now!" With Jim in the lead, Homer in the rear, and Peter in between, the three men sprinted forward across the lobby and up the staircase.

Ghost and Iceberg continued to fire the heavy machine guns in short, effective burst. Occasionally Nolty and Magnum fired their weapons at targets of opportunity.

A center elevator chimed, and the steel doors slowly opened. Iceberg swung the smoking barrel of the .50 caliber. The doors parted no more than a foot when gunshots burst forth from within. Iceberg fired the remainder of the belt, about 25 rounds, through the doors. The perforated steel panels opened to reveal a charnel house inside the elevator.

"Reloading!" he shouted as he opening a new box of ammunition and slapped the belt in the breach.

An eerie silence pervaded the lobby. At least for the moment the shooting halted—there were no more KGB or NPA guards left standing.

The two grand stairways extended only from the lobby to the second floor. The higher floors were accessed through a central box-like stairwell with landings at each floor connected via a doorway to the interior corridors. Given the secrecy surrounding the building, Lieutenant Lacey was unable to email any interior plans to Jim. The best she could offer was a slightly dated satellite photo of the roof showing what were believed to be two access points—one at the front and one at the rear of the massive stone structure—numerous large air conditioning units, and a clock tower. The later was of sufficient height that it was probably visible from any location in the city center.

Peter made it to the second floor landing when he started to slow, breathing deeply, gulping in air. His side was burning, and he thought he may have torn the stiches. Homer relieved him of the duffle bag, noting its considerable heft.

Jim kept moving upward, rifle raised and ready for any assailants. Just as he was closing on the third floor the door opened abruptly and five NPA soldiers turned to descend the stairs. Jim immediately fired before the NPA soldiers even knew he was there, killing all of them before they got a shot off.

Above the third floor the stairs narrowed considerably. The men continued to ascend, though notably slower and more cautiously. They passed the fourth floor without incident, and the staircase narrowed even more in the last flight that connected to what Jim hoped was the roof access door. Behind them, the door at the fourth floor opened, and more NPA militia entered the staircase, not realizing that their enemy was above them.

Jim placed his index finger to his lips, looking at Peter. Homer already knew to be silent. Then he shifted his eyes to Homer, who had two grenades clipped to his load harnesses. Jim pointed to the grenades, and then indicated with hand motions to drop them down the stairs.

Homer silently placed the duffle bag down and slung his weapon. With one grenade in each hand, he extracted the safeties and then popped the pins. Leaning over the railing, he saw the NPA soldiers almost at the third floor landing. They slowed as the bodies of their slain comrades came into view.

That's when Homer threw both grenades down, aiming for

the landing where the NPA were about to step off the staircase.

The grenades landed right in front of the enemy, and they looked around in startled confusion. Some wanted to push forward, others to go back. They had one second to figure it out—not enough time before the explosives detonated.

The concussion instantly killed those within ten feet of the detonation. The men further away were less fortunate as shrapnel tore through their bodies leaving ragged, bloody wounds that none survived.

The boom was still echoing in Peter's ears when Jim shot the lock off the access door and they emerged onto the roof. He was followed immediately by Homer. Both soldiers scanned the roof for any guards. There was no one in sight.

Jim turned back to the stairwell. "It's clear. You can come up."

CHAPTER 42

MINSK

THE EXPANSIVE ROOFTOP was dotted with ten large metal industrial boxes that housed the air conditioning units. Black tar had faded to a shade of weathered gray, except for places easily spotted where leaks had recently been patched.

Gone was the earlier rain.. Although the sky was still cloudy, it looked promising to clear within a few hours. Peter felt a gentle, cool breeze as he stepped onto the flat roof. Homer and Jim were 30 feet ahead.

Jim turned to address Peter. "The aerosol machine could be anywhere."

The three men reached the closest AC unit. Standing about five feet tall and six by six feet at the base, it had metal louvered grills on all four sides. Peter studied the construction, noting that the louvers were door panels. He turned a latch, but it was locked. Quickly, he moved around and tested the other panels—also locked.

"If the aerosol machine is hidden in one of these utility sheds, it'll take some time to force open the locks and search all of—"

Gunshots cut Peter off as bullets perforated the louvers where he was standing. He ducked and dashed to the opposite side of the shed while Jim and Homer hastily returned fire and then joined Peter behind the safety of the structure. With their backs to the louvered panel, they were facing Independence Avenue, which meant that most of the flat roof extended behind them. It was impossible to search while under fire.

"They're coming up the other staircase," Jim said.

More bullets punched into and through portions of the shed, causing Peter to flinch and scrunch lower. Jim cautiously peeked around the corner and saw a large number of enemy soldiers pouring out of the far roof access doorway.

"They're spreading out across the roof," Jim said. "We can't stay here."

A blur of motion caught Jim's eye. He reflexively swung his rifle even before he recognized the four KGB guards exiting the opening that they had used only minutes before.

Black uniforms… heads swiveling, seeking the enemy… rifles at the ready…

Jim's brain processed the visual information in a fraction of a second, because that brief interval of time was often the difference between life and death.

He pulled the trigger, and a stream of bullets cut through the three KGB guards just as they located the two SGIT men and Peter.

"Empty!" Jim shouted as he expertly ejected the spent magazine and rammed home a fresh one. Homer split his attention between the near roof access door and the enemy spreading out across the far side of the roof.

Jim activated his throat mic, enabling his communication with the SGIT team downstairs. "Bull, I need a sitrep."

"So far, pretty quiet out here. No activity."

"Okay. Tell Diaz I need you to cover our back. Cross

through the lobby and double-time up the staircase. Take a defensive position on the fourth floor landing. There's a narrow staircase there that connects to the roof. No one is to access the roof up those stairs. Clear?" Jim knew that as long as Bull was alive no one would get past him.

He looked around the side of the shelter and fired off several shots, taking down two NPA soldiers. Homer was firing from the opposite side, sending a volley of buckshot into an AC shelter where the soldiers appeared to be clustered.

"We can't stay here," Jim said. "Soon they'll flank us and we'll be caught in a crossfire."

Homer nodded.

"Ready?" Jim said, and Homer rose to a crouch. Then Jim leaned around the corner of his cover and fired controlled, short bursts at the KGB and NPA scampering for position. His fire was enough to cause the enemy to duck for cover. Homer dashed to short distance to the next AC shelter. He took up position on the far side, just as a pair of NPA militia broke out onto the open expanse of roof and charged his position. Homer leveled the shotgun and fired, dropping the militia in their tracks.

More gunshots and more bullets peppered the shelter Peter and Jim were hiding behind, a few passing all the way through the metal near the top where there wasn't any machinery to stop them.

"We have to move," Jim said to Peter. "And I don't see how we can search the roof for the aerosol machine."

Peter knew Jim was very close to aborting the mission, but he didn't want to give up, not yet. He was replaying Leonov's words in his mind—something odd about his statement. Time. It is not on your side. Peter looked up and saw the clock tower with new meaning.

He stood and peaked around the side of their shelter, across the roof to the far side, drawing more gunfire. All he saw were more of the AC sheds, and they weren't even close to the height of the clock tower.

"That has to be it," Peter mumbled.

"What?" Jim said.

"Leonov. Remember, when we were interrogating him, he said, 'Time. It is not on your side.' Seemed strange at the moment, nonsensical. But I was wrong."

"We don't have time for riddles, Peter." Jim's admonishment was punctuated by the rapid, booming staccato from Homer's shotgun.

With quickening pulse, Peter pointed to the clock tower off to the left. "That's the highest location on the roof. "That's where the weapon is located."

Two pairs of eyes focused on the tower, trying to discern every detail, large and small. The Tower was square, about 20 feet on each side, with a pyramidal cap to shed rain and snow supported by posts at the four corners. The peak of the tower was 40 feet higher than the flat roof of the KGB Headquarters. A narrow ladder was fixed to the wall of the tower providing an access pathway from the roof, but small windows suggested maybe there was an internal staircase as well. An open platform, or terrace, wrapped around the tower with the clock face on three sides of a cube located at the terrace level. At night, floodlights illuminated the three clock dials, which faced to the front and sides of the stone building.

"When Leonov spoke of time not being on our side, he was referencing the clock tower," Peter said.

"Even if you're right, we can't get there, not with NPA and KGB Guards holding us tight. It's 30 meters from here to the ladder. Anyone not shot running across the open will be shot dead on the ladder."

Another volley of bullets impacted the shelter and Jim

returned fire, conscious of his ever dwindling supply of ammunition. Homer continued to fire at will, effectively blocking any flanking maneuvers.

Peter's countenance was hard, and cold. He'd been here before. Knowing that he had every reason to expect to be killed, perhaps those around him as well. But also knowing what had to be done—for a greater good. To Peter, he wasn't making a choice any more than waking up in the morning was a choice. It's simply what he had to do.

"You're right Jim. We are not going to climb the; I am. You and Homer can hold them off. Give me cover until I'm on the terrace."

Peter shifted his shoulders, adjusting the lay of the flamethrower on his back. He grasped the worn web handles of the duffle bag, measuring its heft while ignoring the sharp stab of pain. The he placed his head and an arm through the straps, suspending the bag across his shoulder, freeing his hands to scamper up the ladder. He looked across the flat roof to the ladder, imagining each stride as he would dash for the tower, jump up to the second rung, and then, hand over hand, scurry up the ladder, finally dropping onto the platform surrounding the clock. Seeing it in his mind's eye almost made it real, but he knew it wasn't.

With no better plan to offer, Jim agreed. He activated his throat mic he said, "Homer, load up that drum of frags."

"Yes, sir." In two seconds Homer's practiced hands had the magazines swapped on the shotgun.

Jim inserted a full mag into his H&K 416 assault rifle and then reached out, stopping Peter. He unlimbered his sidearm, handing the Super Hawg .45 to Peter. He hefted the weapon, visually ensured the safety was engaged, and then stuffed it inside his waistband.

"Ready?"

Peter nodded, and Jim and Homer opened up with a murderous volley. The piercing roar of gunfire was terrifying, but superimposed on the reports were the explosions from the fragmentation rounds Homer was shooting into every obstacle thought to be hiding the assailants. Sheet metal was rent and pieces thrown into the air to be scattered across the roof. The doorway marking the other access stairway was also targeted and ripped off its hinges, the doorframe shattered. NPA soldiers and black-clad KGB guards rose from the mounting pile of corpses, scattering across the roof as they sought protective cover.

Peter never looked back as he dashed for the ladder. At any moment he expected to meet up with a bullet. He jumped, landing on the second rung and started climbing, sucking in air, blocking out the hellish battle behind him, pushing away the fear of being shot in the back.

He grabbed the top rung and yanked himself up and over the ladder, landing on the platform surrounding the clock. Only now could he see that a low stone wall, about two feet high, surrounded the platform. He ducked below the edge. From his position, Peter could not see the other three sides of the cube. To his left was an open hatch in the deck. He looked inside, into a dark shaft with a steep metal stair similar to the type used on ships.

Peter gripped the pistol and silently advanced around the cube, still crouched low. The sharp cracks and deep booms had ceased now that he had reached his goal. As he rounded the corner, there was Gorev. He was behind the aerosol machine in rapt concentration, and didn't acknowledge Peter's presence.

"Stop whatever you're doing, Gorev," Peter ordered with the pistol pointed at the General.

General Gorev looked up, but did not remove his finger from a button on the top of the case—a button that Peter believed was part of the manual timer.

"You are too late, my comedic friend." Gorev laughed. It was short and mocking.

"I disabled the last machine. I'll disable this one too. Now, stand aside."

"Put down the gun, or I'll press this button and activate the device."

"How about I just shoot you now?"

Gorev stared back at Peter with hate-filled eyes.

"Stand aside," Peter said.

"You know, I don't think you are a dangerous man. And I don't think you will shoot me, either." Gorev pressed the button and then quickly rose revealing a pistol. As he raised it, Peter fired.

The bullet hit Gorev low, in the belly. He stumbled back against the stone wall. Again he started to raise his gun, only now more slowly, like he was struggling to lift a heavy weight.

"You should have listened to me General. I have nothing to lose." Peter squeezed the trigger. The bullet shattered Gorev's sternum before blowing out his heart. The pistol clattered as the General fell dead.

Only now did Peter hear the high-pitched whine of the air blower, and he knew the aerosol device was active, spreading the deadly virus.

CHAPTER 43

Minsk

PETER WAS TOO LATE. Now the smallpox virus would spread in a deadly cloud across the most populous part of the city.

As quickly has the thought entered Peter's consciousness, he vanquished it. He had a job to do, and he focused on the task at hand. First priority was to mitigate the spread of the virus spores. Taking stock of his surroundings, he inventoried his resources. The gun was clearly useless unless he was attacked again.

Peter dashed to the floor hatch and slammed it shut. Although he had no way to lock it, at least he thought the squeaky hinges would alert him to someone trying to gain access to the terrace.

The EMP bomb would take at least five minutes to set up and detonate. *There must be something I can do to destroy the virus spewing from the machine,* he thought. He slipped the duffel bag off his shoulder and felt the flamethrower shift against his back. Yes, that's it!

First, Peter ripped the shirt from Gorev's body. Buttons popped and scattered. He tossed the shirt aside and then stripped off his undershirt as well. Grunting from the physical strain, he hefted Gorev's limp body onto the edge of the stone wall so that he was bent over the wall. Next, He took a length of heavy copper wire from the duffle bag and twisted one end around the dead man's belt. The other end was fastened to the hour hand on the clock, stretching the wire over the aerosol machine.

Finally, Peter draped Gorev's shirts over the wire such that the fabric hung down over the aerosol ejection vent. He thought he could smell the aerosol now. It reminded Peter of dusty earth.

The remnants of flammable liquid were dispensed from the flamethrower onto the shirts, thoroughly soaking them, a few drops of liquid slowly finding their way to the sides of the case. Without pausing to admire his work, Peter struck a match and ignited the liquid. Within a second, a raging inferno erupted above the aerosol machine. The intense heat from the blaze sucked in air and spores, incinerating the smallpox virus.

But the fire would not burn long, and Peter still had to rig and detonate the EMP bomb.

"Reloading!" Jim yelled as he slammed in another magazine. Homer was still working through the 50-round drum magazine, but Jim estimated he'd expend the last of the fragmentation rounds soon.

There was more movement on the far side of the roof, and Jim saw the flash of light and white smoke trail before the RPG hit the AC shelter. Although the heavy industrial air conditioning unit protected Boss Man and Homer from the blast, it wouldn't stand up to a second RPG. He sprinted in a low crouch for Homer's position, sliding to a stop behind the cover.

Jim looked over his shoulder and thought he saw wisps

of black smoke coming from the far side of the clock tower. Whatever Peter was doing, Jim hoped he'd get it done soon.

"I'm running low," Jim announced.

"Same here; one drum of buckshot left," Homer answered.

The large industrial AC unit was holding up, but only barely. Jim raised his rifle, aimed, and fired one shot at a time, maximizing use of his limited ammunition supply. "Homer, I'll draw their fire so you can take out that RPG. We need to get back to the access door."

Homer understood that the enemy weapons and ammunition would be their prize.

Jim was firing the H&K 416 between twisted and torn metal. Most of the shots missed, but a few connected and served the purpose of keeping the soldiers down. As expected, one of the assailants popped up with the RPG launcher already shouldered. It would be a snap shot, no time to aim.

Homer shot first, before the RPG was launched. The 12 gauge fragmentation round hit the soldier at the belt line, and exploded. The force split his body in two in a display of violence that was unequaled even on this ferocious battlefield.

Immediately Boss Man and Homer were running for the access door, trying to get there before the shock wore off their opponents.

With no time to waste, Peter opened the multitool Iceberg had given him and started to take apart the closest floodlight. Careful not to short the electrical wires, he discarded the light fixture. He glanced at the fire suspended over the case—still burning, but not as strong; he had to move faster.

Peter began wrapping the copper wire around the length of plastic pipe. He couldn't rush this, and was muttering "slow is fast, fast is slow," to keep his mind focused. His chest and back were soaked from perspiration, and a drop of sweat threatened to fall from his nose onto the coil of wire. Peter brushed it aside with the back of his hand.

Next, he examined the power supply. It was similar to the last one, and Peter connected the copper coil to the direct current output of the power supply after stripping off the wire insulation. He repeated the process to connect one of the electrical wires from the defunct floodlight to the input to the power supply.

Sensing the passage of time, Peter looked up again at the fire. It was almost out! He grabbed the duffel bag and dumped out the remaining contents—copper pipe filled with C4, detonator, and timer—and gently placed the cotton canvas duffel bag over the wire. At first, Peter thought he was too late and that the fire was going to go out, but then the cotton fabric ignited and shortly spread across the bag.

The blower inside the aerosol machine was whining, indicating it was still operating. Peter had no idea how long it would run before the smallpox virus was completely discharged.

He connected the timer and detonator to the second wire from the floodlight, again taking extreme care not to short the electrical power, and then to the other input terminal on the power supply. Finally, he removed the wire coil from the plastic pipe form, and slipped it around the copper pipe. With the detonator inserted into the C4 plastic explosive, the EMP bomb was armed and ready.

All Peter had to do was to set the timer. He punched in a delay of 30 seconds, and then glanced at the dwindling fire from the canvas bag. He estimated that the fire would consume the canvas in less time, maybe only 20 seconds. Quickly, he reset the timer to 15 seconds and activated the device.

Jim and Homer reached the access doorway and pulled the four bodies inside, where they scavenged their rifles, ammunition, and three grenades. From the shelter of the access door Jim could see the clock tower. Peter was nowhere to be seen, and the black smoke was gone.

Jim radioed his team in the lobby on the squad net. "Ghost, it's Boss Man. Sitrep."

"Pretty quiet down here, but they're gonna need to remodel big time. What's your ETA?"

"It got more complicated. We'll be coming down the right staircase in five."

"Roger that."

Shouldering an AK-74, Jim dashed out the doorway and around the corner of the structure to allow a clear line of fire for both Homer and himself.

In the minute they'd used to reposition, the enemy was already moving forward. Jim counted 15. He opened fire and was joined by Homer, who was still using the AA12. The NPA soldiers ducked for cover and returned fire.

That's when Jim saw Peter at the top of the ladder. He was also seen by the NPA soldiers, some of whom began shooting at him. Peter dropped below the stone wall as bullets raked across the facade.

"Peter's up there, but he can't get on the ladder!"

Homer responded by stepping forward into the open, AA12 in one hand and AK-74 in the other. He dove for the shattered shelter they had first used as cover. All that remained was a pile of bent sheet metal and the sturdy base of the air handling system. Homer slid to a stop, propping the two weapons upon the steel base.

And then he opened up on anything and everything in the direction of the enemy.

Jim rushed forward with a second rifle in hand, joining Homer.

"Peter!" Jim yelled, trying to be heard over the gunfire.

"Peter!"

Peter looked over the edge and saw what Jim and Homer were doing—and it was working! None of the enemy soldiers ventured to expose themselves to the brutal onslaught. With the timer ticking and not wanting to find out if he'd survive a half-pound of C4 detonating only feet away, Peter hopped over the edge and started down the ladder.

Half way down, the bomb detonated. The sharp reverberation was accompanied by violent shaking of the tower causing cracks to appear between many of the stones. With his hands already slick from perspiration, that was all it took for Peter to lose his grip. He tumbled to the asphalt-covered roof, landing hard on his back. The air left his lungs with a groan, as his body lay motionless. The stitches in his side ripped from flesh and bright red blood flowed unabated through the fresh wound.

Jim was on the radio. "Bull, Iceberg—get up here now! Peter's down and we're taking heavy fire!"

Commander James Nicolaou, a.k.a Boss Man, considered himself the consummate professional. He even prided himself on his mental discipline, separating emotions from his work. A cool head would always prevail over rash emotions, he had said more than once. Over years of training, and despite the brutal reality of his profession, Jim had done exactly that. He used his intellect, and calm, logical approach to problem solving to get his SGIT team home through innumerable battles in far-away places, some of which didn't even have names.

But this was different. He didn't know why, it just was.

He continued firing both rifles—the passing seconds seeming like hours. When they were empty, he discarded them as the useless tools they had become, and started throwing grenades in the direction of the NPA soldiers. He only had three, and he delivered all of them. The metal balls flew through the air to land with a dull thud and then roll a few meters further before coming to rest.

The swift ferocity of his attack left the enemy stunned as they sought cover. Homer backed up his commander firing an AK, the automatic shotgun empty and joining the growing collection of other now-useless firearms. He kept up the fire, the bullet impacts serving to keep the enemy down.

Jim turned and ran to his friend. He checked for a pulse. Peter was alive, but unconscious. Kneeling, he hoisted Peter onto his shoulders. Just as Jim stood to retreat back to the doorway Bull burst through, blasting away at the advancing NPA .

Seconds later Iceberg emerged behind him. He was armed with a light machine gun, a 200-round ammunition pouch extending below the weapon and another 200-round belt draped around his neck. He stepped into daylight and was firing almost before he had assessed the location of the enemy.

It was a scathing barrage, the NPA soldiers could only hug the roof for a whisper of protection. Round by round, their hiding places were destroyed.

Jim lowered Peter, easing him against the roof access structure. He blinked his eyes twice, then held them open.

Abruptly, the shooting stopped. Iceberg loaded his last belt of ammunition for the light machine gun. Bull rammed in a drum of buckshot, his last.

A pile of empty brass casings and shotgun hulls littered the rooftop for twenty feet around the men—over a thousand spent rounds—testimony to the violence they had undertaken.

"It was activated by Gorev. We've all been exposed."

"We have to contain the virus," Jim said. "Everyone, get into your NBC suits." Jim reasoned that the rubber suits and face masks designed to protect against exposure to nuclear, biological, and chemical agents would serve equally well to keep the smallpox virus on their clothing from causing further contamination.

Jim radioed Ghost again, his throat mic clearly carrying his crisp words. "The device was activated. I need another NBC suit up here."

"Roger that, sending up one NBC suit."

"Don't go above the fourth floor landing. Homer will pick it up there. He's already suited up."

"What about the aerosol machine—is it deactivated?"

"I'll know shortly. Boss Man out." Then he turned to Peter. "You're alive. Wasn't sure you'd made it."

"Me neither." He winced and placed a hand against the burning gash in his side, feeling the warm, thick blood. He shifted to rise to his feet, and immediately reconsidered. "There's someone inside my head swinging a big hammer."

Jim placed a hand on Peter's shoulder. "Stay here. I'll make certain the aerosol machine is deactivated."

With Iceberg, Homer, and Bull keeping a keen eye for any attack from the far side of the roof, Jim scampered up the ladder and disappeared over the short, stone wall. Soon, he appeared again at the ladder holding the device on his shoulder. He lowered himself over the edge and hurried back to his team.

Homer was helping Peter into the rubber suit that Diaz had sent up; it was slow going. A loud explosion split the air, and Peter flinched. Yet the SGIT team knew from the attenuation of the explosive crack that is was not in their immediately vicinity, not an imminent threat.

No more NPA soldiers had showed themselves, leaving Jim to believe they were all dead. In truth, it was unlikely anyone could have lived through the volume of fire unleashed by his team. Looking out over the roof, the air conditioning shelters that had recently provided ample shelter were now all torn and twisted ruins, barely capable of offering protection to a ground squirrel.

CHAPTER 44

MINSK

JIM WAS HOLDING THE CASE closed when he set it down near the access doorway. Homer was just snugging up the clear polycarbonate facemask onto Peter's head. "We need to secure this case and remove it without spreading more of the virus."

Peter produced a length of parachute cord he'd taken along with the copper wire and other supplies from the storeroom. With the SGIT team still on high alert, Peter bound the hard case closed while Jim retrieved two heavy-duty plastic bags from a pocket of his rucksack along with a roll of gray duct tape.

With efficient movements they double-bagged the device, taping all the seams. Jim hauled it onto his shoulder and followed Peter off the roof.

It seemed that all the NPA soldiers and KGB guards had either been killed or had made the decision to retreat. A wise move, Jim thought. Regardless of the reason, no resistance was encountered as Jim's team descended the stairs to the lobby. At the second floor, Jim radioed Ghost to alert him that they were moments away from appearing on the staircase.

"Glad to see you, sir," Ghost greeted Jim. He then deposited the plastic-wrapped case in the back of the Humvee.

"Load up! Let's go!" Jim ordered. With Nolty behind the wheel and Ghost still on the gun, they turned the Humvee around and drove out of the KGB Headquarters building, closely followed by the second Humvee.

Bouncing down the steps Jim saw a Russian BTR-80 armored personnel carrier only 50 meters away. It was on fire with the turret resting upside down in the middle of the avenue, and rounds for the 30mm automatic cannon were cooking off. Severely charred bodies were littered around the back of the machine. Jim reasoned Diaz and Washington had taken out the troop transport with another TOW missile, just as they had the tanks.

The radio squawked and Jim recognized the voice of Captain Diaz. "Where to, sir?"

"Our mission here is completed. We have the aerosol machine. We'll rendezvous with an Osprey at the BSU campus, decontaminate, and debrief at the hotel."

Upon reaching the Renaissance Hotel, the SGIT team was sprayed down with a dilute solution of bleach, effectively killing any virus on their NBC suits. The three Humvees were also sprayed down, inside and out, as was the Osprey. Since the military men all carried current vaccinations for likely diseases—naturally occurring or possible biological weapons—the risk of smallpox infection was slim.

The same could not be said for the civilian population of Minsk, or for Peter.

CHAPTER 45

Washington, DC

PRESIDENT TAYLOR LOOKED around the table at his most senior and trusted advisors. Several of the cabinet members were away on travel, as was the Vice President, but the meeting could not be delayed. Present also were the Joint Chiefs. The emergency cabinet meeting had been called to review the data obtained from the detailed analysis of the first aerosol device.

The fact that General Gorev was shot dead after activating the second aerosol machine was nothing more than interesting trivia, since Gorev could not be tied directly to the Russian military. President Vladimir Pushkin would easily dismiss Gorev as an independent leader of the militia, operating outside any sphere of Russian influence. It mattered little that everyone in Taylor's administration knew that to be a total fabrication.

"Ladies and gentlemen. The past few days have been difficult, to say the least. However, I believe the worst is behind us. I have spoken at length with President Pushkin. It was a frank conversation, and he made it clear that his government believes they have a historical mandate to protect Russian citizens, especially in the Eastern European countries bordering

Russia."

President Taylor paused to select his words before continuing, enough time for Paul Bryan to ask a question that was on the minds of everyone in the room.

"Sir, Russia cannot be allowed to unilaterally turn back the clock to a time of their choosing and expect the United Nations and the international community to accept those historical borders. The precedent would be unacceptable. Just think, what if all of Europe, North Africa, and the Middle East were redrawn to the historical national borders of 1913. Or, heaven forbid, the map of North America was redrawn to as it was in 1800, prior to the completion of the Louisiana Purchase?"

"Relax Paul. Of course I didn't agree with Pushkin's statement, I'm simply telling you his position, and by extension the position of the Russian Federation. We all know who holds the keys to power."

The president continued, "Concerning the limited conflict in and around Minsk, President Pushkin strongly denies any direct offensive involvement from his government. He steadfastly maintains that Russian troops and weapons have not been committed to the fight."

"Those were Russian fighters we shot down, and a column of Russian tanks we destroyed inside Belarus traveling directly for the Minsk airport." This observation came from General Hendrickson.

"No doubt, General." President Taylor's gaze moved around the table again.

"For the time being, President Pushkin has agreed to keep Russian aircraft out of Belarusian airspace."

"I think we bloodied their nose pretty good," said Secretary of Defense Hale, a smirk on his face.

The President allowed the moment of levity, and almost laughed himself. "Yes, I think we did."

"Sir," Bryan interrupted. "You don't really believe him, do you?"

Taylor's countenance became serious once again. "Do you take me for a fool, Paul? No, we will keep our guard up."

"Of course, sir," replied Paul Bryan.

The President dropped his pen on the table and leaned back in the high-back, plush leather chair, eyes focused on his Secretary of State. "Close to 3,000 civilians died in Tbilisi from hemorrhagic smallpox. Although Pushkin denies any involvement, the circumstantial evidence is convincing. I shudder to think how many innocent men, women, and children might have died a horrible death in Minsk had we not been successful. So tell me, Paul, what would you have me do?"

It was a rare moment when Paul Bryan did not have a thoughtful response. So he wisely opted to remain silent. Unable to hold the President's gaze, he lowered his eyes to his tablet.

President Taylor leaned forward and placed both hands on the table. His lips were pursed, and his tired eyes reflected the strain of the past 24 hours. Several of the cabinet members squirmed in their chairs under the penetrating stare of their boss. But not the Joint Chiefs. They were accustomed to facing difficult scenarios and having to make decisions when all of the choices—every last one—was less than optimal. Decisions that would cost lives just as surely as they saved lives.

"Each and every one of you is sitting at this table because you are smart and ambitious. Let's face it; you don't take this job for the pay or the flexible hours."

That brought a round of short-lived laughter. President Taylor was a remarkable politician, and a natural leader. Having passed the halfway point of his first term, he was still polling very strong—to be expected from members of his own party, but also showing good numbers from the Republican opposition. Political pundits had all but conceded the Democratic nomination to Taylor, and he was widely believed to be a shoe-in for a second term.

Joshua Taylor had defied the odds. Born and raised in California to blue-collar parents, he was a successful tech entrepreneur and sold his first company for close to half a billion dollars before age 30. Ready to take on a new challenge, Taylor stepped into the political arena, first winning a Congressional election, then moving into the Senate. He quickly earned a reputation for his hard work and middle-of-the-road sensibility. Although extremists on both sides of the aisle took every opportunity to malign Taylor's character, his supporters spoke louder, and the American electorate, craving common-sense politicians who put the interest of the country above their own personal ambitions, created a tsunami of support that landed Taylor in the White House with an easy victory.

"Does anyone really think this is about the truth?" Taylor held his position and waited in silence until it was obviously uncomfortable.

"Make no mistake. My opponent—our opponent—is a masterful politician." Again he paused.

"If you haven't already figured it out, we have been played. It's time we got smarter, and fast."

Paul Bryan had quickly regained his composure. He lived for the challenge, and the United States had never had a more talented, brilliant, and capable Secretary of State. "With the physical and circumstantial evidence, I can win over support from our European allies. Japan, too. China will be a problem, but, then again, when are they not."

President Taylor smiled. "If I remember correctly, you handled the Chinese Ambassador pretty well in that Alaskan incident involving the Russian submarine. Perhaps the same approach would work again?"

"Yes, sir. It might. I can play off the fears China has of Russian expansionism. The connection to Kazakhstan is important. I can spin this to Russia coveting Kazakhstan and, by extension, the rest of Asia. It shouldn't be hard to tickle China's paranoia."

"Thank you, Paul. Please see to it."

Paul nodded acknowledgement.

"Now, this weaponized smallpox must be eliminated. It presents a very real danger to humanity. Such weapons are not easily controlled, and it is unconscionable to imagine risking further releases of this vile disease."

The President focused on Secretary Hale, his expression one of supreme confidence. In contrast, Paul Bryan's countenance was dour. His face was long, eyelids drooping. Taylor considered this for a moment—his warrior was confident and his statesman was concerned, even worried. The yin and yang; complimentary and yet opposing forces, as it should be.

"I am led to believe we know where these aerosol dispersion machines have been assembled. Is that correct?"

Secretary of Defense Howard Hale was waiting for this moment. "Yes, sir. There is no doubt."

EPILOGUE

Sary-Shagan, Kazakhstan

ULAN BAYZHANOV WAS BUSY pinning wires into a connector. He was working alone, as was frequently the case. He often wondered why the research facility was so large. With few scientists and staff, it didn't make sense to Ulan. Even considering the special laboratories, like the biology lab where he thought they grew certain cultures—maybe to test experimental antibiotics—or the medical research lab where he was told they could perform DNA sequencing for tests on animals, the facility was so large that he seldom had to share his electrical assembly and test lab with any other technicians.

It was lonely at times, but Ulan didn't mind the solitude so much. He had a good job, one that was interesting and paid well. Well enough, in fact, that he would be able to support a family when that time came, as he knew it would.

He had met a young woman a few months earlier. She cleaned many of the rooms including the electrical lab Ulan worked in. He would see her every day, late in the afternoon. After a while, Ulan introduced himself. At first, she was too shy to engage in conversation, but he was persistent, and eventually they became friends.

The squeaky wheels on the mop bucket drew Ulan's attention. He finished with the final pin in the connector and looked up. She was pushing and pulling the mop, cleaning the concrete floor even though it didn't look dirty at all, just as she did yesterday and would do again tomorrow.

Ulan smiled. "Hello, Aida," he said.

She smiled back, her brown eyes shimmering.

Ulan set down the wire harness on his workbench and walked to Aida. "Seeing you is always the best part of my day," he said, drawing a blush.

Aida worked at night, and Ulan worked the day, leaving precious little time for the two to visit outside of the research facility.

"I've been thinking," Ulan continued.

Aida looked up at him, her face radiant and expectant. She, too, had been smitten with Ulan, but she could never be so forward as to say that to him.

"My supervisor said I can have Saturday off, so I don't have to work that day. Of course, I won't get paid either, but I have saved some money."

Her heart was beating faster and her thin lips turned up into a smile. "Yes, and what does this have to do with me?"

Ulan reached out and gently wrapped his hand around hers, still holding the mop handle.

"I would like to meet your father."

She looked at him, her eyes wide.

"Yes," he said more forcefully, "I would like to speak with your father. I have some serious business to discuss with him."

"Oh. And what business would you, Ulan, have with my father?" She played along, enjoying the game as much as Ulan did.

"Well, I intend to ask for your hand in marriage."

She forced her face into a frown. "Perhaps I do not wish to wed? Perhaps I do not wish to be married to you?"

Ulan released her hand and blushed, stung by the unexpected rebuff. "I have a good job and I make enough money for us. You would not have to work."

"Oh, I am only joking Ulan."

"So there is no other man?"

She smiled warmly. "No, my silly Ulan. There is no one else."

He looked deeply into her eyes and smiled. He felt a joy and happiness he had never experienced. Suddenly, all the hardships of his youth seemed distant memories, trivial footnotes to his history.

In all his life, Ulan had never felt this way about another person. Of course he loved his parents, but that was expected. It was a sense of duty and devotion that he took seriously, but he did not choose his mother and father. No, that was the result of fate; of events he had no influence over.

Aida was different. He had chosen her, and she him. Was this love? It must be, for all Ulan thought about when he was not preoccupied with his work was Aida. He wanted to raise a family with her, to grow old by her side.

"I am so happy Aida. Soon I will meet your father. And I will ask for your hand, and he will say yes."

Aida beamed with joy and Ulan didn't want to look away from her. Even when the room was suddenly lit by a thousand suns, he couldn't avert his eyes from hers.

Ulan and Aida shared only one more heartbeat together before their bodies were incinerated, leaving only their ashes to mingle in the savagely swirling torrents of air.

Following a nerve-wracking two weeks, global tensions had finally reduced to a normal level. For three days following the nuclear attack on the Russian research facilities at Sary-Shagan, the United States, Europe, and Russia were on high alert, each side expecting an attack from the other at any moment. Pundits predicted a retaliatory nuclear attack from Vladimir Pushkin's government, but thanks to behind the scenes diplomacy and an unyielding U.S. military presence in Eastern Europe, Pushkin never authorized the strike.

Apparently, the explanation that the attack did not occur on Russian soil had proven sufficient to quell right-wing rhetoric, exactly as President Taylor expected. To carry out such a provocative attack on Russian soil would have been inexcusable, and a retaliation in like would have been inevitable. But once it was clear that the dispersion machines were assembled in Kazakhstan, and given the possibility that more components, probably even more smallpox virus agent, were still inventoried there, President Taylor authorized the strike.

With the American military already mobilized in Europe, the attack was swift, coming only 18 hours following the Cabinet debate and President Taylor's decision. A single B-1 Lancer commanded by Major Lorraine Doyle, escorted by no less than eight Raptor fighters, left Germany and flew south, banking east over the Mediterranean. From there, the flight crossed Turkey and overflew Armenia and Azerbaijan.

Over the Caspian Sea, the specially modified Bone fired a single AGM-129A advanced cruise missile armed with a 150 kiloton nuclear warhead. The terrain-hugging stealth cruise missile flew a preprogramed flight path at 500 miles per hour to its target, just outside the city of Sary-Shagan.

Detonation of the nuclear warhead occurred at optimum altitude above ground. The extraordinarily high temperatures of the nuclear blast incinerated everything within a five-mile radius. Satellite imagery following the attack revealed total destruction of everything above ground at the targeted research site.

Since there was no way to keep an aboveground nuclear explosion secret, the Taylor administration authorized a special, top secret warhead—one specifically designed to emulate a typical 100 kiloton Russian weapon.

President Pushkin's objections were predictable. But with the body of evidence detailing the construction of the virus aerosol machines, plus the direct involvement of General Gorev on the roof of the KGB building, Secretary Bryan was winning support from other nations and undermining Pushkin's popular support.

Presidents Taylor and Pushkin agreed to withdraw military forces from Belarus, and talks between the Russian Federation and the United States regarding the independence of Belarus and the Baltic States were scheduled. President Taylor had made clear his desire that the national borders of Europe—all of Europe—be respected as currently known, and not subject to change by either diplomatic or military measures.

When the national news media picked up the nuclear explosion over Kazakhstan, Peter knew exactly what had transpired, although the cover story that it was a Russian nuclear weapon accidentally detonated by an unknown terrorist group was selling well to the general public.

Peter was still in Germany, at Ramstein Air Base where he had received a smallpox vaccination within hours of exposure in Minsk. He was being held for observation and debriefing when the news broke.

"What did I do?" he asked his friend, Commander Jim Nicolaou. The two men were sitting on a bench and although there was some foot traffic, no one stopped to loiter within earshot.

"Exactly what you were asked to do, what you were expected to do. We gathered evidence regarding the origin of the smallpox aerosol machines."

Peter stared incredulously at his friend.

"What did you expect?" Jim didn't try to hide his exasperation.

"Not this! We nuked that facility. My God, what if we were wrong? What if I was wrong?"

"You weren't wrong. Let it go."

"Let it go? I'm responsible for a nuclear bomb being dropped on Sary-Shagan! You know how many atomic bombs have been used in war?" It wasn't a question and Peter didn't wait for Jim to respond. "Three! Two used against Japan and now this bombing of a small town in Kazakhstan."

Jim waited patiently until Peter finished. When he did, Jim's words were firm.

"You flatter yourself. You didn't authorize the nuclear attack on that research site. That order could come from only one man: President Taylor."

"Yeah. Based on my recommendation."

"Really? As I recall, you analyzed various components from the first aerosol machine. Together, we communicated that data to Colonel Pierson and the President. At what point did you suggest a nuclear cruise missile be launched on the site?"

Peter stared back in silence.

"The evidence you gathered from the electron microscope was only part of the puzzle. There was also the explosive composition and anti-clumping agent." Peter knew this chemical evidence came from the Air Force labs here at Ramstein Air Base. "Plus, we had the written orders you lifted from General Gorev's desk, indicating a direct connection to Russian Special Forces. And don't forget the papers and other information taken from prisoners. It was all pieced together and, when taken in total, President Taylor made his decision."

"Had I known what was at stake, I would have insisted on more data."

"You know that's not true! Science is about unbiased interpretation of data collected from reproducible experimentation. That's exactly what you did; what Lacey and her team did. To suggest you would shade your data if you knew that it might lead to decisions you don't agree with is to betray your belief in, your commitment to, the scientific process. The data and evidence do the speaking—you don't have to."

"And look what happened," Peter said.

"What happened? I'll tell you what happened. A factory responsible for making biological weapons of terror, aimed specifically at civilian populations, for the goal of deceiving world opinion to support Russian expansionist aggression, was destroyed. Not only was the site destroyed, but the method of destruction ensured complete incineration of any virus stockpiles, rather than running the risk that those stockpiles would be dispersed and cause further outbreaks."

Peter sighed deeply. "You make it sound logical."

Jim shrugged. "It is logical. That site had to be removed in order to eliminate the risk. Conventional weapons would have knocked down the buildings, and in the process the smallpox virus, and anything else they might have had, would have been scattered to the winds. That was unacceptable."

"And a nuclear bomb was?"

"The lesser of two evils. The location is very remote. The research site was several miles away from the main city—to enhance security, you know. And the prevailing winds blow from Sary-Shagan to the research compound, so risk of fallout on the small civilian population is minimal."

"You make it sound easy, even sensible."

Jim shook his head. "I never said it was easy. Ever wonder why our Presidents go into office looking young and vital, and within a handful of years, their hair is gray, and they usually suffer heart and other health troubles? I can tell you what you already know: It's not easy making the decision to take another's life."

Peter looked at Jim with a neutral expression.

"But as you also know," Jim continued, "sometimes it is necessary."

Peter decided to change the subject. "How is the population of Minsk being treated? Do they even know of the smallpox exposure?"

"Thanks to your fast thinking and creative ingenuity, it appears very little virus actually made it away from the fire you set above the machine. The Army has been collecting samples from many locations around the KGB building, but only a few, three or four I think, have tested positive. However, as a general precaution, a smallpox vaccination program was initiated. A thousand cases of vaccine have started to arrive and the Belarusian government is administering the program with assistance from Army and Air force doctors and nurses. It should be completed within a couple days, and if any cases of smallpox are reported, the local hospitals are prepared to quarantine the patients and aggressively treat the infection."

Peter nodded. "Good, I'm glad to hear that." But his demeanor remained gloomy.

Jim placed a hand on his friend's shoulder. They had been through a lot together, and Jim understood how Peter ticked; he accepted that Peter was uncomfortable with taking another's life. But he also knew that if Peter was pushed into a corner, he would do just that.

"You did good here, Peter. Your actions saved thousands of lives, innocent lives. Women, children, young, and old. I've seen what smallpox will do—it's not clean or pretty. And this strain of hemorrhagic smallpox has a mortality rate exceeding 90 percent. You were forced to do what you did, as was President Taylor. In this case, I'd say the ends do justify the means."

Peter closed his eyes in thought, his mind swirling with memories and emotions. Quickly they settled on Maggie, her red hair brilliant in the afternoon sun, her face radiant with joy, equally intense in her green eyes and her smile. The scent of pine and water filling his nostrils; his ears registering her laughter. His gazed moved beyond Maggie, to the edge of the lake where Joanna and Ethan, both young children, giggled and splashed in the shallow water.

Then Peter was pouring wine into the cup Maggie held. He saw themselves sitting on a checkered green blanket, in a grassy meadow only yards from the water's edge. He put the bottle down and then picked up his glass. "If all I ever have is a lifetime with you, I'll be the happiest man in the world," he had said.

The words still echoed fresh in his memory.

The sadness and the pain from her loss had never gone away. Her death was like an infection that wouldn't heal.

Eyes still closed, Peter's lips moved as he mumbled softly, "What would Maggie have me do?" He didn't address the question to Jim, didn't even consciously think that Jim heard him. But he did.

"She would say that what you did saved the lives of children just like Jo and Ethan and saved families the pain of loss that you feel."

Although Jim had spoken softly, his words jolted Peter back to reality. He opened his eyes, red and glistening. "And that I always will."

AUTHOR'S POST SCRIPT

THIS IS WHERE I ISSUE MY standard warning—I urge you to read the story first, and then these comments. To do otherwise will deprive you of some of the suspense that I hope you enjoy as the story unfolds.

One of my goals in writing *Deadly Savage* was to bring to light the very real risk presented by the existence of smallpox and other biological weapons. These viruses and bacteria—most notably smallpox and anthrax—are horrible diseases. Smallpox is credited with killing more than 300 million people in the 20th century alone.

I chose to focus on smallpox for three reasons. Firstly, there is presently no known cure for smallpox, and certain strains are very deadly. Secondly, humankind has a history of using smallpox (and other bacteria and viruses) as weapons to inflict indiscriminate death and suffering on an enemy population. That the United States government used blankets contaminated with smallpox to infect indigenous Americans in the 19th century is well documented; one tool of many put to use as our government waged a protracted genocidal war against the native population. Thirdly, stockpiles of weaponized smallpox are still held by both the U.S. and Russia.

It is true that smallpox is the only viral disease to have been declared completely eradicated, thanks to a massive global immunization program that was completed in the 1970s. Since then, immunization against smallpox has not been a regular practice. The result is that we now have multiple generations vulnerable to this highly contagious disease.

So why are stores of smallpox still held by the U.S. and Russia? The obvious answer is so that it can be put to use in weapons of mass destruction, although this has been repeatedly denied by our elected leaders. However, an alternative justification that stands up to logical scrutiny has not been offered.

Supposedly these stockpiles are held safely behind multiple layers of security. However, in 2014 several vials containing viable samples of smallpox, along with samples of other infectious (and sometimes deadly) diseases, were found in a cardboard box in an unsecured storage room on the Bethesda Campus of the National Institutes of Health. The smallpox samples were dated 1954. Although we have been assured that samples of the virus are held at only two locations, the CDC in Atlanta and a laboratory in Russia, obviously that is not true.

Have all samples of smallpox, anthrax, Spanish influenza, and other deadly diseases truly been accounted for? Are they really secured? Could terrorist organizations, or rogue nations such as North Korea, acquire such weapons? And if they did, how would we respond?

At the end of the story, I've imagined the U.S. President using a nuclear weapon. Hopefully, the characters in this novel have reflected adequately the enormity of such a decision—one I hope is never made. Still, the truth of geopolitics is that there are seldom easy choices, and more often than not one must choose between many evils—which is the lesser?

Equally true, I believe, is that it is the innocents who pay the highest price of conflict. Men, women, and children who have no say in, or benefit from, the reckless actions of politicians bent on acquiring power and wealth—or madmen drunk on religious zeal for the purpose of dominating those deemed unworthy.

If for no other reason, this is why force should only be taken after very careful and thorough deliberation. Sadly, this seems to be a lesson all too often pushed to the margins of national debate.

ABOUT THE AUTHOR

DAVE EDLUND is the author of the best-selling, award-winning *Peter Savage* series and a graduate of the University of Oregon with a doctoral degree in chemistry. He resides in Bend, Oregon, with his wife, son, and three dogs (Lucy Liu, Murphy, and Tenshi). Raised in the California Central Valley, he completed his undergraduate studies at California State University Sacramento. In addition to authoring several technical articles and books on alternative energy, he is an inventor on 97 U.S. patents. An avid outdoorsman and shooter, Edlund has hunted North America for big game ranging from wild boar to moose to bear. He has traveled extensively throughout China, Japan, Europe, and North America.

THE PETER SAVAGE SERIES

BY DAVE EDLUND

Crossing Savage
Book 1

Relentless Savage
Book 2

Deadly Savage
Book 3

More to come!

Follow Dave Edlund at www.PeterSavageNovels.com, tweet a message to @DaveEdlund, or leave a comment or fascinating link at the author's official Facebook Page www.facebook.com/PeterSavageNovels.